"Malachi, before the war I was always a lady—"

"Shannon, before, during and after the war, you were always a hellion."

"Malachi, damn you! I just meant that . . . I never would have done . . . what I did. I shouldn't have. . . ."

He hesitated, listening to her fumbling for words. He could sense tears in her voice again, and though he ached for her, he was bitter, too. He didn't like playing substitute for a ghost. He might have forced her to admit she desired him, but the thought of her Yankee fiancé enraged him.

"The war has changed lots of people," he said softly to her. "And you *are* a lady, brat. Still. I'm sorry."

"I don't want you to be sorry, Malachi. I just—it shouldn't have happened. Not now. Not between us."

"A Yank and a Reb. It would never do," he said bitterly.

Dear Reader:

Harlequin offers you historical romances with a difference—novels with all the passion and excitement of a 500 page historical in 300 pages. Your letters indicate that many of you are pleased with this shorter length. Another difference is that the main focus of our stories is on people—a hero and heroine you really care about.

We have some terrific books scheduled this month and in the coming months: Cassie Edwards fans should look for *A Gentle Passion*; the second book in Heather Graham Pozzessere's trilogy, *Rides a Hero*, tells Shannon's story; *Samara* by Patricia Potter is the sequel to her award-winning *Swampfire*; Nora Roberts's *Lawless* is an unforgettable Western. You won't want to miss these and any of the other exciting selections coming from Harlequin Historicals.

Please keep your letters coming. You can write to us at the address below.

Karen Solem
Editorial Director
Harlequin Historicals
P.O. Box 7372
Grand Central Station
New York, New York 10017

Rides a Hero

Heather Graham Pozzessere

Harlequin Books

TORONTO • NEW YORK • LONDON
AMSTERDAM • PARIS • SYDNEY • HAMBURG
STOCKHOLM • ATHENS • TOKYO • MILAN

Harlequin Historical first edition April 1989

ISBN 0-373-28619-8

Books by Heather Graham Pozzessere

Harlequin Historical

Dark Stranger #9
Rides a Hero #19

HEATHER GRAHAM POZZESSERE,

the award-winning author of historical romances written under the names of Heather Graham and Shannon Drake, now begins a new series of historicals for Harlequin as Heather Graham Pozzessere, the name under which she has previously won popular acclaim for her contemporary romances. In addition to being a multitalented novelist, Heather has worked as a model, actress and bartender. Now a full-time wife and mother of four, she considers herself lucky to live in Florida, where she can indulge her love of water sports, such as swimming and boating, year-round.

Prologue

May 30th, 1865   *Kentucky*
The Road Home

It's him, I tell you. It's Captain Slater! Captain Malachi Slater!'' The young man seated on the wagon that blocked the road could hardly control his excitement. "We done got him, Bill," he cried.

Startled, Malachi pulled back on the reins of the bay mare that had taken him through numerous battles, and stared ahead. Two young Union sentries were guarding the road that eventually led to his ōwn home. The sight of the sentries here in Kentucky didn't surprise him. The war was over. The Yankees had won. Yanks were everywhere now, and that was the way it was.

At least he no longer had to be wary. His fighting days were over. He was going home. His unit had surrendered, and he had put his own signature on the paper, swearing an oath of allegiance to the Yankee flag. He should have been bitter, but right now he was just tired. He had seen the death toll, and he was just damned glad that it was all over.

So he didn't need to fear hostility from the sentries. And hell, seeing them, he couldn't feel much fear. The Yanks, it seemed, had been dipping into the bottom of the barrel as the war ended, almost as much as the Confederates had.

These boys were teenagers, green-gilled, and he was certain that neither of them had ever shaved.

Except there was something... something about the way they said his name.

"Captain Slater, you just hold on there," the first boy said nervously.

They shouldn't have known his name. His rank, of course, was apparent from the worn gold braid on the shoulders of his gray wool cavalry greatcoat. But his name...

"You're under arrest," the second boy—the one called Billy—began, and then his mouth started to work hard as if he couldn't seem to remember the right words to say.

"Under arrest?" Malachi roared out in his best voice of command. "What in hell for? The war is over, boys. Haven't they told you yet?"

"You're a murderin' outlaw, Captain Slater!" the first boy said. Malachi frowned and the boy quickly added, "Sir!"

"Outlaw, murderer? I know that you don't give the Rebels much credit, but our cavalry fought as soldiers, same as yours."

"Captain, the poster that's out on you has nothing to do with the cavalry!" Billy said. "And that's a fact. You're wanted for murder in Kansas—"

"I've never been in Kansas!"

"It says right on the poster that you and your brothers are part of the Slater gang, and that you rode into Kansas and murdered private citizens. Yes, sir, you are under arrest!"

Kansas?

Hell.

He'd not been in Kansas for years. But his brother Cole had been in Kansas, and he had waged a single-handed battle against the cutthroat who had murdered his first wife.

Malachi hadn't been anywhere near Kansas during that time, but that was only part of what was taking him aback. Cole was no murderer either. Someone must be out for

them. The Slater gang indeed! That must mean that someone wanted his younger brother, Jamie, dead, too.

The Union boys were trying to ready their breech-loading
rifles. They were both so nervous they couldn't seem to rip
open their powder bags, not even with their teeth.

Malachi's cavalry saber was at his side and he had a Colt
stuffed into the holster beneath his greatcoat. He had
enough time to fill them both full of holes. "Listen to me,
fellows. I am not going to let you put me under arrest," he
said.

The boys looked green. They glanced his way, but they
kept trying to get to their powder. When they did get to it,
they spilled most of it trying to get it into the well of the gun.
They glanced at him again with terror, but they still moved
to their pouches for balls, and tried to ram them down according to proper military procedure.

"Confound it," Malachi said irritably. "Do your moth-
ers know where you are?"

The boys looked up again. "Hank, you got him?"

"Hell, no, Billy, I ain't ready. I thought you were ready."

Malachi sighed deeply. "Boys, for the love of God, I
don't want your deaths on my conscience—"

"There's a big, big bounty out on you, Captain Slater! A
Mr. Hayden Fitz in Kansas is fierce and furious. Says if'n
somebody don't shoot you and your brothers, he's going to
see you all come to justice and hang by the neck until dead."

"Oh, hell!" Malachi swore savagely. "Damn it!" He
dismounted, sweeping his hat from his head and slamming
it against his thigh as he paced back and forth before the
two. "It's over! The war is over! I fought off the Kansas
jayhawkers before the war, and then I fought all those damn
years in the war, and I am tired! I am so damned sick and
tired of killing people. I can barely stand it! The bounty isn't
worth it, boys! Don't you understand? I don't want to kill
you."

They didn't understand. He stopped and looked at them, and they might be still green, but they'd gotten their muskets loaded. Billy started to aim his.

Malachi didn't wait any longer. With a savage oath escaping him, he charged the boy, pulling out his saber.

But he was sick and tired of killing. As he leaped atop the wagon where the boys sat, he could have skewered them through, both of them. But he didn't. For some damned reason, he wanted them to grow old enough to have the wisdom not to pull such a stunt again.

He sliced his saber against the boy's musket and sent it flying.

"Run, Bill, run!" Hank suggested wisely.

But Hank was holding tight to his own rifle. Malachi swore at him and leaped from the wagon and hurried for the bay mare. He leaped on the horse and just barely nudged her. Like a true warrior, she soared forward like the wind, straight for the wagon.

She carried him up and up and they were sailing. But just as they were over the top of the wagon, a burst of pain exploded in his thigh.

Hank had apparently managed to shoot his rifle. Amazingly enough, he had struck his target.

Malachi didn't dare stop. He kept the bay racing, veering into the woods. She was a good old horse, a fine companion, and she had been with him through many a battle. When pain and exhaustion claimed him and he slunk low against her, she kept going, as if she, too, knew the road home, the long, long road home.

Finally the bay stopped before a stream. For a long moment, Malachi clung to her, then he fell and rolled until he could reach the water. He drank deeply before falling back. His leg was burning; his whole body was burning. Surely it wasn't such a deep wound. He needed to keep moving. He had to get to Cole as quickly as possible.

But it wasn't going to be that night. Despite the strength of his will, his eyes closed.

It seemed to him that a fog swirled up from the stream. Pain no longer tormented him, nor hunger, nor exhaustion. The stream was inviting. He stood and shed his worn uniform. Balancing his way out on the rocks, he dived in. The water was cool and beautiful, the day warm with a radiant sun, and birds were singing. There was no smell of burned powder near him, no screams of the dead or dying; he was far, far from the anguish of the war.

He swam through the coolness, and when he surfaced, he saw her.

An angel.

She was standing on the shore, surrounded by the mist, her hair streaming gold and red, sweeping down and around her back. She was a goddess, Aphrodite emerging from the sparkling beauty of the stream. She was naked and lithe and beautiful, with sultry sky-blue eyes and ink-dark lashes, ivory cheeks, and lush, rose-colored lips.

She beckoned to him.

And he came.

Looking at her, he knew that he must have her. Naked, he tried to hurry, thrashing through the water. He had to touch her. To feel the fullness of her breast beneath his hands, caress her with his whisper and his kiss. But even in the strange seduction of the dream, he knew she was familiar. She was his Circe, calling him with magical promises of unimaginable pleasure, but he also knew her.

Nearer, he drew nearer to her, nearer and nearer...

He started to cough. His eyes flew open.

The only Circe that awaited him was the faithful bay mare, snorting now upon his soaking cheek. Malachi staggered to his feet and looked from his sodden clothing to the stream. He had fallen in, he realized, and nearly drowned.

He had been saved by a dream. The dream of a lush and beautiful woman with golden hair that streamed down her back, and eyes to match a summer's day.

He touched his cheek. At least the stream had cut his fever. He could ride again.

He should find attention for his leg, he thought. But he couldn't spare the time. He had to reach Missouri. He had to warn Cole.

"Come on, Helena," he told the mare, securing the reins and leaping upon her back. "We need to head on west. Home. Only we haven't got a home anymore. Can you believe that? All these damned years, and we still aren't at peace yet. And I get shot by a kid who still has to have his mother tell him to scrub behind the ears. And I dream about beautiful blond temptresses." He shook his head, and Helena whinnied, as if she doubted the sanity of her rider.

Maybe he wasn't sane anymore.

He grinned as he kept riding through the night. It had been a funny dream. Curious how his Circe had seemed so familiar. His sister-in-law, Kristin, was a beautiful blond, but it hadn't been Kristin...

Malachi was so startled that he drew in sharply on his reins and the bay spun around.

"Sorry, old girl, sorry!" Malachi told the horse. Then he went thoughtfully silent, and finally laughed out loud.

It hadn't been his sister-in-law in the dream, but it had been Shannon, Kristin's little sister. Kristin's obnoxious little sister! Willful, spoiled, determined, proud...obnoxious! He'd itched to take a switch to her from the moment they had first met.

But it had been Shannon in the dream. Shannon's eyes had beckoned him, sultry and sweet. Shannon's hair had streamed in a burst of sun and fire around the slender beauty of her form. Shannon's lips had formed to issue whispers of passion.

And he had thought when the dream ended that he had lost his temptress! he told himself dryly.

Well, he had not. He was riding toward the spitfire now, and he could almost guarantee that their meeting would not be sweet, nor would she beckon to him, or welcome him.

If he knew Shannon, she wouldn't be waiting with open arms.

She'd be waiting with a loaded Colt.

"Doesn't matter much, Helena," he told his horse. "Damn it!" he swore out loud to the heavens. "When will this war be over for me?"

There was no answer. He kept riding through the night.

Chapter One

June 3rd, 1865   *The Border Country, Missouri*
The McCahy Ranch

Someone was out there.

Someone who shouldn't have been out there.

Shannon McCahy knew it; she could feel it in her bones.

Even though the sunset was so deceptively peaceful!

It was peaceful, beautiful, quiet. Radiant colors soared across the sky, and sweetly kissed the earth. There was a silence and a stillness all around. A soft breeze just barely stirred, damp and sweet against the skin. The war was over, or so they said.

The night whispered tenderly of peace.

Peace . . .

She longed for peace. Just ten minutes ago she had come outside to watch the night, to try to feel the peace. Standing on the wide veranda, leaning idly against a pillar, Shannon had looked out over the landscape and had reflected on the beauty of the night.

The barn and stables stood silhouetted against the pink-streaked sky. A mare and her foal grazed idly in the paddock. The hills rolled away in the distance and it seemed that all the earth was alive with the verdance and richness of the spring.

Even Shannon had seemed a part of the ethereal beauty of the night. Elegant and lovely, her thick hair twisted into a knot at her nape, little tendrils escaping in wisps about her face. Tall and slim, and yet with curved and feminine proportions, she wore a luxurious velvet evening gown with a delicate ivory lace collar that fell over the artfully low-cut bodice.

She was dressed for dinner, though it seemed so very peculiar that they still dressed every evening. As if their pa was still with them, as if the world remained the same. They dressed for dinner, and they sipped wine with their meat—when they had wine, and when they had meat—and when their meal was over, they retired to the music parlor, and Kristin played and Shannon would sing. They clung so fiercely to the little pleasures of life!

There hadn't been much pleasure in years. Shannon McCahy had grown up in the shadow of war. Long before the shots fired at Fort Sumter signaled the start of the Civil War in April 1861, Missouri and Kansas had begun their battling. Jayhawkers had swooped in from Kansas to harass and murder slave owners and Southern sympathizers, and in retaliation, the South had thrown back the bushwhackers, undisciplined troops who had plundered and killed in Kansas. Shannon McCahy had been only a child when John Brown had first come to Missouri, but she remembered him clearly. He had been a religious man, but also a fanatic, ready to murder for his religion. She had still been a child when he had been hanged for his infamous raid on the arsenal at Harper's Ferry.

So she really couldn't remember a time of real peace.

But at least the thunder now no longer tore at the earth. Rifles and pistols no longer flared, nor did swords clash in fury. The passion of the fight was over. It had died in glorious agony and anguish, and now every mother, sister, lover and wife across the nation waited...

But Shannon McCahy hadn't come outside to await a lover, for she had the questionable luxury of knowing that her fiancé lay dead. She even knew where he was buried. She had watched the earth fall, clump by clump, upon his coffin, and each soft thud had taken a bit more of her heart.

The war had robbed her blind. Her father had been brutally murdered in front of her by bushwhackers, a splinter group of Quantrill's infamous Raiders. And in the summer of 1862 Zeke Moreau and his bushwhackers had returned to the McCahy ranch to take her sister, Kristin. But that had also been the day that Cole Slater had walked into their lives, his guns blazing. He had saved them from being murdered and eventually married Kristin. After that his name kept them safe from the bushwhackers, but the war had still gone on. And ironically, she and Kristin had then been arrested by the Yankees for giving aid and succor to Cole, just because once upon a time Cole had briefly ridden with Quantrill.

But Shannon had fallen in love with the Yankee officer who had pulled her from the wreckage of their prison when the faulty old building had literally fallen to pieces. For a brief time, she had believed in happiness.

Until Robert Ellsworth had been slain by the bushwhackers.

In the end, Zeke Moreau and his bushwhackers had come back to the ranch one last time. Cole had ridden in with his brothers and their Confederate cavalry company, and Shannon's brother, Matthew, had brought his Union compatriots. For one sweet moment, there had been no North, and no South, just a fierce and valiant stand against injustice.

But the war was over now.

No...never. Never in her heart, she thought. Then she stiffened, suddenly alert and wary.

There was a movement out by the stables. She blinked and stared again, and felt a quickening in her stomach, a streak of cold along her spine.

Now she was sure.

Someone was out there.

Someone who shouldn't have been out there.

Someone furtive, stealthy, sneaking around the stables.

"Cole? Kristin?" she whispered. She cleared her throat and called their names again a little louder.

Where were her brother-in-law and sister? They should have been in the house, but no one was answering her. She bit into her lower lip, wondering what she should do. There was a pair of Colt six-shooters over the cabinet just inside the hallway; Cole had set them up the very night they heard the war was over.

After that last fight, Malachi and Jamie Slater had ridden back to the war, not knowing that it was already over. Matthew McCahy had known it was over before he left, for he had stayed until his injury had healed, but then he had left also, to return to his Union Army unit. The war might be over, but he knew that peace was yet to be assured. The aftermath of the war would follow them.

And Cole Slater knew that he would eventually have to flee Missouri. He *had* ridden with Quantrill, although only briefly, and certain Yanks with power might consider him ripe for hanging. But Cole intended to wait for Matthew to return home before leaving the ranch. It wouldn't be safe to leave Kristin and Shannon alone. He had friends who would warn him if danger threatened.

Meanwhile, Cole had hung the Colts and had given Shannon some stern advice. "Most of the men coming home will be good ones," he had told her, hammering nails into the wall. "Yep, lots of good men, both blue and gray. Those who have fought with heart and soul for their ideals. And all that those men want to do now is come home. They want to pick up their plows again, open their shops again, start up their businesses once more. They want to hold their wives, and kiss their children, and lick their wounds and try to find a future. They'll come through here. They'll want water, and they'll want meals. And we'll help them when we can, both Union and Confederate."

"So what are the guns for?" Shannon asked, not even wanting to think of helping Confederates, men like the bushwhackers who had killed Robert.

"Because there are men whom the war has maimed, Shannon. Not in body but in mind. Dangerous men. Deserters and vultures. And I can assure you that as many of that type fought for the Union as for the Confederacy. Mind your step, Shannon. You know how to use these guns. Use them well. If anyone threatens you at all, be ready to defend yourself."

"Yes. I will. I can shoot."

"The bad guys, Shannon. Not just some poor farmer in a gray uniform."

"Cole, I have fed and cared for the Rebels passing this way."

"Yes, you have. But not with a great deal of pleasure."

"You make me sound cruel and unreasonable—"

She saw a strange light of pity in his eyes as he answered. "I don't think that, Shannon. The war has done things to all of us."

But he shook his head as he walked away, and she could tell that he really did think she was heartless. He knew that she could never forgive what had happened, even now that the South had been broken. She would never, never forget Robert Ellsworth, his gentle love, his simple honor. Nor could she ever forget his death. She had seen him buried. He had never been laid out in a proper wake, for there had not been enough of him left for the undertaker to prepare. The brutality had made her hard, and very cold.

Cole was wrong, though, if he thought she could no longer feel. She could still feel way too much, it seemed at times. But it was so much easier to be cold, and it was easier to hate. Cole was wrong if he thought she would kill just any Rebel soldier, but she could very easily gun down the men who had so callously gone out and brutally slaughtered Robert and his men. She thought she could have faced it if Robert had died in battle, but what the bushwhackers had done to him had been worse than murder.

Cole was disappearing around the corner, and she longed to call out to him. She did love him, even if he was a Rebel. He had saved Kristin and Shannon from certain rape and probable death, and he was as dear to her as her blood brother, Matthew. But she didn't call out. It wasn't something she could explain.

Cole's first wife had been killed by Kansas jayhawkers, yet now he seemed to have come to terms with life. Maybe Kristin had taught him forgiveness. But Shannon didn't know how to forgive, and it wasn't something she thought she could learn. She just knew that she still lived with the anguish of the past, and she could not put it behind her.

For Cole's sake, though, she would bite her lip and hand out water to the Rebs heading home. This was Missouri; most of the state was Confederate. She might have been a Rebel herself, since the ranch stood on the border between Kansas and Missouri, and the McCahys actually had leaned toward the South at first. But then Pa had been murdered. Matthew had joined up with the Union Army, and everything that followed after that had conspired to make Shannon an avowed Yankee, through and through.

But that didn't matter now.

Over the past days they had been handing out water and meals to boys in blue and to boys in gray. She reminded herself that Matthew was still out there somewhere. Maybe some Reb girl was giving him a cup of water or a piece of bread.

Shannon had handed out water and hot soup without a word. She had bandaged up Rebs, just as she had done on the day when the two cavalry units—Matthew's Federals and the Slaters' Confederates—had joined forces and beaten Zeke Moreau's marauders. For Matthew's sake, she cared for the weary soldiers who passed the house. Somewhere out there, he would be wandering the countryside. And Cole's brothers, too. Perhaps some young woman was being kind to them.

Shannon hoped that someone would deal gently with Jamie.

But if Malachi passed by some strange farmhouse, well, then, she hoped they gave him salt water!

Both Cole's brothers were Rebels. Jamie she could tolerate.

Malachi, she could not.

From the time they had first met, he had treated her like a bothersome child. She didn't know quite what it was that lurked between them, she only knew that it was heated and total and combustible. Every time they met, sparks flew and fury exploded.

She tried. She tried very hard not to let him creep beneath her skin. She was a lady. She had great pride, and tremendous dignity. But Malachi had the ability to strip her quickly of both. She would be pleased with her composure and the calmness of her temper, but then he would say just one word and she would lose all poise and restraint and long to douse him with a pail of water. And when she lost her temper at his needling, he would taunt her all over again, pleased that he had proven her to be a child, and a brat at that.

Not so much now, she assured herself. And it was true. She had grown colder since Robert Ellsworth had died. No one could draw much of a reaction from her anymore.

She thought Jamie might return soon. But Malachi wouldn't.

Malachi had probably thought to join up with General Edmund Kirby-Smith and fight to the bitter finish. But even Kirby-Smith had surrendered now. Maybe Malachi would head for Mexico, or for Central or South America. Good riddance to him. It was difficult to forget the last time they had met. It had been on the day when all hell had broken loose, when Moreau's band had been broken. Even then, in the midst of chaos, Malachi had managed to annoy her. In the thick of it all, he had ordered her around and they had very nearly come to blows. Well, she *had* slapped him, but Kristin and Cole had been there, and Malachi had been forced to calm his temper. Shannon hoped the Federals had picked him up and placed him in a prison camp. It would be good for him to cool his heels for a while. He was going to have to accept the truth.

The Confederacy was bested and broken, and the Glorious Cause was lost.

It was over.

But not yet ended. Some drifter was crawling around in the stables.

Shannon didn't stop to think a moment longer. She stepped back through the doorway to the entry hall and plucked one of the Colts from its crossed position. She reached into the top drawer of the secretary beneath it for the shells and quickly loaded the gun.

"Kristin! Cole! Samson, Delilah, someone!" she called out.

But the house was silent. Where were they all? She didn't know. She was on her own.

Shannon slipped back onto the porch.

The colors of the night were growing darker, deeper and richer. The sky seemed to have turned a deep purple; the land itself seemed to be blue. The outline of the stables stood black against the horizon, and the two loft windows looked like dusky, evil orbs, staring at her menacingly.

Her heart was beating hard, she realized. The coldness remained near her spine.

She should not be afraid. She had been under attack in one form or another several times now. She should have learned courage.

She was still frightened.

But not frightened enough that she would sit like a wounded lamb and wait to be assaulted, she assured herself. No, she would turn the tables. No honest man skulked and loitered in stables. No sincere fellow, Reb or Yank, hid, waiting for the coming of darkness.

She raced from the porch to the paddock, then paused, breathing fast. She listened intently, and heard nothing, but still, she knew. Someone was there. She could feel it in the air now. She could sense the danger.

She leaned against the paddock fence. She was good with a Colt. Damned, deadly good. Cole claimed that she could hit the eye of a fly from a distance of a hundred feet, and that wasn't far from the truth. As long as she held the weapon, she would be safe.

Don't ever tarry, Cole had warned her once. Make your decisions quickly. And if you decided to shoot, shoot to kill.

It shouldn't be too hard, she thought. She had lived through so many years of hell; she had grown up under the fire. In the world she knew, it was kill or be killed, hurt or tortured. She could manage any situation. She always had.

Shannon drew in a deep breath and pushed away from the paddock fence. Where was Cole? He had been born with a sixth sense. He should have known that there was trouble by now, yet he wasn't here. She couldn't depend on Cole. She had to depend on herself.

Shannon raced for the door to the stables. It stood as dark as the windows in the coming night, gaping open like a dark pit.

And she could feel the evil lurking and waiting inside.

She gritted her teeth and carefully flattened herself against the paneling by the stable door, then swiftly, flush against it, she stole inside.

The darkness was complete. For several long moments she stood where she was, her heart thundering, her fingers like steel around the Colt, her breath coming too fast and seeming to rasp more loudly than a twister. He would hear her, she thought. He would hear her, and find her.

She forced herself to be calm; she was not as loud as she thought. But she had to adapt to the darkness, or she would accomplish nothing.

One horse whinnied and a second one snorted. She tried to envision the place with light. The stalls were large and well constructed; there were fifteen of them across from her, but only nine of the horses would be in their stalls, for the men were still out on the range after the cattle. The tack room was to her immediate right, and to her left was a pile of fresh hay and the grain bags. There was more hay up in the loft above her head.

She caught her breath suddenly, barely daring to breathe.

That's where he was—in the loft.

She wasn't in a very good position if the intruder lurked right over her head.

She cocked her Colt and sank low to the floor, then began inching toward the bales of hay. They could provide her with some cover, and make her position a mystery in this stygian darkness, too.

But even as she moved, she heard the soft, careful shuffling above her. A board creaked, and then the building was still again.

Shannon waited.

There was no further movement. Time seemed to tick on endlessly.

All of a sudden she realized what she had to do. Move the ladder.

She ran for it with an impetuous burst of speed, determined to capture the intruder atop the loft.

"Hold!" a voice commanded.

She ignored it and continued racing for the ladder, then wrenched it away from the opening. It rattled to the ground, leaving no means of escape from the loft above.

A shot rang out. It whizzed high over her head and was imbedded into the wall far behind her. Was it a warning shot? Or did the man in the loft have extremely bad aim?

She shot back, aiming for the voice. She heard a low rasp of swearing, and knew then where her target was.

If you shoot, she had been warned, shoot to kill.

She had seen blood and death in wanton numbers . . .

And still she hesitated. The man was trapped in the loft. What could he do?

Even as she asked the question of herself in silence, the answer came to her, and in a most unexpected manner.

He leaped from the loft like a phantom in the night and landed softly in the hay.

Shannon screamed, whirling around and lifting her Colt, aiming toward the bales of hay. She could not see him. He had landed hard, but he had rolled in a flash, and now he hid behind the many bales.

She took aim and fired at the first bale. The shot exploded, loud and crystal clear, in the night.

Why had nobody come from the house? Surely they had heard the shots. But perhaps the noise was muffled by the barn walls and the hay.

And neither could she seem to hear anything from the house or from beyond the stables. She was pitched into a desperate world where she was on her own.

No noise had come from the intruder. No thud, no cry, no gasp of fear or anger or dismay. There was nothing at all.

Had she killed the man?

Shannon stepped forward, moving as silently as she could upon the earthen floor. She moved slowly, pausing with each step. She must have killed him. She heard nothing, nothing at all.

She took another step toward the hay, peering around the side of the tied bale. There was nothing there. She thought she heard something from the stalls. She swung around and realized that it was only the horses moving restlessly.

Then she sensed a movement in the corner. But that was impossible. No one could have gotten by her, not even in the darkness...

It was a mouse in the corner. A mouse, and nothing more. She had shot and probably killed the intruder, and he lay there, somewhere in the hay.

Shannon moistened her lips and tried to still the fear that swept along her spine. She still sensed danger. He wasn't dead. He was hiding, lurking in the darkness. She wanted to shriek and scream and turn and flee in terror. She didn't dare. She had to find him before he found her.

She turned once again and hurried to the next stack of hay, piled higher than the first. She looked to the rear and each side of it...and then a rustle came from just above her head.

She inhaled and jerked back, looking up, trying to aim her Colt. It was too late.

He leaped upon her.

They fell to the ground together. Shannon's Colt went flying through the darkness. He fell hard upon her and she was assailed with the scent of leather and fine pipe tobacco. His hard-muscled arms held her and a wire taut body covered her. A scream bubbled and rose within her.

His hand clapped hard over her mouth.

"Stop," he hissed.

She interrupted him with a savage kick.

He swore in the night, but his hold went slack.

She shoved against him with all her might, and found her escape. She leaped to her feet and dashed toward the door, inhaling for a loud, desperate scream.

"No!" The voice thundered behind her. He caught her by an elbow, wrenching her around. Her scream died in her throat as they crashed to the ground again. This time, he held her with force. He thrust his frock coat back and straddled her prone and dazed form. Shannon lashed out madly with her fists, thudding them furiously against his chest.

"Stop it, Shannon!"

His use of her name did not register in the raw panic that had seized her. She had not come this far to be raped and murdered in her own stables. She gasped for breath to scream again and raked out with her nails, seeking his eyes.

"Stop it!" He caught her wrists and pulled them high above her head. She started to scream, and he secured her with one hand, clamping the other hard over her mouth. She bit him. He swore in a white rage, but did nothing more than grip her jaw so hard between his thumb and forefinger that she could scream no more for the pain that it caused her.

"For the love of God, will you stop it, brat!"

She froze. She wondered how it was that she had not recognized his voice until he used that particular term.

Malachi!

Malachi Slater had come home.

Chapter Two

She stopped struggling and looked up at him. The moon must have come out, for some light was now filtering into the stable. He leaned very close against her, and she began to make out his features.

They were handsome features. She would grant Malachi that much. He was a striking man. His forehead was high and broad, his eyes were large, cobalt blue, sometimes nearly as black as the darkness that now surrounded them. His mouth was full and well defined, his jaw square beneath the gold and red sweep of his mustache and beard, and his nose and cheekbones chiseled in strong, masculine lines. He was a tall man, made lean by the war, and made hard by it, too.

With his face so close to hers, she realized that his beard was not so neatly clipped as it had always been before. There were shadows beneath his eyes. The rough wool of his Confederate uniform was tattered and torn in many places, and the gold braid, the insignia of his rank in the cavalry, was nearly worn away.

She should have known him much sooner. They had tangled often enough. She knew the strength of his arms and the deep tenor of his voice, and the bullheaded determination of his anger. She should have known him.

But he was different tonight. He was still Malachi, but more fierce than ever. Tonight, he seemed brutal. Tension lived and breathed and seethed all around him.

"You gonna be quiet now, brat?" he asked her harshly.

Shannon gritted her teeth. She could not begin to answer him. The gall of the bastard! He had known that it was her. He must have known that it was her from the moment she had entered the stables, and he had knocked her down and dragged her around—twice!—and had no apology for it.

She squirmed hard against him, fighting his hold. His hand pressed more tightly upon her, his breath warmed her cheeks, and she felt a new wave of his ruthless determination.

"Well?" he repeated. His teeth flashed white in the darkness as he smiled with a bitter amusement. "Shannon, are you going to be quiet now?"

He lifted his hand from her mouth. Her lips felt bruised and swollen from his casual disregard.

"Quiet!" she said, and her tone was soft at first, deceptively soft. She knew she should use some restraint. At the best of times, he had little patience with her.

Well, she had no patience with him. Her temper ignited like a fuse. "Quiet?" Her voice rose, and then it exploded. "Quiet? You scurvy, flea-ridden son of a jackass! What the hell do you think you're doing? Get off me!"

His lips tightened grimly and his thighs constricted around her hips.

"Miss McCahy, I'll be happy to do so. Just as soon as you shut that lovely little mouth of yours."

"Get off!" she whispered furiously.

"Shh!"

He was too close to her. His eyes were like pits of blue fire boring into hers, and she was acutely aware of him as a man. He leaned so close that his beard brushed her face. His thighs were hot and tight around her, and his arms, stretched taut across her as he maintained a wary grip upon her wrists, were as warm and threatening as molten steel.

"Malachi—"

"Shannon, I am waiting."

She closed her eyes and ground her teeth. She waited, feeling her heart pound, feeling the seconds pass. Then she smiled with savage sarcasm, but remained silent.

Slowly, he eased his hold. He released her wrists and sat up. He still straddled her hips, but he was no longer pinning her with his touch. Shannon tried counting to keep her smile in place. She longed to explode and shove him far, far away from her.

And still he kneeled there. He crossed his arms over his chest, and watched her through narrowed eyes.

She waited. She could stand it no longer.

"I have been quiet! Now get the hell off me!"

In a flash, his hand landed on her mouth, and he was near her again, so near that this time the warm whisper of his breath touched her cheek, and sent hot, rippling sensations seeping throughout the very length of her. He was tense, so tense that she wondered if she really knew the man at all, and she was suddenly afraid.

"I have been fighting blue bellies a long, long time, and you are the worst of them. Now, I am not going to wind up in prison or swinging from a rope at the end of this because of you. I do swear it. Shut up, Shannon—"

"Don't you threaten me!"

"Threaten! I'll act, and you know it!"

She didn't realize until it pulled and hurt that he had a grip upon her hair. She clenched her teeth, swallowed and tried to nod. Even for Malachi, this was strange behavior.

It was the war, she decided; he had finally gone insane.

"I'll be quiet!" she mouthed.

"Do so, Shannon, I'm warning you."

She nodded again.

He seemed to realize that he was hurting her. He stared at his hand where he gripped her hair, and he dropped it as if it were a golden fire that truly burned. He sat back again, then watched her.

"No sudden movement, no screams."

"No sudden movement," she repeated in a solemn promise. "No screams."

Seeming satisfied at last, he rose, finding his plumed cavalry hat on the floor nearby and dusting it off upon his thigh. He swept it low before her, and Shannon curiously caught her breath.

He was a charismatic man, a tall and arresting one. She knew he rode with elegance and finesse, as if he had been born to it. It sometimes seemed that he embodied some spirit of chivalry, something of a certain gallantry that had belonged to a sector of the deceased, prewar South. He had grace, and he had courage, she did not deny him those. He would never think of personal safety if something threatened someone he loved. He was loyal and devoted to his brother, and to her sister, Kristin.

He also seemed to have gone quite mad, and she needed desperately to escape him at the first opportunity. She didn't know whether to be terrified or furious.

"Miss McCahy," he murmured, reaching for her hand. "Please accept my hand. I admit, my manners were poor..."

It was too much. He had wrestled her to the ground twice, threatened her, bullied her and acted as if he belonged in an asylum. Now he was acting like the last of the cavaliers. She wanted no part of him; she had to escape.

She stared at his hand, creeping away on her elbows and haunches. "You must be completely out of your mind," she told him flatly. Then she leaped to her feet and spun around to run.

"Damn you!"

The oath left him in a fury. This time, when he caught her and dragged her back, he did not throw her to the floor. He curved one hand over her mouth and brought her flush against his chest with the other, his fingers taut beneath her breast. He whispered against her ear.

"Shannon, I am tired, I am bone tired. It has been my belief since I first had the pleasure of your acquaintance that a switch in the barnyard would have done you a world of good. Now, I am going to ask you one more time to behave, and then I am going to take action against you, as I see fit."

Rage and humiliation boiled inside her. "Malachi Slater, don't you ever talk to me like that, ever!"

"Don't push it."

She brought her heel against his leg with a vengeance. It wouldn't do much damage against his boot, she thought regretfully, but it did incite him further.

She gasped as he swung her around to face him, locking her against his body, his arms around her, her fingers laced tightly through his and held taut at the small of her back, as if they were involved in a close and desperate waltz. She opened her mouth to protest, but something in his eyes silenced her, and she stared at him in stony silence instead.

So much for dignity. So much for pride. She did manage to lift her chin.

"Shannon, behave," he said, then paused, watching her. Then he said with a trace of amazement, "You really meant to kill me!"

She inhaled, and exhaled, and tried to count. She tried to stop the trembling in her body, and the thunder in her heart. She was going to speak softly, and with bold, sheer reason. She could not stand being this close to him. She despised her vulnerability, and she hated the shivers that seized her and the way her blood seemed to heat and steam and sizzle throughout her. She hated the hardness of his body, like warm, living rock that she could lean against, when he was every inch the enemy.

"You would have!" he repeated. "You would have shot me. I wonder, did you or did you not know who I was?"

"Malachi, I'd love to shoot you. In both kneecaps, then right between the eyes. But you are Cole's brother, and because of that fact alone, I would never seek to take your miserable life. Besides, you lost, Malachi. I won.'' She paused, savoring the words. ''The war, Malachi. I am the victor, and you, sir, are the loser.''

He grinned, slowly, and shook his head. He leaned closer so that his eyes streaked blue fire straight into hers. His lips were almost against hers, the hair of his mustache teased her flesh, and she felt his words with every nerve of her body. ''Never, Shannon. You'll never, never be the victor over me.''

''You've already lost.''

''We've yet to play the game.''

''Malachi, you're hurting me!''

''You were trying to kill me.''

''I was not! Every deserter and drunk and cutthroat and thief across the country thinks that this is playtime. I didn't know who you were! It's your fault. You should have come straight to the house. You shouldn't have been skulking around in the stables. I wouldn't have come out here if—'' She broke off, frowning. ''You Reb bastard!'' she hissed. ''You knew that it was me! You knew that it was me, but you jumped me anyway.''

''You were wandering around with a Colt. I know what you are capable of doing with one, Miss McCahy.''

''You could have called out—''

''Hell, ma'am, now how did I know that you wouldn't have been damned pleased to use the thing against me, and with such a good excuse.''

She smiled, savagely gritting her teeth, trying to elude his hold. He would not release her. ''Pity I don't have it now. I could be tempted.''

''But you don't have it, do you? My point exactly.''

''Malachi Slater—''

''Stop, Shannon. I told you. I'm exhausted. I'm bleeding and starving and exhausted and—''

''Bleeding?'' Shannon interrupted, and then she wondered irritably why she cared. ''Why didn't you come straight to the house?''

He twisted his jaw, watching her suspiciously. "I thought there might be a Yank patrol there."

"You saw that it was me—"

"Yes. But I didn't quite take the chance that you wouldn't just be thrilled to tears, little darlin', to turn me over to a patrol."

"Why, Captain Slater, you sound as if you believe I hate you."

"Miss McCahy, I am just fully aware that the sisterly love you offer to my brother does not extend to me. So you see, Shannon, at first I had to take care that you did not shoot me with pleasure, then I had to assure myself that you did not have a pack of blue-belly friends awaiting me in the house."

"My brother is a blue belly, you will recall," Shannon told him acidly.

"I said a patrol, and that's what I meant."

"A Yank patrol?" Startled, Shannon quit struggling and spoke curiously. "Why? Matthew isn't even back yet. Why would there be a Yank patrol at the house?"

He stiffened, his hold easing on her a bit. "You mean . . . you haven't heard?"

"Heard what?"

He stared at her for a moment longer and pulled her even closer.

"Swear to me, Shannon, that you're on the level. That you're not going to scream, or run, or try to shoot me again."

"If I had meant to shoot you, Malachi Slater, believe me, you'd be dead right now."

"Shannon, I'm going to let you go. If you scream or move or cause me another problem, I promise, you will live to regret it with all of your sweet heart. Do you understand?"

"There is no bloody patrol at the house!" she told him. Then she lowered her eyes and sighed. "I swear it, Malachi. You're safe for the moment."

Then she gasped, suddenly realizing that Cole's behavior had been a bit strange that afternoon. A friend of his had stopped by, and after that Cole had mentioned very casually that he might have to leave for a day or two to find a hiding place. Just in case, he had assured them. Just in case of trouble. Had Cole known something? It was his nature to be quiet and not alarmist. And he would have played any danger down for fear that Kristin would insist on accompanying him. He would just slip away, and then hurry back once he knew he could keep her safe...

"What?" Malachi demanded sharply.

"There's no patrol. It's just that...an old friend of Cole's stopped by today. And then Cole began to act strangely. Perhaps he does know something he's not telling us." Her heart felt as if it were sinking. Perhaps Cole was already gone. He could have slipped away already, looking for a place to take them. He had wanted to head to Texas before, but he wouldn't leave them for that length of time, Shannon knew. If he had gone off, it would be just for a few days, to find a hiding place deeper into Missouri.

Malachi tilted his head, watching her curiously, but he seemed to believe her. He released her and turned aside. With an uncanny agility in the darkness, he went to the door and found the lantern that hung there and lit it, bringing the flame down low.

And Shannon saw that Malachi was in worse shape than she had at first imagined.

His coat was indeed tattered, his braid frayed. He was very lean, and his handsome features were taut with fatigue. A deep crimson bloodstain marred his trousers high on the inner left thigh.

"You've been hit!" she cried, alarmed. "Oh, my God, I did hit you in the hay—"

He shook his head impatiently, sinking down upon one of the bales of hay. "You didn't hit me. A Union sentry hit me when I passed through Kentucky." He paused, and a gray cloud of memory touched his eyes as he stared into the shadows at nothing. "I could have taken them down," he mused, "but it didn't seem to make any sense. I thought that I could outrun them. They were just kids. They couldn't have been more than seventeen. More killing just didn't seem to make much sense."

None of it was making sense. He must have been in terrible pain, and yet he made his spectacular leap from the loft despite his injury. He must have been desperate indeed.

Curious, Shannon moved carefully over to him. "Malachi, the war is over. Why were they—"

"You really don't know?"

"Know what?" she demanded, exasperated.

"It isn't over. It isn't over at all." He hesitated. "Cole went into Kansas, you know. He killed the man who killed his wife."

Shannon nodded. "I know," she said stiffly. Malachi kept staring at her. "So?" she asked. "Cole knows that he's going to have to leave Missouri for a while. When Matthew comes home, Cole and Kristin will head for Texas."

Malachi leaned against the hay. He winced, and she thought that his leg must be hurting him very badly for him to display even a hint of pain. "Cole can't wait for Matthew to come home. He hasn't got the time. They've got wanted posters up on him. You see, the man he killed has a brother. And the brother seems to own half the property in Kansas. He virtually controls his part of the state. Anyway, he's calling Cole a murderer. He wants him brought in, dead or alive. And he's got enough influence—and money—to see that things are done his way."

Shannon felt weak. She wasn't terribly sure that she could stand. She staggered. She couldn't believe it. Cole had fought long and hard for a chance. He had battled a million demons, and now he had found his peace. He had Kristin and the baby, and with them the promise that there could be a normal life.

And now he was branded outlaw—and murderer.

"He's going to have to head out and hide, Shannon, right away," Malachi said softly. "They'll know to come for him here."

She nodded, thinking that this was what Cole had heard earlier. He had quite possibly left already. But in a second, she was going to go back to the house to check. She would at least have to tell Kristin that the world of peace and happiness that she had just discovered was being blown to bits by the thunder of revenge.

"Why—why were they shooting at you? You weren't in Kansas with Cole," Shannon said.

Malachi grinned, a lopsided, caustic grin. "Why, darlin', I'm the man's brother. A Slater. According to the powers that be, I ran with Quantrill, and I butchered half the population of Kansas."

"But you were never with Quantrill. You were always regular cavalry," Shannon said.

"Thanks for the vote of confidence. I didn't think that you would rush to my defense."

"I wouldn't," Shannon said coolly. "Facts are facts."

Malachi shrugged, leaning wearily back again. "Well, it doesn't matter much anyway. You go on up to the house and get Cole. We'll ride out tonight. You seen Jamie?"

Shannon was sorry to have to shake her head. She liked Jamie. He was always calm and quiet. The peacemaker of the three brothers, she thought. The Slaters were close; she could understand that. She and Kristin were close. Too many times, Kristin had been all that she had had left.

Too many times...

In the days after Robert had died, she had wanted to die herself. She had lain there without eating, without speaking, without the will to move. Kristin had been there. Kristin had given her the desire to survive again.

She lowered her head, almost smiling. Malachi had even helped her then. It had been unwitting, of course. He had never allowed her the peace of silence, or the chance to dwell in self-pity. Since she'd met him he'd been demanding, a

true thorn in her side. But his very arrogance and his endless determination to treat her like a wayward child had
brought out her fury, and with that her passion to live.

"I'm sorry. I haven't seen Jamie," she told him softly.

"Well," Malachi said softly to the lamp. "Jamie is no
fool. He'll lay low. He'll find us."

His words were a lie, Shannon thought. He was worried
sick. She didn't say so, though, for there was nothing that
either of them could do.

"You were in the same company," she said. "Why aren't
you together?"

"Jamie set out a day or two before I did. He wanted to
stop by to see some old friends who had lost a son." He
gritted his teeth. "We've got to run. He'll know how to lie
low."

"You're not running anywhere, not the way that you
are," Shannon told him. She couldn't bear seeing the blood
on his leg. She didn't know why. Most of the time she
thought that not even the Comanches could think up a cruel
enough death for Malachi. But tonight the sight of his blood
disturbed her.

"What do you mean?" he asked her warily.

"Your leg."

"I can find a doc south of here to take out the ball—"

"The ball is still in it?" Shannon said.

He stiffened as he held his breath for several seconds,
watching her. "Yeah, the ball is still in it."

Shannon whirled around and headed for the tack room.
They kept some rudimentary surgical supplies there; it was
a necessary precaution on a cattle ranch.

"Shannon!" he called to her. "What do you think you're
doing?"

"I'll be right back."

She found the surgical box in the lower left hand drawer
of the desk. She paused. They had no morphine; nothing for
pain. Nobody did, not in Missouri. Not in most of the
South.

She pulled open the next drawer and found a bottle of Kentucky whiskey. It would have to do.

Then, as she came out of the tack room, she paused, wondering why she was thinking of doing this for Malachi Slater.

Maybe she didn't hate him so much.

No...she hated him. He was Cole's brother, and if his leg wasn't fixed up, he might slow Cole down. That was it, surely.

She swept back to his side and knelt down. She opened up the box and found a pair of scissors. She needed to slit his pants and find the extent of the wound.

"What do you think you're doing?" he asked her harshly.

"I'm going to cut your pants."

"If you think that I'm going to let you anywhere close—"

"The wound is in your thigh, you fool. Here." She handed him the whiskey. "Drink some of this."

He didn't hesitate to swallow a good shot of the whiskey. He closed his eyes, wincing when he was done. "That was good. It was an inestimable piece of kindness from a Yank to a Reb. Now forget it, I'll find—"

"Sit still, Malachi, and quit whining."

"I'll be damned if I'm whining. Shannon! Shannon, stop!"

He clenched his teeth, but when he went to grip her wrists, he was too late. He hesitated. She already had the shears snipping at his pants, and to make a move might have been dangerous. He inhaled sharply.

She paused and met his eyes. She smiled sweetly. "Sit back now, Captain Slater. Relax."

"You move carefully there, Miss McCahy, or I swear, I'll make you sorry this very night!"

"Why, Captain Slater, I would take great care with those silly threats of yours at this particular moment."

He caught her arm and her eyes once again. "Shannon, I don't make silly threats. Just promises."

"You aren't in any position to make . . . promises, not at this moment, captain."

"Shannon—"

"Trust me, Malachi."

"The way I would a black widow, Shannon."

She smiled and stared at his fingers, which were still locked around her arm. She looked at him again. His eyes remained clear and deep and blue upon hers. Slowly, he eased his fingers, releasing her.

She felt him inhale as she carefully snipped at the blood-stained wool. Seconds later, she pulled the material away from the wound. She could see the ball. It was sunk in just far enough that a man wouldn't be able to remove it himself. One swift slice with a scalpel and a quick foray with the forceps and it would be gone. Then she could douse it with some of the liquor and bind it, and his chances of a clean recovery would be very good indeed.

"Take another swig of the whiskey," she told him, staring at the wound because she didn't dare look into his eyes. "I'll just get the scalpel—"

His hand landed hard upon her wrist, and her eyes were drawn to his. "I don't trust you with a scalpel, Shannon."

She smiled sweetly. "You have to trust me. You have no choice."

"You bring it too close to any part of my anatomy that I consider near and dear, and you will regret it until your dying day."

"Alas, the ladies would be heartbroken!" she taunted in turn. "I will take the gravest care."

He released her wrist, but continued to watch her. There was a warning sizzle in his eyes that brought tremors to her heart. She had to steady her hands. "What the hell," she muttered. "Mr. Ego Reb. Were I to wound anything near and dear there's a likelihood that nobody would even notice."

It was a good thing that the knife had yet to touch his flesh. He caught her wrist again, pinning it, drawing her eyes to his once more. "Sometime, darlin', I just might let you find out."

She jerked away. "Darlin', don't even dream of it. Not in your wildest thoughts."

"Couldn't handle it, huh?"

"I'll handle it right now, if you're not careful, Captain Slater."

"Is that a promise, Miss McCahy?"

"No, a threat."

"Your hands better move with the skill of an angel, got that, Miss McCahy?"

His grip on her wrist was tight. But it wasn't the pain that gave her pause. It was his agony, for all that he concealed it so well.

She nodded. "Give me the bottle."

"What for?"

"To clean the scalpel." She doused the small sharp knife with the alcohol, and then he took the bottle back from her. He swallowed heartily. "Ready?" Shannon asked him.

"You are eager to take a blade against me," he said.

"Right."

"I can't wait to take one against you." His speech was slurred just a bit. When she glanced his way, she saw his grin, lopsided, heartstopping. She closed her eyes tightly against it, against the searing cobalt of his eyes, and the charisma of that smile. He was making her tremble tonight, and she couldn't falter.

She brought the scalpel against his flesh, holding his thigh to keep it steady. He didn't start or move at the swift penetration of the knife, but she felt his muscles jump and contract, and the power was startling.

He didn't make a sound. He just closed his eyes and clamped down on his jaw, and for a moment she wondered if he was conscious, and then she hoped that he was not. She quickly finished her cut, and brought the small forceps out. She had cut well. She quickly secured the ball and dug it from his flesh, then liberally poured whiskey over the wound and began to bind it with linen bandages. There weren't enough to finish the job. She glanced at his face, then lifted her skirt and tore her petticoat.

One of his eyes opened and he looked at her. "Thanks, darlin'." He wasn't unconscious.

"I don't want you getting Cole killed," she said flatly. She came up on her knees, and wrapped the linen around his thigh, moving higher and higher. Both his eyes were open now. She wished that her elegant bodice weren't cut quite so low. He was staring straight at her cleavage, and he was making no gentlemanly move to look away.

"Quit that," she ordered him.

"Why?"

"You're supposed to be a Southern gentleman," she reminded him.

He smiled, but the smile held pain. "The South is dead, haven't you heard? And so are Southern gentlemen. And you be careful right now, Miss McCahy. You're moving real, real close."

She was. She pulled her fingers back as if she had been burned.

"You did a good job," he told her, tying off the bandage.

"Because everything is intact?" she said caustically.

"I do appreciate that. But then, you wouldn't have dared do me injury, I'm certain."

"Don't be so certain."

A soft, husky chuckle escaped him. "Some day, I promise, I'll make it all worth your while."

"What does that mean?"

"Why, we'll have to wait and see, won't we?"

"Don't hold your breath, Captain Slater. And besides—" she widened her eyes with a feigned and sizzling innocence "—I'm just a child, remember? The McCahy brat."

She started to turn away. He caught her arm and pulled her back. She almost protested, but he moved with a curi-

ous gentleness, lifting a fallen tendril of hair, smoothing it.
And his eyes moved over her again, over the rise of her
breasts beneath the lace of her bodice, to her flushed cheeks,
to the curve of her form where she knelt by his feet.

"Well, brat, it was a long war. I think that, maybe, you've
begun to grow up."

"I had no choice," she said, and she was suddenly afraid
that she would start to cry. She gritted her teeth and swallowed the tears harshly. She felt his eyes upon her, reading
her thoughts and her mind and her heart.

"I was very sorry about your Captain Ellsworth, Shannon," he said. "I know what it did to you. But be careful.
If you're not, you'll have scars on your soul, like Cole did
when the jayhawkers killed his wife."

"Malachi, don't—"

"All right, Miss McCahy, I won't talk about sacred territory." He smiled, a devilish smile, taunting her, leading her
away from the memory of pain. "You are maturing, and
nicely. Thank you, Shannon." He paused, his eyes searching her, his smile deepening with a sensual curve to his lips.
She thought that he was going to say something else, but he
repeated himself. "Thank you, you did a good job. Your
touch was gentle, nearly tender."

"I told you—"

His knuckles brushed her cheek. "Definitely growing
up," he murmured softly.

She didn't know what to say. It should have been something scathing, yet she didn't feel that way at all, not at that
moment. She just felt, curiously, as if she wanted to be held.
As if she wanted to burst into tears and be assured that yes,
indeed, the war was over, and peace had come. She wanted
to feel his arms around her, the heat of his whisper as he
caressed her tenderly and assured her that all was well.

But she had no chance to respond at all.

For at that moment, the quiet of the night beyond the
stables was shattered. The thunder of hoofbeats sounded
just outside, loud, staccato, a drumroll that promised some

new portent of danger. Even through the closed door, she could feel the beat she knew well.

Shannon rose quickly, the blood draining from her face.

"Riders, Malachi! Riders coming to the house!"

As if in answer to her worried exclamation, she heard a faint scream of horror from the house. Shannon ran to the door, wrenching it open. The scream came again. Shrill now, then higher and higher.

"Kristin!" Shannon cried. "It's—it's Kristin! Oh, my God, it's Kristin!"

"Wait!" Malachi called.

Shannon barely heard him. Horses had come galloping down upon the ranch again. Numerous horses. The sound of those hoofbeats told her that the uneasy peace that had so briefly settled over the ranch would now be shattered once again.

She started to run.

"Shannon!" Malachi thundered.

She ignored him, unaware that he was behind her, swearing, raging that she should stop.

"Damned fool brat!" he called. "Wait!"

She didn't wait. She burst into the night, staring at the house. In the glow of the light from the house she could see twenty or so horses ranged before the porch. Most of them still carried their riders. Only a few of the men had dismounted.

"No!" Shannon breathed, but even as she ran, she saw her sister. A tall husky man with unruly dark whiskers was coming out of the house with Kristin tossed over his shoulder.

Kristin was dressed for dinner, too, in a soft blue brocade that matched the color of her eyes. Her hair had been pinned in a neat coil, but now it streamed down the giant's back, like a lost ray of sunshine.

Stunned, Shannon stopped and stared in horror.

"I've got her!" the man said sharply. "Let's get the hell out of here!"

"What about Slater?" someone asked.

Shannon couldn't hear the reply, but her heart seemed to freeze over. If Cole wasn't gone, then he was dead. If there was a single breath left in his body, the burly man wouldn't have his hands on Kristin.

Kristin was screaming and fighting furiously as the man walked hurriedly to his horse. Kristin bit him, hard.

He slapped her in return, harder. Swearing. Then he tossed a dazed Kristin onto his horse, and mounted behind her.

"No!" Shannon shrieked, and she started to run in a panic toward the house once again. She leaped one of the paddock fences in a shortcut to the house. She had to stop them. She had to save her sister.

Her feet flew over the Missouri dust, and her heart thundered. She had no thought but to reach the man before he could ride away with her sister. In terror, she thought only to throw herself at the man in a whirlwind of fury.

Suddenly, she was, in truth, flying. Hurtling through the air by the force of some rock-hard power behind her, and falling facedown into the red dust at her feet. Stunned, she inhaled, and dirt filled her lungs. Dizzy and gasping, she fought against the force now crawling over her, holding her tight. Panic seized her. It was one of the men, one of them...

"Stop it, Shannon!"

No! It was Malachi again. Damn Malachi. He was holding her down, holding her prisoner, when the men were about to ride away, ride away with Kristin...

"Let me go, you fool!"

He was lying over her, the length of his body flat on hers, hard and heavy. His chest lay on her back, and his hands were flat upon hers, pinning them down. She could barely raise her head to see.

She could only feel the tension and heat of his whisper as he leaned low against her in warning.

"You fool! You're not—"

"Damn you! Get off of me! He has my sister!" She couldn't even begin to fight; she couldn't twist away from him.

"Shannon! He has twenty armed men! And you're running after him without so much as a big stick!"

"He has—"

"Shut up!" One of his hands eased from hers, but only to clamp over her mouth. He kept them down, almost flat upon the earth. A trough lay before them. It hid them from view, Shannon realized, while they could still see the men and the house two hundred yards away.

"He has Kristin!" Malachi agreed. "And if you go any closer, he's going to have you, too! And if you don't shut up, he'll be after the two of us. We could try shooting down twenty men between us without killing your sister in the fire, but we'd still need our weapons—those wood and steel things back in the hay—to do it with!"

She went still, ceasing to struggle against him.

"My only hope is to follow them. Carefully," he said hoarsely. He eased his hand from her mouth. He did not lift his weight from hers, but pinned her there with him with a sure pressure.

She hated him for it.

But he was right. She had no weapon. She had panicked, and she had run off with nothing, and she could do nothing to help Kristin.

She would only be abducted, too.

"No!" she whispered bleakly, for the horses were moving. The men were all mounted, and the horses were beginning to move away.

With the same speed and thunder, they were racing away, into the night.

And red Missouri dust rose in an eerie fog against the darkness of the night . . .

And slowly, slowly settled.

Chapter Three

When the horses were gone, Malachi quickly stood and reached down for Shannon. She would have ignored his hand and risen on her own, but he didn't give her a chance. All the while, he kept his eyes fixed on the house. As soon as she was standing, he dropped her hands to start limping for the porch. He climbed over the paddock fence.

"Where are you going?" Shannon demanded, following him.

He didn't seem to hear her. He kept walking.

"Malachi!" Shannon snapped. He stopped and looked back at her as if she was a momentary distraction—like a buzzing fly. "Malachi! We have to get guns and horses; we have to ride after them. You're wasting time! Where are you going!"

"I'm going to the house," he said flatly. "Excuse me." He started walking again.

She ran after him and caught his elbow, wrenching him around to face her. Stunned, frightened and furious, she accosted him. "What? You're going to the house. Just like that. Sure, we've got all the time in the world! Let's take a rest. Can I get you dinner, maybe? A drink? A cool mint julep, or something stronger? What the hell is the matter with you? Those men are riding away with my sister!"

"I know that, Shannon. I—"

"You son of a bitch! You Rebel...coward! Good God, I wish to hell that you were Cole! He rode in here all alone and cleaned up a small army on his own! You didn't even fire a shot. You yellow-bellied piece of white trash—"

"That's it!" He stepped back, and his arm snaked out. He caught her wrist and held her in a bruising grip, speaking with biting rage. "I'm damned sorry that Cole isn't here, Miss McCahy. And I'm damned sorry that I didn't have the time to dig through the hay to find my gun or your gun or even my saber. If I had had my gun, I probably could have killed a few of them before they gunned me down. So I'm real, real sorry that I don't feel like dying like a fool just to appease your definition of courage. And, Miss McCahy—" he paused for a breath "—as for Cole, I really, honest to God can't tell you just how much I'd like to see his face. And that, to tell the truth, is what I'm trying to do right now. Those men are riding away with your sister. Well, my brother was in that house, and I—"

He paused again, inhaling deeply. Shannon had gone very pale and very still. She had forgotten Cole in her fear for Kristin. Malachi had not.

He dropped her arm, pushing her from him. "I want to find out if Cole is alive or dead," he said flatly, and he spun on his heels.

It took Shannon a few seconds to follow him, and when she did so, she did in silence. Dread filled her heart. She hoped Cole had left already. But the second that she learned something about her brother-in-law she would be gone. Maybe Malachi could let those men ride away with Kristin—she could not.

He heard her following behind. He spoke without turning around. "I am going after Kristin. If you don't mind, I will arm myself first."

"As soon as we...as soon as we find Cole," Shannon said. "I'll get everything we need. We can leave—"

"*We* aren't leaving. I'm leaving."

"I'm coming with you."

"You're not coming with me."

"I am coming—"

"You're not!"

Shannon opened her mouth to continue the argument, but she didn't get the chance. The porch door swung open again as Delilah came running out. Tall, black and beautiful, with the aristocratic features of an African princess, she was more family than servant, and no proclamation had made her free. Gabriel McCahy had released both her and her husband, Samson, years before the war had ever begun.

Now her features were wretchedly torn with anguish.

"Shannon!" she cried, throwing out her arms. Shannon raced to Delilah, accepting her embrace, holding her fiercely in return. Delilah spoke again, softly, quickly. "Shannon, child, I was so afraid for you! They dragged Kristin from here so quick—"

"Delilah," Malachi said harshly, interrupting her. His voice was thick. "Where is my brother? What happened? Cole would never—Cole would never have allowed Kristin to be dragged from his side."

Delilah shook her head, trying to get a grip on her emotions. "No, sir, Captain Slater," she said softly, "Cole Slater never would have done that. He—"

"He's dead," Malachi said, swallowing sickly.

"No! No, he isn't dead!" Delilah said with haste.

Relief flooded through Shannon. She couldn't stand any longer. She staggered to the porch and sank down on the lowest step. "Where *is* Cole, Delilah?"

"He rode out before—"

"When?" Shannon cried. "I didn't see him go!"

"Let's come inside. You both look as if you could use a little libation," Delilah said.

Shannon shook her head and stood with an effort. "I'm going after Kristin—"

"You're not going after anyone," Malachi said. "I'm going, and I'll do so as soon as I'm ready."

"Don't tell me what I can and can't do, Malachi Slater!"

He walked over to her, his eyes narrowed, his irritation as apparent as his limp. "Shannon McCahy, you are a willful little fool, and you will get us both killed, as well as your sister. I will tell you what to do, and if you don't listen to me, I'll lock you in your room. No, that wouldn't do, knowing you, you'd come right through the window. I'll tie you to your bed. Are we understood?"

She wasn't going to get into another test of strength with Malachi, not at that moment.

Nor was she about to listen to him.

But she inhaled and raised her chin with what she hoped was a chilling dignity. She walked up the steps to the porch and paused before the door. "Yes, let's do go in. I'll get Malachi some of Cole's breeches, and we'll all have a shot of whiskey. Delilah, you can tell us what happened. We do need to move quickly. Malachi needs to get going."

She smiled at him sweetly. She saw his lashes fall as his eyes narrowed, and she saw the cynical curl of his lips beneath his mustache. He didn't trust her. Not a bit. It didn't matter.

She entered the house with a serene calm, walking quickly through the Victorian parlor toward the office. It had been her pa's office; recently, she had begun to think of it as Cole's office. One day, she hoped, Matthew would reclaim it. The country would rebuild after the war, and Matthew's children would come and crawl on his lap while he went over accounts or the payroll.

Delilah and Malachi followed her. She opened the bottom drawer of the desk and drew out a bottle of Kentucky bourbon. With steady hands she found the shot glasses on the bookcase and poured out three servings, then handed one to Delilah and one to Malachi. She took her father's place behind the desk. "All right, Delilah, what happened?"

Malachi was watching her. He perched on the edge of the desk, waiting.

Delilah didn't sit. She swallowed the bourbon neat, and paced the floor.

"Cole left here about an hour ago. He came to speak with Samson and me, explaining that he thought things were going to get hotter a lot sooner than he expected. Some guy called Fitz wanted revenge. Cole didn't think that this Fitz would want to hurt the McCahys—but he knew that Fitz wanted all the Slaters, and just to be safe, he wanted to move Kristin and the baby right away. He didn't want to say anything to Kristin until he had a place to take her and little Gabe, and, well, you know your sister, Shannon, she wouldn't have let him get away. She'd have risked anything, herself and even little Gabe, I think. He meant to come back within a day or two. He didn't want her risking that child or herself." She paused.

"Go on, Delilah," Malachi prodded her. He leaned over the desk and opened the top drawer, reaching for a cigar. "Excuse me," he said to Shannon, smiling politely. She didn't care for the slant of his smile, nor for the touch of blue fire that sparkled in his eyes.

He was, indeed, watching her. And he wasn't about to trust her.

"I gave Cole some food. He gave me a kiss on the cheek, and said that he'd be back, and that everything would be fine. He also said that I shouldn't be surprised to see you coming here mighty soon, Captain Malachi, and that Jamie might be on his way, too. And he left a letter to Kristin on his desk. I brought it up to Kristin right away. She had guessed that he was gone. She ripped the letter open and read it quick, and then she let it drop to the floor. She just sat there, staring at me with her pretty face white as a sheet."

Delilah sighed, slumping down into the leather-covered sofa before the desk. "Then finally she started to cry. 'I knew that he'd have to run, but we meant to run together. He must be desperate, to have gone without me, without the baby! He knew, he knew...that I would follow him anywhere. But he was afraid that they might hurt me or the baby to get to him. Oh, Delilah!' she cried. She cried out my name, just like that. It hurt so bad to hear. I told her that he'd be back for her, just as soon as he could find a place..."

Shannon nodded. So she had been right. Cole had been gone all along. Cole would have heard Malachi in the barn. He would have heard the shots. He would have come to her. Not that it mattered now.

Delilah paused, shaking her head, staring blankly at the desk before her. "Then the horses came."

"And the Red Legs took Kristin?"

"They swept right in here. But Kristin was so glad to tell them that they were too late. Cole was gone, long gone. Then that bearlike bastard brought his knife so tight against her throat that he drew blood. Thank God he didn't seem to know anything about the baby."

"The baby!" Shannon and Malachi cried in unison, jumping up in alarm.

Delilah smiled. If there was one thing in the world that Malachi and Shannon could agree upon, it was their nephew, Gabriel. They both doted on him, and their alarm was clearly written upon their faces. "Gabe is just fine. He's upstairs sleeping with my boy in my room. They fell asleep on the bed together, and so I left them there. I don't think those men even know that he exists." She stared straight at Shannon. "They know about you, though, missy. They were going to look for you, tear the place apart for you, but the dark-haired fellow with the beard said that they should hurry, they had Kristin Slater, they didn't need anyone else."

Shannon inhaled and exhaled slowly. She looked down at her hands. Maybe she had been lucky. If she hadn't been out at the stables with Malachi, she might have been taken, too.

Or she might be dead now, because she would have tried to fight them. She might have shot some of them down, but there had been an awful lot of them. Red Legs...

She jumped to her feet, staring at Malachi in renewed horror. "Red Legs! They were Red Legs!"

Malachi shrugged. "The Red Leg units are all part of the army now, Shannon. Lane and Jennison were stripped of their commands long ago."

His words didn't help her much. Shannon had learned to hate the Southern bushwhackers, but she'd always had the good sense to despise the jayhawkers as they had butchered and plundered and murdered and robbed and raped and savaged the people and the land with every bit as much—if not more—ruthless energy than the bushwhackers.

The Red Legs, as the men were called, were infamous for their brutality. She had seen the uniforms worn by the men in front of the house. But in the darkness, she had not realized who they were. But Malachi had seen them clearly, and he had known right away. He had good reason to know them. A unit of Red Legs had killed his sister-in-law, Cole's first wife.

"We have to get Kristin back," she said.

Malachi rose, too. "I will get Kristin back, I promise you."

"Malachi—"

"Shannon, damn it, you cannot come."

"I'm an ace shot, and you know it."

"And you also panicked just a little while ago. You started racing after them with your mouth wide open and your hands bare. Shannon, the only way I'm going to get Kristin away from those men is to sneak her out of their camp. I can't go in with guns blazing—they will kill her if I even try it."

"Malachi, please just let me—"

"No."

"You don't even know what I'm going to say!"

"Shannon, you listen. Stay here. Take care of Gabe. Wait, maybe Cole will come back, or will try to get a message through to you, or maybe Matthew will come home. Who knows, Matthew just may have some influence with these people. He fought long and hard in the Yank army. If he can get to the right authorities, maybe he can get Kristin back through legitimate means.''

She gritted her teeth, staring at him. ''Meanwhile they could kill, torture, rape or maim my sister.''

He sighed, hands on his hips, and gritted his teeth in turn. ''Shannon, you may not come with me.''

She lowered her head quickly, trying not to let him see her eyes. She was going about this all wrong. She knew Malachi. He was as stubborn as a worn-out mule. He wasn't going to say yes, and she was an idiot to argue it out.

She should let him leave and then follow his trail. He didn't ever have to know that she was near him. And if he didn't manage to get Kristin away from the band of Red Legs, she'd find a way herself.

''Well,'' she said, ''let me go and get you a pair of Cole's breeches.''

''Never mind,'' he told her. ''I know where the room is.'' He turned on his heel and started out of the room.

''Captain Malachi, you'd better have some supper in you before you leave,'' Delilah said. ''You wash up and dress and come on down, and eat something first. And I'll pack you up a little something for your saddlebag.''

''Thanks, Delilah.''

''He needs to hurry, Delilah,'' Shannon said sweetly.

Malachi's eyes met hers across the room, sharp and icy and blue, and he smiled. That chivalrous slant of a grin across his features might have been heart-stopping, she thought, if he had just been some other man.

''Oh, I think I have time to grab a bite,'' he said.

''Certainly. We wouldn't want you to go off hungry.''

''I'm sure that you wouldn't.''

He kept staring at her, so she kept smiling pleasantly. ''You go on then, Malachi. I'll help Delilah see to some dinner.''

''Fine,'' he said. ''Thanks.'' He tipped his hat to her. The brim fell over his eyes, and she wondered once again what he was thinking. But he was quickly gone. She listened to the sound of his boots hitting the parlor floor, then moving up the stairway.

Delilah stood up quickly, eyeing Shannon warily. "What you got on your mind, missy?"

"Nothing that you need to worry about, Delilah."

"Oh, I'm worried," Delilah assured her. "I'm plenty worried." She rolled her eyes Shannon's way.

Shannon ignored her. "Let's go see to something to eat," she said hastily.

Delilah sniffed. "There's plenty to eat out there. Cold roast, cold potatoes and cold turnip greens. Not very nice anymore, but there's plenty. I'll set a plate over the fire. You come pack up some food for Captain Malachi."

Shannon followed Delilah from the office through the elegant little parlor and past the entry to the stairway. She paused, looking up the steps. Malachi would be changing. Then he would eat and leave. She would have to follow quickly. She wouldn't have time to change her clothing. She'd have to roll up a pair of trousers and a cotton shirt, grab a hat and be on her way.

"Shannon?" Delilah looked at her from the doorway to the dining room. "You comin'?"

"I'm right behind you, Delilah," she said, and meekly walked through the dining room to the kitchen. "Is the smoked meat in the pantry?"

"Yes'm, it is," Delilah said, slicing roast beef on the counter and watching Shannon from the corner of her eye. Shannon ignored her and pulled two clean cloths from the linen drawer. She found strips of smoked beef and pork and began to wrap them carefully. Delilah had just baked bread, so there were fresh loaves to pack, too. She turned around just as she was finishing. Delilah was leaning against the door frame, watching her.

"And what are you doing?"

"Packing food."

"I can see that. You're packing up two bundles."

"Malachi is a very hungry person."

"Um. And you're going to give him both of those bundles, right?"

Shannon exhaled slowly. "Delilah—"

"Don't you wheedle me, Shannon. You've been wheedling me since you came up to my knees. You're grown now. I know what you're going to do."

"Delilah, I have to go after Kristin—"

"Malachi will go after Kristin."

"And what if he fails?"

"You think that it will help Kristin if they take you captive, too?"

"Delilah—"

Delilah threw up her hands. "Shannon McCahy, I can't stop you. You're a grown woman now."

"Thank you, Delilah."

"Anyway," Delilah said with a sly smirk, "I don't need to stop you."

"Oh?"

"No, missy, I sure don't. I don't need to at all."

"And why is that?"

"Why, darlin', he's gonna stop you, that's why."

"Don't you dare say anything to him, Delilah."

"I won't. I promise you that I won't. And I can tell you this, it ain't gonna matter none!"

Without waiting for a reply, Delilah turned her back on Shannon, and went to work making up a plate for Malachi, humming as she did so.

Shannon wrinkled her nose at Delilah's back. She knew darned well that Delilah couldn't see, but she might have done so, her next words came so quickly.

"You've got hay in your hair, Shannon McCahy. Lots of it. And hay stuffed right into your cleavage, young woman. You might want to do something about that before dinner."

Instinctively, Shannon brought her hand to her hair, and she did, indeed, pluck a piece of hay from it.

"I thought you weren't terribly partial to Captain Malachi?" Delilah said sweetly.

Shannon found the hay sticking from her bodice. She plucked that out, too, spinning on her heels and walking toward the door. "I'm not, Delilah. I'm definitely not."

"Hm."

She didn't have to defend herself to Delilah. She didn't have to defend herself to anyone.

Then why was she doing so?

"We had an accidental meeting in the stables, and that is all, Delilah. You were right—I'm not at all partial to Captain Slater."

Lifting her chin, she swept out of the kitchen. She paused, biting her lower lip as she heard Delilah's laughter following her. She shook her head and pushed away from the door. She needed to hurry.

She went up the stairs to her room. Beneath her bed she found a set of leather saddlebags. Dragging them out, she quickly stuffed one side with clean undergarments, a shirt and sturdy cotton breeches. The other side she would save for food and ammunition. She made a mental note to bring plenty of the latter, then shoved the saddlebags under the bed.

She stood quickly and hurried to her washstand, pouring clean water into the bowl. She washed her face and hands and realized that she was trembling. She dried off quickly, then moved to the mirror to repair her fallen and tumbling hair. Swearing softly, she discovered more hay. She brushed it out quickly and redid her hair in a neat golden knot at the nape of her neck.

When she was done, she stepped back. Subdued? Serene? She wondered. That was the effect she wanted. It wasn't to be. Her cheeks were very red with color, her eyes were a deep and sparkling blue, and despite herself, she felt that she looked as guilty as hell.

"I'm not guilty of anything!" she reminded herself out loud. "They've taken my sister..."

That thought was sobering. Where was Kristin now? Had they stopped to rest yet? They were heading for Kansas, she was certain. Surely they would keep her safe—until they had Cole. And Cole was no fool. When he heard that they had Kristin, he would take care, of course he would . . .

Her eyes gazed back at her, very wide and misty now. She blinked and stiffened. She needed to find strength. She couldn't possibly sit around and wait. She had to do something to bring Kristin home again.

There . . . not too bad. She folded her hands before her, and a mature young woman with wise blue eyes and a slender face and soft wisps of blond hair curling around her face gazed back at her. A serene young woman, soft and feminine—with no more hay protruding from the bodice of her elegant dinner gown. She was ready.

Shannon started to run swiftly down the stairs, then she realized that Malachi was standing at the foot of them, waiting for her. She quickly slowed her pace, and her lashes swept low over her eyes as she tried to gaze at him covertly. He had that twisted grin of his again, that cocky, knowing grin.

"Miss McCahy, I was waiting to see if you were joining me for supper. We're all set, and all alone, so it seems. Delilah has gone out back to wait for Samson."

She had come to the foot of the stairs. He was very close, watching her face. She swept by him. "Of course, Malachi."

He followed behind her and pulled out her chair. Delilah had already set their dishes on the table. When Shannon sat, Malachi pushed her chair in to the table. He hovered behind her. She wished that he would sit.

He did not. He reached over her, pouring her a glass of burgundy. She look up at him.

"What is dinner without a fine red wine?" he said lightly. Then he gazed at the bottle, and she saw his handsome features grow taut. "I haven't had any in quite some time," he murmured.

Shannon quickly looked away, feeling that she intruded on some intimate emotion. He did not seem to remember that she was there, but if he had, she thought he would not want her watching.

He poured his wine and sat across from her. He sipped it and complimented the fine bouquet. He cut off a large bite of roast beef, and chewed it hungrily and cut another.

"You're not eating," he told Shannon.

"And you're eating too slowly," she muttered.

He looked up, startled, and smiled. "Shannon, I will catch up with them. I'm probably going to have to follow them for several days to learn their ways and find the best time to sneak in among them. Don't begrudge me one hot meal. I haven't had one in ages."

She felt a twinge of guilt. She knew that the Rebel soldiers had been down to bare rations at the end of the war, moldy hardtack and whatever they could find on the land. She lifted her wineglass to him. "Enjoy," she said softly.

Malachi paused in the midst of chewing, lifting his glass to hers, suddenly mesmerized by the girl before him.

Woman. It had been a long war, and she had grown up during the painful duration of it.

And in the soft candlelight, she was suddenly every bit the glorious image he had seen in his dream. Her lips were softly curled, her cheeks were flushed, her eyes were a crystal and beautiful blue, soft and inviting. Golden strands of hair escaped the knot at her nape and curled against the porcelain clarity and softness of her cheeks, down the length of her slender neck and over her shoulders. Her breasts pushed against the low bodice of her elegant gown. She might have been a study of wisdom and innocence, for her smile was soft and young, but her eyes seemed ancient.

Malachi swallowed a sip of wine. She was still smiling. The little wretch. She was up to something. She planned on following him.

He raised his glass in return. "To you, Shannon."

"Why, thank you, sir."

Just as gracious as a Southern belle. He was definitely in trouble if Shannon was being charming.

"You're welcome." His eyes were warm as he gazed at her. He lowered his head, hiding a smile, then he allowed his hand to fall upon hers. She almost jumped a mile.

"Did I thank you for treating my leg?"

"It was my pleasure."

"Oh, I'm sure it was."

Shannon didn't know quite what he meant by that, but she was determined not to argue.

It might be nice not to do so, she thought suddenly.

He was such a striking man. He had washed quickly, and his hair was slightly damp, and he had trimmed his mustache and beard. He had donned a pair of Cole's gray trousers, and a clean cotton shirt, which lay open in a V at the neck, displaying a hint of the bronze flesh of his chest, and the profusion of red-gold hair that grew there. He was achingly masculine in the muted glow of the candles, and she was stunned that his wry smile could bring about a curious beating in her heart.

She had not thought of any man as really attractive...

As sexually attractive...

Not since Robert had died. Then she had dreamed.

For so long those dreams had seemed like dust in the tempest of the wind. She could barely remember Robert's kisses now, or the excitement they had elicited within her. She could scarcely recall the lovely satin and lace gown that Kristin had made for her. Kristin had laughed with mischievous pleasure, assuring her that it would be the perfect gown for her wedding night...

She had ripped the gown to shreds.

When Robert had died, she had ceased to lie awake at night and ponder the things between a man and a woman. The soft, exciting stirrings within her had died.

She had thought that they had died.

But with Malachi's hand so softly atop hers, his eyes with their devil's sparkle so close, his knee brushing hers, she was suddenly feeling them again.

Her cheeks flamed crimson, and she jerked her hand from beneath his, nearly knocking over her wineglass. He cocked an eyebrow at her, and it seemed to her that he was still secretively smiling.

"Something wrong, darlin'?"

"I'm not your *darlin'*."

"Excuse me. Is something wrong, Miss McCahy?"

Wrong? It was horrid. And on a night when Kristin had been so savagely taken . . .

Kristin, remember Kristin, she told herself. That was why she was here, trying to be charming.

"No," she said quickly. "No, nothing's wrong. I'm just so tired. I mean, it's been such a long day. No, no, nothing is wrong at all. What am I saying? Everything is wrong!"

"Hey!" He leaned across the table and caught her chin with his forefinger. She sensed a tremendous warmth within him that she had never seen before, and it touched her, and embraced her. She didn't pull away when he held her, or when he sought out her eyes.

"I will find her, Shannon. I will find her. They—they aren't going to hurt her—"

"They are a Red Legs unit."

"They aren't going to hurt her. Fitz wants her alive. Why do you think they took Kristin?"

"Because they want Cole."

"Right. So they won't hurt her, or else they won't have her to use against my brother. It's going to be all right."

Shannon nodded. He released her, but his eyes stayed on her with a curious speculation, and it seemed that he had to force himself to return his attention to his meal.

And she had to force herself to forget his haunting touch.

"Is—is everything good?" she asked him.

"Delicious," he said briefly.

"I do hope so. More wine?"

"Thank you, Miss McCahy."

"My pleasure."

He sat back, sipping the wine that she had poured. He lifted his glass, and the speculation remained in his eyes. "No, my pleasure, Miss McCahy." He sighed, finished the wine, set his glass down and rose. She jumped up along with him.

"You're going now?"

"I'm going now."

"I'll get your food. And your coat and cavalry jacket." She paused. "You probably shouldn't ride into Kansas with that jacket. Do you want another one?"

He took his jacket and coat from her. "Why, haven't you heard, Miss McCahy? The war is over. Or so they say."

"Or so they say," Shannon echoed.

He grinned. He touched her cheek, and she quickly turned away. "I'll get your food."

"Thanks," he drawled, but when she started to walk away, he caught her hand and pulled her back.

He had put his plumed hat atop his head, and his Confederate greatcoat lay over his shoulders. His eyes were heavy-lidded and sparkled with a lazy sensuality and humor.

"It was a nice dinner, Miss McCahy. You were a beautiful companion. I enjoyed it. Whatever comes, I want you to know that. I enjoyed it."

It was very peculiar talk, coming from Malachi. She nodded nervously and pulled away from him. "I'll...I'll just get your food."

"I'll meet you out front. I want to take a last peek at Gabe, and tell Delilah goodbye."

"Fine."

She fled to the kitchen. She hurriedly secured his bundle of food, adding a bottle of her father's old Irish whiskey from the cupboard. Then she went outside and nervously waited.

Soon he passed by her on the porch. "Just need to get the bay," he told her.

"Of course."

She watched him walk to the stable, a tall figure, dominating the night, with his greatcoat falling from his shoulders and his plumed hat touching the sky.

He was swallowed up by the darkness.

Moments later he reappeared, a masterful horseman, cantering toward her on the bay.

He reined in before he reached the porch and waited as she approached him with the bundle of food and the liquor.

"Is your leg all right?" she asked him with a little pang of guilt. He should have had some rest, but he seemed to be doing well with the wound. As long as infection didn't set in, he should be fine.

But it was true that he should have rested.

"The leg feels good, thanks." He buckled the food into his saddlebag. The bay mare shuffled nervously, wanting to be gone.

Shannon stepped back. Malachi nodded to her, lifting the reins. "Take care of Gabe. I'll be back with Kristin as soon as I can. I hope Cole will hear of this and come back, but we can't rely on that. Be ready. We'll have to take her somewhere. She'll have to hide now, too, or they'll come after her again."

Shannon nodded. "I'll be ready."

"I'll bet you will. Goodbye."

She lifted a hand and waved. He saluted, swung the bay around and rode into the night.

Shannon could barely stand still. The second he was out of sight, she swung around and raced up the steps. She burst into the house and ran up the stairway. She didn't pause to change, but wrenched her saddlebags from beneath the bed and tore down the stairs again and into the kitchen.

Delilah was there. Shannon ignored her as she packed her own food, then she hurried over and hugged Delilah fiercely. "Take good care of Gabe, Delilah."

"Shannon, Shannon, you shouldn't be going! I thought that he would know, I thought that he would stop you—"

"No one can stop me, Delilah. You know that. Please, please, promise to take good care of the baby!"

"You know that I will, missy, you don't need to say a word."

"I know that. Oh, Delilah, you and Samson were God sent! I don't know what we'd ever have done without you."

"You might not be able to run off like this."

"Delilah, she's my sister. I have to go for her."

Shannon kissed Delilah quickly on the cheek, swept up her bags and left the kitchen.

In the hallway she plucked the second Colt from the wall and stuffed her bag full of ammunition. Delilah hovered behind her.

"Shannon, you take care, young lady. Don't go off impetuously and get yourself in trouble, you hear?"

Shannon nodded and threw the door open. She started to hurry out, and she hurried straight into Malachi's waiting arms.

"Malachi!"

"Shannon!"

He set her back on her feet, a broad, smiling barrier in the doorway. He took her saddlebags from her hands. "Going somewhere tonight, Miss McCahy?"

"Yes!"

She tried to snatch the bags from him. His smile faded from his face, and he tossed the saddlebags on the floor of the porch. The sound reverberated, but neither of them heard it. Their eyes were locked.

"Malachi Slater—"

"You aren't coming, Shannon."

"Damn you, you can't—"

"I am sorry, Miss McCahy, but what I can't do is let you get yourself killed."

"Malachi—" She cried out in soft and wary warning. He stepped forward anyway and dipped low, catching her in the midriff and throwing her over his shoulder.

"Put me down, you damn Reb!" she ordered him. He just kept walking. She pummeled his back. "Malachi, Slater, you—"

"Shut up, Shannon."

"Scurvy bastard—"

His hand landed firmly upon her derriere. "This is such a delectable position!" He laughed, his footsteps falling upon the stairs.

She burst out with every oath she knew, beating savagely against his shoulders. He didn't seem to feel a thing, protected as he was by the heavy padding of his greatcoat.

Despite her wild fight, they came quickly to the second floor. His long strides brought them down the corridor to her room. He pushed the door open, and a second later tossed her hard upon her bed. Her skirts and petticoats flew around her, and she scrambled first for some dignity, pressing them down.

"Temper, temper, Shannon," he murmured.

"Temper!" She jumped to her knees, facing him. He arched a brow but didn't take a single step back. He seemed to be waiting for her next move, just waiting.

Shannon smiled and sank down on her pillows, comfortably crossing her arms over her chest. "Go ahead. Lock me in."

"I intend to."

"Aren't you forgetting?" she said sweetly. "This is so very foolish. The second that you're really gone, I will crawl right through that window. Now, it would just make so much more sense if you would be a reasonable man and— what are you doing?"

Shannon sat up, tensing, for he had turned away from her and was prowling through her drawers.

"Malachi?" She rose to her knees again, then leaped from the bed, accosting him. She pulled his hand out of her top drawer. A pair of her knit hose dangled from his hands.

"You're letting me come?" she said curiously. Then she realized from the grim determination on his features that he had no intention of letting her come. She still wasn't sure just what he meant to do.

Then he reached for her, sweeping her off her feet and plopping her down on her bed once again.

"Malachi, no!"

"Shannon, darlin', I'm sorry, yes!"

She let out a spate of oaths again, struggling fiercely against him. She didn't have much chance. He quickly had a grip on her wrists. No matter how she swore and raged and resisted, he tied them to the bedposts with her own knit stockings.

"I'll get you for this, Malachi Slater!"

"Maybe you will."

"I hope that your leg rots and falls off. Then I hope that the infection spreads, and that everything else rots and falls off."

Leaning over her, securing the last of the knots, he smiled. "Shannon, I don't think that was a very ladylike comment."

She narrowed her eyes. "This is no gentlemanly thing to do."

When he was done, he sat back, satisfied. She stared at him in trembling fury. A frightening and infuriating vulnerability drove her to try to kick him. He laughed and inched forward. He touched her cheek gently, almost tenderly.

"You're not coming, Shannon. I tried to warn you."

"Don't you dare touch me. Let me loose."

"You look lovely in bed."

"Get off my bed!"

"All that passion! It's quite—stirring, by God, Shannon, it is. I hope it remains if I'm ever tempted to take you into my bed."

"Malachi Slater, I promise you," Shannon grated out, straining at the bonds that tied her wrists and staring at him with rage and tears clouding her eyes, "the only way you'd ever get me into your bed would be to knock me out cold and then tie me to it!" She jerked hard upon her wrist.

He laughed, rose and bowed to her deeply, sweeping down his plumed hat. Then he came very close, and suddenly teased her forehead with the briefest touch. It might have been a kiss.

"Miss McCahy, I promise you. If I ever decide to bring you to bed, no ties or binds will be needed."

She gritted her teeth. "Get out!"

He swept his hat atop his head and offered her his slanted, rueful smile.

"Take care, Shannon. Who knows? Maybe the possibilities are worth exploring." He paused for a second. "And I promise you, darlin', that I will not let anything rot and fall off."

With that, he turned and left her.

Chapter Four

You can't just leave me tied like this!" Shannon called in amazement to him as the door closed in his wake. She bit lightly into her lower lip. "*I* could rot and fall off and die!"

She heard the husky sound of his easy laughter—and the twist of the key in the door. "Delilah will be up in a few hours. You won't die, Shannon." He seemed to hesitate. "And you might well do so if you were to come with me. Delilah isn't going to let you go until my trail is as cold as ice, so just behave."

"Malachi!"

It was too late. He had gone. She could hear his footsteps as he pounded down the stairs.

With a cry of pure exasperation, Shannon jerked hard upon her wrists, then slammed her head against her pillow. Tears formed in her eyes.

How could she have been so incredibly stupid?

She tried to breathe deeply, to regain a sense of control. She stared at her left wrist, then tried to free it. He was good with knots, she determined. The ties did not hurt her, but they seemed impossible to loosen.

She fell back in exasperation.

There had to be some way out of it. There had to be.

She stared at the ceiling for several long minutes. The best she could come up with was a fairly dirty trick, but she had to try it.

She waited. This time, she wanted to make sure that he was gone. She waited longer.

Then she screamed, high-pitched, long and hard and with a note of pure terror.

Within seconds, Delilah burst in upon her, her dark skin gray with fear. "Shannon! What is it?"

"Beyond my window! Right outside! There's someone here, oh, I know it, Delilah!"

Shannon lowered her lashes quickly. She wondered if God would ever forgive her for the awful scare she was giving Delilah, then she figured that most men and women who had survived the war had a few sins on their consciences— God was just going to have to sort them all out. He would understand, after all they had been through, that she had to go after her sister herself, come what may.

"Outside, now?" Delilah whispered.

"Let me up before someone gets in!" Shannon urged her. She was whispering, too, and she didn't know why. It didn't make much sense, not after her blood-curdling scream.

Delilah hurried over to the bed, clicking her tongue as she worked on Shannon's left-hand knot. "Lord, child, but that man can tie a good knot!"

"Get a knife. There's a little letter opener in my top drawer. It's probably sharp enough."

Delilah nodded, hurrying. She came back and started sawing away at the stocking. "Yes, he sure can tie a knot!" she murmured once again.

"I know," Shannon said bleakly. Then she looked up, and her eyes met Delilah's.

Delilah jumped back, dropping the letter opener and shaking her finger at Shannon. "Why, you young devil! This whole thing was a ploy!"

Delilah had nearly severed the knot. Shannon yanked hard and managed to split the rest of the fibers. The letter opener was within her reach on the bed. She grabbed it before Delilah could reach it, and quickly severed the second bind.

Then she was free.

"Shannon McCahy—"

"I love you, Delilah," Shannon said, quickly hugging her and giving her a kiss on the cheek. "Take care of Gabe."

"Shannon, don't you go getting yourself killed! Your death will be on my conscience! Oh, Lord, but your poor pa must be rolling over in his grave!"

"Pa would understand," Shannon said, then she hurried from the room. She had lost a lot of time. Malachi would ride hard at night. It wouldn't be easy to catch up with him. Not that she wanted to meet up with him tonight. She just wanted to find him so that she could follow along behind him.

She hurried down the stairs. Delilah had picked up her saddlebags from the porch and dragged them into the hallway. Shannon knelt and checked her belongings. She reached into the top drawer beneath the empty Colt brackets and found matches and added them to her bags.

Delilah had followed her downstairs. Once again, Shannon hugged her.

"Come home soon," Delilah said.

"If Matthew comes, you tell him what happened. Maybe, maybe Matt can do something if the rest of us fail."

"Shannon—"

"We're not going to fail." She gave Delilah a brief, hard hug and hurried out of the house.

Entering the stables seemed strange, even just seeing the hay bales where she had fallen beneath Malachi.

She was startled to discover that she had paused and imagined the two of them as they had been that night, so very close in the hay. A curious heat swept over her, because she was remembering him as a man. The touch of his hands, the curve of his smile. The masculine scent of him. The husky tones of his voice.

She pressed her hands against her cheeks with shame. She wasn't in love with Malachi Slater. She didn't even like him. She had hated him for years.

But that wasn't what disturbed her. What disturbed her was a sense of disloyalty. She had been in love. Deeply in love. So in love that when she had heard of Robert's death, she had wanted to die herself. She had ceased to care about the war; she had ceased to care about the very world.

And now her cheeks were heating because Malachi Slater had spent the night touching her . . .

In anger, she reminded herself.

But with laughter, too, and with a new tension. And he had teased and taunted her.

And promised her things.

He had whispered against her flesh, and his words had often been husky and warm. She had never denied him his dashing charm or, in her heart, his bold masculinity.

She had just never realized how deeply it could touch her as a woman.

Her breath seemed to catch in her throat and she emitted a soft sound of annoyance with herself. He was a Rebel, and he was Malachi, and she would never forgive him for being either. She needed him tonight. And she would find him.

She quickly assessed the horses in the stables. She chose not to take Arabesque, her own mare, for the horse was a dapple gray, a color that glowed in the moonlight. She patted the mare quickly. "Not this time, sweetheart. I need someone dark as the night, and fleet as a bullet. Hmm . . ."

She had to hurry.

Without wasting further time, she decided on Chapperel, a swift and beautiful animal, part Arabian, part racer, nearly seventeen hands high and able to run like lightning.

He was also as black as jet, as black as the night.

"Come on, boy, we're going for a ride," she told the gelding, as she quickly saddled and bridled him and led him from the stables.

She looked at the sky. There was barely a sliver of a moon, but the stars were bright. Still, the trail would be very dark. It would be almost impossible for her to track Malachi.

But maybe it wouldn't be so hard to track the twenty horses that had raced before him. They had headed west—that much she knew for a fact.

And they would be staying off the main roads, she thought.

The Red Legs who had taken Kristin might still be a part of the Union army, and then again, they might not. No Union commander in his right mind was going to sanction the kidnapping of young women. No, these people had to be outlaws...

And they wouldn't be taking the main roads. They would be heading west by the smaller trails, and that was what she would do, too.

How much of a lead did Malachi have on her? An hour at most.

Shannon nudged the gelding, and he broke instantly into a smooth and swift canter.

And seconds later, he was galloping. The night wind cooled Shannon's face and touched her with the sweet fragrance of the earth. The darkness swept around her as she crossed the ranch and then the open plain.

Then it was time to choose a trail. She ignored the main road where the wagons headed west and where, over the past years, armies had marched by with their cannons and caissons. There was a smaller trail, rough and ragged and barely discernible, through the trees.

She reined in and dismounted and moved close to the ground, picking up a clump of earth. There were hoof marks all around.

She rose and felt a newly broken branch.

This was the trail she would take.

Malachi knew Missouri like the back of his hand.

He knew the cities, and he knew the Indian territories, and the farmlands and ranches. He could slip through Kentucky and Arkansas and even parts of Texas with his eyes nearly closed.

But these boys were moving west into Kansas. In another hour, they'd be over the border.

And he was an ex-Confederate cavalry captain, still wearing his uniform jacket.

He should have changed it. He should have accepted Shannon's offer of a civilian jacket, but somehow, he had been loathe to part with the uniform. He'd been wearing it for too many years. He'd ridden with too many good men, and he'd seen too many of them shot down in the prime of life, to forget the war. It was over. That was what they said. Abraham Lincoln had said that they must bind the wounds. "With malice towards none, with justice for all."

But then Old Abe had been gunned down, too, and in the blink of an eye, the South had begun to see what was going to be.

She was broken; she was laid to waste. Northern opportunists and plain old crooks swept down upon the fine manors and mansions, and liquor-selling con men were stirring up the ex-slaves to wage a new kind of war against their former masters. Homes and farms were being seized; men and women and children were starving in much of the devastated South.

No...

He probably shouldn't be heading into Kansas in a Confederate jacket. It was just damned hard to take it off. They didn't have a whole lot left. Just pride.

He had fought in the regular cavalry. Fought hard, and fought brilliantly. They had often hung on against impossible odds. They had a right to be proud, even in defeat.

And maybe, even in Kansas, he might have been able to ride through in his uniform if he wasn't who he was. If there hadn't been wanted posters out on him. But if he found himself picked up by the law because of his pride, he wouldn't be able to do Kristin any good, he would probably be hanged, and his pride would definitely be worthless stuff.

Tomorrow, he would pick up some clothes someplace. He'd be much better off traveling as a simple rancher. Displaced, maybe. An ex-Reb. He wouldn't be so damned obvious.

Not that he meant to be in Kansas long. He would get Kristin and get out. There would be plenty of places, deep in Missouri, to hide out until he found Cole and Jamie and decided what to do.

A swift gray shadow seemed to fall over his heart.

They would probably have to leave the country. Head down to Mexico, or over to Europe. The thought infuriated him. The injustice of it was absurd, but no one was going to give any of the Slater brothers a chance to explain. That son of a bitch Fitz had branded them, and because they were Rebs, the brand was going to stick.

Malachi reined in suddenly. In the distance, far ahead, he could see the soft glow of a new fire.

The Red Legs had stopped to make camp for the night.

He nudged the bay mare forward once again. He had been riding hard for hours, and it was nearly midnight, but they still had a certain distance on him.

Carefully, warily, Malachi closed that distance.

When the crackling fires were still far ahead of him, he dismounted from the bay. He whispered to the horse and dropped the reins, then started forward on foot.

The Red Legs had stopped in a large copse right beside a slim stream. Coming up behind them through the trees, Malachi found a close position guarded by a large rock and hunkered down to watch.

There were at least twenty men. They were busy cooking up beans and a couple of jackrabbits on two separate spits. A number of the men had lain down against their saddles before the fire, but a number of them were on guard, too. Three men were watching the horses, tethered to the left of the stream. As he looked across the clearing, Malachi could see two of them against the trees.

They were armed with the new Spencer repeating rifles. They would be no easy prey.

Looking around again, he saw the worst of it.

Kristin was tied to a tree near the brook. Her beautiful blond hair tumbled around her face, but her skin was white and her eyes were closed. She was exhausted, and desolate...

And guarded by two men.

Even as Malachi watched, the situation changed. The tall, burly man who had taken her from the house was walking her way. He bent beside her. Her eyes flew open and she stared at him with stark hatred. The man laughed.

"Sweet thing, I just thought that you might be hungry."

"Hungry for the likes of you, eh, Bear?" shouted a tall, lean dirty blond with a scruffy mustache. He stood up and sauntered toward the tree. He leaned down by Kristin, too. "Sweet, sweet thing. My, my, why don't you come on over and have dinner with me? Roger Holstein, ma'am—"

Kristin spit at him. A roar of laughter went up, and the young man's face darkened with fury. He lunged for her.

The man he'd called Bear pulled him back. "You keep your hands off her."

"Why? We weren't even supposed to bring her back. We were supposed to find Cole Slater. So you tell me why I can't have the woman."

Another man by the fire stood up. "Why should you have her, Holstein? What's the matter with the rest of us?"

"No one's gonna have her, and that's the way I say it is!" Bear bellowed, and Malachi slumped against the rock, relieved. Bear took a step toward Roger Holstein, shaking his fist. "You listen, and you listen good. The woman is mine. I took her. And I'm still the law in this unit—"

"Hell!" Roger Holstein muttered. "We ain't no unit anymore. The war is over."

"We're a unit. We're a unit because we belong to Fitz, just like we always have. And I was there that day Cole Slater shot down Henry and half a troop. He ain't no fool. If he hears that she's already been abused by you pack of trash, he'll take his time. He'll come after us slow and careful. And he won't be alone. He's got a pair of brothers who can pick the eyes out of hummingbirds in the next damn state with their Colts." Bear hesitated, looking at Kristin. "We don't hurt the woman."

"Hell, Bear, I wasn't going to hurt her!" Roger complained. "I was gonna make her have a hell of a good time!"

"You don't touch her. Fitz decides what to do with her. By my mind, leaving the lady her tender flesh and sweet chastity will come in real handy as bargaining power."

For a moment, Malachi thought that fighting was going to break out right then. He prayed silently that it would not; he would never be able to slip away with Kristin if it did.

He didn't think that his prayers would be answered. The tension among the men was as thick as flies on a steer carcass. It escalated until every man in the place was silent, until only the sound of the crackling fires could be heard.

Then Roger Holstein backed down.

"Have it your way, Bear. We'll see. When we get back to Fitz, we'll see."

"Damned right, we will," Bear agreed.

Malachi looked at Kristin. Her eyes were closed again. She was silent and probably grateful that the situation had calmed.

Thank God it was Kristin there and not Shannon. Shannon was incapable of keeping silent. She would be raging and fighting and biting and kicking and creating complete disaster.

Malachi sank against the rock, closing his eyes, exhaling slowly. He wondered what had made him think of Shannon.

The whole damned night had been filled with Shannon, he reminded himself wryly. But she was safe. Delilah would just be releasing her sometime around now. And she would know that there would be no way in hell to follow a trail that cold.

Thank God it wasn't Shannon? he queried himself. Hmph! If it had been Shannon, he wouldn't be here now. He wouldn't be sneaking into Kansas in his Confederate uniform. He'd be headed south. If it had been Shannon kidnapped, he would have pitied the damned Red Legs.

No, she surely hadn't been a Circe this evening. She had been a complete spitfire, stubborn, willful and . . .

Beautiful.

Just like the woman in his dream, the sweet vision who had brought him from the brink of death. She was beautiful, perhaps even more beautiful than Kristin, for she was a searing flame, with a life so vibrant that her golden hair was touched by the fire, as were her eyes, brilliant, sparkling, searing. Her voice was like a lark's, sweet and pure . . . even when she yelled.

Actually, he wasn't thinking about her eyes.

He was thinking about her hands, and the tenderness in her fingers when she had cleansed and bound his wound.

No . . .

He wasn't even thinking about that.

He was thinking about the provocative swell of her breasts when she leaned over him, when she brushed against him. He was thinking of the lithe and shapely heat of her body, the slimness of her waist, the softness of her flesh, the full sensuality of her lips.

Shannon had grown up.

He slunk down into the rock, pulling his hat low over his forehead. She was still Shannon McCahy. The little brat who had been on his tail since he had first walked onto the McCahy ranch. She had fired at him that very first time, and she was firing at him still.

He smiled and leaned back.

He had kissed her once. To shut her up. They were all playing innocent when a Yank officer had come by the ranch, and Shannon, bless her sweet, sweet hide, would have gladly handed him right over.

And so he had kissed her.

It did seem to be the only way to shut her up.

But the kiss had been sweet. Her passion then had been that of anger, but passion nevertheless, and it had feathered against his senses until he had realized who she was, and what he was doing.

But now, tonight, he remembered that kiss.

He opened his eyes and clamped his teeth together. He knotted his fingers into fists and then slowly released them, suddenly aware that he wanted her. That he desired her, hotly, hungrily and completely.

Wanting a woman wasn't so strange, he reminded himself. Over the years, he had wanted a number of women, and, during the war, when lovers were quickly won and lovers quickly lost, many young women, like many men, were quick to seek the solace of the moment. The women he had wanted he had often had. The widow in Arkansas, the desolate, lonely farm woman in Kentucky, the dance-hall girl in Mississippi.

Once, it seemed like a long, long time ago now, there had been a girl he had loved. Ariel Denison. Ariel ... He had even loved the sound of her name. They had been very young. The sight of him could bring a flush to her cheeks, and the warmth of her dark eyes upon him alone could bring forth all the ardor in his heart and soul. Her father had approved, and they were to have been married in June. They spent what May days they could together, hand in hand, racing down to the stream, daring to swim together, daring to come to the shore and lie naked in the sweet grasses, making love. He'd never known anything so deep, or so wonderful ...

But by June, she was gone. A cholera epidemic swept through the countryside, and Ariel, smiling to the last, had died in his arms, whispering her last words of love with the last of her breaths. He had not cared then if he contracted the disease. He hadn't cared at all, but he had lived. Since then, he hadn't fallen in love again. He had given his passion to his land; his loyalty had been to his family and, once the war came, to the Confederacy.

He didn't remember much about love...

But no man lived long without desire. He was used to that. So it was strange to discover with what depth and fervor he desired Shannon.

The brat. His foremost enemy. The ardent, fanatical Unionist. The bane of his every trip to the ranch. Shannon...

"Hey!" came a sudden, loud shout. "Did you hear that?"

Malachi turned around, looking over the rock toward the camp. The guards by the horses were moving. Half the men had begun to settle down for the evening.

Now they were waking up.

Bear strode toward the guards. "What? What is it? I don't hear anything."

"There's something there. Something out in the bushes."

They had seen him. They had heard him, Malachi thought.

But they hadn't. The guard was pointing in the other direction.

"You scared of a bobcat or a weasel?" Bear sneered.

"It weren't no weasel!" the guard protested.

Bear paused, then shrugged. He looked at two of the men. "You, Wills, and you, Hartman, go take a look around. The rest of you, keep your eyes open."

Hell! Malachi thought. If they went snooping around too far, they would find the bay. He cursed whatever creature had been sneaking around the camp. If it was a weasel, he hoped some poor bastard ate the creature.

He sank against his rock. They weren't going to look for him there, not right beneath their noses. He was going to have to sit tight and wait. If they would just settle down for the night, even with the guards on duty, he would be able to reach Kristin. Once the camp was quiet, he would be able to circle around and come at her from the stream. He would have to kill the guards by the horses; he wouldn't have any choice.

Malachi frowned suddenly, feeling the earth beneath his hands. He lay against the ground and listened to the tremors of the earth.

Someone else was out riding that night. Not too far distant, a group of horsemen was coming toward them.

A Union patrol?

He thought they were still in Missouri, but they might have crossed over the border. They had really headed south as much as they had headed west. Not that it mattered much. Union patrols were everywhere.

But it could also be a Southern outfit, heading home.

Maybe it didn't matter. Maybe it did.

He tensed, waiting.

Then a shrill and furious scream caught his attention. He swung around, looking into the center of the Red Legs camp.

"Son of a bitch!" he swore beneath his breath, staring. "If they leave behind just a piece of her, I'm going to skin her alive!"

Shannon had just been thrown into the center of the camp. Hartman and Wills had brought her, and with laughter and gusto cast her with force into the den of rogues.

Wills was limping, swearing away.

"She shot off my toe!" he howled.

"Thank God she can't aim," Roger said, chortling.

"I did aim, you stupid ass," Shannon said with venom. "If I'd have wished it, I'd have shot out your heart."

Wills went silent; even Roger went silent. There was a chill around them all, as if they knew her words to be the truth.

"Get down there, witch!" Wills swore savagely. He shoved her down, hard.

She landed on her knees. She had changed clothing, and wore tight black trousers, a gingham tailored shirt and a pair of sturdy brown boots. She'd worn a hat, a broad-brimmed hat, but now it lay several feet from her in the dust. Her hair had been pinned, but the pins were strewn around her, and her hair was falling, like a golden sunrise, in delicate rays down her back.

Malachi bit hard into his lip as she raised her chin to face Bear, all her heat and fury and passion alive in her eyes. She shouldn't have changed. The perfection of her form was even more apparent in the tight breeches and man's shirt, and he was not the only one to notice. The Red Legs were all rising, one by one, creating a circle around her.

"My, my, my," Roger Holstein drawled. He moved his tongue over his lips. "What have we here?" He stepped out of the circle, coming toward her. Shannon struggled quickly to her feet. Malachi tensed, watching the sizzle in her eyes.

"Don't be stupid, Shannon!" he muttered to himself. "Be quiet, be good, let them tie you up and I can get you out . . . don't be stupid!"

But she was going to be stupid. Roger reached for her, and Shannon moved like lightning, sinking her teeth into his hand. He screamed with pain, then caught her with his backhand, sending her spiraling into the dirt. "Bitch!" he roared.

The men laughed like hyenas. "Least she didn't shoot you, Roge!" Wills said.

Roger came forward again, sucking at his sore hand.

"Get away from her," Bear ordered, coming into the center of the ring.

"Oh, no, you don't," Roger said with hostility. "That one is for Fitz. Fine. This one is mine."

"I'll die first, I swear it!" Shannon hissed from the ground. She seemed to sense that her only hope was Bear. Holding her cheek, she rose and raced behind him. "I'll kill you—"

"Yeah, watch it, man, the little lady will bite you to death!" someone jeered.

"Get out of my way, Bear!" Roger howled. "She's mine!"

"No!"

"You've got Slater's wife—"

"This is his sister-in-law, you idiot."

Roger paused to look from one woman to the other. It was impossible to miss the resemblance. "So they're sisters. So what of it?"

Kristin called out then. "You touch her, and I'll kill myself, you bastard! Then you'll have nothing, nothing at all—"

"Kristin!"

Shannon burst through the throng of men, racing for her sister. Bear caught her just before she could get to Kristin's side. He swept her up by the waist, laughing. "Little darlin'!" he exclaimed. "If you go to anybody, sweet pea, you go to old papa bear!"

He reached up with one of his great hands and clutched the front of her shirt, tearing. Shannon screamed and savagely swung a kick his way.

She did know how to aim.

With a tremendous groan, Bear dropped her and doubled over. Shannon pulled his gun from his holster and swung around, facing the men, who were all on their feet.

"Don't take a chance," she warned them, backing carefully toward Kristin. "I know what I'm doing with this thing."

"You can't kill us all," Roger told her, but he didn't take another step her way.

"I can castrate at least six of you," Shannon promised, and at least six of the men took a step backward.

"Now, all that I want is my sister," Shannon began. She kept talking, but Malachi no longer heard her words because there was movement behind her. One of the guards watching the horses had drawn his knife and was sneaking up behind her.

"Damn!" Malachi mouthed. He couldn't shoot at the man; Shannon was in the way. If she would move...just a hair.

She didn't. The guard came up behind her and slipped the knife around her quickly, right at her throat, against her jugular.

"Castrate us!" Roger chortled as she dropped the gun. "Why, honey, we're all going to make you glad that you didn't—"

The man with the knife moved. Just enough.

Damn her, damn her, damn her, Malachi thought. They were probably all dead now. But he couldn't wait any longer.

He rose and he fired. He got the guard right between the eyes. The man fell.

Shannon reached down for the gun she had dropped. Confusion reigned as men rushed toward her, as men looked around, anxious to discover who had fired the shot.

Malachi kept shooting. He didn't have any choice. He tried to aim and focus and to keep a good eye on Shannon, too. Men fell, and men screamed, and dust flew. But there were too many of them, just too many of them.

Shannon had been holding her own. But in the midst of the melee, Bear stumbled to his feet. He staggered toward Shannon from the rear while another man approached her from the front. She aimed forward...

And Bear took a firm swipe against her arm, sending the gun flying. She turned to fight, and he punched her hard in the mouth. Her eyes closed and she slumped to the ground.

"Get him! Get that varmint in the woods!" Bear ordered.

"Varmint?" Malachi stood up, staring at Bear. "Excuse me, you jayhawking jackals. Captain Malachi Slater, late of Hunt's magnificent cavalry, and still, my friends, a Southern gentleman. Shall we?"

"It's a damned Reb!" one of the guards shouted.

"It's more than that. It's a damned Reb Slater!" Bear roared. "Kill him!"

Well, this is it, Malachi thought. Shannon had wanted him to die for honor, and he would just have to go down that way. He stood, firing again and again as the Red Legs raced toward him, trying to fire, but failing. He ran out of bullets as a pair of them charged over the rocks, but he had his saber with him, and he drew that. He charged in turn, and managed to kill the first two men, but more of them were coming for him, more and more...

He was engaged with one fighter when he noticed a carbine aimed his way. He wasn't even going to have time to ask forgiveness of his sins, he thought. No time to mourn...

A blast sounded.

It was the Yank holding the carbine who fell, and not Malachi. Amazed, he looked around.

Hoofbeats! He had heard the hoofbeats! And now the riders were upon them.

"It's a pack of Red Legs!" shouted a man leaping into the scene on a dapple gray stallion. "Red Legs! Bloody, bleeding, murderin', connivin' Red Legs!"

"Reg Legs!" came another shout.

And they all let out with a sound near and dear to Malachi at that moment.

A Rebel cry went up. Savage, sweet, beautiful to his ears.

He watched as the six horsemen charged the scene. They were in plumed hats and railroad coats, no uniforms, and yet he thought he knew who they were. He was sure that he recognized the young man on the dapple gray mare.

He did. These boys had been with Quantrill. He knew two of them. Frank and Jesse James. Jesse had been a bare kid when he had tasted his first blood, but then lots of boys had become men quickly in the war.

Now this little group was probably headed home, toward southern Missouri. They still seemed young. Even with the war over. But then, Quantrill had depended on young blood, youthful, eager, savage raiders.

Quantrill was dead now. Bloody Bill Anderson was dead, and Little Archie Clement was dead. Archie who had loved to scalp his enemies. Archie had been with the bushwhackers who had so savagely mowed down the contingent of Union officers sent to catch them, the contingent that had included Shannon's fiancé...

Well, Malachi didn't think much of bushwhackers, but these boys had come just in time. Maybe Shannon would accept rescue. Maybe she would keep her mouth closed. But he had to get to her.

He could barely see through the tangle of fighting men and horses, bushwhackers and jayhawkers. He rose, staring over the wavering light of the fires.

He heard a high-pitched scream, and his heart thudded painfully.

He looked between a pair of horses as they danced, a deadly dance for their riders. In the gap he could see Bear. The man was cutting Kristin loose from the tree and throwing her over his shoulder.

Roger Holstein broke away from the battle and joined Bear. Wills, with his bloody toe, ran after them, too.

"Damn it, no!" Malachi swore. Where was Shannon? He couldn't see her. Did the bushwhackers have her, too?

No, they didn't, not that group, anyway. Bear and Holstein and Wills had mounted and pulled away. They were heading fast for the trail, heading west.

"Damn it, no!" Malachi raged again, pushing his way through the warring bushwhackers and jayhawkers, racing toward the Union horses. Bear was gone with Kristin, long gone before he could reach them.

"Malachi!"

It was Shannon. He whirled around in time to see one of the James brothers racing along beside her and sweeping her up onto his mount.

"Hey, you got yourself a girl, Frank!" One of the other riders laughed.

"Not just a girl, Jessie! D'you know who this is?"

"Who?"

"That Yankee-lovin' McCahy brat! Had herself hitched up to one for a while, before we did him in—ouch!" he screamed, looking down at the girl thrown over his saddle, then up at his brother again. "She bites."

"Yellow-bellied bushwhackers!" Shannon screamed. But Malachi sensed something different in her screams, in the sound of her voice.

He heard the pain.

She knew now that these men had been there the day when Robert Ellsworth had been killed, and she would never ask for their mercy.

"Shannon!" he thundered her name over the clash of steel and the explosion of gunfire.

"Let's go!" Frank shouted. He fired a number of shots into the air.

Malachi had swung around, racing toward Frank, when one of the Red Legs jumped in front of him, his sword drawn.

He didn't have time for a fight!

The mounted bushwhackers were gathering together. They had come, they had done their damage. Now they were riding away.

The Red Legs with the sword lunged toward Malachi.

"Ah, hell!" Malachi swore, engaging in the battle. The fellow wasn't a bad swordsman. In fact, he did damned well.

He grinned at Malachi as their swords locked at the hilt. "West Point, class of '58."

"Good for you, ya bloody Yank!" Malachi retorted. He pulled away, parrying a sudden thrust, ducking another.

The riders were pounding farther and farther away, into the night.

"You're good, Reb!" his opponent called.

"Thanks, and you're in my way, Yank," Malachi replied.

"In your way? Why, you're almost dead, man!"

"No, sir, you are almost dead."

Always fight with a cool head...

It had been one of the first rules that Malachi had ever learned. His comment had provoked his opponent. It was the advantage he needed.

The Red Legs lifted his sword high for a smashing blow. Malachi thrust straight, catching the man quickly and cleanly through the heart.

He fell without a whimper.

Malachi pulled his sword clean and leaped away from his fallen foe, swinging to counter any new attack.

But he was alone.

Alone with a sea of corpses.

At least twelve of the Red Legs lay dead, strewn here and there over their camp bags, over their saddles, over their weapons; some shot and some thrust through by swords. Only one of the raiders lay on the ground. A very young boy with a clear complexion.

He groaned. Malachi stooped beside him, carefully turning him over. Blood stained his shirt. Malachi opened it quickly. There was no way the boy could live. He'd been riddled with shot in the chest. Malachi pressed the tail ends of the shirt hard against him, trying to staunch the flow of blood. The boy opened his eyes.

"I'm going to die, captain, ain't I?"

He might have said something else, but the boy already knew. Malachi nodded. "The pain will be gone, boy."

"I can't die. I got tobacco in my pocket. Ma would just kill me. That's a laugh, ain't it? But she'd be awful, awful disappointed in me."

"I'll get that tobacco out, boy," Malachi said.

The youth's eyes had already closed again. Malachi thought that the boy had heard him, though. It seemed that his lip curled into a grateful smile just as the life left his eyes.

Malachi eased the boy to the ground. Someone would come, and someone would find him.

This was border country still. He might be sent to his home.

Malachi dug the tobacco out of the boy's pocket and tossed it over one of the older Red Legs. "Your ma won't find no tobacco, boy," he said softly. Then he stood and he looked around at the sea of dead again.

The clearing was absurdly silent and peaceful now. Its inhabitants all lay quiet, tumbled atop one another as if they rested in a strange and curious sleep. He walked among them quickly, cursing to himself, but he couldn't just leave a man if he was wounded, whether he was a Reb or a Yank.

He needn't have worried. Every one of the Red Legs in the clearing was dead. Dead, and growing cold.

Malachi stepped from the clearing and looked down the road. He stared up at the night sky. The silence was all around him. The sound of horses' hooves had died away in the distance.

"Damn!" he swore.

The Red Legs had taken Kristin in one direction.

The raiders had taken Shannon the opposite way.

Which the hell did he follow?

He didn't take long to decide. He would get Shannon first. He could bargain with the James boys, he was sure. If Shannon could keep quiet for about two seconds he could get her back quickly. He would go after Shannon first.

Though for the life of him, he wasn't at all sure why.

Chapter Five

Shannon could not remember a more miserable night in her life.

The raider party traveled through what remained of it. Somewhere, at the beginning, she had said something that the men really hadn't liked—though she couldn't see where they would like anything that she had to say to them—and she had been bound hand and foot and gagged and tossed over the haunches of the horse.

Then they had begun to ride, in earnest.

They knew their territory. They followed no specific route. They traveled over plains and through tangles of bracken and brush.

They talked about going home, and they talked about the friend they had left behind.

"Willie was dead, shot in the chest, there wasn't nothing that we could do. He went down fighting."

"Yeah, he went down fighting. Well, the war's over. Someone ought to find him and give his body to his ma."

"Yeah, someone ought to find him."

"God help him."

"God help us all."

For a while, Shannon listened to their words, but she couldn't believe that they would try to invoke God's aid, and then, as they kept on quietly conversing, she began to weave in and out of reality. She couldn't understand them anymore. She knew who they were. The remnants of Quantrill's Raiders. They had ridden with Quantrill. They had ridden with Bloody Bill Anderson, and with little Archie Clement.

They might well have been with the raiders on a bloody awful day outside Centralia when the bushwhackers had massacred the small contingent of green recruits sent after them. When they had dismembered the corpses and the dying, scalped them and sliced off ears and noses and privates to be stuffed down their throats...

It was how Captain Robert Ellsworth had died. And as she lay trussed and tossed over the haunches of the horse, it made her feel faint, and it made her feel ill.

The night went on and on.

Then Shannon realized that it wasn't night anymore, it was day. They had traveled miles and miles without rest, or if they had paused to rest, she had been unconscious when they had done so.

It was no longer night. It was day. The sun streamed overhead, and the songs of larks could be heard on the air. Somewhere nearby, a brook bubbled and played.

They had come so far. So very far. She wondered bleakly where Kristin was. She had been so certain that when the Red Legs had settled down and slept, she would have been able to slip in and free her sister.

But then the men had come for her.

And now Kristin was being taken one way, and she was being taken another.

And where was Malachi? He had been there. She had seen him firing and fighting, and then he had disappeared. And then she had seen him again just when she had been swept up into the arms of the bushwhacker.

He had probably followed Kristin, she thought. He had gone for his brother's wife. And she was glad of it, Shannon thought. She was so glad of it, because the men might well hurt Kristin...

What were these men going to do with her?

The gag choked her, making her feel ill all over again. They knew her. They knew that she was old McCahy's daughter, and that her sympathy had been with the North. They surely knew that she was Cole Slater's sister-in-law, but that probably wouldn't count for much. She had been engaged to marry a Union officer, she was the sister of a Union officer, and they knew that she hated them with every breath in her body.

What would they do to her?

And what could be worse than this torture she had already endured, hanging hour after hour over the horse this way, her face slamming against the sweaty flesh and hair and flanks of the animal? She ached in every muscle of her body. It would never, never end.

Then suddenly, at last, they stopped.

Hands wound around her waist, pulling her from the horse. Had she been able to, she would have screamed at the sudden agony of the movement; it felt as if her arms were breaking.

"There you go, Yank," the man said, setting her down beneath a tree. The others were dismounting. They formed a semicircle around her, all of them staring at her.

"What are we going to do with her, Frank?"

The man who asked the question stepped forward. His name was Jesse, Shannon knew that much. And he was Frank's brother. The two of them had spoken occasionally during the endless ride.

Neither of them was much older than she, but they both carried a curious coldness in their eyes. Perhaps they had ceased to feel; perhaps they had even lost a sense of humanity in all the violence of their particular war. She didn't know. And at that moment, she was so worn and exhausted, she wasn't even sure that she cared.

"I wonder what the Red Legs wanted with her," Jesse mused.

"Same thing any man would want with her, I reckon," someone spoke up from the rear. Shannon blinked, trying to see him. He was tall and dark-haired with a pencil-slim mustache, and he smiled at her in such a way that she felt entirely naked.

She closed her eyes. At that particular moment, she just wanted to die. Bushwhackers. The same men who had brutalized Robert might be about to touch her. Death would be infinitely better.

"Better loosen up that gag," the one named Jesse said. "We're losing her, I think. She's going to pass out on us."

Frank stepped forward, slipping the gag from her mouth. Shannon fought a sudden wave of nausea. He leaned over her and slit the ropes tying her wrists and ankles. Her blood started to flow again, but she could still barely move. She rubbed her wrists, backing against the tree, staring at the lot of them. There were five of them left. Jesse and Frank, Jesse with a round young face and dark, attractive eyes, Frank taller and leaner, older. There was the dark-haired man who taunted, and two smaller, light-haired men. Maybe they were brothers, too, she didn't know.

"What's your name?" Jesse asked.

She stared at him in furious silence. They seemed to know everything else. They ought to know her name.

"Shannon. Shannon McCahy," the tall, dark-haired one said. "She was picked up with her sister when the Federals decided to put all the families away. She was there when the house fell apart, when Bill's sister and those other girls were killed and wounded."

"Then she's a Southerner—" Jesse began.

Frank snorted and spit on the ground. "She ain't no Southerner, Jesse. You heard her. She's Yank through and through. Just like her blue-belly pa with the yellow streak down his back—"

Movement came back to her. She felt no pain. Like a bolt of lightning, Shannon flew at the man in a rage. She did so with such force that he went flying to the ground. "You murderers!" she hissed. "You hideous rodents..."

murderers!'' Pummeling the startled man who couldn't seem to fight her fury, Shannon then saw the gun in his belt. She grabbed it and aimed it straight at his nose. The others had been about to seize her. She swung around with Frank's Colt, aiming it right at Jesse. He lifted his hands and backed away.

"We didn't kill your pa, little girl," Jesse said softly. "We weren't there. Zeke Moreau had his own splinter group. You know that."

She gritted her teeth, thinking about Robert, trembling inwardly at the depth of the hate that seared her. She could have pulled the trigger. She would have happily maimed or wounded or killed any one of them. When she thought about Centralia . . .

Jesse knelt in front of her, speaking earnestly. "You're just seeing one side of it, you know. One side. They came in—the jayhawkers, the Red Legs—they came in and ripped us all up really bad, too, you know. We all got farms burned down or kin slain. It always did work two ways—"

"Two ways!" Shannon exclaimed. "Two ways!" She was choking. "I never heard of anything as bad as Centralia. Ever. In the town, unarmed men were stripped and shot down. And outside the town, the things you people did to the Union men shouldn't have been done to the lowest of creatures, much less human beings—"

"You obviously haven't seen much of the handiwork done by your friends, the Red Legs," the tall, dark man said dryly.

"You ain't gonna change her mind," Frank said from the ground.

The dark-haired man moved closer, a wary eye on the Colt. "My name is Justin Waller, Miss McCahy. And I was there, at Centralia—"

"Bastard!" Shannon hissed.

"Justin—" Jesse warned sharply, but Shannon already had the gun aimed straight between Justin Waller's eyes. She pulled the trigger.

And she heard the click of an empty chamber.

"Son of a bitch!" Justin swore. He reached for Shannon. She couldn't escape him quickly enough and he dragged her to her feet. She screamed as he twisted her arm hard behind her back.

"Justin—" Jesse began.

"That bitch meant to kill me!"

"Don't hurt her. We don't know what we're doing with her yet."

"I know what I'm gonna do with her," Justin growled savagely. His free hand played over her throat and the rise of her breasts, which had been left bare when the Red Legs had ripped her shirt. The little pink flowers and white linen of her corset were absurdly delicate against the tattered fragments of the man's ranch shirt.

Shannon recoiled, kicking out desperately. Justin pulled harder upon her arm and she choked back another scream of pain. He pressed her to her knees. "Get me some rope, Jesse. I'm too damned tired to truly enjoy what I intend to do with this little beauty. And she can't be trusted an inch."

Jesse lifted a length of rope from his saddle pommel, but he stared at Justin contemplatively as he walked toward him. "We ain't decided about her yet, Justin."

"We ain't decided what?" Justin had his knee in Shannon's back as he looped the rope around her wrists.

She gritted her teeth against the pain.

"She's kin to Cole Slater," Jesse said softly. "And I never did cotton to the idea of rape and murder, Justin."

"You rode with Quantrill."

"Quantrill didn't murder women."

"All right, Jesse. All right. I ain't gonna murder her."

"You're right, you ain't. I'm in control here."

"War's over, Jesse."

"I'm still in control here, you understand that."

Justin jerked hard on the rope, then shoved Shannon flat on the ground. She tasted dirt as he grasped her ankles and began looping a knot around them.

"Maybe we oughta just let her go," one of the light-haired men said. "Hell, Justin, we ain't supposed to rape our own kind—"

"She ain't our own kind. And if we just let her go, she'll have the law down on us so fast our heads will spin. That is, if she doesn't get hold of another gun. She shot at me, you fools. She meant to kill me. And you all say what you want, she's going to pay for that."

He jerked hard on the last of his knots. He reached for Shannon's shoulders and dragged her face up close to his. "Bitch, when I wake up, we're going to have some real, real fun."

Shannon spit at him.

Swearing, he wiped his face and tossed her down hard beneath the tree. He stared at the four others, who were looking his way. "And you all can watch, join in or turn the other way, I just don't give a damn."

Shannon watched Jesse James set his jaw hard. "I'm in control here, Justin. We agreed. Don't you forget that."

Justin ignored Jesse and went to his horse. He loosened his saddle and pulled it off and threw it beneath the tree next to Shannon. He fumbled through his saddlebags for a canteen. Looking furiously at the other men, he walked down a grassy slope to the fresh-running spring water of a stream.

"Water," Frank James muttered, following Justin.

Jesse remained, staring at Shannon. She didn't know what he was thinking. "Lots of people lost in this war," he told her quietly. "Hell, ma'am, I do not like half the things I learned to do, but I doubt that I'll ever forget them. We all want to remember the weddings and the christenings and the flowers in the fields on a Sunday. Hell, I never really wanted to get so damned good at killing. I just did." He paused. "You shouldn'ta shot at Justin. It was a mistake."

"He's an animal. He was there—at Centralia. You heard him."

"You still shouldn't have tried to kill him. You got his temper up way high."

He turned away from her. Justin was back, drinking water from his canteen. It spilled over his face and trickled down his jaw. It reminded Shannon just how desperately thirsty she was. He stared at her, and she saw he knew of her thirst. He smiled and drank more deeply.

She wasn't going to beg. Not of a man like that.

Frank James was back by then, too. He was drinking from a wooden Confederate-issue canteen with his initials engraved into the wood. He looked at her, then knelt by her, lifting her head.

"Don't give her no water!" Justin said irritably. "I'll give it to her." He smiled, nudging at Shannon's rump with an evil leer. "If she's good, if she's real good, she'll get some water. You'll see, my friends. Old Justin knows how to take a Yankee shrew."

Frank ignored him, lifting Shannon's head, allowing a trickle of water to cool her face and seep into her mouth. She drank it thirstily.

"Frank!" Justin swore.

Frank told Justin what he should do with himself, and Justin jumped to his feet. Shannon watched the two men with interest, her heart thundering. If they would just rip each other to shreds...

Jesse, who was now leaning against the tree, paring off a bite of dried beef from a strip he'd taken from his saddlebags, spoke sarcastically. "That's good, you two. Real good. Kill each other. She's enjoying every minute of it."

Both men stopped. They stared at her.

"Let's all get some sleep," Jesse said. "You want her that bad, Justin, the girl's yours. But don't kill her. I ain't no murderer of women and children, and I ain't ever gonna be."

He stretched out on the ground, leaning his head upon his saddle. Frank swore and chose another tree.

The two light-haired men found their own shade, and Justin smiled as he settled down beside Shannon. She stared at him, her face against the earth, hating him. He laughed and reached out, slipping his arm around her, twisting her over and pulling her close against him. She squirmed and struggled, choking on the tears that threatened to stream down her face. "Bastard, I swear I'd just as soon die!" she hissed vehemently.

Justin laughed at her futile efforts. Tied hand and foot as she was, she wasn't going to do anything.

His hand hooked beneath her breasts as he pulled her against his chest and the curve of his body. His fingers played over her breasts and rested there. He whispered against her ear. "Just a few hours of sleep, honey. I apologize for being so exhausted. But just a little bit of sleep... I wouldn't want to disappoint you. I want to hear you scream and scream and scream..." Laughing again, he leaned his head back against his saddle, seeking sleep.

Shannon closed her eyes and set her teeth. She gave him time to fall asleep, then tried to edge away from him.

His hand tightened around her like a clamp. "Not on your life, my golden Yank. Not on your life." His fingers moved through her hair. Shannon held her breath, praying that he would stop.

He did. He dug into his saddlebags for another length of rope and grimly tied her wrists to his own. Shannon watched him in bitter silence. When he was done, he smiled and touched her cheek. "You're a beautiful Yank-lover, you know that?"

She ignored him. He lay down to sleep again, chuckling.

Shannon lay awake in misery until absolute exhaustion overwhelmed her. Despite her hunger and thirst and discomfort, she closed her eyes, and sleep claimed her.

To the best of Malachi's knowledge, there was no one on the lookout for the James boys.

But they were riding as if their lives depended on getting into the heart of Missouri just as fast as possible.

And they were hard to track. By the time he'd reached his bay and found Shannon's big black gelding, the raiders were already well ahead of him.

And they knew where they were going. Thank God they had turned southward, deeper into Missouri. It was land he knew. If he hadn't been accustomed to the terrain, he'd never have managed to follow them. They cut a course right through forest lands, knowing unerringly where they could take shortcuts and pick up roads again and disappear back into the forests again.

By midmorning he realized that they were following the course of a small stream. Malachi stuck with it.

He was exhausted. His leg was aching, and he was afraid that the fever might be searing through him again. An hour's worth of sleep just might make it a bit better...

But he didn't dare take an hour. He knew Frank and Jesse James only slightly. He'd met them once in the short time that Cole had ridden with Quantrill, and he'd found them to be reckless, sometimes ruthless kids. He thought it might be the Younger brothers traveling with them, another set of reckless youths.

He didn't think that the James boys were especially cruel or brutal. They were still sane, at least, he thought. Like the Younger brothers. They were probably still sane, if nothing else.

But the other man...

His name was Justin. Malachi knew who he was. Cole had seen him in action early on in the war, and the malice with which the man killed and the pleasure he took from his brutal actions had turned Cole away from Quantrill's gang completely.

But to the most decent bushwhacker out there, Shannon would be quite a tonic to swallow. And she wouldn't keep quiet. She wouldn't be able to do so. He had already heard her ranting and raving.

He didn't have time to rest, not for ten damn minutes.

He paused only to give the horses water, and to douse himself with it, and drink deeply. He chewed on the dried meat he had brought, and swallowed some of the liquor Shannon had packed him. It was good, and it helped to keep the pain in his leg at bay.

It was almost night again when he came upon them at last.

He was still a little distance away when he saw the horses grouped in the trees. There were no cooking fires laid out in the camp; in fact, it was barely a camp at all. The bushwhackers had merely stopped along the road.

Malachi was pretty sure that he'd be able to reason with the men; hell, at least they had obstensibly fought on the same side. But the war had taught him to take nothing for granted, so he dismounted from the bay and tethered her with the black gelding some distance down the stream from the raiders. Then he approached them again in silence, coming close enough this time to see the layout in the camp.

They must have been sure of themselves; very sure. No one was left on guard. Each and every one of the bushwhackers was curled up, sound asleep.

Or maybe they weren't so sound asleep. Men like that learned to sleep differently, with one eye open. If a fly buzzed through that camp, the men would probably be aware of it. He'd be a fool to go sneaking in, no matter how silently he could manage it.

And as he had suspected, Shannon was in trouble.

The Younger brothers were stretched out in front of an oak; the others were all laid out beneath other trees, thirty yards apart, and perhaps fifty yards up the grassy slope from the stream.

Shannon was bound hand and foot, and tied to Justin.

He swore inwardly, thinking she must have fought them tooth and nail, because she seemed to have lost Jesse's protection. Jesse, like many other bushwhackers, despite their savagery, still put Southern womanhood on a pedestal. If she had just kept her mouth closed and acted out the part of the Southern belle . . .

But she hadn't.

Sweat broke out on Malachi's forehead and his hands went clammy as he watched her. She was pale and smudged with dirt, but even so, her features retained their angelic beauty, and her tangled hair swept around her face like a glorious halo. Where the sun fell upon it her hair glowed like golden fire.

She was tied to Justin—but at least she was decently clad. She seemed to sleep the sleep of the dead, but even in that sleep, it seemed she strained with all her heart against the man holding her prisoner.

He hadn't touched her yet. Justin hadn't touched her, Malachi assured himself. But he meant to do so.

At the periphery of the circle, Malachi inhaled and exhaled deeply, deciding what plan of action to take. He could try shooting them all, but the bushwhackers were damned good shots, and if he didn't kill Justin right away, he was certain that Justin would kill Shannon for the pure pleasure of it.

No. This wasn't the time to go in blazing away. He needed to play diplomat.

He stood at the periphery of the camp, his saber and his pistols at his side, but his arms relaxed. "Jesse. Jesse James!" he called out sharply.

They moved as one. As soon as he called out, the five of them were awake, staring at him down the length of their Colts and revolvers.

He lifted his hands. He saw five pairs of eyes look over his gray uniform jacket.

By the tree, Jesse stood.

"Malachi!" Shannon called out. "Malachi!" She struggled to rise. Justin jerked on the rope and clamped his hand hard over her mouth.

Malachi nodded toward Justin, trying to burn a message into Shannon's fool head with the strength of his eyes.

"Hey! It's the fool Reb who was taking on the whole of that Red Legs camp by himself!" One of the Younger brothers called out.

"Malachi. Malachi Slater," Jesse said. He walked forward, wary still, but a smile on his face. "You're Cole Slater's brother, right? Hey, they got a whole pack of wanted posters out on you, did you know that?"

"Yeah, I know it. But thanks for the warning."

"What are you doing here about? Heading south? It might be best if you were to take a hike into Mexico."

"Well," Malachi said, "I can't rightly do that yet, you know. I got to tie up with my brothers somewhere. And the Red Legs have got Cole's wife. That's what was going on when you fellows showed up there today. Those men report to a man named Hayden Fitz, and he wants my brother dead. We Slaters stick together; I can't leave yet."

One of the Younger brothers stood up. "Hey, Captain Slater. I seen Jamie. About two weeks ago. He knows about the posters, and he's making his way south. Thought you ought to know."

"Thanks. Thanks a lot. That's real good to hear."

Malachi smiled at the Younger brothers, then turned his eyes on Justin. He strode across the clearing between the trees and lowered himself down on the balls of his feet, staring straight into Justin's eyes.

"I've come for her."

"Well, now, Captain Slater, I'm rightly sorry. She's mine."

Shannon bit his hand. Justin let out a yelp, freeing her mouth, bringing his sore palm to his own mouth.

"Malachi—"

"Shut up, Shannon."

"Malachi—"

"Shut up, Shannon," he said again, smiling with clenched teeth. He stunned her by sending her a smart slap right across the face. She gasped. Tears that she would never shed brightened the blue beauty of her eyes.

"Justin, I don't prowl the countryside for just any woman. This one is mine. We're engaged to be married."

Shannon gasped, and Malachi glared at her.

Justin laughed crudely. "That won't wash, captain. That won't wash one little bit. I know all about this feisty little Yank lover. She hates Rebs. I don't think she even knows the difference between the bushwhackers and the regular army, captain. She just hates Rebs. I thought that I should give her a good taste of Johnny Reb, how about that, captain?"

There was no respect in his tone. There was an underlying hint of violence.

"She'll get a good taste of Reb. She's my fiancée, and I want her back now."

Malachi leaned across Justin with his knife and quickly slit the ropes holding Shannon down. She leaped to her feet, rubbing her wrists, and ran behind him. Malachi stood quickly as Justin leaped to his feet. The men stared at one another.

Malachi reached his hand behind him. "Come here, Shannon. Shannon—darlin'!—get your sweet . . . soul over here, ya hear?"

He grabbed her hand and jerked her up beside him. "Tell them, darlin'."

"What?" she whispered desperately.

"Tell them that you don't hate all Rebs."

She was silent. He sensed the turmoil in her, even as he breathed in the soft sweet scent of her perfume, still clinging to her despite the dirt that smudged her face.

He was ready to strangle her himself.

"Tell them!"

"I—" She was choking on the words, really choking on them. "I—I don't hate all Rebs."

"She ain't your fiancée!" Frank James said.

"She is!" Malachi insisted, his frustration growing. He swung Shannon around, none too gently, and brought her into his arms. "Darlin'!" he exclaimed, and he pulled her close. He stared into her sky-blue eyes, his own on fire.

Her eyes widened; it seemed that at last that she had discovered her own predicament, and realized that her freedom might well hinge on her ability to act.

"Yes! Yes!" She threw her arms around him. Her breasts pressed hard against his chest and her fingers played with the hair at his nape.

And her lips came full and soft and crushing against his.

There was a curious audience before them, and their very lives were hanging in the balance.

And at that instance, it didn't seem to matter.

He locked his arms around her, setting his hands upon the small of her back and bringing the whole of her body hard against his. His lips parted over hers, and in the breath of a second, he found himself the aggressor, heedless of the men watching. He thrust his tongue deep into the sweet crevice of her mouth, feeling the warmth and fever of her reach out and invade him. He held her tighter and tighter, and raped her mouth with the sheer demand of his own. The tension of it seared into the fullness of his body. Then she brought her hands between them, pressing hard against his chest, and he finally lifted his lips from hers, and stared into her wide, startled and glimmering eyes.

Glimmering…with fury, he thought. He only prayed that she had the sense to keep silent until they were away.

If they did get away.

One of the Younger brothers laughed. "Hot damn, but I believe him. That was one of the most sultry kisses I've ever seen. Set me burning for a bit o' lovin', that's for sure."

Shannon's lashes fell over her eyes. Malachi heard her teeth grate together as he swept her around him. "Jesse, she's mine. And I'm taking her."

"You got my go ahead," Jesse said. "Frank?"

Frank shrugged. "The man is still wearing a gray uniform, and he says that the girl is his. Guess it must be so."

There was a sound like a growl from Justin. "Well, captain, I don't say that it's so. The girl tried to kill me. I got a score to settle with her."

"She tried to kill you?" Malachi repeated, playing for time. He didn't doubt one bit that Shannon had tried to kill any of them.

"That's right," Jesse said, sighing. "Why, Justin would be dead right now if Frank's gun hadn't been empty."

Malachi smiled, arching a brow. "What was she doing with Frank's gun?" he asked politely.

Every one of the bushwhackers flushed, except Justin, and he kept staring at Malachi with hatred in his eyes.

"I untied her," Frank James muttered. "I felt sorry for her, gagged and tied. She jumped me."

"She jumped you?"

"Captain, if you know that woman so well, you know that she's a damned hellcat, a bloody little spitfire." He swore again. "She's more dangerous than the whole lot of us."

Malachi lowered his head, adjusting the brim of his hat to hide the smile that teased at his lips. They weren't in the clear yet.

He looked up again, gravely, at Jesse. "Not much harm done, was there? I mean, the gun was empty. Justin looks alive and well and healthy to me."

"You ain't takin' her, Slater," Justin said.

Malachi inhaled deeply. "I am taking her, Justin."

"Maybe she ought to apologize to Justin," Jesse suggested. "Maybe that will smooth things over a bit."

"Oh, yeah," Justin said, tightening his lips, and leaning back with a certain pleasure. "Sure. Let's see this. You get her to apologize, captain."

"Shannon, apologize to the man."

She had been silent for several minutes, a long time for Shannon. She had stood behind him and at his side, quiet and meek. He gripped her fingers, drawing her in front of him. He hissed against her ear. "Shannon! Apologize."

"I will not!" she exploded. "He is a bloody, vicious, sadistic murder—"

Malachi's hand clamped over her mouth. Justin stood in a silent fury. Frank James laughed, and Jesse didn't make a move or say a word at all.

"Your woman don't obey you real well, Captain Slater," Frank observed.

Malachi swept his arm around her, jerking her beneath his chin, laying his fingers taut over her rib cage and squeezing hard. "She's gonna obey me just fine." He lowered his voice, whispering against her earlobe. "'Cause if she doesn't obey me damned fast, I'm going to leave. I'm going to tell Justin to go ahead and enjoy himself to his heart's content—"

"He is a cold-blooded murderer!" Shannon whispered back. He sensed the tears in her voice, but he couldn't afford to care.

"Apologize!" he told her.

She inhaled deeply. He felt the hatred and the fury that swept from her in great waves, and he wondered if he would always be included in that pool of bitter hatred and rage. "I'm sorry that I tried to kill you," she spit out to Justin. She lowered her head. "And I'm sorry that I failed!" she whispered miserably.

Malachi tightened his hold upon her so that she gasped, but as he looked around, he realized, thankfully, that he was the only one who had heard her last words.

He smiled. "All right?"

He didn't want to give them all time to think. "Thanks, boys. I never would have made it against the Red Legs without your help. Be seeing you."

He adjusted his hat and shoved Shannon around, daring to bare his back to the raiders. They wouldn't shoot a Confederate officer in the back.

Even bushwhackers had a certain code of ethics.

He walked several feet, hurrying Shannon ahead of him.

"Slater!"

He stopped, pushing her forward, turning around.

Justin was walking toward him. "Captain Slater, they're letting you take the woman. I'm not."

Malachi stiffened. He stared at Justin. It was a direct challenge, and there was no way out of it.

"No, Malachi!" Shannon cried, racing to him. He shoved her back again, not daring to take his eyes off Justin.

"Then I guess it's between you and me," he said softly.

"That's right, captain. That's what it boils down to."

"Swords or pistols?"

"Draw when you're ready, captain—" Justin began, but he never finished. His eyes suddenly rolled up in his head and he fell to the ground with a curious, silent grace.

Jesse was standing there. He had just clobbered Justin with the butt of a Spencer repeater. He smiled at Malachi.

"I don't know what would have happened, captain, but you've got a powerful reputation as a crack shot. Of course, Justin is pretty damned good himself. One of you would have died. And I'm just sick of the bloodshed, you know. I figure the Yanks killed enough of us that we don't need to run around killin' one another, not now, not when we're all trying to get home for a spell. So you take your little hellcat and you go on, Captain Slater. Head for Mexico, as fast as you can. The best of luck to you, captain."

Malachi turned from the man on the ground to Jesse. He nodded slowly. Then he turned around. Shannon was still standing there, and he grasped her elbow firmly and pulled her along with him. "Come on!" he whispered to her when she seemed to be balking.

Jesse was still watching them. Malachi put his arm around Shannon's shoulder and pulled her close against him. She looked back once and didn't seem to want to protest, not one bit.

He hurried them down the slope to the embankment of the spring, then rushed along the embankment.

Darkness was coming once again. He wanted to sleep...badly. But he wanted to put some mean distance between them and Justin before he paused to sleep.

He didn't need to urge Shannon along. As soon as they had left the raiders behind, she broke away from him and started to run. Her hair streamed behind her, and in the darkening twilight, he heard the soft, sobbing gasps of her breath as she hurried.

Groaning, he ran after her.

She meant to put distance between herself and the raiders, too. She ran so hard and so fast that she was quickly past the spot where he had tethered their horses.

"Shannon!"

He hurried after her. It was almost as if she hadn't heard him. She was probably furious, he thought wearily. She was angry because he had made her apologize. Because he had kissed her.

He had more than kissed her. He had kissed her and touched with an invasion so deep that the intimacy invoked could never be forgotten.

Nor, for her part, he was certain, forgiven.

"Shannon!"

Cursing the pain in his leg, he ran after her with greater speed. At last he caught up with her. She stumbled and fell, rolling down the grassy slope until she was nearly in the water. Malachi followed, dropping down beside her. Her eyes were huge and luminous and moist, a beautiful, glittering blue, still wet with tears. She stared at the sky unblinkingly while he knelt by her.

"Shannon! Damn it, I'm sorry. You fool! You damned bloody little fool. Didn't you understand? I had to get you out of there. Justin is a murdering sadist, and that's exactly why you don't mess with a man like him." He sighed. "All right, hellcat. Stay angry. Tear me up again whenever you get the chance. But for now, we've got to get on the road. We need to ride—"

"Malachi!"

She shot up suddenly and ran straight into his arms. She laid her cheek against his chest, and he felt the terrible beating of her heart and the shivering that seized the whole

of her body. The soft cream mounds of her breasts rose
above the pink-flowered white cups of her corset, brushing
against the rough material of his wool greatcoat. Her hands
seemed frail and delicate where they fell against him.

"Oh, Malachi!"

And she burst into tears.

He put his arms around her and he kissed the top of her
head. He held her tight against him.

Hellcat. It was an apt name for her, but his little hellcat
had broken. The war had made her build an impenetrable
shield around herself. She was strong as steel and tough as
nails, and no one, no one commanded Shannon McCahy.

But now...

Her shield had shattered and broken, and he wasn't sure
that he could stand up to the soft and delicate beauty beneath it.

"It's all right. It's over. It's—"

"Malachi, thank you. Oh, my God, you came for me.
You—you took me from him. Thank you!"

He curved his hand around her cheek, and he smoothed
the tears from her face with his thumb. She stared at him,
and her eyes were earnest and glorious, her hair a shroud of
gold, cloaking her half-bared shoulders and breasts.

He swallowed hard and managed to stand. He reached
down for her, lifting her high into his arms. "We have to
ride," he told her.

She nodded trustingly. Her head fell against him. His
boots sloshed through the stream as he walked toward the
horses.

Chapter Six

When she was set on the black gelding, Shannon seemed well and eager to ride. Malachi was glad of it. He didn't know how long he could stay awake himself, but as long as they could, they would ride.

They crossed the stream, then followed along it. No words passed between them. When Malachi looked back in the darkness, he saw her slumped low in the saddle, but she didn't complain or suggest they stop. He had given her his greatcoat; her shirt was nothing but tatters now, and he didn't want to take the time to dig through his belongings for a new shirt for her. He wanted to move.

It was too late to steal Kristin back before the Red Legs left Missouri. They would have to travel deep into Kansas. The only benefit to that situation was that it was unlikely Justin would follow him into Kansas. There might be a bounty out on Malachi, but at least he had been regular army, not a bushwhacker. A man recognized as a bushwhacker in Kansas might not stand much of a chance.

"Shannon?"

"Yes," she called softly.

"You all right back there?"

"Yes."

"We'll go another hour."

"Fine."

They plodded onward. Where the stream forked, he took the westward trail, telling her to walk the black gelding behind his bay mare in the rocky, shallow water. That way there would be no footprints for the bushwhackers to follow.

With the first light, he reined in. There was a perfect little copse beside the water. It was sheltered by magnificent oaks, and grass grew there like a blanket. On one side of the stream, the water deepened in a small natural pond. It was just like the swimming hole back home where he and Cole and Jamie had roughhoused after working hours, and where the neighborhood girls had come to watch and giggle from the trees, and where, sometimes, the young ladies had boldly determined to join them. He smiled, thinking about those days. They had been so long ago.

Malachi realized that Shannon had reined up behind him. "This is it," he said softly. "We'll rest here."

Nodding, she moved to dismount and missed her footing. She fell flat into the water on her rear and lay sprawled, apparently too tired to move.

Malachi dismounted and hunkered down in front of her, smiling. "Hey. Come on out of the water."

She nodded, barely. Her eyes fell on his, dazed.

He flicked water on her face and saw the surprise and then the anger spark her eyes. "You do need a bath," he told her. Dirt still smudged her face. "Badly. But this doesn't seem to be the right time. Come on, I'll help you out."

His greatcoat had fallen open, exposing the lace and flowers of her corset. When he went to take her hand, his fingers brushed over the lace, and over the firm satiny flush that rose above the border. Warmth sizzled straight to his loins, and he paused, stunned by the strength of the feeling. He shook his head, irritated with himself, and grabbed her hands. "Up, Shannon, damn it, get up."

Sensing the sudden anger in him, she staggered to her feet, using his hand for support.

"You're soaked. Let's get up on the bank."

Thank God he was exhausted, he told himself. Really so exhausted that he couldn't even think about what the sight of her did . . .

She sighed softly as they cleared the water, throwing his coat from her shoulders and sinking down to remove her boots. Her hair, touched by the pale, new light of the coming morning, glowed with a fiery radiance and teased the flesh of her shoulders and breasts. He didn't touch her at all, but the warmth sizzled through him again, making his heart pump too fast and his tired body come alive.

Maybe it was impossible to be too exhausted.

He gritted his teeth and swore.

She paused in surprise. "Malachi, what's wrong?"

When had she learned to make those blue eyes so innocent and so damned sultry all in one? And her hair, just falling over one eye now . . .

"What's wrong?" he yelled at her. "All I was trying to do was get Kristin back from the Red Legs, and instead I'm running over half of Missouri to get you back from a pack of bushwhackers. And did you try to use one ounce of sense in the hands of death? No, Shannon, you just provoke them further, and almost get us both killed."

She jumped to her feet. She was trembling, he saw.

"You don't understand. You don't understand and you can't understand. You weren't there when my pa was killed, and you didn't get to hear, in rumor and in truth, day after day after day, what was done to the men outside Centralia. You don't—"

"Shannon, I fought in the war. I know all about dying."

"It wasn't the dying!" Tears glittered brightly in her eyes, but she wouldn't shed them, she wouldn't break down again, and he knew it. "It wasn't the dying. It was the way that they died. He admitted it; that bastard admitted that he had been there, outside Centralia. He might have been the one who—who . . . Malachi, they had to pick up his pieces! They had to pick up Robert's pieces. I loved him, I loved him so much."

Her face was smudged but her chin was high, and her eyes were even more beautiful fevered with emotion. He felt her pain, and he wished heartily that he had never spoken to her. She still didn't understand. Justin just might want to do the same damned thing to her, if he could get his hands on her again. She'd fought Justin anyway. Or maybe she had understood, and hadn't cared.

She stared at him, her head high, her hands on her hips, her passion like an aura around her. "I loved him, and that bastard helped dismember him!"

"It can't matter!" Malachi told her curtly. "You can't allow it to matter right now!"

"You don't understand—"

"Maybe I don't understand, but you're not going to explain anything to me. No Yank is ever going to explain the horror of this war to a Confederate. We lost, remember? Oh, yes, of course, you're the one who likes to remind me of that fact."

"Maybe you do understand dying and killing. Maybe you just don't understand what love is."

"Shannon, you're a fool, and my life is none of your damned business."

"Malachi, damn you—"

"I don't want to listen right now, Shannon. I'm tired. I have to have some sleep," he said wearily. He didn't want to fight with her. He just didn't want to look at her anymore. He didn't want to see all the fire and excitement and beauty... and the pain and misery that haunted her.

He didn't want to desire her.

But he did.

He turned away from her, heading for the horses. For a moment he thought that she was going to run after him and continue the fight. But she didn't. She stayed still for several long minutes, tense, staring after him. Then she walked down to the water. He tried to ignore her as he unsaddled the horses and rolled out his bedroll and blanket beneath the largest oak. He hesitated, looked at her bedroll, rolled behind the seat of her saddle. He unrolled it, too, beside his own. He didn't want her too far away. He knew that he would awaken if footsteps came anywhere near them, but he was still wary of sleeping. Justin struck him as the type of man who worked hard toward vengeance.

He could hear her, drinking thirstily, splashing water, washing her face. Scrubbing her face and her hands again and again.

He threw himself down on the bedroll, using his saddle as a pillow and turning so he could keep an eye on her. Day was coming fast now. Sunlight played through the leaves and branches, caressing her hair and shoulders and arms. It rippled against the water in a magical dazzle.

"What are you doing?" he demanded.

"Scrubbing. Scrubbing away that awful bushwhacker!" she retorted.

"You can throw your whole body in later and scrub to your heart's content!" he called to her irritably. "Get out now. Let's get some sleep."

She turned around and saw him stretched out, then opened her mouth as if she was about to argue with him.

Maybe she was just tired. Maybe, just maybe, she was still a little bit grateful. Whatever, she closed her mouth and walked toward him.

She hesitated by her bedroll, looking at him. Strands of damp hair curled around her face, and its planes were delineated, soft and beautiful. Water beads hovered over her breasts.

He groaned inwardly and tipped his hat over his face. "Good night, Shannon."

"Perhaps I should move this." She indicated her bedroll.

"Lie down."

"I've never had to sleep this close to a Reb before."

"You slept with Justin just about on top of you yesterday."

She smiled with sweet sarcasm and widened her eyes. "I've never willingly slept this close to a Reb before."

"Willing or other, lie down, brat!"

He watched her mouth twist. He was too damned tired to argue, and if he touched her at that moment, he wasn't at all sure what it would lead to. "Please! For the love of God, lie down, Shannon."

She didn't say a word until she had settled down beside him, but then heard a tentative whisper. "Malachi?"

He groaned. "What?"

"What . . . what are we going to do now?"

He hesitated. "I should spank you, brat," he said softly. "And send you home."

"You—you can't send me home. You know that." There was just the touch of a plea in her voice, and the softest note of tears. "You can't send me back."

"That's right," he muttered dryly. "Justin is out there somewhere, waiting for you. Maybe I should let him have you. The two of you could keep on fighting the war, from here until doomsday."

"Malachi—"

"I'm not sending you back, Shannon. You're right about that; I can't."

"Then—"

"We're going to go onward for Kristin."

"But how will we find her? We'll never pick up the trail again. There's only a few of them left now, but they're so long gone that it would be impossible to find them."

"We don't need to find them."

"But—"

"Shannon, I know where they're taking her. They're taking her to Fitz. And I know how to find the town. We all know something about it, Cole, Jamie and I." He hesitated. "You forget, we've had dealings with the Red Legs before." He was silent for a moment, thinking back to when Cole's place had been burned down and his beautiful young wife killed. Malachi's jaw tightened. "I'm not sure if we can head them off quickly enough, or if we'll have to—figure out something else. We'll find her. We'll reach her.''

"Do you think—do you think that she'll be all right?''

He lifted his hat and rolled toward her. She was staring at him so earnestly. Her eyes seemed old, so very wise and world-weary, and their tiredness added a curious new beauty and sensuality to her features.

He propped himself up on one elbow, watching her across the distance of the mere two feet that separated them.

"Shannon, they're going to take good care of Kristin. She is all that they have to use against Cole. Now, please, go to sleep." He lay back down, slanting his hat over his face.

"Malachi?'' she whispered.

"What?'' he asked irritably.

"Thank you—really.''

Her voice was so soft. Like a feather dusting sweetly over his flesh. His muscles tightened and constricted and ached and burned, and he felt himself rising hard and hot.

"Shannon, go to sleep," he groaned.

"Malachi—''

"Shannon, go to sleep!''

She was silent. So silent then. She didn't try to speak again.

It was going to be all right. She was going to go to sleep; he was going to go to sleep. When he woke up, he wouldn't be so damned tired. He'd have so much more control over his emotions and needs.

A sound suddenly broke the silence of the morning.

He threw his hat off, leaping to his feet. She stared at him, startled.

She sat on her bedroll, cross-legged like an Indian, chewing on a piece of smoked meat. She had bread and cheese spread out before her, too, just like a damned picnic.

"What the hell are you doing?'' he demanded.

"Eating!''

"Now?''

"Malachi, I haven't eaten in ages! It's been almost two full days."

His temper ebbed. He hadn't thought to stop for food last night, and she hadn't said anything, either.

"Just hurry it up, will you, please?"

"Of course," she said indignantly. She stared at him with reproach. He threw up his hands, issued a curt oath and plopped back down on the ground.

He just had to have some sleep.

He didn't sleep. He listened as she finished with the food and carefully wrapped it up to pack in her saddlebags. He listened as she stretched out on the ground, pulling her blanket tight around her shoulders.

Then he just listened to the sound of her breathing. He could have sworn that he could even hear the rhythmic thumping of her heart.

When he closed his eyes, he could see her. Could even see the pink satin flowers sewn into the lace of her corset. He could see her flesh, silky soft and smooth, and he could see the length of her, and the beautiful blue sizzle of her eyes...

He didn't even like her, he reminded himself.

But then again, maybe he didn't dislike her quite so much, either.

Somewhere in time, he did sleep.

He slept well, and he slept deeply. Warmth invaded him. He felt more than the hard ground beneath him, more than the coldness of the earth.

He felt flesh.

He awoke with a start.

He had rolled, or she had rolled, and now she lay curled against his chest. His chin nuzzled her hair; his arm lay draped around her. He was sleeping on her hair, entangled within it. Her features in repose were stunning, a study in classical beauty. Her cheekbones were high and her lips were full and red and parted slightly as she breathed softly in and out. Her lashes lay like dusky shadows over her flesh, enticing, provocative. The scent of her filled him deliciously.

His arm was over her breast, the fullness of one round mound...

He jerked away from her, gritting his teeth. He should wake her up. He should shove her from him, as hard as he could.

He bit hard into his lip, then carefully eased her from him. She didn't whimper or protest. It he hadn't felt her breathing, he might have been afraid that she had died, her sleep was so deep and complete.

He sat up and pulled off his boots and socks and walked down to the water. It was cool and good, and just what he needed. He shucked his shirt, and let the water ripple over his shoulders and back. He came back to his bedroll stripped down to his breeches.

He sighed and laid back. He looked up at the sky. It was midafternoon now. They should ride again by night.

Damn her. He was the one who needed sleep so badly.

He closed his eyes. They flew open almost instantly.

She had rolled beside him again.

He looked at her and then sighed, giving up. He slipped his arm around her and held her close to the warmth of his body. He didn't listen to her heart but he felt it, beating sweetly.

It was so much worse now. He felt her with his naked flesh, and it was good to hold her as a woman. Too good. But he didn't release her. He held her and swallowed back his darker thoughts.

Knowing Shannon, he thought wryly, she would rise in a fury, accusing him of all manner of things. She would probably never believe that she had come to him in her sleep.

Come to him for the simple warmth and caring that she could not seek when she was awake.

We all need to be held, Malachi thought.

He sighed, shuddering against the fragrance of her hair. He would sleep again, he would sleep again. And she would never know just how fully he had played the gentleman, the cavalier...

He would never get back to sleep.

But finally, he did. Perhaps the very rhythm of her breath and heartbeat finally lulled him to sleep. Perhaps abject exhaustion finally seized him.

When he slept, he dreamed again.

He was remembering, he realized. Remembering the day when he had been shot. To the day when he had fallen into the brook.

He was seeing things. Illusions. Soft sunlight playing down from the sky, glittering upon the warm, rich earth. Sunlight touching the earth...and touching upon the woman.

She had risen from the center of the brook like a phoenix reborn from the crystal-clear depths. She seemed to move with magic, bursting with gentle beauty from the depths. Her arms, long and graceful, broke the water first, then her head, with her hair streaming wet and slick, and then her shoulders and her breasts with tendrils of her hair plastered around them. And she continued to rise, rise and rise, until the full flare of her hips and the shapely length of her legs arose.

Venus...arising from her bath.

She was perfection, her breasts lush and ripe and full and firm and achingly beautiful with their rouge-tipped, pebbled peaks. Her waist was supple and slim, her hips...

She was illusion, illusion moving in slow motion. She was the product of a dream, of too many sleepless nights. Maybe she was a spirit of twilight, a creation of sunset. She blended with the colors of the sky, gold and red and soft magenta.

She dipped down again, cupping her hands, dashing the water up within them. She straightened, tossing it upon her face, and the little droplets fell and streamed from her hands like a cascade of diamonds.

He wasn't dreaming.

He was wide awake, he realized. Wide awake and staring at the stream. Obviously, she had thought he would stay asleep.

He rose and walked down to the water.

She paused, seeing him.

Their eyes met across the water, across the sky touched by sunset in gold and magenta and red.

She froze, as if some spell had been cast upon her there. She didn't drop down to the water, nor did she cover herself with her hands. She simply stared at him, her lips slightly parted, some words, perhaps, frozen upon them. She just watched him.

She just watched him.

And he didn't pause or hesitate.

He walked straight over to her. And when he reached her, he put his arms around her, lifted her chin and studied her face and her lips and her eyes, his fingers moving over the ivory softness of her face.

Then he lowered his head slowly over hers, capturing her lips with his own.

And still, she didn't move...

His arms tightened around her. He ran his fingers gently down her cheek to her throat, and he sent his tongue deeply into her mouth, stroking the insides. Desire burst upon him like the crystal shards of sunlight that sprinkled diamond-like upon the water. There would be no turning back for him now. Not now...

He moved his hand over her breast, massaging the fullness, teasing the nipple between his thumb and forefinger and encompassing the fullness of the weight again.

Her lips broke from his. A startled gasp escaped from her, but she didn't fight him. She slipped her arms around him, clinging close to him. Her lips settled upon his shoulder, and her fingers splayed across his back. He continued to play with her breast and she cast her head back as he pressed his lips against her throat, again and again and again. Then he moved downward, and lifted her breast to take it into his mouth, sucking upon the nipple and spiraling his tongue around the aureole.

She cried out, holding his shoulders. He rose to take her lips again, seizing them with hunger, plundering them apart, and seeking her mouth with a fire of passion. She pressed against him, trying to free herself. Her lips rose from his.

"We shouldn't..."

"For God's sake, don't tell me that now!" he said hoarsely, and his mouth closed over hers again, and this time, she made no protest at all. Her arms curled around his neck. He kissed her until he felt her tremble with the same deep desire that burned within him. Until he thought that she would fall.

Then he moved back, and drank in the sight of her again. He reached out and placed his hands around the enchanting fullness of both her breasts, awed by the sensual beauty of their deep-rose pebbled peaks. He touched her breasts, moving his fingers lightly over them, then possessing them with the fullness of his touch.

He stepped even closer, and swept her into his arms.

Splashing through the water, he carried her toward the grassy bank. Her eyes were closed. He knew he should have wondered if she dreamed of another man. He should have wondered if she had any experience with what she was doing, but he didn't wonder about anything at all. Holding her, carrying her to the shore, seemed to be the most natural thing to do, and he would not have ceased with his intent had lightning come from the sky to strike him down.

He laid her upon the soft grass embankment. Her eyes remained closed as the last rays of sunlight played over the beauty of her body again. He fell down beside her, and when the light shadowed magenta upon her, he kissed her, and then where the rays fell golden, he kissed her, too. The beautiful colors and musky light were broken by the dappling patterns of the oak leaves, waving above them in the softness of the breeze.

Holding his weight above her, he kissed her lips gently, then moved down between the valley of her breasts. He ran his hand over the lush curve of her flank as his tongue laved her flesh. She tasted of the water, and of the deep, rich colors of the sun.

Malachi stood, looking down at her, feeling the pulse that lived inside of him, increasing erratically with each touch against her. He stripped away his breeches, watching her still, watching the play of the sunset over her supple form. The world receded; the echoes of gunfire could not touch him here. There was nothing but the glorious, magenta sunset, and the girl, as golden and beautiful as the wavering rays of the falling sun, as naked and primitive as the simple earth where they lay.

He lay down beside her again, half covering her with the blanket of his naked flesh. Her eyes remained closed, and she was nearly motionless. He kissed her temple, whispered against her earlobe, trailed his lips down the snowy length of her throat and over the slender line of her collarbone. His hands teased her breasts again, and she arched against him, a curious cry coming from deep within her throat. He watched with fascination, seeking to judge the responses of her body. The shaft of his desire lay naked against her thigh, warmed there by her flesh and grazed by the evening air, so that the burning ache to have her beneath him soared high and fevered, and still he held himself in check.

He wondered if she even remembered who he was. He wanted her to open her eyes. To see his face, to know his name.

He moved his hands to lazily draw circles along her inner thigh, rising higher and higher. He buried his face against her throat and between her breasts, and feathered her flesh with the soft hairs of his beard. She whimpered slightly and began to undulate against him.

With bold and deliberate purpose, he parted her thighs. A certain resistance met him at first, but he caught her lips again, and his kiss seared and invaded and seduced. He wanted to slide down between them, but he kept his eyes hard upon hers instead. He stroked surely along her thigh until he came to the juncture of it, and swiftly, surely penetrated her with an intimate touch.

Her eyes flew open at last and met his. Wide and blue and beautiful and dazed. He knew how to make love, and his stroke moved with tender, sensual finesse.

"No..." she murmured softly, color flooding her cheeks.

He leaned close against her, speaking a breath away from her lips and keeping her eyes locked with his.

"Whisper my name, Shannon."

"No..." she murmured, and he knew that she didn't protest what they did, but only that he forced her to see the reality of it.

That he forced her to look his way, and say his name.

He found the most erotic places of her body and teased her, then plundered ruthlessly within her once again. She cried out, trying to twist from him, trying to elude his eyes. He shifted, burying his weight deep inside her, and holding himself just slightly away from her. She moved, she moved so sweetly against him even as she denied him.

"Put your arms around me, Shannon, tightly around me!" he urged her, and she did so. It was easy for her to cling tightly against him. Her fingers moved over his shoulders, over his back. Tentative, hesitant, seeking to hold him close as he held her, and seeking to give him a certain pleasure.

"Whisper my name, Shannon," he insisted. He hovered over her, teasing her with the fire of his own body. "Say my name. Open your eyes, and say my name."

Her eyes flew open again. There was a shimmer of fury deep within them. "Malachi!" she whispered tensely.

"Now..." He lowered his head to hers once again, and a ruthless grin touched his features. "Tell me what you want me to do."

She stared at him in astonishment, and a flush as crimson as the sunset touched her cheeks and seeped over her breasts. He couldn't bear it much longer. He had to have her soon. But they had always waged war between them, and this one, at least, he would not lose.

"Tell me what you want."

"No..."

"It's easy." She started to press against his shoulders. He caught her hands, and he laced his fingers with hers, and he drew them high over her head. "Say that you want me. I want you, Malachi." He kissed her. He slid his tongue into her mouth and withdrew it and then raked it along her lips. He drew her hands down and held her firm as he moved low against her, lazily taking her breast in his mouth again, slinking lower and lower against her. She escaped his grasp, and her nails raked into his shoulders. He heard her gasp and felt her fingers on his head when his kiss teased her belly.

She was alive with passion. Her head tossed and her hips moved, and she whispered something, moistening her lips. Her eyes were closed again, and her face lay to the side. They were both entangled in her hair.

"I can't hear you, Shannon."

"I—I want you."

"I want you, Malachi."

"I want you... Malachi."

Her voice was breathy, barely a whisper. It was all that he wanted, all that he needed. She moved against him with grace and exquisite sensuality, and a burst of triumph and fever took hold of him as he shifted, touching her, thrusting deep, deep inside her.

She stiffened, and screamed, and he realized then that he had believed her experienced because he had wanted to believe it. He had been deceived, but only because he hadn't wanted to think...

But he felt. He felt the tear within her body, and the constriction of pain, and the trembling that filled her. He started to jerk from her, but her hands pulled him back.

Her eyes were open now. Tears touched them, but they met his with a curious honesty. "No, no—I said that I wanted you. I said I want you . . . Malachi."

"Damn it, you didn't tell me that you were a—"

"You didn't ask," she reminded him softly. "Please . . ."

Her voice trailed away. He realized that it was too late to undo any harm, and yet perhaps not too late to recapture the magic.

He began to move very carefully. Slowly he entered fully within her, and just as slowly he withdrew. Then he plunged again, slowly . . . slowly.

Minutes later she cried out, straining high against him.

Innately, she seemed to know the craft of womanly art. Supplely, exquisitely, she moved beneath him. He matched his rhythm to hers, to the soft magic of the evening. The breeze rustled the leaves and silently caressed them. Birds cried out, and the water rippled and dazzled still. Malachi cried out hoarsely, giving himself free rein at long last, burying himself again and again with speed and fever within the moist and welcoming nest of her body.

The pressure built in him explosively, and still he held himself in a certain control, whispering to her, touching her bare flesh with kisses, urging her ever onward.

She cried out, straining hard against him, collapsing.

He allowed his own climax to come, and when it seized him it was sweet and violent; he shuddered as wave after little wave of pleasure shook him, and rippled anew. When he had finished at last he gazed down at her.

Her eyes were closed again, her lips were parted, and her breath still came swiftly . . . and he felt the little tremors that touched her. She seemed white, very pale.

"Shannon?" He stroked her hair, smoothing damp tendrils from her face. She moved, trying to free herself from the burden of his body. He shifted his weight, and she curled against him.

"Shannon—"

"Don't. Please, don't . . . not yet," she whispered.

While the twilight darkened, he held her, staring at the trees and watching the silhouette of the leaves against the sky until it was too dark to see them.

Then suddenly, in silence, she pushed away from him. She rose, and her hair fell over her eyes, obscuring them. She walked quickly to the water, and did not pause at the edge, but hurried to where it was deep, and ducked beneath it. Malachi watched her pensively, thinking that the action wasn't much different than the one she had taken that morning when she washed her hands and face as if to wash away the scent and memory of Justin.

He rose and followed her into the water. "Shannon!" She ignored him, and he caught her arm, turning her around. She jerked away from him.

"Shannon, what are you doing now?"

"Nothing."

"Then why won't you talk to me?"

"I don't want to talk."

"Shannon, what just happened—"

"Shouldn't have happened. It shouldn't have happened!" she repeated fiercely. She sat in the water, pursing her lips, scrubbing her thighs and behaving now as chastely as a nun. She sank even lower into the water until the surface rippled against her breasts, and for some reason, the sight irritated him more than her perverse denial.

"Shannon—"

"Malachi, damn you! Could you at least have the decency to leave me alone now?"

"Could I have the decency?" He caught her elbow, pulling her to her feet. He was furious and she was distant. And yet, something was irrevocably and forever changed between them. It seemed natural now to hold her this way, to have her against him sleek and bare and intimate. She couldn't make love the way that she had and pretend that the moments hadn't existed.

"Decency?" he asked sarcastically. "Oh, I see. It was all my fault—"

"I didn't say that."

"It's what you mean."

"Well, you're just one hell of a Southern gentleman! You know something? That's what Kristin always called you. You were the perfect Southern knight, the hero, the magnificent cavalier! Riding to a lady in distress! Well, she's wrong; you're no gentleman. You may have seen me bathing, but you might have turned your back."

"Oh? And you, I suppose, were the perfect lady? Naked as a jay and strutting like a dance-hall girl out there—"

"You could have turned around. I thought that you were a gentleman!"

"Don't ever think, Shannon. Every time you do, someone gets into trouble. And don't you ever deny me, or—"

"Malachi, it was your fault."

"My fault. Right. I didn't exactly drag you screaming from the water."

She lowered her head.

He caught her chin, lifting it. "You just wanted to indulge in a little fantasy. You never made it into bed with the Yank when he was alive, so now you're willing to take on a Rebel captain just to see what it might have been like—"

She struck out at him like lightning, slapping his cheek with a stinging blow, then ducked, afraid that he would extract retribution. Every time she had touched Malachi in anger before, he had repaid her in some way.

But that night, he did not. He touched his cheek, then spun around. "You're right, Shannon. It never should have happened."

He sloshed through the water to the shore and, ignoring her completely, dressed at his leisure. He heard her, though. He would always hear her, he realized. Hear her, and imagine her. Her eyes like the sky. Her grace and energy, her supple beauty. He would hear her, and imagine her, clothed and . . . unclothed.

He heard her coming to the shore, and imagined her slipping into her thin cotton pantalets and beautiful corset with the pink roses sewn into the lace. He sneaked a glance, and saw she had plunged into her jeans, and now sat on her bedroll pulling on her boots.

He dug into his saddlebags and found a clean checked cotton shirt. He tossed it to her.

"Thank you. I don't—"

"Put it on. If you ride around in that corset thing, every man jack we run into will fall under the illusion that you're ready and willing, too."

She slid the sleeves of the shirt over her arms and began to work on the buttons. Her head was high. "I wasn't going to refuse the shirt, Captain Slater. I was going to suggest that you should wear something similar. That Confederate coat of yours is pretty distinctive."

Malachi didn't reply. He turned around to pack up his bedroll, setting his greatcoat and jacket in with his blanket. His trousers were gray, but his shirt was plain blue cotton.

He couldn't quite part with his hat yet, so he set it atop his head, and stared at Shannon, waiting. When she had buttoned her shirt, she dug into her bag for a comb. She started trying to untangle the long strands of her hair.

Malachi saddled the horses, and she was still struggling. He walked over to her impatiently, snatching the comb from her fingers. "Get down on your knees," he told her gruffly.

"I won't—"

"It's the only way that I can handle this mane!"

She complied in silence. He quickly found the tangles, and eased them out. When he was done, he thrust the comb back to her. "May we go now, Miss McCahy?"

She nodded, lowering her head. They mounted and started out.

Malachi rode ahead of her, silent as death, wrapped up with his own demons. He felt as if they had been on the road for hours when she finally tried to catch up with him, calling to him softly.

"Malachi?"

"What?"

"I—I want to explain."

"Explain what?"

"What I said. I didn't mean to deny—"

"That's good. Because I won't let you deny the truth."

"That's not what I meant. I want to explain—"

She was still behind him. He couldn't see her face, and he was glad. It was easier to be cynical and cool that way. "Shannon," he said, with a grate to his voice, "you don't have to explain anything."

"But you don't understand—"

"Yes, I know. I never do."

"Malachi, before the war, I was always a lady—"

"Shannon, before, during and after the war, you always were a hellion."

"Malachi, damn you! I just meant that . . . I never would have done . . . what I did. I shouldn't have . . ."

He hesitated, listening to her fumbling for words. He could sense tears in her voice again, and though he ached for her, he was bitter, too. He didn't like playing substitute for a ghost. He might have forced her to admit that she had desired him, but the thought of her Yankee fiancé enraged him.

The ghost had never had what he had had, he reminded himself. He cooled slightly. "The war has changed lots of people," he said softly to her. "And you *are* a lady, brat. Still, I'm sorry."

"I don't want you to be sorry, Malachi. I just—it shouldn't have happened. Not now. Not between us."

"A Yank and a Reb. It would never do," he said bitterly.

She cantered up beside him, veering into his horse so that he was forced to look at her. She was soft and feminine now, her beautiful features and golden hair just brushed and kissed by the pale dusky moonlight.

"Malachi, please, I didn't mean that."

"I hope you meant something," he told her earnestly. "Shannon, you changed yourself tonight. Forever. You cast away something that some men deem very precious. You can't just pretend this didn't happen."

Even in the dim light he saw her flush. She lowered her face. "I know that. But that's not at all what I meant. What I meant is that..." She hesitated.

"Shannon, I did not drag you down, I did not force you into my arms. I seduced, maybe, but not without your ready cooperation."

He thought she might hit him. She didn't move. Only the breeze stirred her hair. They had both stopped, he realized.

She looked up at him, smiling painfully. Tears glazed her eyes. "I did want you, Malachi. I shouldn't have. I knew it was you, and I wanted you...and I shouldn't have. Because I did love Robert, with all of my heart. And it hasn't even been a year. I..." She shook her head. "I...I'm the one who is sorry."

She moved ahead of him. He suddenly felt exhausted, tired and torn to shreds.

He had never imagined, never, through hellfire, war and his meager taste of peace, that Shannon McCahy could come to brew this tempest in him. Anger, yes, she had always elicited his anger...

But maybe, just maybe, she had always aroused this fever in his loins, too. And maybe he was just beginning to see it now.

She was searing swiftly into his heart, too.

Maybe they could be friends. Maybe every war deserved a truce now and then.

"Shannon."

She reined in and looked to him.

"Let's camp here and get some sleep. We'll move more westerly tomorrow night, away from the water, so let's take advantage of it now."

He thought she raised her eyebrows, and he remembered clearly just what advantages the water had given them. "To drink and bathe," he told her dryly.

She nodded and dismounted, removing her saddle. He would have helped her, but she had grown up on a ranch and knew what she was doing, so he decided to leave her alone. They both needed some privacy right now.

He unsaddled his horse, set her to graze, and hesitated. At last he decided it was safe, and he moved close to the water to build a small fire. Shannon watched him as the flames caught. He looked at her. "I need some small rocks. I've got a pan; we'll have coffee." And brandy, he added to himself. Lots of it.

He was the one who needed to keep away from her. This was going to be hard, damned hard now. He couldn't look at her, have her near, and not imagine her in his arms again. Maybe if she hadn't known how to move and arch and undulate and please a man, all by instinct . . .

She came back with the rocks, and he arranged them around his fire and set the pan so that the water would boil without putting out the flame. He stared at the water while she undid the bedrolls, setting them up for the remainder of the night.

The coffee was soon done; Shannon laid out bread and cheese and smoked meat. They barely spoke to one another as they ate, and when they were done, silence fell around them again.

"Why don't you go to bed," he told her.

She nodded. "Yes. I guess that I will." She rose and started for their bedrolls, then paused, looking at him.

She seemed angelic then. Soft and slim and wistfully and painfully feminine. She smiled at him awkwardly. "Malachi?"

"What?"

"Does it matter to you?"

"Does what matter to me?"

"A—er—a woman's . . ."

"Virginity?" He offered.

She flushed, and shook her head. "Never mind—"

"Shannon—"

"Never mind. Forget it. Sometimes I forget consequences and . . ."

He took a long sip of coffee, watching her over the rim of his cup. "Have you forgotten them this time?"

"What?" she murmured. It was her turn to be confused.

He stood and walked over to her. Malachi was irritated by the touch of malicious mischief in his own heart. He would set her to thinking and worrying for days, he thought.

But then he had spent these last hours in a type of hell, and he would surely spend all their moments together in torment from this day forth.

"Consequences. Procreation. Infants. Sweet little people growing inside a woman's body . . ."

Her eyes widened. She hadn't thought about it at all, he saw, and he was right—now she would worry for days.

He kissed her on the forehead. "Good night."

She was still standing there when he walked back to the fire.

Chapter Seven

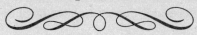

"What do you think?" Shannon murmured. It was late the next afternoon, and they had spent the day riding westward, avoiding the major roads, and had slipped quietly through the countryside.

"I think it's Kansas," Malachi replied flatly, turning toward her.

They sat on their horses looking down a cliff to a small, dusty town. On the distant rolling plains they could see farmhouses and ranches. Before them they could see a livery and a barbershop and a saloon. A sign stretching across the top of a long building advertised Mr. Haywood's Dry Goods and Mercantile, and next to it was a smaller sign, advertising Mrs. Haywood's Haywood Inn, Rooms to Let by the Day, Month, Year.

"Haywood, Kansas," Shannon murmured. She could still feel Malachi looking at her, and she couldn't bring herself to look his way. She'd had trouble looking at him ever since...

She couldn't believe what she had done. She hadn't had a single drop of liquor inside her. She hadn't been dragged, forced or coerced. She had done it all of her own free will, and if it were possible to live a thousand years, she would never be able to forget it. Or Malachi...

She could not look at him anymore and not remember everything. When his eyes touched her now she started to tremble deep inside. When she watched his hands resting on the reins, she remembered them against her body. The low male tenor of his voice moved against her now as if it touched her every time, as if it stroked the length of her back, just brushing over her flesh. And too often, way too often, she would grow hot and shivery all at once, and at the very core of her, and she would be ashamed to remember the feeling of unbelievable ecstasy that had burst upon her at the end.

She had never denied him his appeal, even in her moments of most vehement hatred. Even as the war had waged on and on, even as he dismissed her again and again as a child. And now she knew even more about him that she could not deny. That he was wonderfully muscled and sleek and bronze. His back was riddled with scars, and she knew that they were the result of cavalry battles, that he had been nicked time and again, and that he fought on, because a man just didn't walk away from a war, or from his duty as he saw it.

She knew that his chest was tufted with short red and gold hair, and that the hair narrowed enticingly at his hips, and that it flared out again to frame a demanding... masculinity.

He was an attractive man.

But she should have never been attracted, and each time she thought of her own behavior, it hurt. She knew that he thought that she had wanted to see him as a substitute for Robert. But he hadn't allowed it, and by then... she hadn't cared. She could make excuses. Maybe she had been striking out against the loss. Maybe she had just felt the need to be held.

No, the need to be loved.

But there really was no excuse. They hadn't even been friends. Passionate enemies, at best. What he must really be thinking of her, deep down inside, she couldn't even imagine...

And then she suddenly knew what her greatest fear was—that it had been a swift, casual fling for him, when for her it was a nightmare that changed her entire life and left her wondering if she had any morality whatsoever. And of all men to humiliate her so, it just had to be Malachi . . .

She had to be mature about it. She had to learn to forget it, and she had to learn to . . . quit worrying. Malachi had brought up a consequence that hadn't even passed through her mind. She'd never been that innocent, not on the ranch. She always knew what men and women did to create sons and daughters. It was just that she couldn't afford to think about it. She had to put it behind her now as well. Kristin was out there, somewhere. And Shannon did need Malachi's help. She didn't know the first thing about Kansas, or the awful man, Fitz. She needed Malachi.

"We need to go down," he said slowly, reluctantly. "We need to buy some food, if there's any to be had. And I'd give a hell of a lot to see a newspaper and try to find out what's been going on in the world."

"I'll go—" Shannon began.

"Don't be a fool," he told her impatiently. "I can't let you go down alone."

"I would be perfectly safe, and you wouldn't be."

"No one is safe anywhere around here. It wasn't safe before the war, and it surely isn't safe now."

"But I'm a Yank, remember?"

"Yeah, but they may not see it like that. To some, anyone from Missouri is a bushwhacker. Anyone at all."

"So what do you suggest?"

He gazed at her, lifting a brow. "Why, we pretend like hell, Miss McCahy, what else. We go in together—man and wife. Our place has been burned out. We're looking to keep on moving westward. Don't mess up, you hear?"

She eyed his hat pointedly. "You're riding in with a lantern of truth atop your head, captain," she said sweetly.

He swept the hat from his head and looked at it for a long moment, then dismounted and walked toward some bushes. He set the hat carefully in the midst of them.

"Is this a funeral?" Shannon asked sarcastically. "Maybe we should run down and bring the preacher out to mutter a few last words."

His face was savage when his eyes lit on hers. She swallowed, wishing that she hadn't spoken. He didn't reply. He walked around and mounted the bay again and reached out for her horse's reins, holding the horse there before him. "Follow my lead, Shannon. I don't mind dyin' for Kristin, and I don't even mind dying for you—when it can't be helped. I will be bloody damned, though, if I'll die just because you can't keep a civil tongue in your body."

His words fell into silence. Shannon stared at him without a word for what seemed like an endless time. She had only been teasing him. She hadn't realized how her words might wound, and she didn't know how to explain that or apologize.

"What about your saddle?" she asked him coldly. "Are there any Confederate markings on it, or on any of the other trappings on your horse?"

"My saddle came off a dead Ohioan's plow horse," he said. "And the bridle is from your ranch. No markings at all."

"Shall we go then?" she said tautly.

He released her horse's reins and they started down the slope. "We're going to buy some supplies and get some information," he told her. "You keep careful."

"Me?" she inquired sweetly. "You should be grateful to have me along, Malachi Slater. They aren't going to take your Confederate currency here. I've got Yankee dollars."

He turned to stare at her. "You keep your Yankee dollars, Shannon."

"Oh?"

"I've got gold, Miss McCahy. Last I heard, they're still taking that stuff everywhere. Come on now, I want you close."

He continued down the slope. Their horses broke into smooth canters as they crossed the empty plain and entered the town by the single road that cut through the line of buildings. Malachi reined in, nodding to Shannon to do the same. They dismounted in front of the mercantile and tethered their horses on the wood rail that ran the length of the place, then started up the two dusty steps to the open doorway.

There was a portly, balding man behind a counter that stretched in front of a wall with rows and rows of just about everything. There were rolls of fabric, mostly cottons and linens, but there were brocades and silks and satins, too, and smaller rolls of elegant laces. There were sacks of flour and coffee and tea and sugar, and there were sewing goods and farm supplies, leather items, blankets, sheets, canteens. The whole store was composed of shelving, and Shannon saw jars of jams and preserves, pickled vegetables and smoked and dried meats. As small as this town was, it seemed to be a prosperous place.

"Howdy," the portly man said to the two of them.

Malachi grinned broadly, walking up to the man. "Howdy, sir."

"What can I do for you, young man?"

"Well, the wife and I are heading out west. We just need ourselves some food supplies."

"We can take care of that, Mr.—"

"Uh, Sloan," Malachi said.

"Gabriel," Shannon said quickly at the same time.

Malachi frowned at her, his jaw locking. The balding man looked from one of them to the other. "It's Sloan Gabriel, sir," Malachi said. He jerked Shannon over to his side. "And this is my wife, Sara."

The man looked from Malachi to Shannon. Shannon smiled and escaped Malachi's punishing grip, wandering away to look over the merchandise in the store. "Nice to meet you, Mrs. Gabriel."

"Likewise, I'm sure," she murmured demurely.

The man leaned toward Malachi. "My wife's got herself a little tea parlor next door, young man. Maybe the lady would like a cup?" He winked. "And you could take a walk on over to the saloon and have yourself a pint or two."

"That sounds mighty nice," Malachi told him. A saloon was always the best place to hear whatever news was passing around. He looked at Shannon.

"Sweetheart." She was looking at a roll of calico and didn't pay him the slightest heed. He walked over to her, catching her hands and spinning her around and into his arms. "Darlin'! That nice man, Mr.—"

"Haywood," the balding man supplied.

"That nice Mr. Haywood says his wife has a little tea shop next door. Wouldn't you like to have a cup of tea, complete with milk and sugar? It's been a long, hard road."

She smiled sweetly. "Are you going to have a cup of tea, darlin'?" she asked him. She came up on her toes, slipping her arms around his neck.

"I had reckoned that I might have a beer across the way," he told her, his jaw twisting. Her smile had been dazzling, and her eyes were absurdly large and innocent. Her body was pressed tight to his and he could feel all the curves and soft slopes that he had recently come to know so well.

His eyes narrowed. "Careful!" he mouthed. She couldn't be that innocent. She had to know what she was doing to him.

"Why, darlin'," she drawled sweetly. "I don't mind. I'll come over to the saloon with you." She wrinkled her nose up prettily. "I don't rightly care for that nasty old beer, but—"

He untangled her arms from around his neck. "Sweetheart," he said firmly, "you go on and have tea. It might be a rough place. There might be some . . . talk . . . I don't want you to hear."

"If you're there, my love, I'm sure that I'll be safe."

"You'll be much safer, sweetheart, having tea."

"But I don't mind hearing talk, beloved."

He was losing control. There was a definite note of irritation in his voice. "Honey love, sometimes a man just don't talk as freely when there's a lady present. You'll have tea."

"But, darlin', I—"

He didn't let her finish. He could hear Mr. Haywood snickering behind him, and he'd had about enough. She was the one pressing it. He pulled her even closer and slammed his lips down hard upon hers in a bruising, punishing kiss. He held her so tightly that she could barely breathe, and that was what he had intended. When he released her, she was silent, gasping for breath. He spun her around so that his back was toward Mr. Haywood and he whispered with vehemence. "Go over and have tea. Now. You ruin this—"

"But I want to hear, too—"

"Go. Now. Smile, kiss me sweetly, and damn you, go have a cup of tea. I mean it, Shannon."

He could hear her teeth grinding, but she went still. Malachi spun around. "Next door, you say, Mr. Haywood?"

"Sure thing. The little lady can go right through this door here."

Shannon didn't see a door. Then she realized that even the door was lined with shelves that were filled with merchandise.

"See you soon, sweetheart." Malachi pulled her into his arms, kissing her on the forehead. She longed to slap him, hard. She smiled instead, and threw her arms around him again, rising up on her toes, and quickly threading her fingers through the hair at his nape. She kissed him . . .

She kissed him with purpose . . . and with menace, pressing her lips fully against his, and teasing his lip with the thrust of her tongue. Startled, he gave way. She pressed her tongue fully into his mouth, slowly, provocatively, filling it.

Then she withdrew, dropping back on her heels with her body tight to his, rubbing him with the length of it. She saw a dark sizzle in his eyes, but ignored it despite her own breathlessness. She turned to Mr. Haywood and smiled brightly. "Newlyweds, you know!" she explained, flushing and batting her lashes. "I can't bear to see him go, even for a second. It's just been so hard, what with the war and all. The cows scattered, then the fields were trampled, and then the whole ranch was burned down one day. But now we're finally together, heading west, and it is just so hard to let my darlin' out of my sight . . ."

Both men were silent. Malachi was as stiff as a poker, not saying a word. But when she looked at him, his eyes were narrowed. Real narrow. The way he looked at her caused her heart to jump and shiver, and she decided then to make a hasty retreat. She offered Mr. Haywood another smile and quickly passed through the shelved door that he held open for her.

She found herself in a large parlor. For a moment, it reminded her so much of her home that she inhaled quickly, feeling a little dizzy. It was lovely. A piano stood on a braided rug before a polished wood staircase. Beautiful Victorian chairs sat all around the piano in pleasant angles, a grouping of three here, two there. There was a grouping around the fireplace, and there were lovely little marble-topped tables all around.

"Hello?"

A short, buxom woman with small brown eyes, iron-gray hair and warm, rosy cheeks came through a doorway, wiping her hands on a towel. She smiled at Shannon, then eyed her outfit.

She didn't fit in the beautiful little parlor, Shannon realized. Not in her dusty breeches and checked shirt.

But the woman didn't hesitate long. It was ranch country, farm country, and Shannon's outfit was not completely alien here.

"Hello, miss . . ."

"Uh—Gabriel," Shannon said quickly. "Sh—Sara Gabriel, Mrs. Haywood. Your husband sent me over."

"Oh, how lovely. Well, do sit down. I'll bring you in some of our finest, young lady." She extended her arm around the parlor. "As you can see, we're not terribly busy at the moment."

Shannon nodded, wondering if they were ever busy. It seemed to be such a small town to support the shop and boardinghouse.

"Sit, sit!"

She shooed Shannon into one of the chairs by the fireplace and disappeared. Shannon barely had a chance to get her breath and look around before Mrs. Haywood was back, carrying a large silver tray. She set it down on one of the marble-topped tables. She poured tea from a pot through a strainer and looked at Shannon. "Sugar, cream?"

"Yes, please," Shannon said.

As Mrs. Haywood continued fixing the tea, Shannon looked over the curve of her chair toward the street. Malachi was just going into the saloon, pushing his way through a set of swinging doors.

"Is that your husband, dear?" asked Mrs. Haywood, following Shannon's eyes.

"Yes," said Shannon, a little grimly.

"Now, now, don't worry about him, Mrs. Gabriel," Mrs. Haywood advised her. She sighed with an expansive smile and patted Shannon's knee. "You're such a pretty young thing, you needn't worry a bit. Newlyweds, eh?"

"Er, yes ma'am. How did you know?" Shannon said.

"The war, my girl, the war. Young ladies here and there are snatching up their fellers the second the boys come home. Too many young men dead. Too many young women left without husbands or intendeds. Those who can are marrying quick. Did your husband fight in the war, Mrs. Gabriel?"

"Yes—yes, he did," Shannon said quickly. She prayed that Mrs. Haywood wouldn't ask her any more questions.

She didn't. She pointed to the pastries on the plate. "Meat pies and cinnamon swirls and raisin muffins. And I'm the best cook this side of the Mississippi, I promise you. Help yourself, young lady."

Shannon hadn't known how hungry she was until she bit into the first pie. It was still warm from the oven, and the pastry was fluffy and light and delicious, and the meat was tender and seemed to melt in her mouth. She hadn't had anything nearly so good in ages, and it felt as if she and Malachi had been on the road forever, despite the fact that this would only be their fourth night away. Everything about the parlor felt good, from the elegance of the chairs to the fine food and sweet tea. It was nice to stop, even if Malachi had been his usual dictatorial self when he had refused to let her go to the saloon.

Mrs. Haywood kept talking as Shannon ate. She explained that Haywood was kept busy by the traffic that went through. There were roads all around the town. Some of them went south, Texas way, and some of them went to Missouri, and some of them headed toward the north, while an awful lot of them headed out west. "People are headin' for California, right and left, already. Almost as much as back in '49. The war . . . it left so many without a home, or without a home they could call their own anymore."

Shannon nodded vaguely. She found herself looking over the rear of the chair, out the curtained windows and across the street to the saloon. Heat suffused through her as she thought of the way she had kissed Malachi in the store, and she wondered why she had done so. If she were playing a game, it was a dangerous one. If she was hoping to taunt him or hurt him, she was risking herself by doing it. She didn't know what had seized her; she didn't seem to know herself at all any more.

Nor did she understand why she was so anxious over the length of time he was staying at the saloon. What was he doing over there?

Drinking it up with the whores, no doubt, she thought, and a flush of anger filled her. She didn't care; it was none of her business.

But she did care. It made no sense. She did care. Maybe it was the idea that he could move on from her to a whore so quickly. Maybe it left her with doubts about her abilities.

She almost bit through her cup with that thought, and she reminded herself fiercely that she really loathed Malachi, loathed him with all her heart, and she had never set out to please him, she had never set out to be with him at all. And she didn't want to be with him now; it was a matter of necessity.

Maybe he wasn't being entertained by a woman at all. Maybe he was in trouble, Shannon thought.

"You two staying the night?" Mrs. Haywood asked her.

"Uh—no, I don't think so," Shannon said. "Ma—my husband, Sloan, wants to keep moving. He says the sooner we get where we're going, the sooner we'll get settled down."

"But a little rest never did nobody any harm, either," Mrs. Haywood said. "Pity, I've got the coziest little room upstairs. Pretty lace curtains, a big wool comforter, a fireplace and—" she winked, leaning toward Shannon "—I got the most unbelievable hip bath you ever seen up there. It's a two seater, wood and copper, just right for a young mister and his new missus."

Shannon nodded, her face growing red despite herself. "I'm sure it's very, very nice, Mrs. Haywood—"

Mrs. Haywood jumped up, grabbing her hand. "Do come on. Your young man seems to be enjoying himself. You come on up here, and I'll show you my honeymooners' retreat!"

Shannon didn't have much choice. She stared across the roadway one more time, wishing she could give Malachi a good punch right in the gut. What did he think he was doing? Was he enjoying himself at her expense, or...

Was he in trouble?

She wished she knew.

It was a typical saloon, the type that had been cropping up in Kansas ever since the white man had first started to claim the land. Two men served behind the bar, and a beautiful brunette with a feathered hat and shoulderless gown played tunes at the piano. There were two lone drinkers at round tables, and a poker game going on in the rear of the room. Three of the players were ranchers; they had come with their dusty hats and kerchiefs and chaps and spurs, and they were swigging on whiskey bottles. A fourth man seemed to be a clerk or a banker. He was wearing a neat pin-striped suit with a crooked tie and white shirt.

The other two had a somewhat professional air about them. Both wore vested suits and tall hats. One was lean with a thin curling mustache, and the other was heavier set with small, very dark and very alert eyes.

Malachi wandered over to the bar, and one of the barkeeps hurried to serve him. "Beer," Malachi said briefly, throwing a coin on the bar. The man smiled and drew a foaming brew from the tap. Malachi nodded his thanks.

"Passing through?" the barkeep asked.

Malachi nodded again. From the corner of his eye, he saw that the gamblers were being served by a tall, buxom redhead. The sight of the woman gave him a start, and he almost forgot to answer the barkeep. "The wife and I are heading out for California. Seems the only thing to do now." He remembered Shannon's words and added, "We were burned out. End of the war, you know. Seems to make sense to up and start all over."

"Yep, seems to make sense. Lots of people heading west these days. You staying in town long?"

"Nope. Just came in to wet my whistle."

The barkeep smiled. "And your wife is over at Mrs. Haywood's having tea."

"Yeah, how'd you know?"

"Cause this is Haywood's saloon. His town, really. He entertains the lady folks on that side of the street, and the men on this side. Darned good scam, ain't it, Mr.—"

"Gabriel. Sloan Gabriel."

"Matey. Matey MacGregor. It all seems to come out clean in the wash here. The Haywoods are right nice folks themselves, and that seems to make it all right."

Malachi grimaced. "Yeah, maybe it does." He turned around, leaning against the bar, watching the tall red-haired woman again. He swore inwardly. It was Iris Andre from Springfield, and he did know her.

He thought he should turn around and hurry out of the saloon, but just at that moment, the woman looked up and saw him. Surprise and pleasure appeared on her attractive features, and she straightened, ignoring the poker players, and hurried toward him. She was going to call out his name, he knew it.

"Iris! I'll be damned!" He went to her quickly, hugging her and squeezing the air from her before she could speak. He picked her up to swing her around, whispering in her ear, "Sloan. Sloan Gabriel. Please."

She nodded swiftly—Iris always had been a bright woman. She meant to have her own business one day, and Malachi was sure that when she did, it would be a financial success.

"Sloan!" she said enthusiastically.

"You two know each other, Iris?" the barkeep called.

"Sure do, Matey. We're friends from way back. Sloan, grab your beer and come over here to a table for a moment."

He'd always liked Iris. She might be a whore, but she was a whore with class. He didn't miss a beat. She was almost as tall as he was, and though she wasn't beautiful, she was attractive with her strong features, blazing red hair, green eyes and regal height.

"Come on!" she urged him, pulling him farther and farther into the back. She sat him down at one of the small tables, far away from the others, far away from probing eyes. "Malachi! What the hell fool thing are you doing in Kansas? Wait a minute, don't answer that. Buy me a drink so this will look like business. Matey!" she called out. "We'll take a bottle of whiskey over here. The good stuff."

"Coming right up."

Iris dangled her fingers sensually over the back of Malachi's hand while they waited for Matey to come over with the whiskey. When he was gone, Iris lowered her head close to Malachi's. "Malachi! They've got wanted posters up all over the country! They say you were in on a raid with your brothers, that you went into Kansas and shot some guy named Henry Fitz, and that you're wanted on all kinds of other bushwhacking activities, too. I heard about what Fitz did to your brother, so I wasn't too surprised—"

"Iris, I wasn't with Cole, not that I wouldn't have gone with him if I could. But the war was ending right then. I had a whole contingent of men under me, and I couldn't just go running off to Kansas. Cole was a scout. I was regular cavalry. I went where I was ordered to go."

"Malachi." She moved even closer to him. "I know that none of you has done anything to be hanged for, but you don't know Hayden Fitz."

"And you do?"

Iris nodded. "Never met a meaner son of a bitch in my entire life. There's something evil about him. He likes bloodletting, and he likes to watch men die. He's worth money, too, Malachi. Big money. He invested with arms manufacturers during the war and made himself even richer. He owns Sparks—"

"Sparks?"

"The town where he lives. I mean, he owns it." She smiled, waving a hand around. "All right, so the Haywoods own Haywood. But this is a two-bit rest stop, Malachi. Sparks is big. The stagecoach goes through. It's always filled with Conestogas. There's a jail and a circuit court, and if he manages to get you into that jail, he'll hang you, too. You fool! You gotta get out of Kansas."

Malachi shook his head. "I can't. Hayden Fitz sent men to my sister-in-law's place. Cole wasn't there, so they carried her away. I've got to find her."

Iris sat back. "At least you got rid of your Reb uniform," she said softly. "You don't look like the poster so much anymore."

"I still have the uniform," he said, pouring out shots of the whiskey. "It's stuffed in my saddlebags. And my hat—well, I left it out in some bushes. It was kind of hard to part with, you know?"

She nodded. "Old times," she murmured, then she looked at him. "Oh, Malachi!"

"What, Iris?"

"Malachi, I did hear something about Fitz holding a woman. Just the other day, some of the boys were talking about Fitz having a blond woman in his jail. Said she was part of a conspiracy to murder Union soldiers."

His heart sank, but it was what he had been expecting to hear. The Red Legs would have carried Kristin straight to Fitz. And Fitz surely knew that he was holding the key to Cole's whereabouts.

"You think he'll—hurt her?" Malachi asked.

She shook her head strenuously. "I—uh—I don't think so. He could kill her, Malachi, if he does anything. But hurt her? Not if he's using her for bait."

"You hear anything about my brothers?" he asked her.

She shook her head. "Not a word. Sorry, Malachi." She was silent for a minute. "But I can help you."

"What?"

"Like I said," she told him dryly, "I know Hayden Fitz. I know his sheriff, Tom Parkins, real well. The town ain't twenty miles from here, Malachi. I can take a trip over and bring you back some information."

"Iris, that's good of you. That's real good, but I can't stay here—"

"You can stay here if you can stay anyplace on God's good earth. I tell you, Malachi, for Yanks, these are real good people here. Stay. Just give me one or two days. I can ride over tomorrow, spend some time and ride back.

"I can't have you do that—"

"I do it now and then anyway, Malachi."

He hesitated. If anything happened to Iris, he would never forgive himself. But if she could help him free Kristin and he didn't let her, he'd never forgive himself, either.

"Iris, I can't believe I'm saying this, but all right. You think I'm really safe here?"

"As safe as you're going to be."

He exhaled slowly.

"I won't let nothing happen to me, Malachi, I swear it," she insisted. "It's all right. It really is."

He still hesitated, then he sighed. "All right. It's good to see you, Iris. So good. You stayin' on here?"

"Don't look at me like that—I'll feel like I want to stand up and sing 'Dixie,' and that just ain't no good anymore. No. I'm going to California. The war is too close here, Malachi. I want to leave it behind. My father fought with Grant, and he's dead. My brother was with General E. Kirby-Smith down south, and now he's dead, too. I want out of this hatred, Malachi. It ain't going to end here. Not in my lifetime."

He laced his fingers through hers and squeezed them. They were very close and intimate, two friends who had run the same gamut.

That's how they were sitting when the saloon doors burst open and Shannon came into the room.

She had a Colt shoved into her belt, and she looked around the saloon carefully, looking for any danger. He saw from the position of her hand that she could have grabbed the gun in a split second, and fired, with great accuracy, in less time than that.

Her eyes fell on his.

"Ma—Sloan!" she said, startled. Her eyes took in the two glasses, the whiskey bottle and his hand, his fingers interweaved with Iris's on the table. She took in Iris, from the little flare of her hat to her black petticoats peaking out from beneath her crimson gown. She looked from the poker players to the bar, where Matey was staring at her expectantly.

Her eyes narrowed, dark lashes falling over her brilliant blue eyes. Her hair was loose and beautiful, spilling all around her shoulders. It was one of those occasions when her masculine apparel made her look all the more feminine, for her slender legs seemed very long, and her derriere was defined by her trousers just as her breasts were full and defined by her cotton shirt.

She was furious. Malachi wondered why. Just because he had left her for so long, hadn't allowed her to take an equal part in this venture? Or was there, maybe, just maybe, more to it than that?

Thinking about it made a pulse beat hard against his throat. He wanted to be with her somewhere alone, then, at that moment.

He swallowed down his desire and fought the tension. She was striding his way. They were going to do battle again. Her claws were bared; he could almost see them. He nearly smiled. A woman didn't get that way unless she was jealous. At least a little bit jealous.

"Darlin', I'm so very sorry to interrupt," she drawled. Her voice dripped with honey. She smiled sweetly at Iris. Then she knelt close to Malachi. "You son of a bitch! You left me over there scared to death...never mind. Bastard! Well, darlin', at least the whole town will be expecting a marital dispute. I'm checking into Mrs. Haywood's. I assume you have other arrangements." She stood. "Nice to meet you, Miss—" she said to Iris.

"Iris, honey. Iris Andre. And you're...?"

"I'm—" Shannon paused and shot her very sweet and dazzling smile at Iris once again. "I'm Mrs. Sloan Gabriel,'' she said, and she picked up Iris's shot glass and tossed the whiskey into her face.

Matey inhaled in a massive gasp; even the poker players went dead silent.

Malachi leaped to his feet, reaching for Shannon. Iris was on her feet, too. Malachi knew Iris, and Iris didn't take that kind of thing from anybody. He jerked Shannon around behind him. "Iris, I do apologize for my wife's manners—"

"Don't you dare apologize for me to any who—"

He spun around, clamping his hand hard over Shannon's mouth. "Iris, I apologize with all my heart." He jerked Shannon's wrist and twisted her arm around so that she couldn't possibly fight him without feeling excruciating pain. "Darlin', please, Iris is an old friend, and we just have a few things to say to one another." He dropped his voice and whispered against her ear. "Darlin', you are acting like a brat, and I promise you, if you don't act grown-up real quick here, I'm going to peel those breeches and tan your hide, just to prove that the man wears the real pants in this family. I'll do it, Shannon, because I'll have to." He hesitated. "She knows something about Kristin. She can help us, Shannon!"

He released her, very slowly. He waited expectantly, ready to snatch her back into his arms if need be.

For once in her life, she seemed to have believed his threat. Perhaps she was so concerned that she would grab at any scrap of information about her sister. She faced Iris.

"Miss Andre, it was a pleasure," she said. Her voice was the softest drawl, her manner that of a charming, well-mannered belle. She swept from the saloon like a queen.

A cheer went up from the poker crowd. One of the ranchers stood. "Mister, I sure salute you! That's one heck of a spirited filly, beautiful to boot, and you handled her like a man!"

"Buy him a drink!" the heavyset professional gambler called. "If I'd been able to manage my wife like that, I might be a rich man by now!"

Malachi laughed, sitting down and waving a hand in the air. "She's going to be mighty mad later, gents. We'll see how I handle her then." He looked at Iris. She sat beside him. He gave her his kerchief to wipe the whiskey from her face. She seemed more confused than angry.

"Malachi, that really was your wife?"

He shook his head. "Iris, she is my sister-in-law's sister. She wants Kristin back. I couldn't seem to stop her from coming with me, and that's another long story, too."

Iris sat back, smiling. Malachi poured her more whiskey, and she swallowed it.

"Thanks for not ripping her hair out."

"Don't kid yourself, Malachi. I saw that Colt in her pants. I'm willing to bet she knows how to use it."

"Like a pro—except that she has a bad time aiming at people."

Iris was smiling at him with a peculiar little grin. "She might not make you such a bad wife after all, my friend."

Malachi frowned. "Iris—"

"She's got spirit, and she's got courage. A little raw around the edges, as if she's got some scars on her. But we've all got scars. I can't see you with a namby-pamby woman, and she ain't that."

"No, she isn't that. She's a pain in the damned—"

"Butt!" Iris broke in, laughing. "Yes sir, she's that. But I can see something in your eyes there, Malachi. She ain't going to be checking into Mrs. Haywood's place alone, is she?"

Malachi smiled, idly twirling his whiskey around in his glass. Miss McCahy had seen fit to comment upon his actions **and** whereabouts.

He was damned ready to comment upon hers.

"I think I should give her time to check in and settle down and get real, real comfortable. What do you think?"

Iris laughed at the sizzle in his eyes.

She wished that it was her. But it wasn't. He was more like a married man than he knew. The beautiful little blonde with the delicate features and the tough-as-nails stature had those golden tendrils of hers wrapped tightly around him.

Still, Mrs. Sloan Gabriel's manners did need a little improvement.

"Let her get real, real comfortable," Iris advised him sagely. "A game of poker might be right in line here. Come on over, I'll introduce you to the boys."

"All right. I'm glad to meet the boys."

The heavyset gambler was Nat Green. The slimmer man with him was Idaho Joe, and the ranchers were Billy and Jay Fulton, Carl Hicks and Jeremiah Henderson. It was a good game. Iris held onto his shoulders, laughing, while he played. She brought him drinks.

Around supper time, she disappeared and came back with big plates of steak and potatoes and green beans.

He lost at cards—a little bit—and the meal cost him almost as much as the liquor, but he didn't care much. He had a good time.

And through all of it, he anticipated his arrival at Mrs. Haywood's Inn, Rooms by the Day, Month or Year.

He was just dying to see his darlin' wife.

Just dyin' to see her.

Chapter Eight

He knew that the door would be locked.

He even suspected that Shannon might have gone to Mrs. Haywood with quite a sob story about being ignored so that her husband could play around with another woman.

Shannon was a good little actress. He was learning that quickly.

And he was learning, too, that things had changed between them, irrevocably. Maybe they would always be at battle, but the battlegrounds were subtly changing. He might still spend ninety percent of his time thinking Mr. McCahy should have dragged his daughter into the woodshed a number of times at a far younger age, but he couldn't deny what she had done to him. Exactly what that was, he wasn't sure yet. And he didn't want to think about it; he didn't want to analyze it. He fixed it in his mind that Shannon had started this one. Either down in the store when she had kissed him with that pagan promise, or when she had come striding across to the saloon to douse Iris in whiskey. This one, she had begun.

But he was going to finish it.

He had his own fair share of acting ability.

"Mr. Gabriel!" Mrs. Haywood said with censure when Malachi came to ask for a key to the room. "Now, I know, sir, that a man has got to have a few simple pleasures of his own. And a saloon's a good place for a man to have whiskey and a cigar—keeps the scent out of his own parlor, you know. But when it comes to other things . . . when he leaves a beautiful little bride . . .'' She shook her head in reproach.

"Iris is just an old friend, ma'am." Mr. Haywood was in the kitchen, eating his supper. Malachi raised his voice a hair, determined to work on them both. "I don't know what my wife told you, Mrs. Haywood, but there was nothing going on. I had a few drinks, and I lost a few hands of poker. Ma'am, you got to understand. If a man lets his wife make a fool of him like that, well, then, he just ain't a man anymore."

"That's right, Martha." Mr. Haywood dropped his napkin on the butcher-block kitchen dining table and strode to the door. "Martha, if the man wants a key to his own room, we'd best give it to him. She's his wife, and that's that."

Mrs. Haywood was still uncertain. "Mr. Gabriel, I probably ain't got no right to keep man and wife apart, but—"

"I'm going to try to make her understand, Mrs. Haywood. Honest, I am."

"You give him the key, Martha," Mr. Haywood said.

"You're right, Papa, I suppose. Oh, Mr. Gabriel, I was just giving my husband a piece of apple pie. Won't you have some?"

"Why, that's mighty kind of you. Thank you, ma'am."

He had the key, and he had a cup of good strong coffee and some of the best apple pie he'd tasted in his entire life. And it was the middle of summer.

"I jar and preserve all my own fruits," Mrs. Haywood told him proudly.

"Well, it's the finest eating I've done, ma'am, since way before the war."

As Mrs. Haywood blushed, the door to the parlor opened. A pretty young girl in a maid's cap and smooth white apron walked in. She bobbed a nervous little curtsy to Malachi and looked at the Haywoods. "Mrs. Gabriel is all set for the night, Mrs. Haywood. She had me fetch her some of the lavender soap, and asked if we'd be so good as to put the price on the bill. She thanks you kindly for the use of the tub.''

His heart started ticking a staccato beat. If he'd gone by instinct, he would have knocked the table over, brushed the maid aside, burst through the door and raced up the stairs.

Primitive, he warned himself reproachfully.

That wasn't what he wanted. Slow torture was what he had in mind.

He sipped his coffee like a gentleman. "My wife's in the bath?" he inquired innocently.

"Oh, why, yes, Mr. Gabriel," Mrs. Haywood said. "Don't worry, young man, you're welcome to stay here in the kitchen if you're worrying about disturbing her."

"Why, ma'am, I was thinking that I might steal a little of her water, and save someone having to haul more up the stairs." He spoke sincerely, rising.

"That's thoughtful of you, Mr. Gabriel," Mrs. Haywood said. Around her ample figure, Mr. Haywood looked up at Malachi with his brow arched and a skeptical smile slipping onto his lips.

"Mighty thoughtful, son," he said dryly.

Malachi flashed him a quick grimace. "Mr. and Mrs. Haywood, thank you again. Good night, now."

He nodded to the young maid and swept by her. He forced himself to walk slowly through the parlor and up the stairs. He glanced at the key. Room five.

It wasn't hard to find.

He took a deep breath outside the doorway, smiled again, and slipped the key into the lock. He heard her key fall out of the door on the other side as he pressed his in. He pushed open the door.

The most outrageous bathtub he'd ever seen sat before the fire. It was a long wooden tub with headrests rising up at both ends. It was decorated with copper and delft tiles, and at that particular moment, it was laden with bubbles...and with Shannon.

Her hair was curled high on top of her head, leaving the slim porcelain column of her neck bare. Her shoulders and just a peak of her breasts rose out of the bubbles.

She turned on him, her eyes wide and startled and very blue. She almost leaped up, but then seemed to realize how much worse that would be. "Get out!"

"Darlin'!" he said softly, with taunting reproach. And he stepped into the room, closing the door behind him, leaning against it. His eyes stayed on her while he twisted the key in the lock.

She must have put on one hell of a performance with the Haywoods, he thought. She hadn't expected him that night. It was a pity that he hadn't gotten to see it.

Shannon sank farther into the tub, watching him as he sauntered coolly into the room.

"Don't you dare get comfortable," Shannon warned him. She felt herself burning all over, and it wasn't from the steam in the bath. It was caused just by the way his eyes fell upon her.

The nerve of him. How dare he be here. How dare he look at her like that. When he had just left his redheaded slut!

He tossed the key onto the side table and dropped down on Mrs. Haywood's beautiful crocheted bedspread, lacing his fingers behind his head and staring right at her. He smiled.

"Don't let me disturb you."

"You are disturbing me." She narrowed her eyes. "You've no right in this room. The Haywoods—"

"The Haywoods know that a man has a right to be with his wife—beloved."

"The Haywoods know that the man is a scoundrel and cad, seducing women from the Mississippi to the Pacific. They understood completely that you deserved a night in the livery stables."

"Tsk, tsk." His apparent relaxation had been deceptive. He moved all of a sudden, sleek and easy, twisting to stretch out on his stomach, facing her from the foot of the bed.

There was no more than six feet between them. She could see the tension in his features and the pulses beating furiously against his throat and temple. There was a dangerous gleam in his eyes, and she was aware that he was angry with her—furious, probably, for her behavior in the saloon—and that he seemed to have forgotten any rules of fair play for the night.

She sank lower in the tub. He wouldn't force her into anything. She knew him, and she knew that he would never force any woman.

But what would he do?

And what would she do? If he touched her, she would scream, she thought, and not with horror, but because her flesh seemed to cry out to know his hands again. She was hot inside and out, and trembling fiercely. The scent of the lavender soap was all around her, the softness of the bed awaited . . .

And he had just spent hours and hours with a whore.

"Malachi—" She paused. "Sloan," she hissed. "This is my room. Get out."

He smiled, giving her a flash of white teeth against the golden strands of his mustache and beard. "I'm sorry, sweetheart. I may be a cad, but I wouldn't dream of leaving my sweet young wife alone for the entire night."

He rose and sat at the foot of the bed, nonchalantly kicking off his boots and peeling away his socks. Shannon watched him, stunned, as he proceeded to pull the tails of his shirt from his pants and unbutton his shirt and cast it aside.

"What are you doing?" she asked him quickly.

"I'm going to take a bath."

"No, you're not. This is my bath."

"Darlin', we've got to talk, and it looks like it's just the right place, to me."

"Malachi, if you touch me, I'll scream."

"You're my wife. They might shake their heads a bit downstairs, but they won't interfere."

"I'm not your wife!" Shannon swore, panicking. The look in his eyes caused shivers to streak along her spine. The sight of his bare chest, sleek and gleaming, brought her body alive with memory. She lowered her head, determined not to look at him.

But she could hear him.

She heard his pants fall to the floor, and she heard his footsteps as his bare feet padded behind her. He dropped to his knees and his lips touched her shoulders like a burning brand. She jerked away from him and wished she hadn't, for when she turned to him she saw his hungry eyes on her newly exposed breasts. Her nipples hardened instantly and flames seemed to rise to her cheeks, then sink back and lie deep in her core. She sank into the water. She wanted to be angry, indignant. Her voice came out as a husky whisper. "Malachi, I am not your wife!"

He was on his feet, naked as a jay, and his manhood flying proud and firm. She was determined not to stare, but her teeth were chattering, and she felt compelled to watch him, like a marionette jerked by strings. She loved the look of him, she realized. She felt some ancient and instinctive fascination, which lay deep below the level of her mind, something that caused her blood to race and heat and her breath to catch and come too quickly and that made her flesh come alive at the very thought of him. She could not draw her eyes from him. She could not help but respond to the naked length of him. She found him magnificent. From the breadth of bronzed shoulders to the lean hardness of his thighs, she found him so boldly and negligently male that she could not turn away.

He stepped into the tub, sitting behind her so that his feet brushed her bottom. He leaned back against the rim of the tub and sighed deeply. "This is just wonderful." He closed his eyes in complete comfort.

Hating him, hating herself, Shannon swore furiously. "Malachi, I am not your wife!"

His eyes flew open, glittering and dangerous. "That's not what you told Miss Andre when you so rudely doused her."

"I—I had to appear upset."

"Did you now?" He leaned forward. His hands dangled over his knees. His fingers almost brushed the flesh of her breasts. She leaned against the tub, as far as she could go. It made no difference. "You're lucky she controlled her temper."

"You're damned lucky that I'm controlling mine right now."

"Am I? Why, beloved, is that a threat?"

She didn't answer him. She was shaking all over and she only hoped she had the bravado to make an escape. "If you're going to stay, Malachi, then I'm going to go." She started to rise. He was on his feet in an instant. He set his hands on her shoulders and pressed against them with relentless determination. Water and bubbles swished all around them. Her rear landed hard against the bottom of the tub, and he followed her quickly back down.

"Sit. You're not going anywhere."

"Don't you dare manhandle me! I've had it. I've simply had it! I'm not going to sit—" She tried to rise again. He caught her foot this time. She felt his free hand roaming the water for the soap. His fingers brushed her thighs and her rear and her flank and she gritted her teeth to keep from screaming out.

"Malachi—"

"Sit," he said pleasantly. "Just sit, darlin'."

"Malachi, you son of a bitch!" She tried to pull away. His grip upon her foot was firm. Softly humming "Dixie," he washed her foot with the lavender soap.

She leaned back and spoke through a clenched jaw. "Malachi, I want you out of here! Now! You left me cooling my heels to run off to a saloon. You spent the whole afternoon and evening with a whore. I had to act the way I did—"

"Jealous, darlin'?" He taunted huskily. She opened her eyes. Her foot was free and he had come close to her. Very close. Their limbs were all entangled. She could feel the shaft of his sex against her ankle, the hardness of his thighs against her toes. It was unbearable.

And she could see the pulse beating, beating, against his throat. His lips were close to hers as he spoke.

"Never!" she promised him in a heated panic. "I just can't stand the thought of being sullied by your touch."

"No?" He cocked his head, and his lashes fell lazily over his cheeks. "You didn't mind down in the store this afternoon."

"That was—that was necessary."

"No, I don't think so. I don't think so at all. Shannon, I haven't ever, not even by the most practiced whore, been kissed so provocatively in my entire life."

She leaped up. It had gone too far. Her cheeks were blazing and her breasts were heaving. The bubbles and water sluiced from her, bathing her in a seductive white foam.

Malachi leaned back. His eyes fell on the hardened dark peaks of her breasts as they thrust through the white foam of the bubbles. She saw that look in his eyes again, and she cried out softly as she stepped from the tub. She grabbed for the towel, but she had barely dried her face before he was up behind her. He lifted her cleanly from the ground and tossed her upon Mrs. Haywood's crocheted spread. She gasped for breath, trying to rise. It was impossible. He was down beside her within a split second, a leg cast over her hips and thighs, his arm a bar of steel across her.

"That kiss wasn't necessary at all," he told her.

"I am going to scream, Malachi. I'm going to scream so loudly that you'll be sorry."

"If you scream," he promised her, "it isn't going to be for help."

"You bastard!" She surged against him. "You can't come from a fancyhouse to me—" She broke off, straining against the muscles that held her. She tossed like a wild creature, but it served no purpose. It just put their bodies more fully in contact. Her breasts rubbed against his chest, and her limbs became more and more entangled with his. She felt the hard, searing heart of his desire against her thighs, against her belly. She tried to kick him and failed, but he swore softly, knowing her intent. He straddled her, keeping himself safe from her rancor, and caught her hands, pinning them to her sides. Exhausted, she twisted her head from his, gasping desperately for breath.

She heard him chuckle softly and she opened her eyes, staring at him in fury. "I will scream, Malachi! You bastard!" Tears glazed her eyes. "Gentleman! Southern cavalier! The last of the flower of knighthood—"

"Shannon, I didn't touch her."

"What?" she breathed.

"She's a friend, and a good one. She's going to do some spying on Fitz for me."

"Fitz?"

"We're not far, not far at all now. Fitz has Kristin. She's in jail."

"Oh, no, Malachi!" She surged against him, bit her lip and fell back.

"But she's all right. Iris is going to go see her. She's going to help us."

"Or else turn you in," Shannon said softly.

He shook his head with irritating confidence. "She's a friend."

"I'll bet she is."

He lay over her, his head close to hers. "You are jealous, Miss McCahy. I told you; I didn't touch her."

"That—that doesn't mean anything at all," Shannon whispered against his lips. "I don't—"

His mouth closed upon hers with a curiously tender force, parting her lips, searing them, causing them to part sweetly beneath his. She lost contact with everything but the fire of his tongue, so hot and hard, thrusting into the depths of her soul and desire. She didn't feel the bed beneath her, or know

that gentle candlelight filled the room. She could only taste
the fever of his kiss.

She ceased to fight him. Her fingers curled around his.
His mouth lifted from hers, and touched down again upon
the column of her throat. The brush of his mustache and
beard feathered softly over her flesh, and she moaned,
arching hard against him. He lowered his head, sweeping his
face over her breasts, slowly encircling one mound with the
tip of his tongue, then taking in the fullness of her nipple
with the whole of his mouth. His teeth grazed the pebbled
peak as he licked it in slow and leisurely fashion.

Her heart was beating like thunder; her blood seemed to
hiss and boil and cascade through her, and she could not
think of anything but the exquisite pleasure of his touch.
Something deep inside her tried to warn her that it was
wrong, that no great and everlasting love lay between them,
that theirs was the heated and tempestuous passion forged
from the hatred borne between sworn enemies.

But she did not hate him. Not at all . . .

She craved his touch with a basic, undeniable need. She
felt the huge pulse of his passion, thundering against her,
and she was sweetly excited, pleased that this time there
would be no pain at all. She wanted to touch him. She
wanted to explore his shoulders and run her fingers over his
chest, and she even wanted to venture decadently downward, and touch with fascination the place from which his
darkest desire sprung . . .

His lips moved over her, down to her belly. His tongue
laved her with hot moisture, and his beard continued to caress her flesh and evoke a greater surge within her. She
wanted him so desperately . . .

Suddenly he rose above her. His features were tight, but
he smiled and he spoke lightly. "Good night, Shannon."

She stared at him in utter disbelief, then the color surged
to her face and she tried to strike him in a raw fury. Once
again, he secured her hands. He fell to her side and swept
her against him. "We need to get some sleep."

"Sleep! I will never sleep with you, you Confederate snake! You rodent, you knave, scalawag! You bastard, you—"

"Enough, Shannon."

"Vulture, diseased rat! Rabid dog!"

"Enough!" He managed to land his hand on her derriere in a sharp slap. She swore again with the venom and expertise of a cowhand, and this time his hand landed over her mouth. "Darlin', let's go to sleep, or I will forget that I'm a gentleman."

"Gentleman!"

"A gentleman," he repeated. "You're the one who wants to be left alone," he reminded her gruffly.

She was quick and twisted around to see his face. His eyes were unreadable, his features taut, his jaw locked. And his eyes... he stared at her as if he hated her, and she found herself lowering her eyes in misery.

It was true. She had wanted to be left alone because...

"Oh, Malachi!" she said miserably, a sob catching in her throat. He was the one who had brought them to their present untenable position, but she had provoked him earlier. She had meant to stir him down in the store, and she had meant to provoke him over at the saloon. She had been sick, imagining him in the arms of the redhead...

"Malachi, I did love Robert," she whispered. "And if I did, then it can't be right, it just can't be right... I don't mean by Sunday-school morals, I mean in the soul, in the heart..."

She was near to tears. She couldn't possibly be speaking to Malachi this way, especially not when she lay naked in bed with him.

But something in his eyes softened, and his touch was very gentle as he drew her against him. "Shannon, I know that you loved him. You've taken nothing away from him by needing to feel warm again." He sighed. His beard brushed the top of her head. His hand lay against her midriff, but it was a tender touch, and not meant to seduce or capture. "Tell me about him."

"What?"

"Tell me about him. When did you meet? What was he like?"

She shook her head. She couldn't begin to imagine Malachi being interested in her deceased Yank fiancé. But he whispered against her hair softly. "Talk to me. It may feel good. You met when the house in Kansas City fell down."

She nodded, absurdly content to lie there, held by him. "I was arrested along with Kristin—for my relationship with Cole. I was arrested for harboring bushwhackers!"

"The Slater men haven't done much for you, have they?" he murmured quietly.

"I didn't mind that. Cole saved us. I always liked Cole. From the first moment I saw him."

Just like she always hated me, Malachi thought. He smoothed back a strand of her hair. What the hell was he doing here? He'd never been that much of a gentleman. Why had he let her go when she was welcoming him against her? He sighed softly.

"It was awful," Shannon said, shivering. "They had so many of us, stuffed into that terrible decrepit building. When the roof collapsed . . ." She paused. "I thought I was going to die. I was just hanging through the roof when the rafters broke apart. I could hear everyone screaming. And then Robert was there. He and Kristin made me jump. And he caught me. He was so brave and wonderful—a hero. I'll never forget looking into his eyes then. And then...then we heard all the screams again. Five of the women were killed. So many were hurt badly... It was odd. We were friends then, all of us. The other girls knew where my sympathies really lay, and they understood. Josephine Anderson was my friend. When she died, her brother went mad. That's when he really became Bloody Bill, after she died. Oh, Malachi! So many people died!"

"It's all right," he said softly. She was crying. Not sobbing hysterically, just crying very quietly. "It's all right," he said again.

He kept stroking her hair. She didn't speak again, and he didn't speak, either. He closed his eyes, just holding her. It was too painful for any of them to think of the war. Northerner, Southerner, it was just too damned painful to look back. Great men, kind men, good men, all of them dead. Gallant men, alone and moldering in gallant graves. He sighed and closed his eyes. He couldn't let it go on any longer. He had to find some way to free Kristin.

And then he had to find his brothers.

And run.

He opened his eyes. The candles were burning low. He had drifted to sleep. The room was cast in very soft shadows, and the light was pale and ethereal.

He wondered why he had awakened. Then he knew.

Her fingers were moving over his chest. Her nails lightly raked his flesh, and her hair fell over him like a brush with angel's wings. She traced tentative, soft patterns over him, exploring his rib cage and breast and collarbone.

He lay still. He kept his eyes open a slit, watching her. She rose slightly, watching him, watching the movement of her fingers. Her breasts peeked out from the golden glory of her long hair, and as she watched her fingers moving over him, she lightly moistened her lips with the tip of her tongue.

I'll be damned if I'll be a gentleman, he thought. Even cavaliers and knights of old surely had their needs.

He reached out, catching her hand where it lay over his heart. Her eyes darted to his in alarm.

"Go on. Touch me," he whispered.

"I—I didn't mean to wake you," she stuttered. They were both whispering. She must have known that he could not let her go, not this time. She was exquisite in the light, her breasts full and firm and ripe and her skin silky, shining in the candles' pale glow. Her eyes were so very blue...

"I'm awake," he told her.

"I've disturbed you—"

"Disturb me further, darlin'...please." His eyes remained locked with hers. He drew her hand along the length of his body. He heard her breath go ragged in her throat and her eyes followed the motion of their hands with a deadly fascination. Her fingers trailed over his flesh, over the soft hair that nestled around his sex. She tensed, and he felt her trembling. He sensed a certain fear within her, but he held her tight. She curved her hand around it hesitantly.

Rockets seemed to burst within his head and into his body. She gasped softly as she felt him swell huge and hard. She cried out softly. He reached up, slipping his hand around her neck to cup her head. He rose up on an elbow and kissed her slowly and fully, taking her lips, releasing them, hovering over them again just to brush them with the taste of his mouth and the seductive jut of his tongue.

Then he laid her flat and crawled aggressively over her. He kissed her again, easing away her hesitance.

He felt her fingers upon his shoulders again. Her body found a slow undulation beneath his. He set his hand upon her breast, and followed his touch with his kiss. He stroked her thighs and invaded her intimately with his touch.

With raw purpose he moved his body in a slow, bold sweep down the length of hers. He kept his eyes hard upon hers until he came to the juncture of her thighs, when he replaced his intimate touch there with the searing violation of his tongue.

She called out his name in a gasp as he brought her to the very edge of ecstasy, then withdrew. He found her eyes once more and she choked out incomprehensible words, reaching for him. She pulled him to her, seeking his shoulders with her lips and teeth. He pushed away again, demanding that she meet his eyes as he parted her thighs with the wedge of his knee and thrust deep and swiftly inside her.

She shuddered and whispered his name again.

That night, he gave little heed to finesse, and passion rose like a tempest within him. He caught her lips again with a savage passion, and as their bodies arched in an urgent rhythm, he caressed her with rough and demanding hunger.

Her legs wrapped high around him and her kisses fell upon him as she tasted the textures of his face and his throat. Her fingers trailed down his back to knot into the rigid muscles of his buttocks. At the end he cast back his head as a fierce shudder gripped his body, a hoarse cry escaping his lips. She sobbed out in turn, barely aware of the night, of time or place, barely conscious of reality.

Seconds later, she felt his touch, so absurdly gentle once again. Their harsh breathing could still be heard, and they were both covered in a soft sheen. "Malachi—"

"It's all right," he said gently. "You don't have to say anything." He lay back, bringing her down beside him. He whispered softly against her ear. "Just don't think to hop up and leave me. Don't deny me."

She lay there in silence. The darkness closed around them as the last of the candles burned out.

Much later, they crawled beneath the sheet. Shannon knew a moment of panic at this new intimacy, but then she relaxed again. There was nothing left to fear for that night. She hadn't meant what had happened. At least she didn't think that she did. She had thought he slept soundly, and she had not been able to resist temptation.

And temptation had definitely led to sin, she thought.

With his arms closed around her, she felt as if she might start crying again, because it felt so good. His arms offered warmth and security and a steel-hard strength, and she found she loved that. Just as she was coming to love the slant of his grin. And the way he would never let a man—or a woman—down. He had his code of honor.

And in his sweeping way, he was a cavalier.

She loved his courage, and his daring, just as she was coming to love the bronzed power of his arms, holding her close now. Just as she was coming to love the breadth of his golden-matted chest, and the hard, muscled length of his thighs...

And his impossible, immoral intimacy. She could not believe the way that he had touched and caressed her, and neither could she believe the sweet, unbearable ecstasy that he brought her with his sheer decadent purpose and determination. She was coming to care for him too much...

"Malachi," she whispered softly.

"What?" He moved his hand gently against her, beneath her breasts, idly, tenderly upon them.

"Have you ever been in love?"

He went still, then he moved away from her, his arm over his forehead as he rolled to his back, staring at the ceiling. "Yes. Once. Why?"

"I just... wondered."

He grunted, giving her no further answer.

"Malachi?"

"Yes?"

"Who was she?"

"A girl." It was a short, terse answer. He sighed. "It was a long, long time ago."

"What happened?"

"She died."

"The war—"

"A fever."

"I'm so sorry."

"I told you, it was a long, long time ago."

"It hurt you, though. Badly."

"Shannon, go to sleep."

"Malachi—"

"Shannon, go to sleep. It's night, and I'm tired." He started to rise. In the darkness, she saw the glitter in his eyes. "Unless you plan on entertaining me again, I suggest you go to sleep."

She closed her eyes quickly, turning from him and hugging her pillow. She couldn't... do it again. Not that night.

She had to hug what had happened to herself, and she had to try to understand it, and live with it.

She felt him as he eased back down.

And later, when she was drifting off to sleep, she felt his arm come around her again, strong and sure, bringing her body close against his. It was warm, and it felt better than she ever might have imagined.

It felt . . . peaceful.

She opened her eyes and looked down at his hand, brown against the whiteness of her flesh in the moonlight.

It felt right, and though it might not be, she was tired. She was tired of the war, and tired of fighting. She didn't want to worry anymore. She wanted to take moments like these, and cling to them.

Her pa would be twisting and turning in his grave if he knew anything about her behavior in bed with this man, she thought ruefully. Gabriel McCahy had been a strong man—in his beliefs, in his ideals, in his morality. He'd liked his Irish whiskey, and he'd always been able to spin a fine tale, but he'd loved their mother, and when she had died, he'd been determined that his daughters would be ladies.

Of course, he'd never reckoned on the war.

And then, she reflected wistfully, maybe he wouldn't be so upset after all. He'd had an ability to judge men, and he might have understood that she had stumbled upon a good one, albeit, he came clothed in gray.

She closed her eyes and slept, her fingers falling lightly over Malachi's where they lay across her midriff.

"It is him! I told you it was him, Martha!"

Malachi woke abruptly, his eyes flashing open.

The bore of a sawed-off shotgun was stuck right beneath his nose. He jerked up. Shannon, curled against his chest, moaned in protest and went silent again. Instinctively, Malachi pulled the sheets high over her naked form as he stared respectfully into the face of the man carrying the shotgun.

"You're Malachi Slater," Mr. Haywood said. He barely dared glance at his wife, plump and pink in her nightgown and cap behind him. "Martha, you look now. It is him."

"Do you make a habit of bursting into your guests' bedrooms in the middle of the night?" Malachi demanded icily.

Beside him, Shannon stirred. Her eyes flew open and she saw the shotgun. "Oh!" she gasped, grasping the covers. She stared from Malachi to Haywood, and past him to his wife. She stiffened, raising her chin, and her voice came out as imperiously as a queen's. "What is the meaning of this?"

"There's wanted posters out on him all over the countryside," Haywood said. "You're a dangerous man, Captain Slater. Captain! Hell! Bushwhackers shouldn't get no titles or rank!"

Shannon leaped from the bed, dragging the covers with her, and heedlessly leaving Malachi bare. "He isn't a bushwhacker!" she swore. "It's all a lie! You want to shoot somebody, you ought to go out and shoot Fitz!"

Malachi grimaced at her sudden, passionate loyalty and pulled his pillow around to his lap. "Mr. Haywood, what she's saying is true. I was never a bushwhacker. I was a captain under John Hood Morgan until he died. I signed surrender forms with my men, and we were all allowed to keep our horses, and I was even allowed to keep my arms. I didn't know anything about this until some Union sentries shot at me." He indicated the wound on his leg. The bandage had been lost during his impromptu swim in the stream, but the evidence of Shannon's quick surgery was still there, a jagged red scab.

"Well, I don't know, young man. You're worth an awful lot of money, you know. If this is the truth, you can tell it to Mr. Fitz," Haywood said.

"Fitz will hang him and ask questions later," Shannon said.

Both the Haywoods looked at Malachi again. Malachi barely saw Shannon move, but suddenly she was behind the chair and she was aiming her Colt at the two of them.

"Drop the shotgun," she said.

Mr. Haywood frowned. "Now, come on, little girl. You put that thing down. Those Colts can be mighty dangerous."

"You ever seen close hand what a shotgun does to a man?" she inquired sweetly.

Malachi was afraid of the outcome.

"Can she shoot that thing?" Haywood asked him.

"Better'n General Grant himself, I'm willing to bet," Malachi replied sagely.

He still didn't think it wise to wait. He leaped from the bed.

Shannon watched in amazement as he swooped down on Mr. Haywood, bare as birth, and procured the shotgun. Mrs. Haywood gasped in astonishment, but didn't look away from the swaggering male body. Malachi bowed in response to her gasp. "Ma'am, excuse me." He tossed the shotgun to Shannon, reached for his pants and quickly limped into them.

"Oh, my goodness!" Mrs. Haywood gasped again. Her eyes closed and she promptly passed out.

"Oh, no!" Shannon wailed. Wrapping the sheet around herself, she hurried over to the fallen woman. Malachi stopped her, grabbing the Colt from her fingers. Shannon dropped down by Mrs. Haywood. "Malachi, Mr. Haywood, I need some water."

Mr. Haywood moved suddenly, as if rousing himself from shock. "Water. Water." He hurried to the washstand and brought over the pitcher. Nervous and disoriented, he poured the water over his wife's face. She came to, sputtering and coughing. She looked up at her husband. "Mr. Haywood!" she said reproachfully.

"Are you all right?" Shannon murmured.

"We've got to get out of here, Shannon!" Malachi warned her gruffly.

She ignored him. "Mrs. Haywood, I swear to you, I was telling you the truth. You've got to understand the whole story. Mr. Fitz had a brother who led a unit of jayhawkers, Mrs. Haywood—''

"I never could abide jayhawkers," Mr. Haywood said. "Never could abide them! Why, they were just as bad as the bushwhackers themselves."

Shannon nodded. "They killed Cole Slater's wife, Mrs. Haywood. She was expecting a child. She was innocent, and they came and they killed her, and they burned down the ranch... And, well, Cole ran into Henry Fitz toward the end of the war. It was a fair fight—even the Yanks there knew it. Cole killed him."

"So now Hayden Fitz wants the whole lot of you Slaters, is that it?" Mr. Haywood asked Malachi.

Malachi nodded. "But that doesn't matter. I want Hayden Fitz. He has Shannon's sister, Cole's new wife, in his jail. He's going to use her, another innocent woman, to lure my brother out of hiding. I'm sorry, Mr. Haywood, but I ain't going to be hunted down and murdered by the likes of Fitz. And I'm mighty sorry, 'cause you and your wife are fine people, but I'm going to have to tie you up so that Shannon and I can get out of here."

"Shannon?" Mr. Haywood looked her way, then sank down on the bed. He looked to his wife. "What do you say, mother?"

"I never could abide those jayhawkers. Killing women and innocent children. And that poor dear girl, locked in a jail cell. It ain't decent!"

"Ain't decent at all."

Malachi looked uneasily from Shannon, kneeling by Mrs. Haywood, to Mr. Haywood, calmly sitting on the bed.

"What—"

"You don't need to tie us up, Captain Slater."

"I'm sorry, but—"

"You're going to need us, I think. We're not going to turn you in. If what you tell us is true, we'll try to help you."

"Why?"

"Why?" Mrs. Haywood stood up, strangely noble despite the water that dripped from her nightcap over her bosom. "Why? 'Cause somewhere, Captain Slater, the healing has to start. Somewhere, it has to quit being North and South, and somewhere, we have to stand against the men going against the very rules of God!"

"Malachi!" Shannon urged him. "We need them, if they will help us. We need this base. We need . . . we need the information that we're supposed to get in the next few days."

Malachi thought furiously. Iris said that these were good folks. And Iris said that she could get to Fitz, and she could probably help him with information that he could never get on his own.

"Malachi! We have to trust them."

Slowly, he lowered the Colt. Then he tossed it onto the bed.

"Shannon, I pray you aren't going to get us both killed," he said savagely.

"Hmph." Mr. Haywood stood, as stout and proud as his wife. He went over and picked up his shotgun. He didn't wave it at Malachi, but he held it in his hand, shaking it.

"So you ain't a bushwhacker and you don't deserve to hang for that! But you aren't this young lady's husband, either, and you should be strung up for seducing an innocent, and that's a fact."

Shannon was surprised to see the flush that touched Malachi's cheeks. "That's none of your business, Mr. Haywood," he said.

"It is our business, captain," Martha Haywood warned him severely. "You were living in sin, right beneath our roof. What do you say, Papa?" she asked her husband.

"I say that he hangs."

"What?" Malachi exploded. He made a dive for the Colt. Mrs. Haywood moved faster. She grabbed the gun and aimed his way. "Now, captain, where are your manners? I never did meet a more gallant boy than a cavalry officer, and a Southern gentleman at that. You should be ashamed of yourself."

"Ashamed! Where have the values gone?" Mr. Haywood said fiercely. "Pride and gallantry and good Christian ethics. The war is over now, son."

"Sir—" Malachi took a step forward. A shot exploded in the room, and he stood dead still. Mrs. Haywood knew what she was doing with a Colt, too, so it seemed. The ball went straight by Malachi's head, nearly grazing his ear.

"Shannon," he said through his teeth, keeping his eyes warily upon Mrs. Haywood. "Shannon, I am going to wring your neck!"

"No, captain, you're not. You're going to marry that girl, that's what you're going to do."

"I'm not going to be coerced into any marriage!" Malachi swore.

"Well, son, you can marry her or hang," Mr. Haywood guaranteed him. "Mrs. Haywood, would you like to go for the preacher? A Saturday morning wedding seems just right to me."

"No!" Shannon called out.

Malachi looked at her, startled. She was wrapped in the sheet, her hair a wild tangle around her delicate features and beautiful sloping shoulders.

Her eyes were filled with flashing blue anger. "Don't bother, Mrs. Haywood. I won't marry him."

"Well, well, dear, I'm afraid that you'll have to marry him," Mrs. Haywood insisted. "Right is right."

"That's right, young lady. You marry him, or we'll hang him."

Shannon smiled very sweetly, glaring straight at him. "I will not marry him. Mr. Haywood, you'll have to go right ahead. Hang him."

"Shannon!" Malachi swore. He swung around to stare at her in a fury. He was unaware of Mr. Haywood moving around behind him. He really did want to throttle her. His fingers were just itching to get around her neck.

His fury did him in.

He didn't see Mr. Haywood, and he certainly didn't see the water pitcher.

He didn't see anything at all. He simply felt the savage pain when the pitcher burst as Mr. Haywood cracked it hard over his skull.

He was still staring at Shannon, still seeing her standing there in white with her hair a golden, glowing halo streaming angelically all around her . . . when he fell to the floor.

And blackness consumed him.

Chapter Nine

Two hours later Shannon found herself in the store, standing on a stool, while Martha Haywood fixed the hem of the soft cream gown that Shannon wore.

It was a beautiful, if dated, bridal gown.

It had been Martha Haywood's own. A lace bodice was cut high to the throat with a delicate fichu collar over an undergown of soft pure satin. Ribands of blue silk were woven through the tight waistline, and the lace spilled out over the full wide skirt. Tiny faux pearls had been lovingly sewn into much of the lace.

"Mrs. Haywood, you don't understand," Shannon said urgently. She dropped down at last, catching the woman's nimble hands upon the hem. "Mrs. Haywood, you and your husband can't keep threatening Malachi. I don't want to marry him. And I don't believe you. You can't hang him if I refuse to marry him."

"We can, and we will," Mrs. Haywood said complacently.

"But I don't want to marry him. Please!"

Mrs. Haywood stared at her with her deep brown eyes. "Why? Why don't you want to marry him? You seem to be with him by choice."

"I am with him by choice. No...I mean, yes! But it's more circumstance than choice."

"That still doesn't explain why you don't want to marry him."

"Because . . . because he doesn't love me. I mean, I don't love him. It's just all—"

"Love comes," Mrs. Haywood told her. "If it isn't there already," she muttered. "The way you two came in here, the way we found you together . . . You explain yourself to me, young woman."

"I . . ."

"You just crawled into bed with him just like that . . . because of circumstances?" Martha Haywood's tone sent rivers of shame sweeping into Shannon. She felt as if she was trying to explain things to a doting and righteous aunt.

"You must have felt something for him. But then again, I'm not arguing that. Did you hear what you told me? You said that he didn't love you. So maybe you do love him. And maybe you're just afraid that he doesn't love you."

Shannon shook her head vehemently. "I promise you that he does not love me. And I do not love him. I was in love, once, during the war. I was engaged to marry a Yankee captain. He was killed . . . outside Centralia."

Mrs. Haywood finished with the hem and stood. "So you can't love again, and that's that. Why? You think that young man who did love you would want you spending your life in misery." She shook her head slowly and gravely. "The world has a lot of healing to do. And you should maybe start with your own heart. This Captain Slater seduced you under my roof, young lady. And you were curled up to him sweet as a princess bride this morning, so you're halfway there."

"Mrs. Haywood—"

"Papa has gone for the preacher. He is the local magistrate, so he's the law here. Oh, don't you worry none. Papa and me won't ever let on to anyone that we know your man's really a Slater. And the reverend will keep the secret, too. That is, if you two do the decent thing and marry up."

"You can't hang him for not marrying me!"

Mrs. Haywood laughed delightedly. "Maybe not, but there ain't no law against hanging a criminal. Captain Slater understands. Papa explained it to him real clearly."

"Mrs. Haywood—"

"Lord love us, child, but you do look extraordinarily fine!" She stepped back from the stool, gazing over Shannon and her handiwork with rapture. Tears dampened her eyes.

"Mrs. Haywood, this dress is beautiful. Your kindness to me is wonderful, but I still can't—"

"I had meant to see my own daughter in it one day. She was such a pretty little thing. Blond, with blue eyes just like you. And if I'd a caught her in bed with a Rebel captain, it'd have been a shotgun wedding, too, I promise."

"You . . . had a daughter?"

"Smallpox took Lorna away," Mrs. Haywood said softly. She wiped a tear from her cheek. "Never did think I'd put a young lady in this dress, so it's quite a pleasure."

Shannon sighed deeply. She should have just run away. She should have run from the house, screaming insanely, and then maybe the Haywoods would have understood.

But she just couldn't tell if they really intended to hang Malachi or not. If they weren't going to hang him for being a wanted man, surely they wouldn't for not being the marrying kind.

Still, she couldn't just run away. Not when they had locked him up. Not when they were holding all the weapons.

"Mrs. Haywood, please try to understand me—"

"Did you ever stop to think that Hayden Fitz just might get his hands on your man?" Martha asked her.

"What . . . do you mean?"

"Your man is going after your sister, his brother's wife. He ain't going to stop until he has her. He'll succeed with his mission, or he'll die in the attempt. I know his type. I saw all kinds during the war. Men who would run under fire;

men who carried their honor more dear to their hearts than life. Your boy is one of the latter, Miss Shannon. So you tell me, what if Fitz gets his hands on the boy?''

"He . . . he won't," Shannon said.

"He could. I promise you, lots of folks wouldn't have paused like Papa and me. Fitz has power in these parts. Lots of it. He owns the mortgage on a dozen ranches, and he owns the ranchers, too. He owns the sheriff and he owns the deputies. So you tell me, what if Fitz gets his hands on this boy and kills him? What if you were free of us, and Fitz caught him and killed him anyway?''

"I don't . . . I don't understand what you're trying to say," Shannon protested.

"What if you're carrying that man's child and they hang him? What'll you tell your son or your daughter?''

Shannon felt herself growing pale, and she wasn't sure just what it was that Mrs. Haywood's grim words did to her. She had known all the while that they were entering into a dangerous world.

She knew that people died. She had been watching them die for years.

She felt ill and flushed and hot. Was she such a fool? Did everyone else think so rationally? The odds seemed so foolishly against them . . .

She still couldn't marry him. Not if she carried ten of his children, not if they were both about to be hanged in a matter of seconds. And suddenly she realized why.

She did feel for him. He had created a tempest deep within her heart, and it was with her always.

She didn't know how to put a name on the feeling. She didn't know if it was love or hatred or a combination of both. The thought of him with another woman had made her insanely jealous, and it had been humiliating to see how quickly he could still arouse her in the wake of her anger. Maybe their hatred had been mixed with love from the very beginning. Maybe circumstances were letting all her emotions explode here and now.

But she couldn't marry him.

She had heard herself. He didn't love her. And if he was forced into marrying, he would never forgive her. Not in this lifetime, or the next, and he would escape her as soon as he possibly could. She didn't want the misery for either of them.

If she was ever to have him, it had to be of his own free will.

"Mrs. Haywood, I can't—"

"Let's go into the next room. I hear voices. Papa must be in there with the preacher, and it's high time that we got on with the ceremony."

"Mrs. Haywood—"

The woman stopped and turned to her, her hands folded serenely before her. "Papa is not a patient man, young lady. And I'll wager he's got the shotgun aimed right at your Captain Slater's heart. Don't tarry, now. I don't want him getting nervous. The poor fellow might move in the wrong direction and Papa might decide to shoot him in the knee-cap just to make sure that he sticks around."

With a smile she turned and opened the shelved door and proceeded into the parlor. Shannon hurried behind her. They didn't mean it. They wouldn't shoot Malachi, and they wouldn't hang him, either.

Would they?

She stopped short when she came to the entrance of the parlor.

Malachi was there. He was standing right in the center of the parlor.

Mr. Haywood had apparently decided to dress Malachi for the occasion, as well. He was wearing a ruffled white shirt and a pin-striped suit with a red satin vest and a black-lapelled frock coat. She'd never seen him dressed so elegantly, and her breath caught in her throat as she saw him. The beauty of his costume was offset by the raw menace in his eyes and the rugged twist of his jaw. She had never seen him so coldly furious, nor had his eyes ever touched upon hers with such glaring hatred and with such a raw promise of revenge.

For a moment she couldn't move farther. She couldn't breathe, and she believed that her heart had ceased to beat. Panic made her seize hold of the doorway, meeting the savage fury of his glare.

"Come in, come in!" Mr. Haywood called.

She still didn't move. Then she realized that the preacher was moving behind Malachi. He was a tall thin man with a stovepipe hat and black trousers and a black frock coat. He nodded to her grimly.

She heard a peculiar sound and looked at Malachi again . . . and saw that his wrists were shackled by a pair of handcuffs.

"Oh . . . really, please," she murmured. "Please, you all must understand . . ."

"Talk to her, captain. Talk to her quick," Mr. Haywood advised Malachi. He, too, was all spruced up in a silk shirt and brown trousers, which gave him a dignity he had lacked earlier. One arm was around his wife's shoulders; in the other, he carried the shotgun.

"Get over here!" Malachi snapped to Shannon.

The deep grate of his voice brought her temper surging to the fore. "Malachi, damn you, I am trying—"

She broke off with a gasp because he was striding her way with purpose and hostility. He might have been shackled but he managed to get a grip around her wrist, jerking her hard against him. She shivered as she felt the fire and tension and fury within him and felt his heated whisper against her cheeks.

"Get over here and marry me."

"Malachi, I don't believe them. I don't believe that they'll hang you if we don't marry."

He glared at her. "So you want to wait—and see?" he asked her slowly.

"I don't think—"

"You don't think! Do you want to wait until they tie the rope around my neck? Or maybe we should wait until I'm swinging in the breeze!"

"We could—"

"Shannon! Get over here and marry me now!"

"No! I will not—"

"You will, damn you!"

"I won't! Malachi, it wouldn't be right—"

"Right! You're talking about right? At a moment like this you're worried about right?"

"I don't love you!"

"And I don't love you, so maybe we're perfectly right!" His eyes narrowed to a razor's edge, raked hers with contempt. "They'll hang me, you bitch! Get over here and do it."

"What a wonderful way to ask!" she hissed sweetly.

His jaw twisted and set. "I'm not asking you, I'm telling you."

"And I'm afraid I'm not listening."

His fingers tightened around her wrist with such a vengeance that she cried out softly again.

"Captain Slater!" Martha Haywood protested, calling from the center of the parlor.

He didn't ease his hold. She found herself watching the pulse at the base of his throat with a deadly fascination. She felt weaker than she had ever felt in her life. She had thought she knew how to match her temper to his.

But maybe she didn't.

He pressed her up against the door frame, hard. "Shannon, you can get out of this later. You can say that you were coerced. But for the love of God, get over there now."

Some demon steamed inside her then, and she didn't know quite how to control it. All of her seemed awhirl in a tempest of hot blood and raw emotion. His anger fed her own. And for once, he was powerless against her.

"I don't like the way you're asking, captain," she told him icily.

He wasn't powerless, not in the least. With a swift turn on his heel, he dragged her along after him into the center of the room. She was stunned when he fell down on one knee, maintaining his firm grip on her before the preacher and the Haywoods. "Miss McCahy!" he hissed, the words dropping like sharp icicles from his mouth. "Dear Miss McCahy—beloved. Do me the honor this day of becoming my lawful wedded wife!"

"That wasn't exactly voiced the way I always thought that I'd hear the words!" Shannon retorted.

"Please, please, please, my beloved darlin'!" he said, rising swiftly, his eyes like knives that sliced through her. She was shaking, knowing that she pushed him. But he could have protested, too. He could have done more than he was doing.

"One more please, captain. And make it a good one."

"Please," he said. She had never heard anything that sounded less like an entreaty. He looked like some savage creature, and he didn't just want to chew her all up, he wanted to skin her alive first. But her demons told her they shouldn't be doing this.

He didn't wait for her answer, but turned to the reverend. "Go ahead, preacher man," he said dryly. "Get to it."

"No!" Shannon protested.

Mr. Haywood cocked the shotgun. The preacher began the ceremony.

Shannon listened to him in a daze. She could no longer run screaming into the street, because Malachi held her in a vise. Nor could she really risk it. Maybe Haywood would hang Malachi. She just didn't know.

The preacher was nervous. Looking at Malachi would probably make anyone nervous. Only the Haywoods seemed complacent.

Malachi answered the preacher in a cold raw fury, biting off each of his words. He spoke loudly and with a vengeance, enunciating each word. Love, honor and cherish. Till death did them part.

When her turn came, Shannon couldn't answer. She turned to him with one last fervent plea.

"Malachi, we can't do this—"

"Love, honor and obey!" he snapped at her.

"Malachi—"

"Say it!"

Shivering, she turned to the preacher. She stuttered out the words.

"The ring," the preacher said, clearing his throat.

"The ring?" Malachi said blankly.

"I've got it, Reverend Fuller," Mr. Haywood said. He stepped forward and placed a small gold band in Malachi's hand. Malachi stared at the man for a moment, fingering the gold. Then he slipped the ring on Shannon's finger, despite the fact that she was shaking so badly that her hands weren't still at all.

"We owe you again, Mr. Haywood," Malachi muttered.

"Don't worry. Price of the ring will be on your bill," Mr. Haywood said complacently.

"Hush, Papa! This is a beautiful rite!" Mrs. Haywood murmured.

It fit her tightly, snugly. Shannon felt the gold around her finger as smoothly and coldly as Malachi must feel the steel of the cuffs around his wrists. His eyes touched hers with a searing blue hatred and she thought that she could not wait to remove the ring.

Seconds later the preacher was saying that by the authority vested in him by the law of the great State of Kansas, and the greater authority vested in him by the glory of God on high, he now pronounced them man and wife.

Mrs. Haywood let out a long sob, startling them all. They stared at her. She blew her nose and smiled wistfully. "Don't mind me, dears, I always cry at weddings. Papa, release the groom from those shackles. He probably wants to kiss his bride. Reverend Fuller, could you do with a touch of Madeira? We've no champagne, I'm afraid. Maybe we've some across the way."

Reverend Fuller said that Madeira would be just fine. Malachi stared at Shannon venomously as Mr. Haywood came to him with a small key and freed him from the handcuffs.

"Captain Slater, a glass of Madeira?" Mrs. Haywood began.

But Malachi, freed, paid her no attention. He dragged Shannon into his arms and forced his mouth hard against hers with brutal purpose. His fingers raked her hair at her nape, holding her still for his onslaught. His tongue surged against her lips and forced them apart, raked against her teeth and invaded the whole of her mouth with ruthless abandon. Finally his mouth left hers and his lips touched her throat where it lay arched to him with deliberate possession. Then his mouth demanded hers again. His fingers trailed over the white lace of her gown with idle leisure and abandon, cupping lightly over her breast. The savage fury and heat of his kiss left her breathless, and with a searing sense of both clashing, tempestuous passion, and of deep, shattering humiliation that he would touch her so before others.

She felt the wrath in him deeply. It burned around him, and emitted from him in waves. She was amazed that he had married her; that he hadn't told the Haywoods to go ahead and hang him, and be damned. She hadn't thought that Malachi could be coerced into doing anything that he didn't want to do, but it seemed that they had managed to coerce him.

She tore away from him; he let her go. The back of her hand rose to her lips, as if she could wipe away his touch. "They should have hanged you!" she hissed.

He blinked, and opaque shadows fell over his eyes. He bowed to her in a deep mockery of courtesy.

"You were trying hard enough, weren't you?"

He didn't give her a chance to answer. He swung around to Mrs. Haywood. "I thank you for your hospitality, ma'am," he drawled with a sure trace of sarcasm, "but I think I've a mind for something a little stronger at the moment." He strode toward the front door, then paused, looking back. "I have fulfilled your requirements to escape the hangman, haven't I?"

"Sign your name on the license, and you're free to go," Mrs. Haywood said.

Malachi walked to the marble-topped table where the license lay. He signed his name with an impatient scrawl and looked at Mr. Haywood, his jaw twisted hard, his hands on his hips.

Mr. Haywood nodded to him grimly. Malachi cast Shannon one last glare and then he threw open the door, slamming it in his wake. Shannon stared after him as cold fingers seemed to close over her heart.

"Madeira?" Mrs. Haywood offered her with a winning smile.

Shannon mechanically accepted the glass of wine. She cast back her head and swallowed it down in a single gulp. It wasn't enough. Malachi was right about one thing—they both needed to head straight for the whiskey.

She set her glass down. The wine tasted like bitter acid in her present mood. "I'll give you your dress back, Mrs. Haywood," she said simply. She turned, nodded to the preacher and to Mr. Haywood, and ran up the stairs. She found both keys on the bedside table, and picked them up, biting into her lower lip with such force that she drew a trickle of blood.

Malachi might really be her husband now, but he wasn't coming into this room again. Ever.

Ever!

She couldn't admit it, not even to herself, that her fury came mainly from the fact that she was afraid that he wouldn't even try.

He had slipped a ring upon her finger, forcing her to issue vows, and then he had left her.

For a red-haired whore.

No, he wouldn't be coming in the room again. Ever...

"Why, Ma—Sloan!" Iris called out to him as he entered the saloon. She never would get accustomed to calling him by another name.

He nodded her way and walked up to the bar, tossing down a coin. "Whiskey, Matey, if you would, sir. Whiskey, and lots of it."

Iris, pretty as a picture in a quiet gray dress and blue shawl, hurried over to him. She slipped her arm through his. "I was about to leave. I'm going to take the buggy and head for Sparks and see what I might find out about your sister-in-law. Is it still safe for me to leave? What's happened?"

He looked at Iris, at the concern naked in her eyes. He felt her soft touch on his arm, and some of the anger eased out of him.

"It's safe." He caught her to him and tenderly kissed her forehead. "You're a fine woman, Iris. Funny, ain't it? You really are such a fine damned woman no matter what your vocation. And her..."

"Your...traveling companion?"

"The little darlin'...yes. Shannon." He grimaced, staring at the ceiling, then he laughed bitterly. "My traveling companion. The curse of my life! The sweet little—hellcat!"

"What did she do now?"

"Damned little witch. I should have let you floor her yesterday, Iris. Hell." Matey put the whiskey bottle in front of him and he took a long, long swallow, gasping as the liquor sizzled its way down his throat to his stomach. He looked at the bottle reflectively. "I should have floored her myself."

"Malachi..." Iris realized that she had used his name, and she looked quickly around. The saloon was nearly empty. Only Matey might have heard her, and Matey minded his own business. "Let's go to my room, Mr. Gabriel," she said softly.

Malachi looked at her speculatively and picked up the whiskey bottle. "Yes, Iris, let's go to your room."

She led him up a flight of stairs in the rear and opened the first door.

She had a real nice room for a working girl, Malachi thought. There was a big bed with four carved posters and a quilted spread, a braided rug on the floor, a handsome dresser and a full-length mirror on a stand.

"Nice," Malachi murmured. He drank more of the whiskey. He drank deeply, then he crashed down on the bed. He reached out for Iris with a slow smile curving into his lips. She sat down by his side, but watched him speculatively. He stroked her arm, and soft, feathery tendrils of desire swept along her flesh. She wanted to be touched by him. She had almost forgotten the feeling of wanting to be touched.

She pulled her arm away. He swallowed more whiskey, leaving one last slug in the bottle. Then he just lay there, staring at the ceiling.

"I want to kill her, Iris. I want to close my fingers right around her lovely white throat, and I want to squeeze until she chokes. I want to take my hand..." He raised his right hand as he spoke, studying the length of his fingers and the breadth of his palm, flexing his fingers. "I want to smack my hand against her flesh until it's raw... I want to shake her until her damned teeth crack!"

"Malachi, what happened?" Iris asked him softly.

His eyes fell upon her. His lip curved into a twisted, wry grin. "I married her. For real."

Iris lowered her eyes, swallowing. "Why?"

"They said they'd hang me if I didn't. They're convinced that she's a sweet young innocent and that I seduced her."

"Didn't you?"

"No. Yes. Hell, she's almost twenty now, she's as sweet as raw acid, and as to her innocence..."

"Yes?"

"She seduced me equally. No one innocent has a right to look the way she does... naked."

Iris would have laughed if she didn't feel such a peculiar hurt deep inside.

It wasn't that he had married the girl. It was the way he spoke about her.

"Now who is it who thought that you weren't married to begin with? Who thought that she was . . . seduced?"

"The Haywoods. They said they'd hang me."

"Of course they would want to hang you! You're worth a lot of money, dead or alive. There's a bounty on your head. If they know that you're not married, then they know—"

"They don't care who I am. They don't intend to let the knowledge go past themselves—and the reverend, of course," he added bitterly.

Iris exhaled softly. "Thank God for that!"

Malachi grimaced. "They weren't going to hang me for being a Confederate, a bushwhacker, or Cole's brother. They wanted to hang me because I seduced Shannon!"

Iris inhaled deeply. She couldn't believe that she was going to defend the other woman, that beautiful young woman with the sky-colored eyes, alabaster skin and the sun-drenched fall of long, curling hair.

But she was.

"Malachi, if the Haywoods forced you into a marriage, you can't really blame her." She paused, frowning. "Did she tell them . . . who you really are? Did she demand that you marry her? I mean, they are real God-fearing folk. Did they do it? Or did she force and coerce you?"

"What?" He stared at her blankly.

"Malachi, you can't hate her if they forced it. Maybe you can't even really hate her if she did make them force you into it. She isn't . . . well, she isn't my kind of woman. If you took advantage of her, maybe she had a right to force you—"

"She didn't force me."

"Then—"

"The bitch!" he exploded. "They're sitting there swearing up and down that they will hang me—and she's refusing! She's sitting there arguing with a shotgun. I was barely able to make her spit out the words! She would have made me hang."

"Then..."

"She's a witch, Iris," he said softly. He swallowed the last slug of whiskey. Iris hoped he wasn't heading for one heavy drunken stupor; even an experienced drinker like him would have trouble with the amount he had swallowed in the last ten minutes. "She's a witch," Malachi continued. "I mean to touch her, and I'm furious, and I want to hurt her. And I don't quite understand it, 'cause I'm hurting myself. I dream of her eyes. I dream of her reaching out to me. And then sometimes she touches me and I feel everything in me exploding just to touch her back, to feel her softness, to see her smile, to see her eyes glaze with wanting... She teases and she taunts, and she loves like a wildcat, like a pagan temptress, then she bares her claws and she swipes out and she draws blood, Iris, blood."

Iris smiled slowly. He still wasn't looking at her. He was staring at the ceiling. He turned around and suddenly grasped her hand. He kissed her fingers, and she shivered, feeling the sensual movement of his lips and beard against her flesh. "She's not like you, Iris. She's not like you at all. You can't ever talk to her, you can't reason with her. She's a witch... I've been fighting her forever and forever, Iris. Always fighting. She would have let me hang, can you believe that?"

"They wouldn't have hanged you," Iris said.

"She didn't know that."

"Maybe she did."

"She didn't, and that's a fact." He sat up. His eyes glittered. "Well, she has married me now. And she's going to pay for it!"

"Malachi, you were mad because she wouldn't marry you."

"She wanted them to shoot my kneecaps, the witch! But now, now she's mine..."

He fell back. His eyes closed.

Iris watched him for a minute. He was asleep. She smiled ruefully. "She may be a witch, but you're in love with her," Iris said softly.

She set the empty whiskey bottle on the dressing table, and decided to leave him where he was. Let him sleep off the bottle of whiskey he had swallowed in ten minutes, and maybe he'd go back to his tender young bride in a better state of mind.

She picked up her portmanteau and hat, walked to the door and blew him a kiss sadly. "I'll be back tomorrow, captain," she said softly. "Even if you do love her, I've got to help you."

She turned around and left him. If she hurried, she could make it to Sparks, spend plenty of time there and still be back in Haywood by the morning with all the information she could gather. She had friends in Sparks. Friends of the best variety for what she needed now. They were smart, beautiful women. And they knew the men of Sparks.

She looked back with a wistful smile.

Malachi slept peacefully.

Iris shrugged. He probably needed the rest.

She left, letting him sleep on.

And on . . .

Shannon changed and returned Martha Haywood's gown immediately, thanking her. She didn't want to wear Malachi's shirt any longer than she had to, so she determined to go into the mercantile and find another. Martha followed beside her, talking about her own early years of marriage.

"They were a hoot and a holler, I do tell you. Why, we were madder 'n wet hens at each other time and again, but then, I don't really remember what one of those arguments was about."

Shannon found a pretty soft blue blouse with teal embroidery along the bodice. She set it on the counter with boxes of ammunition. "First off," she told Martha Haywood softly, "we've got the same conflicts between us that just set a whole country to war."

"The war is over," Martha reminded her.

"Secondly, I knew a man once who was always gentle. He never had a temper about him."

"You'd have been miserable in a year."

Shannon gasped in horror. "That's not true! I was in love with him, I was deeply in love with him—"

"And you can't let it go. Still, it's true. You'd have been miserable in a year. Now, I don't think that you and Captain Slater will be getting along real well for a long time to come. But I think you'll come to realize that you have more in common than can be seen."

Shannon flushed. She set her hands on her hips. "He's been over at the saloon all day, Mrs. Haywood."

"Well, go on over and get him then. If you want him back, go on over and get him."

Shannon bit her lip, pretending to study the beautiful new blouse. "It's wonderful embroidery," she said softly. Then she smiled at Mrs. Haywood. "I don't want him, Mrs. Haywood. I don't want him near me again, and I mean it. He's been over in that saloon all day..." She swallowed fiercely. "Mrs. Haywood, could I have a tray sent up to me? I think that I want to retire early."

"It was a hard tonic for him to swallow, Shannon, being manipulated by us and all. I'm amazed that he was as docile as he was. And it must have been darned hard on him when you turned him down—"

"He didn't want to marry me."

"You refused to marry him when we might have hanged him!"

"You wouldn't have hanged him. Thank you for trying, Mrs. Haywood. I need to lie down for a while."

"It's very early," Martha told her anxiously.

"Yes, I know. Now, you're running a tab on everything, right? I should be ashamed. We came out of the war much better than many folks. I do have money."

"We're running a tab, Mrs. Slater."

Mrs. Slater. The name sounded absurd, and she hated it!

Malachi had been in the saloon for hours and hours now. And if he tried to tell her that he wasn't with the redhead this time, she'd probably scream and go mad on the spot.

Impulsively, she kissed Mrs. Haywood on the cheek. "I really need to lie down," she said softly. "Thank you so much for everything."

Shannon stepped into the parlor. She realized that she was absently twisting the ring around her finger. She tried to wrench it off. It was too tight. Soap might take it off.

On impulse, she hurried to the door to the street and pushed it open. Things were quiet, very quiet. An old bloodhound lifted his head from his paws across the way on the saloon veranda. He looked at Shannon, then dropped his head again. Two men idly conversed down the way before the barber's shop, and that was it.

Shannon strode down the steps and across to the saloon. She entered the building, assuring herself that she wasn't going to do anything but order herself a brandy.

She pushed through the swinging doors. The saloon, she saw, as her eyes adjusted to the darkness, was almost as quiet as the street. A lone rancher sat in the back, his hat pulled low over his eyes, hiding his face. A blond harlot in crimson silk sat upon the bar, absently curling a strand of hair around her finger.

The barkeep was drying glasses. He looked at Shannon warily.

"May I have a brandy, please? And could you put it on my husband's tab?"

He shrugged uncertainly, found a glass, filled it and set it before Shannon. She nodded her thanks and swallowed the brandy down. She looked around the saloon again. Malachi was definitely not there.

Kristin would be horrified that she was standing in the saloon, Shannon thought. But then Kristin had always been more conventional, and Kristin had always had a better hold on her temper. Well, maybe not. Kristin had waged a few battles with Cole, and Cole was such a lamb in comparison with Malachi. None of that would matter to Kristin. A lady shouldn't be in a saloon like that.

Even if she was wondering what her husband of five hours was up to.

He wasn't in the saloon.

"Have you seen, er, Mr. Gabriel?" she asked the bartender sweetly.

The blond woman answered, looking her up and down and smiling sweetly. "He's still sleeping up in Iris's room, last I heard."

Shannon felt dizzy. It was as if the whole room went black, then seemed to be covered in a red haze.

"Thank you very much," she said pleasantly. "When you do see him again, please tell him that he is most welcome to remain where he is, and that he will not be at all welcome elsewhere. Thank you."

"Wait," the woman began.

But Shannon cut her off with a clipped, commanding tone, her chin high, her eyes a cutting, crystal blue. There was a note of warning in her voice. "Please, just see that he gets my message." She'd had no idea that she could speak quite so commandingly, but the woman's next words died on her lips and Shannon turned and left the saloon. In the middle of the street, she suddenly paused, doubled over and let out a deep, furious, and anguished scream.

Martha Haywood came running out of her parlor. "Oh, dear, oh dear, what is it?"

Shannon straightened. "Nothing. I'm fine, Mrs. Haywood."

"You're fine!" Mrs. Haywood exclaimed. "That didn't sound at all like fine to me!"

"Well, I wasn't fine until I did it. Now, I am fine. I promise you." She wasn't fine at all. She felt as if she was being ripped apart on the insides by sharp talons. She wanted to kill Malachi. Slowly. She wanted to stake him out on the plain and allow a herd of wild buffalo to trample him into the dust. She wanted to watch the vultures come down and chew him to pieces. She wanted...

She wanted him to come back so she could tell him just how furious she was. And how hurt. How deeply, agonizingly... hurt.

"I am fine, Mrs. Haywood," she repeated, smiling, stiffening. She clung to her temper. She would never forgive him. Never. She stood as tall as she could, straightening her shoulders. "Just fine. If you'll excuse me... Can you please see to it that I'm not disturbed until the morning?" She pushed past Martha and hurried into the house. She raced up the stairs and went into her room, locking the door and assuring herself that she had both keys.

She gasped, trembling, as she looked around.

Martha Haywood had tried so hard to make it welcoming!

Hot water steamed in the bath and there were fresh flowers beside the bed. A silver tray with cold meat and pastries sat on a table, and across the bed lay one of the most beautiful white satin nightgowns she had ever seen. There was a note on it. Shannon picked it up. "Every bride deserves a new thing of beauty. Wear it with our warmest wishes. Martha and Hank."

She set down the note and sank onto the bed, and suddenly she was softly sobbing. Every woman harbored and cherished dreams of just such a gown on her wedding night. And every woman cherished her dreams of a man, magnificent and gallant and handsome. A man who would hold her and love her...

She had the gown, and she had the man. But the dream had dispersed in the garish light of reality.

Malachi did not love her.

She lay on the bed and gave way to the flood of tears that overwhelmed her, and then, when her tears dried, she stared at the ceiling and she wondered just how long she had really been in love with Malachi. They'd never had a chance to be friends. From the start the war had come between them.

But she would never forgive him for this. Never. Come what may, he would never touch her again.

Whether he'd been coerced into marriage at gunpoint, it hadn't been her doing; she'd tried her best to stop it all. He'd had no right to go straight to the red-haired whore, and she would never forgive him.

After a while, the shadows of twilight played upon the windows. The bath had grown chilly, but she decided to indulge in it. She carefully set a chair under the doorhandle first; she wasn't taking any chances.

There was a bottle of wine with the food on the table. Shannon sipped a glass as she bathed quickly.

She even donned the beautiful satin gown.

In time, she stretched out in bed. She closed her eyes and she remembered him the evening before, coming into the room with a vengeance and a purpose. Sweeping her up, holding her.

Claiming his rights, when they weren't in truth married.

But now she was his bride.

Eventually, she closed her eyes. She had her Colt by her side, fully loaded. If he tried to return, she would demand that he leave quickly enough, and she would enforce her words.

But this night, their wedding night in truth, he did not return.

Toward dawn, she cried softly again.

He was her husband now. He did have certain rights.

But he wasn't coming back. Not that night.

Chapter Ten

At two in the morning, Malachi stirred. His head was killing him; his mouth tasted as if he had been poisoned, and his tongue felt as if it was swollen in his throat. A clock ticked with excruciating, heavy beats on the mantel.

He staggered out of bed and peered at the clock. When he saw the time he groaned and looked around the room. Iris was gone. She was a good kid. She had gone to Sparks, trying to help him. He was sleeping in her room, while Shannon...

Oh, hell.

His head pounded with a renewed and brutally savage fury. Shannon...

Shannon would be sleeping, too, by then. If she wasn't sleeping, it was even worse. She'd be furious, hotter than a range fire.

He threw himself back on the bed. The hell with her. They were going to have one fabulous fight, he was certain. It couldn't be helped.

He was going to be a rational man, he promised himself. He was going to be level and quiet. He was going to be a gentleman. Every bit as much a gentleman as the Yank she mourned.

The hero...

Well, hell, at this moment, it was easier for a Yank to be a hero. Rebs weren't doing very well. Just like she liked to tell him—they had lost the war.

Darlin'...the South will rise again, it will, it will, he vowed to himself. Then he remembered that he had just promised himself that he was gong to be reasonable.

They were married to one another.

His head started pounding worse as his blood picked up the rhythm, slamming against his veins. He was married to her...for real. If he had a mind to, he could walk right across that street and sweep her into his arms. He could do everything that the rampant pulse inside him demanded that he do. He could meet the blue sizzling fire in her eyes and dig his hands through her hair and bury his face against her breasts. He could touch her skin, softer than satin, sweeter than nectar, he could...

Rape his own wife, he thought dryly, for she sure as hell wasn't going to welcome him.

She would have let him hang! He was the one with the right to be furious. Granted, he would have come for Kristin with or without Shannon—he had meant to come without her—but it was still her sister he had traveled into enemy territory to save.

He could have been in Mexico by now. He could have been living it up in London or Paris. There was no more cause, no South left to save. It was over.

It should have been over.

He exhaled. He wasn't going to go to her now. She'd surely bolted the door against him. And the house would be silent. Dead silent. It just wasn't the time for a brawl, which is what it would be.

If she didn't just shoot him right off and get it over with.

She wouldn't shoot him. She was his wife now.

Yeah, a wife pining for a divorce, or pining to become a widow quick as a wink.

The turmoil and tempest were swirling inside him again. He didn't want to start drinking. He rose and went to the washstand and scrubbed his face and rinsed out his mouth, availing himself of Iris's rose water to gargle with. He felt a little better. No, he felt like hell. He felt like ...

Racing across the street and breaking the door down and telling her that she was his and that she would never lock a door against him again, ever ...

He groaned, burying his head in his hands. They were just a pair of heartfelt enemies, cast together by the most absurd whims of fate. She was in love with a dead man, and he wasn't in love at all. Or maybe he was in love with ... with certain things about her. Maybe he was just in love. Maybe there really was a mighty thin line between love and hate, and maybe the two of them were walking it.

He walked to the window and stared at the night.

The new moon was coming in at long last, casting a curious glow upon the empty street.

They were forgetting their mission. Kristin ... they had come all this way and met with physical danger, culminating with the last encounter with the Haywoods. They had come together in a burst of passion, and they had exchanged vows, and now they were legally wed, man and wife, and despite it all, they were still enemies, and despite it all, he could still never forget her, never cease to want her.

He walked over to the bed and lay down, folding his hands behind his head, staring at the ceiling. Iris would come back, and then he would have a better idea of what to do next. Cole must have heard what was happening by now. Jamie, too. And once they had heard about Kristin, they would have started moving this way.

He and Shannon had to start moving again. They had to cease the battle and come to a truce and worry about their personal problems later.

It was the only logical move ... the only reasonable one.

He gritted his teeth hard against the fever and tremor that seized him again. He steeled himself against thoughts of her. He wanted her so badly ... he could see her. He could see her as she had been in his dream, rising from the water, glimmering drops sluicing down her full, full breasts...water running sleek down the slimness of her flanks, down her thighs...

He could see her eyes, dusky blue, beautiful as they met his in the mists of passion. He could almost feel her moving against him, sweetly rhythmic. He could hear her whispering to him...whimpering, crying out softly and stirring him to a greater flame, a greater hunger...

Logical, reasonable. This was insane.

He was a gentleman, he reminded himself. He had been raised to be a Southern gentleman; he had fought a war to preserve the Southern way of life, perhaps the great Southern myth. He didn't know. But he had been taught certain things. He loved his brother; he would always honor his brother's wife. He believed in the sanctity of honor, and that in the stark horror of defeat, a man could still find honor.

Logic...reason. When the morning came, he would defy the very fires within him. She would not be able to ask for a more perfect gentleman. As long as she didn't touch him, he would be all right.

The perfect gentleman.

If not quite her hero.

Someone was turning the knob of her door.

Shannon didn't understand at first just what was awakening her. Something had penetrated the wall of sleep that had come to her at last.

She lifted her head and she listened. At first, she heard nothing.

Then she heard it. The knob was twisting. Slowly. Some weight came against the door. Then the knob twisted and turned again and again. Someone was trying to be quiet; stealthy.

She rose, biting into her lower lip.

It was Malachi, at last.

She leaped out of bed and ran to the Haywoods' lovely little German porcelain clock. She brought it close to her eyes and looked at the time.

It was almost three in the morning.

She spun around. The knob was twisting...

Malachi. Damn him! He had finished with his whore, and now he wanted to come back to her to sleep! On her wedding day!

Oh, granted, it was no normal wedding day!

But still...

She hated him! She hated him with a vengeance! With everything inside her. How could he? How could he drag her—force her!—into this horrid mockery of marriage, and then spend the day with a harlot. After last night...

It was foolish to give in to him, ever.

She hadn't meant to give in to him.

Ever.

She had simply wanted him, and therefore, it had never been so much a matter of giving, it had been a matter of wanting. Of longing to touch, and to be touched in turn. Of needing his arms. Of needing his very height, and his strength. Of hearing his voice with the deep Southern drawl, of feeling his muscled nakedness close to her...

She had loved once.

And she loved now, again. Perhaps he could never understand. And if she valued not only her pride but her soul and her sanity, he could not know.

Not that it mattered. She could never let him in; she could never let him touch her again. He couldn't come straight from his whore to her. Whether emotion entered into it or not. He just couldn't do it, and that was the way that it was.

Her eyes narrowed; she was ready for battle.

But the doorknob twisted one last time, and then she heard footsteps—soft, soft footsteps!—moving away from her, down the hall and then down the stairs, fading away into the night.

"Malachi!" she murmured in misery.

So there would be no fight, and no words spoken. She could not go to battle, and she could not give of herself or take, for he was gone, leaving her again.

She lay down and cast her head against the pillow in misery. She stared straight ahead and ached for what seemed like hours and hours.

He had gone back to her. Back to his old friend. Back to the red-haired harlot.

She could not sleep. She could only lie there and hurt.

At three in the morning, the last of the locals threw down their cards, finished off their beers or their whiskeys and grunted out their good-nights to Matey and to Reba, the golden blonde who played the piano at the Haywood saloon.

Reba started collecting glasses. Matey washed them, telling Joe, his helper, to go on and clear out for the night. Joe had a wife and new baby, and was grateful to get out early for the evening.

Reba tucked a straying tendril of her one natural beauty, her hair, back into the French knot she wore twisted at her nape. She looked across the saloon to the dark shadows and paused.

They had both forgotten the stranger. It was peculiar; she had thought that he had left earlier.

But he had not. He was still there, watching her now. She could feel it.

He raised his face, tilting back his hat.

He was a decent-looking fellow, Reba thought. Sexy, in a way. He was tall and wiry and lean, with dark hair and strange, compelling light eyes. The way he looked at her made her shiver. There was something cold in that look. But it made her grow hot all over, too, and there weren't many men who could make her feel anything at all anymore.

This one made her skin crawl. He also made her want to get a little closer to him. There was something dangerous about him. It was exciting, too.

"Mister," she called to him. "We're closing up for the night. Can I get you anything else?"

He smiled. The smile was as chilling as his eyes.

"Sure, pretty thing. I'll take me a shot and a chaser..." His voice trailed away. "A shot and a chaser and a room—and you."

"You hear that, Matey?" Reba called.

"Got it," Matey replied with a shrug. The drinks were his responsibility. It was Reba's choice, if she wanted to take on the drifter this time of night.

Reba brought the shot and the beer over to his table. He grasped her wrist so hard that she almost cried out and pulled her down beside him. She rubbed her wrist, but thought little of the pain. Lots of men liked to play rough. She didn't care too much. Just as long as they didn't get carried away and mar the flesh. If he wanted to be a tough guy, though, he could pay a little more.

"You got a room?" he asked her.

"That depends," she said.

"On what?"

He was a blunt one, Reba decided. She flashed him a beautiful smile, draping one long leg over the other, and displaying a long length of black-stockinged thigh. She ran a finger over the planes of his face, and found herself shivering inside again. His eyes were strange. They were so cold they might have been dead. They calculated every second. They were filled with something. She didn't quite recognize what it was.

Cruelty, maybe...

She shook away the thought. A lot of men looked at women that way. It made them feel big and important. Still...

She started to pull away from him. She almost forgot that she made her living as a whore, and that she didn't mind it too much, and that the pay was much better than what she had been making as a backwoods schoolteacher on the outskirts of Springfield.

Should she? She was tired; she wasn't in any desperate need for money. She should just tell him that it was too darned late for her to take a man in for the night.

"I got gold," he told her. "Is that what it depends on?"

Gold. He wasn't going to try to pawn off any of that worthless Southern currency, and he wasn't even going to try to pay her with Union paper. He had gold.

"All right," she told him at last.

And unknowingly sealed her fate.

He stroked her cheek softly, and looked toward the stairs. He smiled at her, and Reba silently determined that she had been mistaken—he was just a tough guy, not a cruel one. And he was handsome. Not nearly as handsome as Iris's friend Sloan, but he had all his teeth, all his hair and all his limbs. And that wasn't so common these days.

A working girl could always use a little extra cash.

"Where's your friend?" he asked her.

"Who?"

"The redhead."

Strange, he was talking about Iris. Reba started to answer, but then she paused, stroking his arm. "Iris is occupied for the evening." She smiled.

The stranger lifted his glass toward the saloon doors. "The husband, eh? That the blushing little bride was looking for."

Reba chuckled. "It's a good thing the groom is occupied. The maid over at the Haywoods' told Curly—Curly's the barber—that Mrs. Gabriel has bolted down for the night. Sloan Gabriel would need four horses to ram the door down."

"Is that a fact?"

"'Course, Iris says he'll do it. When he—when he's good and ready, he'll go over and break right in. Determined type. He doesn't take nothing off of her."

"Doesn't he, now?"

"Not Sloan Gabriel."

The stranger's lip curled. "Sloan Gabriel, eh?"

"That's right. That's the man's name. Why?"

"No matter. It's just a good story. I watched the woman earlier. She needs a lot of taming." He paused, sipping at his whiskey. "You think Mr. Gabriel will just break the door on down to get to her, eh?"

"To teach her a lesson."

"And he's here now. Right here in this fine establishment."

"Ain't that a laugh."

"Yeah. It's a laugh. But, hey, now..." He swallowed the whiskey in a gulp, then drained his beer. He set the glass down on the table hard. "No matter at all. What matters now is you and me. Let's find that room of yours, all right?"

Reba nodded swiftly, coming to her feet. She took the stranger's hand and called good night to Matey as they walked up the stairs. She passed by Iris's doorway and hid her smile of secret delight.

Sloan Gabriel was in there, all right. Still sleeping away, after consuming his own bottle of whiskey. Iris had asked her to look in on him now and then, and she had been glad to comply. He was still sleeping peacefully, and his golden wife assumed he was enjoying the daylights out of himself. She didn't know why she didn't tell the stranger. It was a funny story. It was great.

But Iris had acted as if she didn't want too many people to know where she was going.

Reba shrugged and hurried to her own door.

When they entered her room, the stranger closed the door. Reba turned around, smiling at him. "Want to help me with a few buttons, honey?" she asked. She sat down at the foot of the bed, a woman practiced with her craft, and slipped off her shoes. When that was done she slowly slid off her garters and started peeling away her stockings one by one. He watched her, standing by the door. Reba smiled with pleasure, certain that she had this drifter well in hand.

"What's your name, honey?" she asked him.

"Justin," he said.

"Justin what?"

"Justin is all that matters."

"All right, Justin, honey." She smiled and licked her tongue slowly over her lips, as if she gave grave attention to her stockings. He was quiet, then he spoke suddenly, pushing away from the door.

"Turn over," he told her.

"Now, honey, no funny stuff," she said. He didn't smile. She added nervously. "Honey, any deviation—any slight, slight deviation—will cost you a fortune." Little pricks of unease swept along her spine, but she kept smiling anyway.

Her smile faded when he suddenly strode across the room and jerked her around by the arm, pressing her down into the bed, face first. He tore at her chemise and petticoats, ripping them from her with a vengeance. Gasping, smothering, she tried to protest.

"Shut up," he warned her.

"No! No, please—"

Reba tried to twist around. He slapped her hard on the cheek, sending her head flying against the bedpost. Stunned, she still tried to resist. She hadn't the power. He shoved her over and down.

A scream rose in her throat when he sadistically drove into her. But her scream went unheard, muffled by her pillow.

In time, either the pain dulled, or she passed out cold.

When she awoke, it was morning. She felt the sun coming in through the window.

She tried to move, but everything about her hurt. Her cheek and eye were swollen where he had beaten her. She hurt inside, deep inside. She would have to see the doctor, and pray that nothing was busted up too bad. God, she was in agony.

She was afraid to open her eyes; he might still be there. She didn't feel him, though. She lifted her lashes just slightly. Then she dared to twist around.

He was out of the bed. He was dressed, and he was staring out her window, toward the Haywoods' store and hotel across the street.

Suddenly, he stiffened and straightened. She saw him set his hand on his gun at his hip.

"There he goes," he murmured. He swung around, as if sensing that Reba was awake. She closed her eyes, but not fast enough. He came over to her, wrenching her up. "You shut up, bitch!"

"I didn't say—"

He slapped her again. Reba gasped, screaming for all that she was worth. Matey would be up and about; someone would hear.

"Oh, no you don't!" He slammed her pillow down on her face, pressing hard. Reba twisted and gasped, and the pain entered her lungs as she could draw no air. He kept talking. As she grew dizzy, she could hear him. "You ain't ruinin' it for me, honey." He started to laugh. "What's one little whore, when the golden girl is right across the street? If you're right, Slater is in there, getting through to her for me right now. I tried to get to her last night, but I was afraid to bust the door down myself. I might have had the whole town down on me. I slipped out, and I slipped back in, and nobody knew it at all. I came back to the saloon...and to you, too, honey. I'm gonna kill Slater, and I'm gonna make her wish that she was dead. You can imagine how good I am at that, huh, honey?" Dimly, she heard him laugh. "You can imagine. You can just imagine." He pressed harder and harder upon the pillow.

Her struggles ceased.

Finally, he tossed the pillow aside. She was still and silent. "I wouldn't have had to kill you if you'd just known how to keep that whore's mouth of yours closed." He tipped his hat to her. "It's closed now, honey. Sure am sorry. It's just that you don't compare. No, ma'am, no way, you just don't compare. I'm gonna have me that girl, and I'm gonna kill that man."

He looked outside. Malachi Slater was heading across to the livery stable. Looked like time to take a walk himself.

"Shannon!"

She had awoken, hearing him call out her name in annoyance. He banged on the door. She pressed her fingers against her temple and ignored him.

"Shannon, open this door."

"No!"

"Don't give me a hard time now, Shannon McCahy. I've got to get in."

"It isn't McCahy anymore, is it?" she demanded bitterly through the door. "Get away from here!"

She waited. There was silence for a moment. "Shannon, open the door. Now."

"You arrogant Reb bastard!" she hissed at him. "Go away. I'll never open the door."

She heard his sigh even through the door. "Shannon, I am going to try not to fight with you. I am going to do my best to get along with you, Shannon, because—"

"Your best! Malachi, go!"

"Shannon, I really am trying. Now, open the door and—"

"You're an ass, Malachi. A complete ass!"

"Shannon, I am trying—darlin'. But keep it up, and you'll pay. I promise," he said very softly.

"Go away!"

"Shannon, I'm giving you ten seconds. One—"

"You should have knocked when you came last night."

"I didn't come here last night. You're dreaming."

"Nightmare, Mr. Slater. If I was dreaming, it was a nightmare." She paused, then said with disgust, "You liar!"

"I didn't come near you last night, Shannon. But so help me, I'll come near you now!"

It was a threat. A definite threat. After everything that he had done!

She spat out exactly what he should do with himself.

He slammed into the door. The noise brought her flying up in panic, searching for the Colt. The wood splintered and sheared around the lock, and the door soared open.

Malachi stood in the doorway, looking much the worse for wear. His clothing was rumpled, his eyes were red, and his temper hadn't improved a hair.

Not that the night had done much for Shannon's.

She lifted the Colt and aimed it straight at his heart. "What do you think you're doing here?" she demanded huskily. She couldn't quite find her voice.

He eyed the Colt but ignored it. He stepped into the room, kicking the door shut behind him. "Shannon, I am going to try and talk reasonably. I—"

"Malachi, get out of here. Or else I will shoot you. I will not kill you. I will aim—"

"Don't you dare say it!" he snapped at her.

"Say what?"

"You know what!"

"All right! I'll shoot at—"

"Shannon!"

"Malachi, I don't want you here. I married you to save your damn neck and you can't even stay with me for two seconds."

"I had to beg you to—"

"You forced me to say those words."

"You know, I'm remembering right now just how bad it was. Dropping down on my knees to beg you to—"

"Beg! You get out, now! Or I will put a bullet right where it might count the most!"

"Why, darlin'," he drawled. "You are my beloved wife, and I can come to you whenever I choose."

"The hell you can."

"The law says I can," he told her softly.

"The law plans on stringing you up—darlin'. Maybe we ought not tempt fate."

"Well, then, Mrs. Slater, I say that I can." He crossed his arms over his chest, leaning back against the broken door.

His lashes fell with a lazy nonchalance over his eyes, but she could see the slit of blue beneath them, wary and hard.

She was trembling. She couldn't let him see it. She kept her hand as steady as she could manage on the Colt.

"You chose your bed, captain. You just go on back to it."

"Darlin', I'm tired of you spying on me, and I'm damned tired of your being a brat. I didn't come to fight—"

"You shouldn't have come at all."

"Put the gun away, Shannon."

"Get out!"

"I can't, not now—"

"Malachi, get away from me, now!"

"Put the gun away, Shannon. Put it away now! I'm warning you as nicely as I can, but I mean it." It sounded as if he was growling at her. She gritted her teeth and smiled sweetly.

"Malachi, since I am the one with the gun, I'm warning you."

"You'll be damned sorry when you don't have the gun."

"Don't threaten me."

"You vowed to obey me."

"You vowed to cherish me. It was all lies. So no, captain, you go on back across the street to your whore. You're not going to touch me."

"You're one Yank I do intend to touch, my love."

She pulled back the trigger on the Colt, letting him hear the deadly click. "Get out. You know that I can aim."

"I haven't come to do anything to you. I've come because this is my room, and you are my wife. Put the gun down. I have every right here, and you won't shoot me."

"You have no rights here, and I will shoot you!"

He took a step toward her. She fired, with deadly accuracy. The bullet whizzed by his face, so close that it clipped his beard before embedding itself into the thick wood of the door behind him. He stopped, staring at her, the muscles in his jaw working. He was surprised, but he was not afraid.

"You shot at me!" he said, his voice harsh and low. "You actually shot at me!" He took another step toward her.

"You fool!" Shannon warned him, backing away. She fired again, and drew blood this time, nicking his ear.

But it did no good. He was upon her, wrenching the Colt from her hand. His fingers dug around her upper arms with a trembling force, and he picked her up and tossed her like a sack of wheat upon the bed. She struggled to rise, but he caught her and pushed her back. He straddled her, pinning her down, and she saw the naked amazement and wrath in his eyes. "You little bitch! You really would have killed me!"

She wriggled and kicked, struggling fiercely. "If I'd meant to kill you, you'd be dead, and you know it."

He eased his hold on her to touch his ear, feeling the trickle of blood. She used the opportunity to surge against him, freeing her hands and swinging at him. She caught him on the jaw with a good punch, and he swore savagely, securing her beneath him again. The beautiful white satin bridal nightgown was twisting higher and higher around her hips with every fevered moment. "Let me go, Malachi."

"Oh, no, Shannon, you're the one who wanted to play rough. Well, let's play rough, shall we?"

And he wrenched the gown up high on her thighs with his free hand. He released her to unbuckle his trousers, and she screeched, jumping up. He caught her arm, twisting her down.

"You shot at me!" he hissed at her.

She swung forward, trying to hurt him, trying not to cry. "And you slept with the red-haired harlot, so leave me alone!" She slammed against his chest and thrashed out with her legs. She heard him groan in pain and she knew that she had gotten him good.

But he fell against her again, and her hair caught and pulled in his fingers. "I didn't sleep with her—"

"Oh, no! Don't try to play me for a fool, Malachi."

"I did not sleep with Iris. She's a real friend, an old friend. I should sleep with her. She is kind, and caring. And warm. But I wasn't with her last night. I slept in her bed, but not with her."

"Liar!"

"No!"

He pushed her flat against the bed. Tears stung her eyes and she writhed and struggled against him. "Liar!" she accused him again. But his lips met hers, and she didn't understand what happened at all.

"I am not lying!" he swore, and his hatred contoured and marred his features.

"Please..."

He assaulted her...but she met his fury with her own. His mouth forced down hard upon hers...but her lips parted to his, and she met the invading thrust of his tongue with the passionate fury of her own. When his lips broke from hers, she cried out his name. She didn't know if it was a plea, a broken whisper, a beseechment that he leave her...or a prayer that he stay with her.

Whatever it was, it changed his touch. He went very still. Shannon was amazed that she had freed her hands, only to wind her arms around him, only to rake her fingers through his hair. She felt the touch of his fingers, slowly curling around her breasts over the satin of the gown.'

"I am not lying!" he vowed again, and softly. He rubbed her nipple between his thumb and forefinger and felt it swell to his touch. She felt the softness of his beard, and the sweet, burning tenderness of his kiss. He ravaged her body still, but with care, with passion, but with some strange lust gone, so gentle that she arched and writhed and twisted toward him, maddened to feel more and more of it...

Then he thrust into her, deep, full, grinding, and defying all his previous gentleness. Bold, determined, sure, his fingers and his eyes locked with hers as he claimed her completely and cast her shuddering to her depths with the ecstasy of feeling his body within her own, burning within her, a part of her mind, her heart, her frame . . . her soul.

"Malachi." She whispered his name again as he began to move within her. She held him, embraced him, caressed him. Fever and tempest were with them as they whirled and whirled in a dark and furious and timeless storm that stripped away pretense . . .

And even hatred . . .

Satisfaction burst upon them, as volatile as the burning cannon fire of the war that had raged around them.

He pulled from her when it was over. She lay silent; he lay looking at the ceiling.

"What are we doing to one another?" he said softly. But he didn't look her way. He rose. Shannon could not move, not even to adjust the satin of the gown over her hips. She heard him doffing his borrowed clothes, donning his own trousers and shirt and boots. She still did not move.

He paused at last. "We've got to go. Get up. Get dressed. I'll explain when you come down, but I've got some good news as far as freeing Kristin is concerned. Hurry. We need to get moving."

He walked to the door. When he reached it, he paused for several seconds.

"I'm sorry, Shannon. Really sorry. It . . . it won't happen again."

He was gone. She listened dully as his footsteps faded away on the staircase. Listlessly, she curled into herself. She had to get up. She had to get dressed and ready. They were going after Kristin. This was what it was all about . . .

She dragged herself up. Then she leaped up from the bed, anxious to call him back because she realized now she could still hear his footsteps. She had to tell him that she was sorry, too, so very sorry . . .

"Malachi!"

He was coming up the stairs, coming back to her. She raced to the doorway.

A man was coming up the stairs. He was wearing a feather hat, and his head was bowed low, and the brim covered his face. But it wasn't Malachi. A sense of danger suddenly sheared along her spine.

At that moment he reached the top step and raised his head.

She stared straight into the evil leering face of the bushwhacker, Justin Waller. "Howdy, Shannon. Excuse me— howdy, Mrs. Gabriel," he said softly. "My, my, my, I have been anxious to catch up with you. And you do look particularly pretty this morning."

"You!" she cried, swinging around to dive for the Colt.

"Me! Justin Waller, Mrs. Gabriel. Why, yes'm, I've turned up again, and I am . . . anxious!"

The Colt was on the floor somewhere. She groped frantically, opened her mouth to scream. The sound that issued from her was a breathy gasp. He caught her around the waist. She opened her mouth to scream again, and his hand clamped tight over her mouth. "No, no, my little darlin'," he crooned, his face taut against hers, his pleased grin displaying his teeth. "You do have to hush! The captain might have gone for the horses, but the Haywoods are downstairs, and I planned to leave kind of quiet like. I do want to deal with Malachi Slater, but not here. Not now. You're going to be real, real quiet for me."

Shannon tried desperately to inhale and bite his hand. He laughed, reaching into his pocket with his free hand, and produced a soaking, foul-smelling scarf. He removed his hand from her mouth. She gasped in quickly to scream, but before she could issue a sound, he dropped the scarf upon her face, and she inhaled the potent drug upon it.

The room spun and faded and went opaque, and then disappeared entirely from view.

Justin Waller waited. Her eyes fell shut; she went limp beneath him. He pulled the scarf from her face at last, and lifted her dead weight over his shoulder.

At the top of the staircase, he hesitated. He heard Slater talking in the kitchen.

Quickly, quietly, he ran down the stairs and out the front door. The street was quiet. He smiled. He walked calmly to his horse, tossed Shannon over the animal's flanks, and mounted behind her lolling body.

And rode serenely out of town.

Chapter Eleven

When Malachi returned with the horses, Iris was already waiting for him, seated in a small buckboard wagon. She was wearing green brocade with a cocky little feathered hat, and the green went exceptionally well with her red hair.

Malachi tethered the horses and looked at her. "You're a beautiful woman, Iris," he told her.

She smiled and didn't flush. "Thanks, Malachi. You didn't need to say that."

"You don't need to come."

"Yes, I do," Iris said. "You don't know anything about the back entrance to Cindy's house. And you won't be able to run around in the town of Sparks, I promise you. You won't be able to do your brother one bit of good if you're arrested along with his wife."

"I don't like putting you into danger," he said softly.

"I won't be in any danger. Cindy's a friend of mine. I come into Sparks often enough. I'm known there."

"Still—"

"Malachi, I swear that I will be in no danger.

Malachi still didn't like it, but he knew he had no right to dictate to Iris. And her trip to Sparks had been monumentally important.

She had found Cole. He'd been sitting in the local saloon, his hat pulled low over his head. She hadn't recognized him herself at first, not until she'd leaned back and seen his silver gray eyes. He'd been wearing ranch clothes and a Mexican serape and his face had been covered with the rustic start of a beard and mustache. He hadn't looked at all like Cole.

He'd recognized Iris, though. Before she could talk to him, he'd come up quickly to buy her a drink, then he had told her he was going by the name of Jake Egan.

Iris had brought him to Cindy's place, a big gabled house her friend owned on the outskirts of town. It was a cathouse, of course, and Shannon was sure to hate it, but that was where they were going now.

Cole told Iris that Jamie was just over the border, and he had gotten word to him. The three of them planned to converge in Sparks, and take matters from there. Thanks to Iris and her friends, they would have a good place from which to plan and work.

Iris glanced toward the Haywoods. "Your wife ain't pleased, I take it?"

He shrugged. "I haven't told her yet."

Iris frowned. "But—"

"We had an argument. We didn't get that far," Malachi said briefly.

Iris lowered her head and a smile stole over her lips. "I hope you told her that I wasn't with you—"

"Iris, it doesn't matter—"

"It matters to me! I'd just as soon she not shoot me."

"She's not going to shoot you, Iris."

"Malachi—"

"Iris, the matter is solved."

"I don't think so, Malachi."

"And why is that?"

"Well, as you might have noticed, Mrs. Slater isn't out here yet."

Malachi swore softly. He started up the porch steps toward the front door.

"Malachi!" Iris called to him. "I'm going to run back in. Reba might be up by now and I want to thank her for covering things for me yesterday."

Malachi nodded to her and hurried up the steps and opened the door to the parlor. Mrs. Haywood was just coming out of the kitchen with a big parcel in her hands. "Here you are, Captain Slater. Some of my best summer sausages and biscuits. And when you're heading back through, you make sure to come and see us."

Malachi nodded stiffly. "Surely, ma'am," he said, and he looked up the stairway. "Has she come down yet?"

Mrs. Haywood shook her head. "Maybe you should go on and hurry her along."

He nodded again. Mrs. Haywood was still staring at him.

"We wouldn't have hanged you, captain, you know."

"I'm glad to hear that, ma'am."

"And we couldn't have forced you into marrying your lady—not unless you wanted to."

He hesitated, staring at her. "Now, Mrs. Haywood—"

"Never mind. Maybe you're not ready to admit that. You go up and hurry her along. I'll take the vittles out to the buckboard. Iris is going with you?" Mrs. Haywood's eyes danced with merriment. "What a lively trip. I wish I were going. I wish that I was twenty years younger!" she said, and she laughed.

A slow smile curved Malachi's lip. He saluted her. "Yes, ma'am, it would have been nice to have you along."

Mrs. Haywood, chuckling, headed toward the door. Malachi went to the steps and started up them, two at a time.

He came to the door and noticed the splinters around the broken lock. He had already paid Mr. Haywood for the damages, but seeing the door made him feel ill. He had sworn he wasn't going to lose his temper, and he had. He had sworn that he wouldn't touch her in anger...and he had. He wanted to leave this place now. More than anything, he wanted to leave this place. Nothing could really be solved between himself and Shannon until Kristin was rescued, or...

Until they all died in the attempt.

"Shannon!" he called out sharply.

He stepped into the room. She was nowhere around. Other than that, the room was exactly as he had left it, not half an hour ago. "Shannon?" he called out again.

Damn her. She was angry, and she was playing some trick. Never! He never could trust her, not for one damned moment! He thought she had understood how close they were coming to Kristin.

He wandered to the foot of the bed and sank down upon it with a weary sigh. Where had she gone? Mrs. Haywood hadn't seen her downstairs. And...

He looked across to the hall tree. Shannon's shirt and trousers were still hung on it.

He rose, a frown knitting his brow. He went over to their saddlebags and ripped hers open. Her dress was still there. Wherever she had gone, she had gone wearing the slinky satin nightdress she had worn this morning.

He jumped up, trying to tell himself that she might have run into the mercantile store to buy something. More underwear, a new shirt, perhaps. Another one of the embroidered blouses like the one on the hall tree...

Malachi ran down the steps. Just as he reached the parlor, he heard screaming from the street. He burst out of the door and ran down to the street, his booted footsteps clattering over the wood of the steps until he hit the dust.

Iris was in the middle of the street, her arms around the blond, Reba.

Reba was lying in the dust, wrapped in a blanket, and held tenderly by Iris. Her eyes were closed. Her face was parchment white. A trickle of blood seeped onto the blankets.

The Haywoods were there, bending over.

"What happened?" Malachi demanded.

"She shouldn't have moved. She was trying to get to you. She wants you to kill him," Iris said, her voice rising hysterically.

"Kill who?" He looked from Iris to Reba. Her eyes remained closed. He leaned down and picked her up. He glanced at Martha Haywood for assent, but the sturdy matron was already shooing him toward the house. "Right into the parlor, Malachi. Bring her to the couch. I'll send Papa for the doctor."

He hurried inside with the blond whore and laid her carefully on the sofa. He knelt beside her as Iris followed, smoothing back her hair. She had been beaten. Her lip was swollen, and one of her eyes was almost shut.

Her other eye opened slowly. She almost smiled, a caricature of a smile. "He wanted your wife, Mr. Gabriel. He wanted your wife."

"What?"

His heart thudded, then seemed to stop for a moment. Cold fear fell harshly upon him. He took Reba's hand in his. "Please, we know you're... hurting." The way the blood seeped from her, she was probably dying. Maybe she knew it; maybe she didn't. "Try to tell me."

She moistened her lips, nodding. "Kill him. You have to kill him. I saw him watching you. He was waiting for you to get to her; he couldn't make the noise to reach her. He tried... last night. Then he came up to my room with me." She paused. Tears trickled down her cheeks. "He's got your wife, Mr. Gabriel. He thinks I'm dead. He thinks he's safe... Get him. Kill him. He—" She tried to find breath to speak, and made one final effort. "He said that his name was Justin."

Malachi shot up. Iris and Mrs. Haywood stared at him. "Justin Waller," he said. "He followed us. I underestimated him. I thought I'd lost him."

He turned and strode toward his horse, checking that his Colts were in his gun belt. When he reached the bay, he leaped upon the animal, and then just sat there. He didn't even know which way to ride.

East. Back the way they'd come.

Justin Waller wouldn't dare head farther west into Kansas. He'd killed a lot of men in Kansas. Maimed and wounded them. Someone might recognize him.

East. He had to return eastward.

He set off at a gallop, and realized a second later that he was being followed. He turned and saw that Iris had mounted Shannon's big black gelding. With her skirts and petticoats flying, her fine green dress bloodstreaked and ruined, she was racing after him.

He reined in. "Iris, go back! What do you think—"

"Malachi, she's dead. Reba just died."

"So go back! This man is an animal. I'm better off alone."

"Your wife may need me," Iris said quietly.

Malachi locked his jaw, he was suddenly shaking so hard. That Shannon might be touched by the madman hurt...hurt so badly that he couldn't help her...

"All right, come on," he told Iris.

He leaned forward over the bay's neck, urging the animal forward, and they galloped eastward again at a breakneck pace. How much time did Justin Waller have on him already? How much time did Justin Waller need?

He didn't dare think. He rode.

It was the sickness in Shannon's stomach that finally woke her. She didn't know what he had used in his scarf to knock her out, but the smell of it had invaded her system, and her mouth tasted horrible, and she was certain that she was going to be sick any minute. She didn't care much about being sick. It might make her feel better. Except that there was a gag in her mouth, tied so tightly over her lips that she was afraid that she would choke to death upon her own fluids.

She tried opening her eyes carefully. The sunshine shot into them like knives. She had thought that she was moving; she was not. Her wrists hurt her because she was tied to a tree. The sun was overhead, streaking through the leaves. She was in a copse, surrounded by rocks and foliage and trees. She couldn't move at all, for rough nooses looped both of her wrists, and her arms were pulled taut around the circumference of the tree.

She closed her eyes again. The dizziness still assailed her. She willed it to go away.

There was a sound in the woods. She opened her eyes quickly. Justin Waller was coming through the bushes. There was nothing she could do. Absolutely nothing but stare at him, and hate him with everything in her.

"Hello, little darlin'," he crooned. He hunkered down by her, smiling as he tossed his rifle down at her side. He ran his hand over her thigh, moving the satin of her gown upward to her hip. She kicked and thrashed at him, and the motion almost made her sick. He laughed, enjoying her inability to really do anything, anything at all.

"I'd like to remove that gag, honey, and hear everything that you have to say to old Justin. You're going to apologize, do you know that? You're going to tell me how sorry you are for everything you ever did to me. And then you're going to tell me that you'll never leave me again. And you're going to tell me how much you want me, you're going to ask me to be nice to you."

He lifted his hand to her cheek, and ran a finger down her throat. He idly stroked a line down to the rise of her breast, and he laughed again at the rage that filled her eyes when he cupped the mound.

"You're thinking that Slater will come and kill me, aren't you? Well, he's going to come. That's why you're here. I'm going to meet him on the road, and then I'm going to kill him. And then I'm going to come back for you. But do you know why you're here in this nice little cove? 'Cause if I die, Miss McCahy, you're going to die, too. He'll never find you.

Only the snakes and the buzzards will know where you are. Maybe a rattler will come by. And maybe not. Maybe you'll just bake slowly in the sun...and you'll be glad to die, you'll want water so badly. Then the birds will come down and you know what they like to do first? They like to pluck out eyes..."

He sighed, letting his hand drop. "I'd really like to stay. But—"

He broke off, listening. From somewhere, Shannon could hear the sound of hoofbeats.

Justin's face went dark. "How the hell did he know so damned fast?" he muttered. "Must not have done in that whore properly..." He stared at Shannon. "No matter, darlin'. Don't fret. Don't miss me too much. I will be back."

He rose, clutching his gun, and thrashed his way through the undergrowth. The sound of the hoofbeats was coming closer and closer. Shannon closed her eyes.

Malachi.

He would never abandon her, she thought. No matter how mad she made him, no matter how they fought...

Even if he hated her. He would never abandon her.

But would Malachi be expecting Justin to ambush him? And Justin meant to do just that. Sit in wait to prey upon Malachi, shoot him down in cold blood from the shadows of the bracken on a summer's day.

Malachi was coming closer. Shannon could feel the hoofbeats pounding the earth. There was more than one horse. He wasn't alone. Maybe that was something that Justin hadn't counted on.

She tugged at the ropes that held her, but Justin could tie a secure knot. The more she twisted, the more hopelessly tightly she was bound. Tears stung her eyes. If she could just call out. If she could warn him that it was going to be an ambush.

Willing herself not to panic, not to give up, she twisted her head, biting at the gag. At first, she felt nothing.

Then she felt it loosening.

The sound of hoofbeats had slowed as the riders had entered the narrow trail through the forest. Shannon bit desperately against the material slicing her mouth. There was a give and then a tear. She twisted and spit again. The gag slipped enough for her to draw in a huge gulp of sweet air, and then scream for all she was worth.

"It's a trap, Malachi! Don't come any closer! It's an ambush! Be careful, for the love of God—"

As she screamed, Justin Waller suddenly appeared through the shrubs, and she saw the murderous hatred in his eyes.

"Stupid bitch!" he swore. His palm cracked across her cheek so hard that she was dazed.

She felt a little trickle of blood at her lip but that didn't deter him in the least. He stuffed the gag into her mouth and secured it, winding a strip of rawhide tightly around her head. It cut searingly into her mouth, and she could barely breathe, much less issue the softest cry.

He smiled, pleased with his handiwork. "Our time is coming, sweet thing," he promised her.

He jumped to his feet, carelessly holding his repeating rifle. The sound of hoofbeats had ceased. The forest seemed quiet.

"Slater!" Justin screamed.

Shannon took some small pleasure in realizing that she had ruined his original plan. He couldn't possibly ambush anyone. He was the one whose whereabouts were now known.

"Slater, I'm going to shoot her. Right through the head."

She couldn't help the shivering that seized her. Justin Waller would do it. He would shoot a human being just as quickly and easily as he would swat a fly. There would be very little difference to him.

He aimed the rifle at Shannon. She caught her breath, and her heart seemed to cease to beat. She wanted to pray; she wanted to ask God to forgive her all her sins, but she didn't seem to be able to think at all.

Malachi's face filled her thoughts. His slow, cynical smile curling into his lip beneath his mustache. His eyes, bluer than teal, deeper than cobalt, secretive beneath the honey and gold arches of his brows. In those seconds, she imagined his face. And she wished with all her heart that she could see him. She prayed at last, and she prayed that he not be fooled into giving his life for hers...

The rifle exploded with a loud blast. Dust flew up, blinding Shannon. But she wasn't hit. He had aimed at the ground, right beside her feet. He aimed again, and she quickly closed her eyes as pieces of bark sheared from the tree and flew around at the impact of the explosion. Shannon choked and screamed deep in her throat. More shots exploded against the tree. She almost longed for him to hit her so that the torture of waiting for a bullet would end.

"Come on out, Slater. One of these shots is going to hit her! Or maybe one of them already has. Maybe she's screaming deep, deep down inside, and you can't hear her...but you can hear me. Come on out, Slater, you coward, damn you!"

There was a rustling sound behind them. Justin swung around, shooting at the bushes. Bracken broke and flew, and the earth was spewed up in a rain of dirt. But when the noise died away, there was nothing. Nothing at all.

Justin hunkered down in the dirt, looking anxiously around. The silence was awful. It dragged on forever.

Shannon thought that she might have passed out again. It seemed that she closed her eyes and opened them again, and the sun was falling. The sky was streaked with beautiful, dark colors. Twilight was coming on.

And she was still tied to the tree. Justin was less than ten feet away from her, his rifle over his knee. He still stared out into the bracken as the night fell.

A fly droned around Shannon's face, and landed on her arm. She leaned against the tree, desolate, despairing.

"I think I've killed him. I thought he was out there, but maybe I've killed him," Justin muttered to himself.

He twisted around and looked at Shannon and saw that
her eyes were open. Low on the ground, he crawled to her.
He reached up with his knife toward her head, and she
wondered with horror what he intended to do. She tried not
to shrink from him, but she was terrified, and she couldn't
help it. He smiled, liking her fear.

But he didn't cut her. He slipped the blade into the rawhide tie that he had bound so tightly around her head. He
slid it, and let the scarf gag fall from her face. She inhaled,
gulping in air. She would have screamed, but it seemed like
such a foolish thing to do. There was probably no one to
hear her.

Maybe Malachi *was* dead. Justin had mowed down half
the foliage around him, and sheared away rock and trees. He
could easily have hit Malachi. He could be out there anywhere, lying injured, dead, dying...

Justin stretched his length against her body. She didn't
kick him and she didn't speak. She stayed still, her head
against the tree, and stared at him. He was insane, she decided. Some men would come back from the war and tremble through the night at the memories of the horrors they
had seen...of the death they had themselves delivered. But
Justin Waller had used the war. He had loved it, reveled in
it. It had allowed him to rape and murder freely. And now
it seemed that he had learned murder and rape as a way of
life.

She would give him no satisfaction, she swore.

"You've nothing to say, sweet thing?" he whispered
against her flesh. He touched her cheek and ran his hands
down to her breast again. "Our time has come. Your lover
is dead, and we have the whole night ahead of us. Your
mouth is free. You can scream and scream and scream..."

She gazed at him. "You're pathetic," she said softly.

He grabbed her thigh, pinching it mercilessly. She wasn't
going to cry out, but the pain came so fiercely that she did.

"Talk to me nicely, little girl. Talk to me nicely. Tell me that you won't take off again. No more tricks. And maybe, just maybe, if you're good, real, real good, I'll let you live."

She lifted her chin. She ignored his hand upon her thigh, inching up the satin of her gown. "Death might be very simple, Justin," she said.

He started to laugh again. "Yeah, it just might be. But you ain't going to die. Not until I'm through with you." He cupped her chin in a cruel grip and moved his face close to hers.

She managed to twist away. "I will throw up on you," she threatened. "I swear, I will throw up all over you. That drug is heaving up and down inside of me."

He jerked away from her as if he had been burned. He stared at her, and then he chuckled and stroked her chin again. "You are a one, Miss Shannon McCahy. I've waited a long time for a woman the likes of you. A long time."

He leaned toward her again. She prayed that the earth would open up and swallow them whole.

The earth did not open up, but there was suddenly a massive rustling in the bushes near the road. Justin jerked away from her and stood up on the balls of his feet with his rifle ready. Shannon watched him with renewed fear. "Son of a bitch! Sit tight, sweetheart. I'll be back, and we won't waste any more time." He jumped close to the tree, then bent down and disappeared into the low brush.

Shannon strained frantically against the ropes that bound her. Maybe Malachi lived. Maybe he was out there thrashing around, needing help. Justin would hunt him down. He would hunt him down and shoot him between the eyes. Justin Waller might be a raving lunatic, but he had fought with the bushwhackers, and he had learned a lot about guerrilla warfare. He was wiry and athletic. He was an able opponent. And Malachi...

"Watch out!" she screamed aloud. "Malachi! If you're there, watch out!"

Justin did not return to shut her up. She bit her lip, looking into the bracken. Night was just starting to fall.

Suddenly, from around the tree, a hand fell over her mouth. Fear curdled within her again. With wide, startled eyes she twisted around.

It was Malachi. He had found his hat. It sat jauntily atop his head, the brim low, sheltering his eyes. He brought a finger to his lips, and she exhaled, so dizzy with relief that she nearly fell. Hunched down low beside her, he smiled the crooked, rueful smile that had stolen her heart.

"Are you all right?" he asked her swiftly.

She nodded. "Malachi—"

"He didn't—he didn't hurt you?"

"He hasn't had much time. He's been watching for you through the day. Oh, Malachi! Be careful! Please, just get me out of here. He's dangerous. He's sick. He's—"

"Shh!" He brought his finger to his lips again. He seemed to hear something that she could not. "Can you make it just a few minutes longer?"

"Malachi—"

"Can you?"

"Yes, of course, but—"

"Shh!" He didn't untie her. He slunk back into the brush behind the tree.

"No!" Shannon whispered. She heard the branches breaking and a soft tread upon the earth. Justin Waller was returning. He was returning, and Malachi had left her for him . . .

"Weren't nothing," Justin said. "Weren't nothing at all but a rabbit or a squirrel. I left you for a rabbit. Can you beat that? My nerves are raw, honey, but you're gonna fix that."

Laughing, he dropped the rifle. He fell down on his knees beside her, and he stroked her calf. She kicked out in a rage. He fell upon her, the whole of his length covering her, smothering her. She started to scream and writhe, and Justin smiled, bringing his leering features level with hers.

"Moment of truth, honey darling mine—"

He broke off at the sound of a gun cocking, right at the base of his ear.

"Moment of truth," Malachi said harshly. "Get up. Get off my wife."

Shannon watched as Justin Waller went as stiff as a poker and slowly rose. Malachi didn't miss a beat. The barrel of his Colt remained flush against the man's head.

"She ain't your wife. Not for real—Mr. Gabriel."

"She is my wife—for real, Mr. Waller. And I don't take kindly to you touching her. In fact, I don't take kindly to much that you've done."

There was another rustle in the trees. Malachi didn't move a hair. Justin sneered, and despite herself, Shannon stiffened. Iris Andre stepped in among them. She had a small pearl-handled knife in her hands. She hurried toward Shannon, knelt beside her and started sawing the ropes that held her.

"Just how many woman do you need, Slater?" Justin taunted.

Malachi walked around in front of him, aiming the Colt at his heart. Shannon looked gratefully to Iris as the red-haired woman freed her. Maybe she was a whore. Maybe she had been sleeping with Malachi. But they had come together to save her, and for that, she had to be grateful.

Iris flashed her an encouraging smile. Shannon rubbed her wrists.

"Can you stand, honey?" Iris asked.

"I—I think so."

But she couldn't. When she tried to rise, she fell back upon the tree. She was parched; she hadn't had water in hours. The nauseating taste of the drug remained.

Iris lent her an arm.

"Boy, captain, you do have it made. A whore and a wife, leaning on each other. That's mighty cute, Miss McCahy."

"It's Mrs. Slater," Shannon told him.

"Poor little fool. Can't you see what he's doing to you?"

"Iris, tie up his hands," Malachi directed.

Iris nodded, leaving Shannon against the tree. Shannon stood there, chafing her wrists, shivering as darkness fell and the coolness of the night came upon them. She watched as Iris walked toward Justin with firm purpose. Malachi tossed her a skein of rope.

But before Iris could reach him, Justin reached out, and grasped her and pulled her against him. He produced a knife from his calf, and caught it against her throat.

"Malachi, shoot him!" Iris called out.

Malachi didn't dare shoot; Justin would have slit her throat as easily as he breathed.

"Drop it, Slater," Justin advised.

Malachi reached out and dropped the Colt. But as he did so, he lunged.

Justin thrust Iris away from himself just as Malachi stormed against him. Justin had his knife; Malachi was unarmed. They rolled together. Malachi leaped to his feet. Justin swiped at him with the knife, and Malachi leaped again. The knife sliced through the air.

Malachi landed a blow against Justin's chin, but then Justin was swinging with the knife again.

Malachi was good. He was fast on his feet; he could whirl with the wind. But Justin was armed. Unless he was disarmed swiftly.

Shannon could barely move. She shook her head, trying to clear it, needing strength. Iris lay on the ground before her, trying to stagger up.

"Iris!"

The woman turned to look at her.

"The Colt. Give me the Colt."

"You'll hit . . . Malachi."

Shannon shook her head. She had to clear it. She crawled past the tree before falling to the ground. She couldn't quite reach Malachi's Colt.

Iris reached for it and swept it along the dirt to Shannon. For a brief moment their fingers touched. Shannon bit her lip, then smiled swiftly, encouragingly. Her fingers curled around the butt of the gun.

The men were still locked in deadly combat. Justin was on top of Malachi; Malachi was straining to hold the man's arm far above him, to escape the deadly silver blade of the razor-edged knife. Shannon blinked against the darkness and against her trembling fear and the nauseating aftereffects of the drug.

She aimed carefully, and then she fired.

She was a crack shot, and she proved it that night. She hit Justin right in the hand. His knife went flying as he screamed in pain, his fingers shattered.

Malachi pushed him away and reached for the knife. Stunned, he came up on the balls of his feet and looked at Shannon. He smiled slowly, smoothing back a lock of hair that had fallen over his eyes.

"Thanks... darlin'," he murmured.

He stood, dusting off his pants. Justin Waller was rolling on the ground screaming.

"Bitch! I'll kill you, I swear, I'll kill you—"

"You aren't killing anyone else, Waller," Malachi said softly. "We're taking you back to Haywood, and they'll see that you hang."

"There ain't no wanted posters out on me, Slater."

"They're going to hang you for murder. Reba died this morning," Malachi said.

Justin let out a howl. "Your wife wanted it, Slater. She was smooth as silk to touch. She was better than that blond whore back in town. She screamed and cried and asked me for more and more."

Malachi stood still.

"But then, you can't imagine that whore. She wanted to live so badly. She begged me to stop."

"I'm not going to kill you, Justin," Malachi said. He walked over to where the man lay. "I'm not going to kill you. The war is over. I'm done killing. They'll hang you, and you aren't going to say anything to make me kill you now and cheat the hangman."

"You shoulda seen her scream."

Malachi ignored him. He started walking toward Shannon again.

"I'm going to kill you, Slater!" Justin raged. He stumbled to his feet and came running toward them. Cupping his bleeding hand beneath his good arm, he stumbled toward them and fell upon his rifle where it lay by the tree. Malachi started to spring for him.

Then a shot rang out. Justin Waller fell down dead.

Malachi and Shannon stared at one another, then turned and looked at Iris. She had a little ivory-handled pistol in her hand. A small waft of powder floated from it.

She looked from the dead man to Malachi. "You couldn't kill him, Malachi. I had to."

Malachi nodded at her. He walked over and retrieved his hat from where it had fallen in the dust, then he came back to Shannon.

"Can you ride with me?" he asked her.

She nodded.

"What about him?" Iris asked, referring to Waller.

"We'll put him on his horse and bring him back to Haywood. They can do what they want with him there. If they happened to know that he was at Centralia, they might butcher him up and feed him to the crows. I don't know. We're done here. We've got to get moving."

Iris nodded. Malachi brushed Shannon's forehead with a kiss, then nodded to Iris. Iris came forward and slipped her arm around Shannon while Malachi picked up the dead man, throwing him over his shoulder.

Shannon looked at Iris sickly. "He—he killed a woman?"

"A friend of mine," Iris said.

"The blond woman?"

Iris nodded. "Come on, honey. Let's get out of these woods. It's been a long day, and it's going to be a longer night."

Arm in arm with Iris, Shannon made her way through the bracken and trees. Malachi walked ahead of them.

They came to where a trail showed in the moonlight. The bay and her black gelding were there. Malachi tossed Justin's body over the bay and looked at the women. "I'm going to give the woods a look for his horse. Will you be all right?"

"Of course, sugar—er, uh, I mean, sure, Malachi," Iris said.

"I'm fine," Shannon added. She wasn't fine at all. She was sick to death and cold and shivering, but Justin was dead, and the danger was over. And Malachi had cared enough about her to come for her.

She had loved Robert Ellsworth. She had loved him very much.

But that didn't stop her from loving Malachi now. No matter what his relationship had been with Iris.

She couldn't even hate Iris anymore.

Malachi walked into the bushes and disappeared. Shannon must have weaved in the night breeze, because Iris quickly made a clucking sound. "Let's sit. It's all right here, I'm sure. We'd hear a rattler if there was one around anywhere."

"Iris," Shannon said softly, sitting down beside the redhead.

"What? I'm sure that there's really nothing to worry about—"

"Iris, I'm really sorry about the whiskey."

Iris inhaled sharply and her eyes fell on Shannon. "It's all right." She grimaced ruefully. "Most ladies do feel that way about whores."

"Oh, Iris, trust me! I didn't act like a lady!" She smiled, and then she laughed, and she realized she was glad because she had wondered if she would ever laugh again. Then she was afraid, because perhaps her laughter sounded hysterical. "Too bad you couldn't have met my pa, Iris. He would have explained in no uncertain terms that a lady wouldn't do things like that." She hesitated, then she smiled. "Pa would have said that you were quite a lady, Iris. Thank you for coming for me. You don't owe me anything. Even if you—even if you do sleep with my husband."

Iris squeezed her hand in return. "I didn't sleep with your husband. Well, not now, anyway. I had a thing on him once, years ago, in Springfield. It was before the war. It was—it doesn't matter what it was. It's over."

"You know that we're not really married," Shannon said softly.

"You are really married now, if I understand things right."

Shannon flushed. "He had to marry me or hang."

Iris shook her head, and her sage green eyes glittered knowingly. "You don't know your man very well, Mrs. Slater. No one ever forced Malachi to do anything that he wasn't willing to do already, deep down inside." She brought her finger to her lips. "Sh! He's coming back. And men are funny. They just hate to have women talk about them."

Shannon smiled. Malachi thrashed his way through the bushes with Justin Waller's buckskin horse.

"Shannon, can you ride with me?"

"Yes."

"Iris? You'll be all right on Shannon's black?"

"Yes, Malachi."

The two of them were meek, Malachi thought. Damned meek, for a pair of hellcats.

He walked over to Shannon and reached down to her, wishing that his hands would quit shaking. It had been the longest day of his life. He'd had to wait and watch and steel himself to be patient lest Waller killed them both. He had barely managed to keep still when Waller had started shooting at the tree and the ground.

He pulled Shannon to her feet. The once beautiful satin nightdress was mud-stained and torn. "We'll get you into a warm bath and dressed as soon as we get to the Haywoods'," he said gruffly.

She smiled tremulously and stumbled against him. Her eyes shone with their own crystal-blue radiance, and he couldn't look away from them. They had never been so softly blue upon him. They carried a look of innocence and knowledge, older than the hills, and they had never carried such tenderness.

He swept her into his arms. Her eyes remained locked with his. Her arms curled trustingly around his neck.

He set her atop his horse and mounted behind her. She leaned against his chest, and they were a silent party as they rode back to Haywood.

Chapter Twelve

Shannon was certain, upon their return to Haywood, that she had never been more cherished in her life.

They had been met on the steps of the inn by Martha and Mr. Haywood and what seemed like half the town. Cheers went up as they rode in. Malachi handed Shannon down to Matey. A woman quickly brought a blanket to wrap her in, and Martha Haywood brought her water, which she gulped down until Malachi warned her that she must go slowly. That was the last she saw of Malachi. The men dragged him off to the saloon.

It was the last she saw of Iris for the moment, too, but she didn't dwell on the thought.

Martha clucked like a mother hen and took her immediately beneath her wing. She fed her roast beef with hot gravy, potatoes and carrots. Hot tea was made with brandy, and the bathtub was filled with steaming water and French bubble powder.

Shannon bathed with a vengeance. She wanted to wash away so much. The dirt, Justin's touch upon her...and the blood that marred not only the night, but so much of the countryside. She scrubbed her flesh and her hair, and she wasn't happy until she had scrubbed both a second time. Martha stayed with her, helping her rinse out her hair. And when Shannon stepped out of the tub at last, Martha was there with a huge fluffy towel to wrap around her. When she was dried, Martha offered her a new nightgown.

It was entirely different from the first. It was soft flannel with little pink flowers and it buttoned all the way to the neck. It was warm and comfortable, and Shannon loved it. Combing out her clean but snarled hair, Shannon thanked Martha. "You've been so very good to us."

Martha waved a hand in the air. "We haven't done a thing, dear."

Shannon laughed. "You're harboring a man whose face graces dozens of wanted posters and you've treated me like a daughter."

Martha looked at the bed as she straightened the sheets and plumped the pillows. "I'd like to think that if my girl had lived, dear, she would have been a great deal like you."

Shannon came over and kissed her cheek. "Thank you. That's so very sweet."

Martha blushed. "Crawl in here now. Someone wants to see you."

Her heart fluttering, Shannon crawled into the bed. Malachi was coming. There were things she wanted to say to him. Things that she needed to say.

Martha smiled and left the room, closing the door behind her.

It didn't lock anymore.

Shannon sat back against her pillow, biting her lower lip and smoothing her fingers nervously over the covers. She heard a slight sound as the door opened and she looked up with anticipation.

Iris Andre walked into the room.

Shannon tried not to show her disappointment. She smiled as Iris came to the bed, pulling a chair over from the hearth. "How are you feeling?" Iris asked her. She smiled, and her eyes were bright with concern.

A moment's jealousy rose within Shannon, and she tried to swallow the feeling. Iris had such lovely flame-colored hair and bright green eyes. She had changed into a soft blue cotton dress, high-necked, decorated with rows of soft white lace. She looked beautiful and worldly and sophisticated, and somehow angelic, too. And once, Malachi had had a love affair with her. Iris denied that she had slept with him this time, but he had been with Iris far more than he had been with Shannon.

"I feel fine, Iris, thank you. The nausea has all gone away. Food helped."

"So you're none the worse for wear?"

Shannon ruefully pulled the sleeves back on her gown and showed where her wrists were chafed. She shivered, and her smile faded. "He killed your friend. I am so sorry."

"So am I," Iris said softly. "No one deserved to die that way, not even a . . . whore."

"Oh, Iris!" Shannon sat up and reached out for the woman's hand.

Iris smiled. "You are very sweet, do you know that?"

Shannon flushed. "There isn't a sweet bone in my body." She hesitated. "Ask Malachi. He'll tell you."

"Malachi!" Iris said, laughing. There was a sparkle about her eyes.

"Why are you laughing?" Shannon demanded.

"I'm enjoying this, I suppose," Iris said, and then she sighed. "He does say that you have a temper. And you are good with a Colt. I'm glad I never tempted you to shoot."

"I was very tempted to shoot when we met," Shannon admitted.

"I'm glad that you didn't," Iris said. She stood up abruptly. "I guess I had better go. Malachi is anxious to see you—"

"Iris?"

"Yes?"

"I don't understand." She had to force herself to look at the other woman. "He didn't come back here last night . . ." She couldn't help it. She lowered her eyes, and her voice trailed away.

"I wasn't here, honey. I went over to Sparks."

"Oh!" Shannon looked at her again.

"It's a long story. I'm sure that he wants to explain it to you himself. I'll see you tomorrow. Malachi is anxious to get on his way tonight—"

"He's leaving?"

"There I go again. He'll explain—"

"He's leaving me here?"

"No, not exactly. Please, let him explain." Iris didn't give Shannon another chance to question her. She smiled and hurried out of the room. Shannon's mind began to race. Something had happened, something that she didn't know about. They were getting closer and closer to Kristin, and Malachi meant to leave without her.

She started to crawl out of bed. If he was leaving that evening, so was she.

She started at the sound of a tap on the door. Malachi? She glanced at the door, remembering what had happened when she tried to keep him out. And now he was tapping quietly?

He didn't wait for her answer. He stepped into the room. Shannon quickly glanced his way. He had been at the saloon, but he hadn't been drinking, not much, anyway. He still wore his cavalry hat. He was taking chances here, she thought. But then, maybe it didn't matter in Haywood. Maybe the war had really ended here.

She loved him in that hat. She loved the way the brim shadowed his eyes and gave mystery to his face, and she loved the jaunty plume that flew with Rebel fervor.

She loved him...

His shirt was torn at the sleeve and covered with dirt from his fight with Justin Waller on the ground. His shoulder was visible through the tear, bronzed and muscular. There was a masculine appeal to him that made her heart ache to look at him—mussed and torn in her defense, ramrod straight and tall and lean and rugged. She felt that she stared at him for ages, but it could have been no more than seconds. He frowned as he realized that she had been about to crawl out of bed. "What do you think you're doing?"

"I'm going to get dressed. If we're leaving—"

"I'm leaving."

"But—"

"Shannon, I'm just going ahead of you by a day. I have to go tonight." He smiled, and his lip twisted with a certain amount of amusement rather than anger. He strode across the room to her and caught her by her shoulders, pushing her gently back down on the bed and sitting by her thigh. She opened her mouth to say something, but no words would come to her. She didn't feel like fighting him at that moment. She didn't feel like fighting at all.

She reached up and stroked his cheek, feeling the softness of his beard.

He caught her hand and kissed her fingers. "I was so damned scared today," he told her.

She smiled. "So was I."

"Are you really all right?"

She nodded. "You came in time."

He folded her fingers and set them down upon her midriff. He stood and wandered idly over to the window, leaning against the wall and staring out at the street. "Did Iris tell you? She found Cole."

"What?" Shannon shot up with pleasure. "Oh, Malachi, I'm so very glad. Where? Is that what—"

He turned around and walked back to her. She was kneeling at the end of the bed. Her hair was drying in soft, waving tendrils that curled over her shoulders and breasts and streamed down the length of her back. Her eyes were beautiful with enthusiasm. She looked completely recovered from the day, and exquisitely alive and vital.

She loved Cole, she reminded herself. She always had loved Cole. The bright enthusiasm in her eyes was for his brother.

"Cole is in Sparks."

"Oh, no!"

"It's all right. He's safe. Iris has a friend there named Cindy who has a—er—house . . . on the outskirts of town. Cole is there. He's safe. He's gotten word to Jamie. That's why I have to leave tonight."

Shannon started to crawl out of bed again. "Whoa!" he told her, catching her arm. "You aren't coming. Not tonight."

"But Malachi—"

He caught her chin and lifted it. He met the dazzling sapphire blue of her eyes, and smiled. "I'm not leaving you, Shannon. It's too much trouble to try. But I want you to stay here tonight, please. I want you to get one good night's rest. Iris will bring you in the morning with the buckboard. All right?"

"But Malachi—"

"Shannon, we have to figure out a way to free Kristin. There isn't going to be anything that you can do until we form some kind of a plan. Please, get some rest tonight. For me."

The last words were softly spoken. They were husky, and they seemed to touch her with tenderness.

If he had yelled or ordered her around, she would have fought him. But he wasn't yelling; he wasn't angry. His hand upon her was light, and she longed to grip it and kiss his fingers in return.

"Stay?" he said.

She nodded. He stroked her cheek before turning away from her. He tossed his hat onto the chair.

"Will you take good care of that for me? Bring it tomorrow in the buckboard. Pack it. They probably won't think too much of it in Sparks."

"I'll pack it carefully."

"Thanks."

He started to unbutton his shirt, then realized that it was torn beyond salvation. Grinning at her, he ripped open the buttons. "This one has bit the dust, don't you think?"

She nodded. She didn't care in the least about his shirt. She cared about his shoulders, bronze and hard and glimmering in candlelight. And dried blood showed on a cut on his arm.

Shannon leaped out of the bed. He started to frown at her again.

"Your arm," she told him softly, as she hurried past him to where a clean cloth lay over the rim of the bath. She picked it up and wet it and came back to his side, suddenly hesitant to touch him. She looked up, meeting his eyes, and she flushed.

"It's nothing," he told her. She nodded, then gently started to bathe the wound. It wasn't deep. She wiped away the blood, then she found herself rising on her toes to press her lips against his back, against his shoulder. He twisted around to look at her. She kept her eyes upon his, and kissed his upper arm, then jutted the tip of her tongue to spiral it slowly upward to his shoulder.

He turned and caught her elbow and pulled her against him. Against the flannel of her gown and through his breeches she felt the pulsing hardness of his body. She laid her head against his chest and touched the mat of hair that lay there. She brought her palm against his chest, over the muscle, and found his hard nipple amidst the mat of gold hair. She teased it between her fingers, then tentatively reached forward with her tongue and bathed it with warmth. His groan gave her new courage and a soaring, exciting sense of her own power. She pressed her lips against the furiously beating pulse in his throat, and over the width of him and breadth of him, burrowing low against him to tease the steel hardness of his midriff, and delve her tongue into the fascinating pit of his navel.

He groaned again, dragging her back to her feet, winding his fingers into her hair.

"You've had a rough day," he said jaggedly. "You're supposed to be in bed."

She smiled wickedly. "I'm trying to be in bed."

It was all the invitation that he needed. He smiled in response and swept her up high, depositing her on the bed. He leaned over her, working upon the nightgown's dozen tiny buttons. They gave at her throat, and she arched back as he kissed and stroked the length of the soft column while working away at the next buttons, those that went lower and lower against her breasts.

There would never be another night quite like it for her. Soft moonlight played through the window and a soft cool breeze caressed her flesh. He made her warm despite it.

He made love slowly, with a leisurely abandon. She touched him and he caught her hands. He kissed each finger individually, and he raked his tongue between them, and then suckled them gently into his mouth. He kissed her arms, and her knees. He loved her feet, and cherished her thighs, and he ravaged her intimately with his touch and with his tongue until she cried out, shaking, soaking and glistening with her release. Then he touched her again . . .

And they sat and stared at one another, their bodies glowing in the soft light. When they reached out again, it was like tentative strangers, allowing slow exploration. She knew she could dare anything, and found the thrill of feminine power. She shivered and died a little bit with the delight of hearing him groan as she possessively stroked his body, and held him with her hands, and with her kiss, and with all the warmth and welcoming heat of her body. Time lost all meaning. His whispers were sweet, and often urgent. Passion was stoked to a never-ending flame, but for that night, tenderness reigned.

Somewhere in it all, she fell against her pillow, and in exhaustion, she slept. She awoke, though, when he moved away from her.

She watched him dress in the moonlight, loving the length of him. His shoulders, broad and gleaming, his legs, long and muscular, his buttocks, tight and hard . . .

She smiled as her thoughts continued to his most intimate and personal parts, then her smile faded, because he was leaving her, and she was suddenly very afraid.

"Malachi."

Startled, he looked at her. He pulled on his breeches and went over to the bed. "I'm glad you're awake," he said softly. He kissed her lips. "Do you mind coming with Iris?"

She shook her head. "I mind that I'm not coming with you."

"You'll be safer coming with Iris." He rose and donned a clean shirt, buttoning it quickly and tucking the tails into his pants. "Shannon, I'm a wanted man. You're not, and neither is she. Just in case there turns out to be trouble."

"Malachi—"

"Shannon, we'll be staying in a brothel, you know."

"And that's where you're going now?"

He nodded.

She didn't say a word. She watched him finish dressing. He kept his eyes on her, and when he had pulled on his boots, he came over to her with the Colt. "If anyone bothers you on the way, shoot him. Don't hesitate, and don't ask questions, just shoot. You understand?"

She nodded, her lashes hiding her eyes. He caught her hands and pulled her into his arms. He kissed and touched her, as if he memorized her flesh and curves. Then he kissed her again and slowly released her. Shannon picked up her pillow and watched him as he walked to the door.

"Behave," she whispered softly at last.

He turned back, grinning slowly. "Why, ma'am, I'm a married man. I intend to be an angel."

She smiled, wanting to send him on his way without worry. It was difficult to smile. She didn't feel good about his leaving. She didn't know why, but she was scared.

"Be careful," he warned her.

"You be careful yourself."

"I'll be careful," he promised. He hesitated, as if he was going to say more. "I'll be very careful," he said after a moment, and then he turned away.

"Malachi!"

She leaped out of bed and raced to him naked. She didn't want him to go because there were so many things to say. But suddenly, she couldn't say them. She simply threw herself against him and he held her very tightly for a moment.

"I'm afraid," she told him.

"Afraid, vixen?" he whispered. "The hellcat of the west is afraid?" he teased in a husky voice. "Darlin', if you had just been on our side, the South might have won the war."

"Malachi, I am afraid."

"We're going to get Kristin, and then we'll all be safe," he vowed softly. Then he kissed her swiftly on the lips again and was gone.

Shannon closed the door in his wake and slowly, mechanically went to the bed and slipped into the flannel nightgown. She sat on the bed, then stretched out, and she tried to tell herself that she would be with him soon. Her eyes would not close; she could not sleep. She stared at the ceiling, and gnawed upon her lower lip, and worried regretfully about all the things she had not said. She was in love with him. It would have been so easy to whisper the truth. To tell him that she believed in him . . .

He was on his way to a whorehouse, she reminded herself dryly, and he had spent two nights in a saloon. But Shannon believed Iris, and she believed Malachi, whether it was foolish or not.

That wasn't what mattered, she thought, staring out the window at the moonlit night. What mattered were the things that lay between them. He had been forced to marry her, and his fury had been obvious. She couldn't whisper that she loved him because he didn't love her. She might have forgotten her hatred of the past, but she didn't think that he could forget the years that had gone before. She was his wife, and they had exchanged vows, but that wasn't enough for a lifetime. She couldn't hold him to a marriage.

She didn't mind loving him; she craved to be with him. But she couldn't hold him to the marriage.

She twisted around, determined that she would sleep. She started to shiver. All of a sudden, she was very afraid. She didn't like him out of her sight.

He was safe, she told herself.

But no matter how many times she repeated the words, she could not convince herself, and it was nearly dawn when she slept.

Mrs. Haywood was perplexed to see her go in the morning.

"You don't need to go traipsing off, young lady. Let the men settle things. You should stay right here, in Haywood."

Iris was already in the buckboard and they were packed. Chapperel was tied to the rear of the wagon, and they had a big basket of food and canteens of water and even a jug of wine.

"We're going to be just fine, Mrs. Haywood," Shannon assured her. "Iris and I can both take care of ourselves."

"Hmph!" Martha sniffed, and she wiped away a sudden tear. "You come back when things are all right again, you hear?"

Shannon nodded and gave her a fierce hug. "We'll come back, Martha, I promise." She hurried down the steps then and over to the buckboard. It was going to be a long ride.

She climbed into the buckboard and waved to Mrs. Haywood. Mr. Haywood was with her now, his arm around her. "You send for us if you need us!" Mr. Haywood called.

"Thank you! Thank you both so much!" Shannon returned. She smiled. What more could they possibly do for her? No one could help a man condemned as an outlaw without so much as a trial.

"Ready?" Iris asked her.

"Ready," Shannon said. Iris lifted the reins. They started off. Shannon waved until they had left the little one-road town behind them, and then she turned and leaned back and felt the noon sun on her face.

She felt Iris watching her and she opened her eyes. "Are you really all right?" Iris asked her.

"I am extremely well, really. I've never felt healthier. Never. Honest."

"It's a long ride, that's all."

"I've already come a very long way," Shannon told her.

They rode in silence for a while. Then Iris asked her about her home, and about the war, and Shannon tried very hard to explain the tangled events that had led her to be living in the South—and being a Union sympathizer.

Iris was silent when she finished. Shannon looked at the other woman curiously. "You knew Malachi before. And if you found Cole, I assume that you knew him before, too."

Iris smiled. "And Jamie. They all used to come into a place where I worked in Springfield. Before the war."

"I see."

Iris looked at her curiously. "No, you probably don't see. You were raised by a good man, and you loved him, I hear it in your voice when you talk about your pa. I was raised by a stepfather who sold me to a gambler on my thirteenth birthday. You can't begin to see."

"I'm sorry, Iris. I didn't mean to presume to judge you." She hesitated. "You speak so beautifully, and when you dress like you so often—"

"I don't look like a whore, is that it?"

Shannon flushed, but she didn't apologize. She looked at Iris and smiled. "I just think that you are too good and too fine a woman to end up...like Reba."

"You're going to try to make me go straight, huh?" Iris asked.

"You could, you know."

"And do what?"

"Open up an inn."

"Miss Andre's Room and Board for Young Ladies?" Iris asked.

"Why not?"

Iris laughed and flicked the reins. "All right. I'll think about it. And what about you?"

"What do you mean?"

"When it is over, what about you?"

"I—er—I'll go home."

"Alone?"

Shannon lowered her face. "You know he didn't mean to marry me," she murmured.

Iris was quiet for a minute. "I know that you're in love with him."

"He doesn't love me."

"How can you be so sure?"

"He—he's never said so. And ... Iris, you can't imagine, we were enemies. I mean bitter enemies. Remember, the North and South will still clash for years to come. His favorite name for me is brat. There isn't a chance ..."

Iris laughed delightedly. "You listen to me, young woman. If he were mine, if I had this chance, I would hang on for dear life. I would fight like a tiger. If you've any sense, and if you do love him, you'll do the same."

"But, Iris, I can't force him to stay with me!"

"Then sleep with your pride. Lie awake night after night, and remember that you have the cold glory of your pride to lie with you instead of the warmth of the man you love."

Shannon fell silent. They rode awhile longer, then Iris suggested they stop for lunch.

They found a brook, and as they dangled their feet in it, Shannon entertained Iris with stories about growing up with Kristin and Matthew.

"You'd like my brother," she said impulsively.

Iris sniffed. "A Yankee."

"I'm a Yankee, remember? And you're living in Kansas. Yankee territory."

"No. The whole country is Yankee territory now," Iris said. "And I'm a working girl. Confederate currency doesn't put much food on the table these days."

They left soon after.

They didn't pass a single soul on the road. Close to sunset, they came to a rise overlooking a valley. Shannon climbed down from the buckboard to look down at the town of Sparks.

It was obviously thriving. There were rows of new houses, and more rows of businesses. Ranches spread out behind the town, and the fields were green and yellow and rich beneath the sun. In the distance, she could see railroad tracks, and a big station painted red. Iris told her that the town was a major junction for the stagecoaches, too.

She came back to the buckboard and looked at Iris. "It's a big place," she murmured uneasily. "A very big place. And Hayden Fitz owns it all now?"

Iris nodded gravely. "He owns most of the land. And he owns two of the stagecoach lines. And the saloon and the barbershop. And the sheriff and the deputies. Come on. Climb back in." She pointed down the valley to a large house surrounded by a stable and barns. It was a fair distance from the town. "Cindy's place."

"Cindy's place," Shannon echoed. She shrugged, and a smile curved her lips. "Let's go."

In another thirty minutes they reached the house on the plain.

It was a beautiful, elegant place with cupolas and gables, numerous stained-glass windows, and even a swing on the porch. It looked like the home of a prosperous family.

But when Iris reined in, the front door opened and a woman burst out, running down the stairs and dispelling any vision of family life.

She was clad in high heels and stockings and garters and little else but a short pink robe. She had midnight-black hair and a gamine face, and it wasn't until she was almost at the buckboard that Shannon realized that she was not a young girl at all but a woman of nearly fifty. She was beautiful still, and outrageous in her dress, and when she laughed, the sound of her laughter was husky and appealing.

"Iris! You did make it back. And this must be Malachi's blushing little bride."

"I'm not little," Shannon protested, hopping down from the buckboard. She extended a hand to Cindy. She might be slim, but she was taller than Cindy by a good inch or two.

"I stand corrected," the woman said. "Come on down, Iris. Do come in before someone notices that Mrs. Slater here is a newcomer."

"You're right. Let's go in," Iris said.

They hurried up the steps to the house and came into a very elegant foyer. Shannon could hear laughter and the sounds of glasses clinking. Cindy cast her head to the right. "That's the gaming room, Mrs. Slater. I don't imagine you'll want to wander in there. And there—" She pointed to the left. "That's the bar. Don't wander in there, either. Not that you're not welcome—the men just might get the wrong idea about you, and I don't want to have to answer to Malachi. Come on, and I'll show you to your room. Then I'll show you the kitchen. You're perfectly safe there. It's Jeremiah's domain, and no male dares tread there."

Cindy started to lead them up a flight of stairs. Shannon caught her arm, stopping her.

"Excuse me, but where is Malachi?"

"He's, er, he's out at the moment," Cindy said. "Come on now, I've got to get you settled—"

Shannon caught her arm again. "I'm sorry, but he's out where? Is Cole here? Has Jamie slipped in yet?"

"Cole is just fine, and Jamie looks as good as gold," Cindy said.

She came to the second-floor landing and hurried down the hall, pushing open a door. "It's one of the nicest rooms in the house. See the little window seat? I think that you'll be very comfortable in here, Mrs. Slater."

Shannon stood in the center of the room. It was a beautiful room with a large bed, a marble mantel, chairs, and the promised window seat. It was missing one thing. Her husband.

"Thank you for the room, and for your help and hospitality, for myself, my husband and my brothers-in-law. And excuse me for being persistent, but where is my husband, please?"

Cindy looked uneasily from Iris to Shannon.

"He's..."

"You might as well answer her," Iris advised. "She won't give up asking you."

"I won't," Shannon said.

"He's holding up a train."

"What?" Shannon gasped in astonishment.

"Wait a minute, I said that badly, didn't I?"

"Is there a good way to announce to his wife that a man is holding up a train?" Iris demanded.

"Well, he isn't really holding it up—"

"What are you saying!" Shannon demanded.

Cindy sighed and walked over to where a pretty little round cherry-wood side table held brandy and snifters. There were only two snifters—the room was planned for a party of two, and no more.

"We'll share," Cindy told Iris, and she drank a glass of brandy before pouring out two more and handing one glass to Shannon and the other to Iris.

"Cindy, explain about Malachi," Shannon insisted.

"All right. All right. Kristin is being held in the Hayden house. They've got bars on the windows, and at least twenty guards in and around the house. There was no way for the three men to break in and carry her away." She hesitated. "The boys just might have some friends around here, but we don't really know that yet. A lot of decent folk aren't pleased that Hayden Fitz is holding a lady, no matter what legal shenanigans he tries to pull. Anyway, Jamie heard tell that some bushwhackers on the loose were planning to hold up the train south. And there's a Federal judge on that train. They're going to seize the train from the bushwhackers and then try to explain the whole story to the judge."

"Oh, those fools!" Shannon cried. "They're going to get themselves killed."

Iris slipped an arm around her. "Honey, come on! They aren't fools. They know what they're about."

"If the bushwhackers don't shoot them, the judge will!"

"Well," Cindy said dryly, "you can be sure of one thing."

"What's that?"

"If Cole Slater is killed, Hayden Fitz won't need your sister any more. He'll let her go."

"I don't know," Iris murmured miserably, staring at her glass. "Knowing the perversions of Hayden Fitz, I imagine—"

"Iris!" Cindy said.

Iris quickly looked at Shannon and flushed. "Oh, honey, I'm sorry. I really am . . ."

"It's all right, Iris. You don't need to hide the truth from me," Shannon said. She sank down on the bed. "Oh, God!" she murmured desperately. "He said that we'd be together tonight. He said that we'd be back together."

Iris and Cindy exchanged looks over her head. Shannon leaped up suddenly. "Iris, I can't just sit here. Let's go into town."

"What?"

"Iris, you can get in to see Kristin, can't you? I would feel so much better if you saw her."

"Shannon, I don't know—"

"Iris, I can't just sit here. What if—" She hesitated, feeling her heart thunder hard against her chest. "What if Cole and Malachi don't make it? Iris, we have to discover some other way!"

"Malachi would hang me if—"

"Iris, I'm going with or without you."

Cindy shrugged, lifting her brandy glass. "You both look like respectable young women right now. Can't see how a ride into town could possibly hurt. Besides, if Hayden is around, he probably will let you in to see Kristin, Iris."

"Iris, I'm going with or without you. Iris, please. I'll go mad sitting here wondering about Malachi and Jamie and Cole and that stupid train!"

Iris sighed. "All right," she said at last. "All right. Shannon, I hope to God that this works out! He'll flay me alive if it doesn't."

"We'll be fine," Shannon assured her. "Just fine."

She would have plenty of time later to rue her confident words.

Maybe, if Shannon could have seen Malachi, seated comfortably in the club car of the train along with both his brothers, she might have felt a little better.

The three Slater brothers were seated in velvet-upholstered chairs around a handsome wood table drinking whiskey from crystal glasses at the judge's invitation. Cole was intense, straddled across his chair, leaning on the back, his eyes silver and his features taut as he spoke. Malachi leaned back, listening to his brother, more at ease. Jamie was, for all appearances, completely casual and negligent, accepting his drink with ease. He wore a broad-brimmed Mexican hat, chaps and boots, and looked every bit the rancher. Only the way his eyes narrowed now and then told Malachi that his younger brother was every bit as wary this night as he and Cole.

Two friends of Jamie's from Texas were playing lookout while the brothers spoke with Judge Sherman Woods. Cole, seated to Malachi's left, was earnestly explaining what had happened at the beginning of the war, how his wife had been killed, how the ranch had been burned and how, sick with grief, he had joined up with the bushwhackers for vengeance.

"But I never gunned down a man in cold blood in my life, judge," Cole said simply. "Never. I always fought fair. I wasn't with Quantrill more than a few months, then I went regular cavalry. I was assigned as a scout. I took my orders directly from Lee. I was in Kansas, and I did kill Henry Fitz, but it was fair. Any man who was there could tell you that."

Judge Woods lit up a cigar and sat back. Malachi liked the man. He hadn't panicked when the masked bushwhackers had seized the train, and he had barely blinked when the Slaters had reseized it from the robbers at gunpoint, sending them on their way into the night. He was a tall thin man with a neatly trimmed mustache and iron-gray hair. He wore a stovepipe hat and a brocade vest and a handsome black frock coat and fancy shoes, but he seemed to be listening to Cole. He looked from one brother to the other. "What about you?" he asked Jamie.

Jamie smiled with innocent ease. "Judge, this is the first time I've been in Kansas since 1856. I was damned stunned to hear that I was a wanted man. And amazed that any fool could think that my brother was a murderer."

The judge arched one brow. He turned to Malachi. "And what about you, captain?"

Malachi shrugged. "I wasn't in Kansas. I spent most of the end of the war in Kentucky, then in Missouri. I would have come to Kansas, though, if I had thought that Cole might need me. Fitz was a murderer. He killed my sister-in-law. He killed lots of other people. And it seems to me, sir, that if we're really going to call a truce to this war, we have to prosecute all the murderers, the Yank murderers, too. Now Hayden Fitz is holding an innocent woman. God alone knows what he could want with her, and so help me, I can't understand what law he is using to get away with this legally."

The judge lifted his hands. "You do realize that what you're doing right now is illegal?"

"Yes, it is," Cole admitted.

"But we did stop those other fellows from robbing you blind," Malachi reminded him.

"Of course. All right, I've listened to your story. And God knows, gentlemen, I, for one, am anxious to see an end to the hostilities! I'm afraid we won't live to see it, but I'm a father of four, and I keep praying that maybe the next generation will see something good come to this land. You had best slip off this train and disappear into the night, the same way that you came. I give you my word of honor that I will look into this situation immediately. If you're patient, I'll see that your wife is freed, Cole Slater. But I suggest that the three of you remain out of sight for the time being. Understood? And, oh—stay away from Fitz. We don't want him finding you."

Malachi looked at Cole, and Cole looked at Jamie. They all shrugged. They *were* in hiding. Just because they were hiding right beneath Fitz's nose . . .

They shook hands with the judge. Outside the club car, Jamie waved to his friends, and they jumped from where they were standing on the engine platform and the mail car. The five men hurried quietly for their waiting horses, then galloped away into the darkness of the night.

A half mile from the train, they left Jamie's friends, Cole and Malachi voicing their thanks earnestly. The two men had served with Jamie during the war. "Don't mind helping a Slater," said the older of the two. "Jamie pulled me out of a crater in December of '64. I owe him my life."

"Thanks just the same," Jamie said, tilting his hat. Malachi and Cole echoed the words.

Then the brothers were alone together, riding through the night.

Malachi flashed Jamie a smile. "Well, I admit, it seemed like a reckless plan to begin with, but it went fairly well."

"Nothing really gained," Jamie murmured.

"Nothing lost," Cole said, sighing. Malachi saw his brother's frown in the moonlight. "And we're close enough. If Fitz does threaten Kristin . . ."

"Then we are close, and we just get a little more reckless," Malachi said. He urged the bay along a little faster.

"Hey!" Jamie called out to him. "What's your hurry now? We're not being pursued."

Malachi reined in. "I . . . Shannon is supposed to be coming in tonight."

Jamie started to laugh. "That hellcat in a whorehouse? You're right. Let's hurry."

Cole grinned. "It will be good to see her," he said softly. "I've missed Miss McCahy."

Malachi hesitated, then he muttered. "Mrs. Slater."

"What?" Both brothers queried him.

"Mrs. Slater," he repeated. He looked from Jamie to Cole. They stared at him in amazement.

"They were going to hang me," Malachi explained lamely. "I—er, we kind of had to do it."

"She married a Reb?" Jamie demanded.

"She married—you?" Cole said.

"I told you, they were going to hang me if we didn't. Damn it, quit staring at me like that!" He swore. He urged the bay forward. "It's a long, long story and I'm not in the mood for it tonight."

"Cole, come on now, hurry!" Jamie laughed. "I am anxious to hear this! The hellcat married to my brother! Mrs. Sweet-little-hellcat Slater, holed up in a whorehouse! I can't wait."

Malachi ignored his brother and urged his horse faster. He wanted to see Shannon. His heart was pounding; his body was aching. They would have to take some time. She would need to see and hug and hold Cole, and she would laugh and maybe cry and then hug Jamie fiercely, too. But then they would be alone.

And he was realizing more and more that he had come to live for the moments when they could be alone.

She was his wife . . .

And he was very anxious to lie down beside her that night.

He had no idea until they rode into the yard in the darkness of the night that he would be denied that simple pleasure.

Chapter Thirteen

Shannon breathed a sigh of relief as they reached town. No one thought to molest two women riding in a buckboard, and when Iris reined in just to the right of Hayden Fitz's massive dwelling, with its barred windows and guards, they were still left entirely alone. The man before the door raised a hand to Iris, and a grin broke out on his features.

"Why, Miss Andre. Nice to see you."

"Herb Tanner," Iris told Shannon with a sniff. She reached in back of her for the basket of food they had packed. "I think that you should sit tight—"

"Who's that you got with you?" the man called out.

"Never mind," Iris said beneath her breath. "You keep quiet. Let me do the talking." Iris looked at her and shook her head mournfully. "A beautiful young blue-eyed blonde. You could be in trouble just by being here. I wish I had a sheet to put over your head. Keep your mouth shut, you hear?"

"I'll be silent as a mouse," Shannon promised.

She crawled out of the buckboard behind Iris and followed the older woman toward the house. Herb Tanner was holding a repeating rifle, but he seemed to consider his guard duty a bit of a joke. He set the gun down to sweep his hat off to Iris.

"Hello, Herb," Iris said sweetly.

"Hello, Iris!" Herb said happily. "The boss man is engaged this evening, if you come to see him." He spoke to Iris, but he looked over her shoulder to Shannon, offering her a broken-toothed and lascivious grin.

"Well, Herb, I really came for curiosity's sake."

Herb's grin widened. "You curious about me, Iris?"

Iris laughed and patted his chest and moved close to him. "Why, Herbie, you could make a woman just as curious as a prowling cat, you know that, boy? But that wasn't what I meant. Not at this particular moment." She moved closer against him. "I want to see the woman that old Fitz has locked up in the house. I have a bet with my friend Sara here that we can get in to see her. They say that she's the wife of that awful outlaw, Cole Slater. What do you think, Herbie? Could we get in? Just to give her some apple pie and chicken from Cindy's house."

"I don't know, Iris," Herbie said.

"Oh, Herbie, come on! Isn't it funny? A couple of girls from Cindy's place bringing vittles to that little bushwhacker's lady? Why, it's just plain ironic, it is. Fitz would laugh himself silly, I'm certain."

"Iris, Fitz is in a meeting with some of his boss people—"

"Herbie, I could promise you a real good time."

Shannon saw that Herb jumped and trembled like a dog with a juicy new bone, just from the sound of Iris's voice. She clamped a hand on Iris's arm. Annoyed, Iris turned to her. Shannon pulled her down the steps.

"Iris! I don't want you promising that man sexual favors to get us into that house!"

"It's probably the only way, Shannon."

"Iris—"

"Shannon, it's what I do for a living!"

"You told me you just might think about changing occupations."

"Honey—"

"Iris, don't make any promises, please."

Iris grinned and shrugged. "All right, honey. You can promise him the sexual favors."

"What!"

"Oh, for heaven's sake. I'll promise him for a later date, and we'll never get to it, all right?"

Shannon exhaled slowly. "All right."

They hurried back to Herb. "Little financial negotiation," Iris said sweetly to him. "Sara doesn't think I should be giving the business away. But if you can get us in to visit that bushwhacker's woman, I'll promise you . . . I'll promise you the time of your life next Friday night. What do you say, Herbie?"

Herb's Adam's apple bulged and he exhaled in a rush. "Gee, Iris, I didn't think I could ever afford you. Not in a month of Sundays!"

"Well, curiosity, you know . . ."

Herb's eyes narrowed in calculation. "It's a deal, Iris. But I want you both." He looked over at Shannon like a cat who had swallowed a mouse, a pleased gloat on his face.

"What?" she gasped.

Iris elbowed her in the ribs.

"Sure, Herbie. Let us in, huh?"

"Let me see your basket," Herb said. Iris produced the basket. Herb searched through it. Satisfied, he nodded. He stepped aside, opening the front door.

There was another armed man in the entryway. "Let 'em in, Joshua. They're all right. They're just bringing the prisoner a bite of food."

"All right, Herb."

Joshua nodded to them. Iris dazzled him with a sweet smile, and he pointed them up the steps.

Shannon ran alongside Iris. On the landing was another man sitting in a chair reading the newspaper. Joshua called up to him. "Fulton, it's just a pair of—er, ladies to see the prisoner."

Fulton looked up and spat tobacco into a brass spittoon. "Herb say it was all right?"

"Honey chile, Herbie let us in," Iris told him sweetly.

Fulton stood up and moved close behind her. "Is there anything left that you can promise me?" he asked with a yellow-toothed smile.

"We'll see, darlin'," Iris promised. "Now, if you'd just show us the bushwhacker's wife..."

Fulton shrugged and produced a set of keys. He walked down the hall to a door and twisted a key in the lock. "You're looking good, Iris. So is your friend." He paused, staring at Shannon. "You new in town, girl?"

Shannon nodded.

"Learning the ropes of the business," Iris supplied.

Fulton's eyes swept over Shannon. "Well, I'll be savin' up my dimes, young lady. You can bet on that."

"Fulton, for you, there will be a big discount," Iris promised.

Fulton smiled and pushed open the door. "Company!" he called. Iris hurried into the room. Fulton caught Shannon's arm. "I'll be expecting a big discount, little lady."

Shannon wrenched her arm away, then remembered to smile. "Sure, sweetie," she promised, and batted her lashes his way. Iris grasped her arm and jerked her into the room. "Enough is enough, Shannon!" she hissed. "You want to wind up serving the man right here in the hallway?"

But Shannon wasn't listening. While Iris closed the door, Shannon stared across the room.

Kristin was standing by the foot of the bed, tall, stiff and proud, and every inch the lady. Her facade broke as she saw Shannon. Both women cried out and raced across the room and into one another's arms.

"Shh!" Iris begged them. "They'll hear you!"

Shannon and Kristin went dutifully silent, but continued to grip each other fiercely. Finally Kristin drew away. Shannon surveyed her sister as anxiously as Kristin studied her.

Kristin seemed to be all right. Someone had supplied her with a change of clothing, and she wore a cotton day dress in a soft rich burgundy with a cream lace collar. She was thin and pale, but she was smiling, and there didn't seem to be a mark on her.

Kristin held Shannon's hands as she made her sit down at the foot of the bed. Amazed, she looked from Shannon to Iris. Then she whispered, "What are you doing here? Shannon, I have been ill with worry! I saw the bushwhackers take you away—"

"Malachi rescued me," Shannon said quickly, not wanting to talk about that experience or Justin Waller.

"Oh, Shannon, you see, he has a good heart."

"Yes, Kristin—"

"Shannon, you shouldn't be here," Kristin said anxiously.

"Kristin, if I hadn't followed, Malachi might have slipped you away from the Red Legs. So I have to make up for that. Iris and I had to come!"

Kristin looked at Iris again, smiling. She stood up and offered Iris her hand. "How do you do? I'm Kristin Slater," she said softly. "Whoever you are, thank you!"

"Iris Andre," Iris offered.

"How did you get in here?" Kristin asked.

Shannon looked at Iris and Iris looked at Shannon. "We made a few deals," Shannon said ruefully.

"What? Oh," Kristin said. Her eyes, wide and very blue, fell upon Iris.

"I'm sorry, Mrs. Slater, but you should know. I'm a whore. And your husband and her husband have been staying out at Cindy's place. It might not be fittin', you two being ladies and all, but we're willing to help, and —"

"Sh!" Kristin cautioned, hurrying to Iris with a crooked smile. "I don't care what you do, Miss Andre. I thank you for caring. Did you say my husband? Cole? Is he there? He can't be!" She whirled around and stared at Shannon. "Nor Malachi. They wouldn't allow Shannon to do such a foolish thing as come here."

A small smile teased Iris's lips. "Mrs. Slater, I'm willing to bet that both Cole and Malachi are aware that there is not much that can stop your sister when her mind is set. But, yes, Mrs. Slater, your husband has been in town. So has Shannon's and so's your brother-in-law Jamie. They went out tonight to try to un-hold-up a train."

"What?"

"Kristin, I had to come. I had to see you. We must come up with a way out of this awful situation!" Shannon said.

Kristin was still staring at Iris, a frown marring her features. "My husband," she murmured. She stared at Shannon. "And her husband . . . Miss Andre, what husband?"

"Why, Malachi."

"Malachi!"

"Shh!" Shannon jumped to her feet.

Kristin sat at the foot of the bed, staring at Shannon incredulously. "Malachi!" she gasped. "Shannon, that's impossible! The two of you are incapable of sharing a room for ten minutes without all hell breaking loose. You and . . . Malachi?"

Shannon smiled uneasily. "It—er—it seemed like the thing to do at the time."

"They had threatened to hang him," Iris supplied with a shrug.

"But—" Kristin began.

"I'll tell you all about it at some other time," Shannon promised quickly. "Kristin, are they treating you well?"

"Well enough."

"No one has—"

"No one has physically abused me," Kristin said flatly. "Fitz thinks that if he can't get Cole to come out of hiding by just holding on to me, he'll pass a rumor that he's willing to deal." She hesitated. "So Cole is here. Oh, God, Shannon, don't let him do anything stupid! What is this about a train? Please, talk to him. Make him see that he can't win. Tell him to go home and get the baby and leave the country. Tell him—"

"Kristin! You know that he'll never do that."

"I have the perfect plan," Iris said softly.

Kristin and Shannon spun around to look at her. She smiled. "It will be easy enough to find another night when Fitz is occupied. And if not, I know how to occupy Fitz. Then we come with more of the girls. And we bring a few shawls and the like. And we all leave together. We just walk away, all of us, together. I guarantee you, none of the men will feel like moving."

Kristin stared at her in silence, then burst into laughter. "Oh, Iris, it's wonderful. But I couldn't let you do something like that! Fitz would surely get even with you—"

"With all of us? What could he do?"

"Fitz would find something."

"No. Because he would never be able to prove it. He wouldn't discover you missing until the next morning, and you could all be halfway to Texas by then. He wouldn't know which of us were involved, and it would be hard to hang a whole whorehouse. I think the men of this town would finally rebel."

"Neither Cole, Malachi or Jamie will let you do it, either," Kristin warned.

"They won't know!" Shannon said.

"But—" Kristin began.

"Shh! We'll be back," Shannon told her.

"Be ready," Iris warned Kristin. She grabbed Shannon's arm and pulled her to her feet. "We've got to move now, or they'll suspect us of something tonight, and we don't want that."

"Take care!" Shannon warned her sister, and hugged her fiercely again. "We'll be back."

"Come on!" Iris tugged on her sleeve.

They hurried to the door together. There was no one on the upstairs landing and they hurried down the steps. When they reached the bottom, Fulton was blocking their way. Iris smiled at him. "Thanks, Fulton. We'll be seeing you soon."

"You bet you will, Iris."

"Why, Fulton, what's wrong with you, honey?"

Fulton stepped aside. Shannon gasped, stunned.

Bear stood there. He was the massive jayhawker who had carried Kristin away after the fighting between the jay-hawkers and the bushwhackers, and it was obvious from the glint in his eyes that he remembered his brief glimpse of Shannon.

"What's going on?" Iris asked uneasily.

Shannon didn't say anything. The big man walked toward her with a wide grin plastered against his beefy features. "It is her," he said flatly. His arms crossed over his chest, he walked around Shannon. "Saw you when I was coming down the street, little miss. I thought I recognized you." He spun in a sudden fury and banged Fulton on the head with his hat. "Couldn't you see how much she looked like that Slater woman? They're as like as two peas from the same pod, you damned fool."

"Don't go beating at me, Bear!" Fulton protested. "Herbie said that the women were all right."

"Well, Herbie's going to have to answer to the boss, and that's that," Bear said. He grinned at Shannon and Iris. "Let's go and see the boss man, little lady."

Bear grasped Shannon by the arm. Iris slunk back against the wall. Shannon bit hard into Bear's fingers. When he screamed, Iris pulled out her small pistol.

"Let her go, Bear," Iris said.

Bear lifted up his hands. Shannon grabbed the Colt she was carrying from her skirt pocket. She drew the gun and held it on Fulton. "We're going to walk away. I'm going to go back up and get my sister out, and we're going to walk away."

"I think not, ma'am," a deep male voice called out.

Shannon spun around and looked up the stairs.

Kristin stood on the top step now, biting into her lip.

Behind her stood a tall, lean man with snow-white hair and cold gray eyes. He wore an elegant brocade vest and a frock coat and he held a small silver pistol to Kristin's skull. "Drop the gun," he told Shannon.

"Don't do it!" Kristin charged her. "Get out, Shannon, just get out—oh!"

The man cracked Kristin hard upon the head and she fell at his feet. He smiled at Shannon and aimed the gun toward her sister's back. "Drop it."

"Do it, Shannon," Iris advised wearily. "That's Fitz. And he will shoot her, without a thought."

"Why, thank you, Iris," Fitz drawled softly, "for that fine commendation. Girl, drop the gun."

Shannon inhaled and exhaled. Fitz cocked the gun. Shannon slowly bent and lay down her Colt.

"That was a very fine idea, young woman." He nodded to Bear. "Bring her to my office."

Bear set his arms upon Shannon. She tried to shake him off. "I can walk on my own!" she spat out.

"Fitz, you can't hold this girl—" Iris began.

"Iris, I am so disappointed in you!" Fitz said, shaking his head with a half smile. "Fulton, escort our friend Iris to my chamber, will you? Iris, I don't know what promises you made to get in here, but we'll just discuss them all. Later. And you will pay up."

Fulton grabbed Iris, sweeping her little pistol from her hands and jerking her around. "Come on, Iris. You heard the boss."

"Fitz, you can't hold her! Fitz, you—"

"I can, and I will, Iris," Fitz said. He stepped over Kristin and started down the stairs. "Get her out of here, Fulton. You'd better start worrying about yourself, Iris. Harboring a known criminal like this one here. Why, we could just shoot you down on the spot, Iris, and no court of law in the country could have a thing to say about it. Fulton, get her out of here!"

"Fitz, you'll pay!" Iris vowed as Fulton wrenched her arm behind her back. Iris cried out in pain. Shannon couldn't bear seeing Iris so hurt on her behalf. She flew at Fitz, her nails gouging his flesh.

"Let her alone, you bastard!" she hissed.

She didn't expect the iron grip of the man. He caught her flailing fists and pressed her against the banister. When she tried to kick him he lashed out, slapping her so hard that she staggered to her knees. He jerked her to her feet and prodded her before him. He threw her through a door in the foyer, and she fell to the ground.

He followed her into the office, stepping over her skirts. He closed the door behind him and walked around his desk to sit, idly watching her for several moments.

Shannon barely dared move. She stared at the man and waited.

"Well, well, well," he murmured at last. "My net is closing fast around all the little fishes."

"I don't know what you mean," Shannon said.

"Don't you?" he said, arching a distinguished white brow. "I think that you do. After all, my dear, you are here now, aren't you?" He smiled. "I hear things, you know. Nothing much happens in these parts that I don't hear about. Captain Malachi Slater was with you in Haywood."

Shannon shrugged. "I'm here on my own."

"Come, come, my dear. Malachi Slater gunned down half my men in the woods along with his bushwhacker friends. Bushwhackers. You never can trust them. I even heard that Malachi Slater gunned down a fellow Reb just the other day."

"He didn't gun down anyone," Shannon said.

"Ah, but he is near!" Hayden Fitz said. He smiled. "And your name is Shannon, and you're a Slater now, too. Is that true?"

Shannon shrugged. "Malachi despises me. If you hear everything, you must know that he and I are enemies. We were on different sides during the war, Mr. Fitz. Perhaps you should know, too, that my brother is a highly respected

Union officer. When he gets his hands on you, you'll be really sorry."

Fitz laughed, delighted. "Don't fret, girl. Your brother will be too late to help you. Oh, young lady! I can't tell you just how happy I am to have you. The net does draw tighter and tighter. And I know you *are* Mrs. Malachi Slater." He stood up, coming around the desk. He looked down at her. "You're even prettier than your sister, and I didn't think that possible. My men would really enjoy you. And they just might, you know. I could enjoy an evening with you my-self—" He broke off, shrugging. "But I want the Slaters first. I want every last one of them dead."

"You'll never do it," Shannon said defiantly. "They'll kill you, and you know it. You're so damned afraid of them that you can barely stand it!"

"Those Slaters are cold-blooded murderers!"

"The Slaters! Your brother swept in and murdered in-nocent women! How dare you talk about cold-blooded murder?"

"Bushwhackers deserved to die."

"There weren't any bushwhackers back when Cole's wife was killed! Just bastards like your brother!"

Fitz clenched his teeth and struck out at her with his booted foot. She screamed with the sudden pain.

The door burst open. Bear and Fulton rushed in.

"Trouble, boss?" Bear asked. Fulton was frowning, staring at Shannon.

"Boss, you know you can't hold another woman here. Someone will protest—"

"Shut up, Fulton."

"But boss, if this gets out, too, now . . ."

"Mary Surratt was hanged for complicity in the Lincoln assassination," Fitz said quietly, staring at Shannon. "I'm sure that I can pin complicity on these lovely ladies, too."

"But boss, what about Iris?"

"Fulton, are you questioning me?"

"Sir, it's just—"

"Bear, go out, will you? Check the street and see if we've got any other visitors running around tonight."

"Yes, sir."

Bear ran out. Fulton asked, "Mr. Fitz, should I go out with him?"

Shannon should have seen the curious cold light in Fitz's strange gray eyes, but she wasn't prepared for what happened next.

"No, Fulton, you stay here," Fitz said. "I need you." Then he pulled out his little pistol and aimed it at Fulton.

"No!" Fulton gasped, his eyes widening with horror.

Fitz fired. Fulton dropped to the floor.

And Hayden Fitz threw himself on top of Shannon, pretending to struggle with her.

The door burst open. Bear was back.

"She shot him!" Fitz cried. "The little bitch came flying at me and stole my pistol and shot Fulton, shot him down dead, in cold blood."

"Liar!" Shannon raged, trying to free herself. Fitz held her tightly, meeting her eyes with a cold smile.

"Murderess!" He stood and dragged her to her feet. "Damned bushwhacker's murderess!" he swore. He held her very close in a deadly challenge. "You'll hang for this!" he promised, and shoved her toward Bear. "Lock her up. Lock her up with her sister. They can both hang for murder, and for conspiracy to do murder!"

"You can't get away with this!" Shannon cried.

"Watch me, Mrs. Slater. Just watch me. You'll feel the rope around your neck and then you'll know."

She escaped from Bear and flew at Fitz with such a rage that she managed to rake bloody scratches down his cheeks with her nails. He hissed out something, and Bear came up behind her. He struck her hard on the head with the butt of his gun.

Hayden Fitz went hazy before her. Then the world went black.

"Lock them both up," Fitz said. "And make sure poor Fulton is brought over to Darby's funeral parlor. See that he's done up right. Stupid, murdering bitch."

"Yes, sir, yes, sir," Bear said. He scooped Shannon up into his arms and left the office.

Hayden Fitz stepped over Fulton's body. He walked to the stairs and looked up them. He smiled.

Iris had yet to pay for her part in the night's proceedings. She had yet to pay...

But she would pay very dearly.

He set his hand upon the banister and started up the stairs.

"That's—that's all I know," Cindy said unhappily, staring at the three Slater brothers. "A friend of Bear's come in here about midnight, and told everyone what happened. We've got to move the three of you—they'll come here looking for you, and I'm gong to have to pretend to be innocent. I—"

Malachi stood up. "Cindy, you don't have to do anything. I'm going in tonight," he said softly.

"No! Malachi, no, that's just what Fitz wants!" Cindy protested. "If you go raging in—"

"He's got my wife," Malachi thundered.

Cole stood and clapped Malachi on the shoulder. "He's had my wife, Malachi, don't forget that. I admit, bursting in, guns blazing, was my first thought. But Fitz will kill them, Malachi."

Malachi slunk back into his chair. He stared across the room.

"We have to bide our time," Jamie murmured.

"There will be some kind of a trial," Cindy said. She looked unhappily at Malachi. "But Hayden's telling everybody that Shannon McCahy Slater shot one of his men in cold blood. The trial will be rigged. She'll be condemned, and unless he gets his hands on you, he will hang her. He'll hang them both."

Malachi stood again. He strode across the room and came back to stand before Cole.

"A hanging. A big crowd, ropes. Lots of confusion."

Cole smiled slowly. "A few sharpshooters could do a fair amount of damage in a crowd like that."

Malachi grinned his slow, crooked smile. Cole laughed, and as Cindy watched, even Jamie smiled with a leisurely pleasure.

"You've all lost your minds!" she told them.

"No, darlin'," Malachi drawled softly. "I think we've just found our way out of this mess."

"What are you—"

Cindy broke off. Someone was knocking at the door. A voice called, "Cindy! It's Gretchen. I need to see you."

The Slaters quickly stood. Malachi came around behind the bar. Cole and Jamie sank against the pillars. Gretchen pushed open the door. She was followed by a tall man clad in the dark blue uniform of the Union cavalry man.

"Cindy, this man insists he get to you!" Gretchen said, rubbing her wrist and looking at the stranger in the shadows. "He said that he knows the Slaters are around here somewhere, and he wants Cole to know that the baby is fine." Pretty, sandy-haired, freckle-faced Gretchen looked at the man resentfully. "He said something about a house shouldn't be divided, not a family, and that the Slaters ought to know what he was talking about."

Malachi came around the bar. He looked closely at the stranger. He started to laugh. "Matthew! Matthew McCahy! How are you?"

Matthew stepped forward. "Well, Malachi!" Matthew pumped his hand firmly. "What in God's name is going on? I've been following a trail of the most absurd stories to get here. Red Legs and bushwhackers, corpses all over. I've got friends investigating Fitz, but I don't seem to be able to get to my sisters. What the hell is going on? I hear tell that they arrested Shannon today, too, for murder."

"It's all right," Malachi said. "We've got a plan."

Cole and Jamie stepped out of the shadows. Cindy sighed with relief. "Well, I think that this calls for drinks all around," she murmured.

"Drinks, then we've got to get out of here before we cause Cindy any trouble," Cole said.

He took a seat at the round table. The other men followed him. Matthew McCahy looked hard at Malachi. "All right. What's the plan?"

"It's dangerous, Matthew. We might get ourselves shot up."

"They're my sisters," Matthew said. "My flesh and blood. I'll darned well get shot up for them if I feel like it." He narrowed his eyes. "Kristin is Cole's wife. But I've got more of a stake in this thing than either of you have, Malachi and Jamie."

Malachi shook his head. "Shannon is my wife," he said, finding with surprise that breaking this news got easier with practice.

"What?" Matthew said incredulously.

"Malachi married Shannon," Jamie answered, smiling with amusement.

"Yes, I married Shannon!" Malachi said dryly. "Now, if you all don't mind, think we could get on with this?"

"Sure," Matthew said.

Malachi leaned across the table and started talking. Matthew listened gravely. When Malachi was done, he sat back, nodding. "Think we'll have any help on it?" he asked.

"Jamie's got a couple of friends from Texas here," Malachi said.

"And I've met some people in the area," Cole added. "Maybe they won't take a stand against Fitz alone, but if we give them half a chance, they'll help us."

"It doesn't matter what we do or don't have," Malachi said. "As far as I see it, it's our best shot. Are we agreed?"

All around the table, they nodded to him one by one. Jamie lifted his whiskey glass. "What the hell. A man's gotta die sometime," he said cheerfully.

Malachi stood. "Let's get out of here. Cindy, you'll keep us up on everything that happens. Everything."

"Of course, Malachi. You know that."

An hour later, the Slaters and Matthew McCahy had slipped away into the night.

When Fitz's men came to the house, there was no sign that they had ever been near.

The only benefit to being held was that she was with her sister.

For the first day, Shannon nervously paced the room, but she was grateful that they had at least been kept together. She hadn't really meant to say much about her own strained relationship with Malachi, but the hours dragged on and Shannon found herself telling her sister almost everything.

Almost . . .

She didn't tell her how easily she had fallen into her old enemy's arms, or how she had longed for him to touch her again and again. She didn't tell her that even as they waited now, prisoners in the room, she thought of her husband, longing to be with him, aching to see his slow, lazy grin and the spark it ignited in his eyes. She didn't speak about that longing . . .

But watching Kristin's smile, she thought that her sister read her mind, and her heart, and that she knew.

"Actually," Kristin said mischievously, "I think you just might be perfect for one another."

Shannon shook her head. "Kristin, I don't know. I should let him out of the marriage. But Iris says that I'm a fool if I don't fight for him."

"I agree with Iris," Kristin said. She took Shannon's hands. "I'll never forget how miserable I was about Cole! I was tied up in knots, hating him, loving him. But it worked out for us, Shannon. I didn't think that he would ever forget his first wife, but he did fall in love with me. Shannon, even when I gave birth to Gabe, I was so afraid that Cole would never, never love me. You have to fight sometimes, for anything in life that is good. Look at the two of us now. Things have worked out—''

She broke off and Shannon bit her lip, watching her sister. Nothing had worked out for any of them. They were in the midst of disaster.

"I'm so scared!" Kristin said softly.

Shannon threw her arms around her. "It's all right. It's going to be all right!"

The two sisters hugged one another, shivering. They didn't know if it would be all right at all.

The next day was the mock trial, which took place in the town courthouse. Hayden Fitz sat on the bench as judge; the jurors were selected from among his men. Shannon was accused of murder. She stood at the witness stand and listened silently to the charge, then turned scornfully upon Fitz.

"I didn't murder anyone. You shot down your friend, Mr. Fitz. You shot him down in cold blood because he was protesting your cruelty to me. You may own this town, Mr. Fitz, but I can't really believe that you own everyone in it. Someone will get to you. The war is over, Hayden Fitz. No one will let you do murder endlessly!"

There was a murmur among the crowd. Fitz stood, pointing his gavel at her. "You murdered Fulton. I saw you with my own eyes. You murdered him to free your outlaw sister. You shot down men in Missouri, too. You're in league with your husband, and the two of you rode around the country in Cole Slater's gang, bushwhacking, murdering innocent Union women and children."

"Never," Shannon said quietly.

Fitz slammed his gavel against his desk. "You may step down, Mrs. Slater."

She didn't step down; she was dragged down. Kristin was brought up. Kristin denied everything, and threw at Fitz his brother's activities as a jayhawker. She described graphically how Cole's first wife had died.

A murmur rose in the courtroom, but Fitz ignored it. Kristin was handcuffed and led back to Shannon. They were both returned to the room with the barred windows at Fitz's home while the carefully selected jury came to their decision.

By night, the verdict was brought back to them. They were both convicted of murder and conspiracy against the Union.

They were to be hanged one week from that night at dawn.

"One week," Kristin told Shannon bitterly. "They want to make sure to give Cole and Malachi and Jamie a chance to show up."

Shannon nodded. One week. She looked at her sister. It had already been three days since she had been captured.

"Kristin?"

"Yes?"

"Where do you suppose they are? I'm scared, too, Kristin. They *were* in town. And now it's so silent! What if they've already been caught, and been taken . . ." Her voice trailed away miserably.

"They haven't been taken," Kristin told her dryly. "Fitz would have men walking through the streets with their heads on stakes if he'd caught them."

That was true, Shannon thought.

But as the days passed, they still heard nothing. An ominous silence had settled over the town. A harsh, brooding silence, as if even the air and the earth waited . . .

And prayed.

Slowly, excruciatingly slowly, the week passed. Finally, the night before the scheduled hanging came. Kristin sat in the room's one chair; Shannon stood by the window.

The scaffold had been built beneath the window, right in the center of the street, because Fitz had wanted them to watch its building. Shannon stared at it with growing horror.

It was a long night.

Morning finally came. "I—I can't believe that they haven't tried to rescue us!" Shannon told Kristin.

Kristin stared at the ceiling. "I was wrong. They must be dead already," she said softly.

Shannon felt as if icy waters settled over her heart and her body. She had endured too much. If Malachi was dead, then so be it. She wanted no more of this earth, of the awful pain and suffering. He had just taught her how to live...

And now, it was over.

When Bear came for them, he tied their hands behind their backs and led them out. Kristin smiled at her sister as they walked into the pearly gray dawn. It was going to be an absurdly beautiful summer's day. "Pa will be there, I'm certain," she said. "It won't be so hard to die. Mother will be there, too. And Robert Ellsworth. Oh, Shannon! What about Gabe, what will happen to him?"

"Delilah will love him. Matthew will come home, and he will raise him like his own."

"Shannon, I love you."

"Courage!" Shannon whispered. She was going to start to cry. Courage was easy in the midst of safety. But as they walked up the steps of the scaffold and beneath the dangling nooses, it was much harder to find.

Fitz sat in front of the scaffold on his horse. "Have you any last words, ladies?" he asked them.

Shannon looked over the crowd. The people weren't smiling or cheerful; they looked troubled. "Yes!" she called out. "We're innocent! Your hatred and your vengeance have made a mockery of justice, Hayden Fitz. And if you do not pay, sir, in this lifetime, I am certain that you will pay in the next, in the bowels of hell forever!"

Fitz's cold eyes narrowed. "Hang them!" he ordered.

The ropes were fitted over their heads and around their necks.

Shannon bit back tears as she felt the rope chafe the tender flesh of her neck. In a second, it would be pulled taut. She would dangle and choke. If God were merciful, her neck would snap. And if he were not merciful, she would die slowly of suffocation. Her tongue would swell and protrude and she would die hideously...

Hayden Fitz lifted his hand. The executioner walked over to the lever that would snap open the trapdoor.

Hayden Fitz read off the charges, and the order that Kristin and Shannon Slater be hanged by the necks until dead.

He lifted his hand...

And let it fall.

The executioner flipped the lever, and the floor gave beneath them.

Suddenly, the street was alive with explosions.

Shannon was falling, but the rope did not tighten around her neck. Someone had cut it. She kept falling, and crashed hard upon the ground. Cindy was there, slitting the rope that bound her wrists. Shannon twisted around in the dust.

"Get up! Get out of here!" Cindy cried.

"Kristin—"

"I'm freeing Kristin. Get up, go! Both of you!"

Kristin did not ask questions. She grabbed Shannon's hand and the two of them crawled out from beneath the scaffold. Shannon peered through the rain of gunfire. The streets had gone mad. People were screaming and running.

And a group of horsemen was bearing down on them.

She raised her hand over her eyes to shade them from the sun.

Malachi rode straight at her on his bay mare, his cavalry sword glinting in the sun, a Rebel cry upon his lips. He wore his plumed hat, and his full gray and gold Confederate cavalry dress.

He was coming for her, fighting his way down the street. Any man fool enough to block his way was cut down. As he neared her, she saw his teal-blue eyes blazing.

"Shannon! Get ready!" he yelled, striking down the last of Fitz's men to stand between them. He was a golden hero, riding to save her.

The bay was rearing over her. He reached down and swept her up onto the saddle before him, and they thundered down the street together.

Chapter Fourteen

The morning had burst into madness as they fled the town. There were explosions of gunfire. Women were screaming; men were shouting. Held tight against Malachi on his bay, Shannon was dimly aware of a number of horses riding beside them. Her hair kept whipping against her face, blinding her, but she managed to see at last. Cole was to her left with Kristin, her brother Matthew was to her right, and numerous men she'd never seen before were riding behind her. Some of them were in tattered remnants of uniforms, both blue and gray. Some were dressed as ranchers.

They all rode grimly, not stopping until they were miles from the town. Then Malachi reined in, shouting over Shannon's head to Cole. "We'll kill the horses if we keep this up. Think we've come far enough?"

Cole shrugged, his arms tight around his wife, and looked back along the trail they had just taken. "Here's Jamie," he said.

Jamie Slater, on a huge dapple gray stallion, raced up behind them. He waved his hat in the air, a look of triumph on his face.

"Fitz is dead. And there isn't the first sign of pursuit. I think we can take it easier now."

"Not too easy!" A woman called. Shannon gasped as she saw Iris on a dark roan, riding up behind Jamie. "Fitz may not have been tremendously popular, but someone may seek to avenge him.''

"Iris!" Shannon gasped when the redhead looked her way. She was, as always, impeccably dressed, and her hair was unrumpled. She looked unscathed by her imprisonment, except for the large blue circle beneath her right eye.

"I'm all right, honey," Iris said softly. "Thanks to Jamie. He pulled me away from Fitz."

"Jamie, bless you!" Kristin said.

"Always willing to oblige," Jamie drawled softly.

Shannon leaped down from in front of Malachi and ran over to Jamie, who also hopped down off his horse to meet her. "Hey, brat!" He laughed, sweeping her up in a fast hug. Matthew and Kristin dismounted as well, and they all hugged one another with laughter and relief.

"Shannon, get back over here!" Malachi commanded sharply. She glanced at him and saw that his features had become as threatening as a winter storm. She stiffened. Cole wasn't yelling that way. She stared at Malachi, defiant and hurt at once. Safe in the warmth of his arms, she had felt that the war between them was over. But now it seemed that nothing had changed. Did he still hate her?

"We do have to keep moving," he said.

Kristin turned and hurried back to Cole. He lifted her up before him. Jamie and Matthew mounted up again.

Shannon turned to the strangers who surrounded them. "I don't know who you are, but thank you, all of you. With all my heart, I thank you."

"We all thank you," Kristin echoed.

Malachi looked around at the curious assortment of men with them. "Shannon is right—thank you all." He pointed to the right. "These are Sam Greenhow, Frank Bujold, Lennie Peterson and Ronnie Cordon—all friends of Jamie's from General Edmund Kirby-Smith's command down in Texas. And those boys there—" he pointed to the left "—are from Haywood."

"Howdy," said one of the Confederates to Shannon, and he tipped his hat to Kristin. "I don't mean to be telling you all your business, but you were right, Malachi. You should keep moving. You need to put some mean space between you and Sparks."

Malachi nodded. He and Cole and Matthew thanked the men. Then Malachi called to Shannon again. "Shannon, get over here."

She didn't like his tone, but she could acknowledge he was right. She lifted her head and walked back to Malachi. He reached down for her, encircling her waist with his arm and pulling her up before him. They waved to the men who had risked their lives to fight against the corrupt rule in Sparks.

A silence fell as their curious little party started off: Cole and Kristin, Matthew, Jamie, Iris and Malachi and Shannon. Jamie rode in the lead, taking them south.

Shannon waited as the morning wore on, wanting to speak, not knowing what to say. She stared at Malachi's hand where it rested on her knee, and thought of how she had come to love that hand, how the texture of the bronze skin, the tiny tufts of gold hair on his long fingers now meant everything in the world to her.

She thought of the warmth of the man behind her, and she thought of the danger they had faced together time and time again. When she remembered the past she wanted to cry out all her pent-up fears and sorrows, but her recollections also made her think gravely of the future, too. Life was precious. It was dear, and could be so swiftly stolen away.

She and Malachi had life. This morning, they both had life. They had the sun over their heads, and the radiance of the blue sky, and they rode with people near and dear to them. God had been good to them that morning.

But Malachi was still as stiff and cold as steel. Shannon thought that perhaps he had decided that now he had carried out all obligations to her. He was angry, that much she knew. Maybe he was anxious, too, to be free.

But Iris had told her to fight for him. Could she do that?

Shannon moved her fingers gently over his hand. "Thank you," she told him softly.

He grunted in return. She thought that he would say no more, but then he growled in her ear. "I should thrash you within an inch of your life, young woman."

"What?" she demanded, startled.

"You were told to come to Cindy's. But oh, no, that wasn't good enough for you. You had to put yourself and Iris into a damn fool dangerous position—"

"*I* was foolish! You three were out holding up a train—"

"We went to un-hold-up that train—"

"There is no such thing as un-holding-up a train, Malachi Slater. If you had been killed, Kristin would have been on her own. I would have had to have done something—"

"You did real well," he drawled sarcastically.

Shannon clenched her teeth, trying not to break into ridiculous tears. She stared down at his hand, and noted that he was shaking. With anger, she assumed. "I was doing fine," she stormed. "Ask Iris. Then that horrible Bear recognized me."

"You could have been killed."

"And you could have been killed—un-holding-up a train!"

"I know what I'm doing, and you don't!"

"Lower your voice. Everyone can hear us."

"Can they now?"

"You're humiliating me, Malachi Slater."

"Humiliating you? I wish I had a switch."

"You're the one who should be taken to a woodshed, Captain Slater. Let me down."

"Let you down? You going to walk to Texas?"

"I'll go and ride with my brother."

"You'll ride with your husband, Mrs. Slater," he said, and the words were hard but the husky tension in his voice swept sweetly over her. There was a note of possession in his words that captivated and thrilled her. She didn't mind the demand in it at all.

She looked down at her own hands. They were trembling, too.

Jamie pulled up suddenly in front of them, extending his arm to point. "There's a river up here, and a natural cove. Shall we take a break and ride with the cooler air in the evening?"

"Yes, please!" Kristin answered him. They had ridden so hard at first, and now they had been in the saddle for hours and hours.

"All right with you, Matt? Malachi?" Cole asked.

Malachi nodded. Shannon leaped down quickly. Malachi dismounted behind her.

"Someone get a fire going," Jamie said. "I'll see if I can find something in the woods to cook."

He nodded to them all, pulled his rifle from his saddle and started into the woods.

"I'll join you," Matthew called after him. He looked at Iris, eyeing her from head to toe. "Start the fire."

"I don't know how to start the fire."

"Learn," Matthew said curtly. He started off after Jamie. Iris kicked the dirt.

"Learn!" she muttered. "Damned—Yank!"

Shannon started toward Iris, wanting to assure herself that the woman was all right and to help her build the fire. She didn't get far. Malachi caught her by the arm. She stared at him indignantly.

"We're going for a walk," he told her.

"But I don't want to go for a walk," she began.

She broke off with a startled scream as he swept her up into his arms. "I said that we're going for a walk."

Stunned, Shannon remained silent, staring up into his teal-blue eyes. In the background, Kristin laughed softly. She'd obviously heard the exchange.

Stung by her elder sister's amusement, Shannon started to protest, but Malachi was already carrying her off. With long strides he followed the river's edge, beneath the shade of the huge old oaks. The sun rose high above them, the sky was blue, and the water was tinkling a delightful melody.

Shannon's arms had curled around his neck for self-preservation. She kept staring at him as he moved, unhurriedly but with purpose.

"Malachi...let me down!" she entreated him softly. They were far out of sight of the camp now, around a curve in the river. There might not have been a living soul in miles, and there was no sound except for the melody of the rushing water and songs of the birds and the whisper of the breeze through the leaves of the oaks.

"Malachi, put me down!"

This time he responded, laying her on a grassy spot upon the slope, and immediately throwing himself down next to her. He placed his knee casually over her legs, supported his weight on an elbow, and touched her cheek.

"I should tan your hide," he said softly. His fingers trailed over her flesh. He stroked her face and her throat. He leaned against her and kissed first her forehead, then the tip of her nose. He buried his face against hers, and kissed the lobe of her ear, nibbling the soft flesh, warming it with the heat of his breath.

She wrapped her arms around him, holding him close.

"Malachi..."

"I should... I should really tan your hide."

His face rose above hers. His eyes searched hers, and she smiled slowly, her own eyes wandering over his beloved features, his clipped beard, his mustache, seeing the fullness of his lips, the character in his eyes.

"Malachi..."

She reached up and threaded her fingers through his hair and pulled his head down to hers. She kissed him, then broke away, then teased his mouth with the tip of her tongue, then kissed him passionately once again. His lips parted to hers, and he took control with a tender and savage aggression that swept through her like heat lightning across a summer's sky.

She felt the passion deep within him, simmering, threatening to burst. He leaned over her intimately, his fingers trembling as he worked at the tiny buttons of her bodice.

Shannon caught his hand. Her lashes fell low and sultry over her eyes. "Malachi, you are something, you know. You're always yelling at me."

"I'm not always yelling at you." He shook away her hand. She made no further protest as he peeled back her bodice and kissed her breasts above the froth of her chemise. Shannon stroked his shoulders, inhaling swiftly as shivers of delight cascaded along her spine.

"You are always yelling at me," she corrected. She placed her hands on either side of his face and lifted his eyes to her.

"You are always doing foolish things," he said softly. "And if I yell at you . . ."

"Yes?"

He smiled slowly. "What do you want? A signed confession?"

Shannon nodded.

"If I yell at you . . ."

She caught her breath, waiting.

"It's because I love you."

"Oh, Malachi!" She threw her arms around him and they rolled in the grass, laughing. "Malachi, say it again!"

He caught her beneath him and laid his hand upon her breast over the thin material of the chemise. He stroked the nipple with his thumb until it hardened to a coral peak, and she moaned softly. "Malachi . . ."

"You were willing to let me hang rather than marry me!" he told her reproachfully.

"I didn't want you to be forced to marry me!"

"You didn't want to marry me."

"But I did. I really did."

"You were in love with a ghost. Are you still?"

She shook her head, biting into her lower lip as she met his eyes. His hands were still roaming sensually across her body. "I did love him. But...even on the awful day that we were married...I did want to marry you."

"Did you?"

He laid his head against her breast and used his tongue to stroke her through the soft fabric. Shannon forgot the question. Malachi did not.

"Did you?" he repeated.

"What?"

"Love me. You haven't said it, you know."

She smiled, trembling beneath him. "I love you, Captain Slater. I think I loved you all along."

"From that very first time you tried to shoot me?" he teased.

"Maybe. Malachi..."

"What?"

"Love me."

"It's been forever," he said huskily, lacing his fingers with hers, stretching out over her.

"It's been a week."

"A long week," he corrected her. And when he took her lips with his own, she saw he spoke the truth.

"Love me," she whispered to him once again.

So he did. The sound of the river came as the sweetest melody, and the grass beneath offered up the softest bedding. He laid his coat upon the ground and stripped her of her clothing piece by piece. She barely dared to move while he touched her, feeling as if time had come to a standstill between them, and that she might shatter some fantastic spell if she were to breathe. She waited. She waited for him to finish with her, and then to doff his own clothing, and to lie down beside her.

She wondered if anything would ever again be as beautiful as that day at that moment. The sun was warm upon her and the air was cool, and his body was a fervent flame of fire within and around her. He touched her with tenderness, and with searing passion. He led her to the brink of ecstasy, and back down, merely to stroke the flames one more time.

Then there was nothing while she soared. Climax burst upon her, and she felt the sweet rush of his release.

Once again, the earth existed. The sky, the river, the ground beneath them.

Shannon looked to her side and saw that his hat lay upon the ground, his fine, plumed Confederate cavalry captain's hat. She smiled, wondering how she had ever allowed the war to stand between them. She realized then that she loved him for everything that he was. A man, a Rebel, a knight in shining armor.

A hero.

No matter how many times she had needed him, he had come for her. He had never let her down.

She touched his cheek. "I do love you. I love you, Malachi Slater."

"Captain Slater."

She smiled.

"I can't change my part in the war, Shannon. Nor do I want to. I fought for what I believed."

"I know."

He hesitated, pulling her close beneath his chin. "The fighting isn't over, Shannon. Fitz is dead, but they'll still come for us." He paused again. "Matthew is going to ride for home tomorrow, Shannon. I'm going to send you with him."

"No!" she protested, sitting up.

He smiled and lazily ran a finger over her bare breast. "Shannon, Cole and Jamie and I have to leave the country. I don't know where we're going. I don't—"

"Kristin will go with Cole."

He shook his head gravely. "Kristin is going home to the baby, Shannon."

"Malachi—"

"No!" he said firmly. Standing up, he started to dress, tossing her her stockings. "Shannon, I have to know that you're safe. Do you understand? Get dressed. We should get back to the others.''

''And what are we supposed to do?'' Shannon demanded bitterly. ''Just go home and wait for the years to go by?''

''We'll find a way to return.''

''When?'' Shannon demanded, wrenching her dress over her head. ''Malachi, I don't mind—''

He caught her against him and kissed her. He broke away from her, smiling ruefully. ''That is the only way to shut you up, you know.''

''Malachi—''

''No.'' He kissed her again, then caught her hand, pulling her along.

''Wait!'' Shannon cried. She pulled back, flushing as she did up the numerous little buttons on her gown.

He paused, looking around. Shannon was about to argue again when he suddenly went very tense and brought his fingers to his lip. He drew his gun, and pulling her behind him, crept along the trees.

A few minutes later, Shannon began to hear the sounds as well. There were men and horses deeper in the woods. She crept along beside Malachi until they neared a small encampment.

There were about fifteen of them, all dressed in clean blue uniforms. They were a cavalry unit, and a young group at that. Two of the men were cleaning their carbines; one leaned against a tree reading, and the others were finishing a meal, laughing and talking idly.

''Damn!'' Malachi muttered. ''We've got to slip back and get the others to move.''

Shannon nodded. She turned around to hurry with him, then hesitated and looked back, anxious to see if they had been spotted. They had not. The men didn't even look up. She turned again to follow Malachi, well ahead of her now and running in a half crouch through the bracken. Suddenly, she screamed, crashing straight into a blue-clad soldier who appeared from behind a tree.

He gasped, as startled as she, and she realized that he had been taking care of personal business in the bushes.

"Excuse me!" Shannon muttered.

"Excuse me, ma'am," the man apologized. Then his eyes narrowed. "Hey, wait a minute," he began, his hand falling upon her shoulder.

"Let her go!" Malachi called out. He stood ahead of them, leveling his gun calmly at the man.

But by then all the young cavalry boys were up and stumbling around looking for their weapons, and the most prepared were already through the trees.

"Let her go!" Malachi insisted.

"Slater!" Someone called suddenly. Shannon saw that it was the officer in charge. And he must have known Malachi, because he raised his hands, displaying that he carried no weapon, and he walked forward.

"Captain Slater," the officer called, "I know you—"

"I don't know you."

"I know your brother Cole. I'm Major Kurt Taylor. We were together in the West before the war broke out." He hesitated. "I saw him in Kansas. Before he went up against Henry Fitz."

"Ain't that nice," Malachi drawled softly. "I don't want to hurt anybody, major. Tell him to let my wife go."

"Captain Slater, I know that you could shoot down half my boys in a matter of seconds."

"That's right. So let her go."

"Captain, we were sent to find you."

"What?" Malachi asked warily.

"Judge Sherman Woods sent us out. I can't make promises—"

"I wouldn't trust a promise from a Yank anyway," Malachi interrupted.

"You've got a beautiful wife, captain. Do you really want to spend the rest of your life running? Or do you want to take a minute and listen to me?"

"Start talking."

"I can't leave, captain. So to get away from me, you're going to have to kill these men. If you come in with me, I'll promise you and your brothers a fair trial."

"What's to make me think the Union will keep this promise?"

"You'll have to trust Judge Woods, Captain Slater. You went to him for help, and he wants to help. But you have to give him the chance to do so."

"I'm sorry—" Malachi began.

"Malachi!" Shannon cried in anguish. "Please! For God's sake, please! Give us this chance."

He was very still for a long time. Tall, proud, his Confederate greatcoat over his shoulders, his plumed hat waving in the breeze. His jaw was hard, his eyes cold, his chin rigid and high.

Then he exhaled and tossed his gun down.

"I couldn't shoot those boys anyway," he said quietly. "I just couldn't kill any more damned children. They say that the war is over. Major, we'll have to see if it is."

Major Taylor nodded. "Captain, will you do something for me?"

"What's that?"

"Go talk to your brothers. If I can, I'd like to avoid being a target for a Slater."

Malachi nodded. He reached out a hand to Shannon, and she ran to his side. Together, they walked through the woods with Major Taylor behind them.

When they reached the others, Jamie instantly drew his gun. Cole and Matthew followed suit.

"Kurt!" Cole said, slowly lowering his Colt. "What's going on?" he asked Malachi.

"You do know this fellow?" Malachi asked Cole.

Cole nodded. "What—"

"Judge Woods sent me out to find you. We'll give you a fair trial in Missouri. It will be fair, I swear it on my honor."

Cole looked at Malachi, a question in his eyes.

"I'm tired of running," Malachi said. "And honor is honor. Blue or gray. I believe this man has some. I've already surrendered to him."

"Well," said Cole, "it's what we wanted when we talked to Judge Woods. Jamie?"

Jamie shrugged his shoulders. "I don't trust Yankee honor much, but I'll go with you and Malachi, Cole."

The two men dropped their guns on the ground.

"I just hope I don't end up hanging," Jamie muttered.

"You won't hang!" Shannon cried. She clung to Malachi's hand. She wouldn't let him hang. She couldn't.

Malachi turned to her. He swept off his hat and took her into his arms and kissed her long and deep for everyone to see. Then he broke away from her, replacing his hat on his head. He strode over to the bay and mounted. "Whenever you're ready, major. Your prisoner, sir." He saluted sharply.

Major Taylor saluted in return.

Cole kissed Kristin, and he and Jamie followed Malachi's lead, mounting their horses.

Then they rode away, without looking back.

Kristin started to sob. Matthew came up to her and put his arm around her, and then he gathered Shannon to him, too. "It's going to be all right. I swear to you, it will be all right."

"It will be!" Shannon agreed fiercely. "It has to be."

Iris cleared her throat. "I managed to make the fire, and Jamie managed to shoot the rabbits. Let's sit down and eat. And then we can head back and plan some strategy."

"She learns really fast," Matthew said with a grin. "Let's eat."

She tried to smile. She could not. But she slipped her arm around Kristin's waist and led her to the fire.

They did eat. When they were done, Kristin mounted with Matthew and Shannon sat behind Iris, and they started their cold, lonely trek back home to Missouri.

Chapter Fifteen

The trial took place in Springfield. The courthouse was crowded with spectators, and with artists from *Harpers* and from every other leading paper and magazine.

Shannon had visited Malachi in jail, and she hated the experience. He was distant from her there. She knew that he loved her, and that he was in jail for her sake. But not even for her would he deny any of his brothers, and he explained to her that the brothers had determined to stand together. They would not opt for separate legal representation, nor would Jamie and Malachi seek lesser charges.

Malachi smiled ruefully to Shannon through the heavy iron bars of the jail. "We are all innocent."

"Cole wouldn't want you to hang because he rode with Quantrill."

"Tell me, Shannon, could you bear it if Cole were to hang because he sought to avenge the death of a beautiful and innocent bride? His wife, a woman carrying his child? She was my sister-in-law. I would have joined Cole at any time; I was already in the Confederate cavalry."

"Malachi—"

"If you love me, Shannon, you must love me for the man that I am. My brothers and I stand together."

She turned away, tears in her eyes. Cole already would have tried to convince Malachi and Jamie to save themselves. The Slaters were a stubborn lot.

And no...she could not bear it if Cole were to hang! They had all paid enough; the war was over. She could not accept any further horror—they had to win.

The first day of the trial was wretched, although their lawyer, Mr. Abernathy, was a skilled defender, with a sure belief in the Slater brothers' innocence. Shannon was pleased with him, even if he didn't pressure the men to stand alone. But Taylor Green, the prosecuting attorney, scared her. He seemed to personally want the Slater brothers to hang, all three.

When the trial started, Green immediately struck upon Cole Slater's association with William Quantrill. There were dozens of witnesses to testify to that association. But they weren't necessary, for at the end Cole quietly admitted to it. In a low, controlled voice he described the scene at his own ranch, years before, at the very outbreak of the war, when the jayhawkers had come to kill his wife. Shannon listened to him, and ached for him. He did not break or falter, but she saw it all through his eyes. She saw his young wife, she heard the woman screaming, and running, running, trying to reach her husband. He made them feel what it was like, to catch her as she fell, to feel her blood upon his hands...

The court was still when he finished. Not even Mr. Taylor Green managed to speak for several seconds.

And then there was a recess for the day.

Kristin came to the witness stand the next day and described in graphic detail how Zeke Moreau had murdered their father, and how Cole Slater had ridden to their rescue.

"Against the bushwhackers?" the prosecuting attorney asked her scathingly. "You want us to believe, Mrs. Slater, that your husband rode against his old comrades at arms? Maybe they just made a deal there instead, isn't that possible?"

"No, sir, it isn't possible at all," Kristin said. "He came and saved our lives. And he returned with Malachi and Jamie Slater to save the lives of half a Union company when Zeke Moreau came back again.''

Kristin was fierce and beautiful and unfaltering. Taylor Green did not care to have her on the stand long.

Malachi was called.

He walked to the witness stand in full dress uniform, and Shannon's heart felt as if it had been torn. He was tall and straight, distinguished and ruggedly indomitable, and he was the handsome cavalier who had captured her heart.

"Captain Slater—well, of course, you are a civilian now, aren't you, sir?"

"The war is over," Malachi said flatly.

"But you choose to wear that uniform."

"We fought with honor."

"You still deny the Union?"

"The war is over," Malachi repeated.

"You would like it to continue? You still think that the South can rise again and whip the North, eh, captain?"

"No, sir. I think that the war is over, and I damned well would like it to end for good!"

A loud murmur rose in the courtroom. Shannon smiled. It seemed the first ray of hope. The people were with her husband.

"Did you ride with Quantrill?"

"No."

"Never?"

"No, never. But I would have ridden with my brother. If you'd seen his wife, lying in a pool of innocent blood, you'd have ridden, too."

"Captain, you seem to be an ornery sort."

"I'm telling you the truth, and that is all. This is a court of law, and we are sworn to the truth, right?"

"You're bold with your brand of truth."

"I have to be. And I have to believe that there is still justice in this land. If justice has not been lost, then my brother Cole is innocent, and so are James and I."

"You were regular army."

"Southern cavalry. Under John Hunt Morgan."

"Sounds like you avoided the border war, captain. So tell me, why don't you come clean, and give us the truth about Cole Slater."

"The truth is, Mr. Green," Malachi said, his eyes narrowed sharply, "that my brother is one of the finest men I've ever met in my life. In the North or the South. And if Cole is guilty for wanting to hunt down the man who murdered his wife, then I'm guilty, too. I would have been with him if I could have been."

"An admission, gentlemen of the jury, there you have it! You may step down, Captain Slater!"

"Admission!" Shannon didn't know that she was the one who had shouted until everyone turned to look her way. "Admission! Why, you Yankee bastard!"

There was an instant uproar. Some people were laughing, and some, the northern sympathizers, were offended. The judge slammed down his gavel. "Young woman, one more such outburst and I shall hold you in contempt! Are we understood?"

She sank into her chair. Only then did she realize that Malachi was watching her, too, and that a smile curled his lip. She lowered her eyes, then met his once again, and the smile warmed her and gave her courage.

Malachi walked down from the stand, and Jamie was called up for questioning. He was barely civil, but Taylor Green didn't manage to get a single rise out of him. Jamie could be as stubborn and proud a Slater as either of his brothers.

Shannon sat in the court with Kristin and Matthew and Iris, listening to it all. When the session broke, she was allowed to see Malachi for a few minutes.

"Yankee bastard?" Malachi teased her, his eyes dancing. "Did I hear you say that? You, Shannon McCahy Slater, called that man a Yankee bastard?"

"Malachi!"

"I could die happy, hearing those words upon your lips!"

"Don't you dare talk of dying!"

"I'm sorry."

"Damn your pride!" she told him savagely, tears glistening in her eyes. "You are innocent, and it's as if you're trying to make yourself sound guilty!"

He smiled, tilted her chin and kissed her. "I can only tell the truth, Shannon."

She wanted to say more. She wanted to argue and hit him and make him see reason, but an officer of the court came and took him away, and she wasn't able to say anything more.

The days went on, and the situation began to appear bleaker and bleaker.

It wasn't that it didn't seem to be a fair trial. It was just that Taylor Green seemed to know how to make a simple statement of fact sound like a full confession. And the fact remained that Cole *had* ridden with Quantrill. No matter how briefly he had done so, it was enough to condemn him in many hearts. Still, she knew that his first speech had also touched the hearts of many. The brutal slaying of a young woman was a heinous act to any ordinary man, be he a Yankee or a Rebel.

On the fourth night of the trial Shannon went to see Mr. Abernathy. He was at dinner, and his housekeeper nearly stopped her from reaching him, but she pushed by. He was just about to start eating his dinner—a lamb chop, peas and a roasted potato.

"What are you doing?" Shannon demanded. She was so distraught that she picked up his plate and tossed it into the corner of the room.

He arched his snowy brows, and cleaned his fingers on the napkin that was tied about his throat and covered his chest. He smiled slowly at her and glanced remorsefully toward his lamb. "Mrs. Slater, I could call this assault! At the very least, it's a case of assault against a very fine lamb chop!"

"I'm sorry," Shannon murmured swiftly. She was sorry. She drew up a chair at the table. "I'm just so worried—"

Mr. Abernathy smiled again and took her hand, patting it. "Trust me, Mrs. Slater. Trust me."

"They could hang, sir!"

"I'm not going to let them hang. Now you'll see, you'll see."

"When?"

"Why, tomorrow, I do believe. The prosecution seems to have finished. I'll start with my case tomorrow. And I'll wager you two lamb chops that I'll need but a day!"

Shannon couldn't believe that he could possibly undo all the harm that Mr. Green had done. But he gave her a glass of sherry, and shooed her out the door.

Shannon went back to the hotel, where she found Kristin red-eyed and puffy-faced from crying. Shannon hugged her sister and lied through her teeth. "It's going to be all right. Mr. Abernathy has it all well in hand. Why, he says he can have them freed by tomorrow!"

"He can?" Kristin wanted so badly to believe.

In the morning, Mr. Abernathy stood before the court and addressed the judge. "My defense is simple. I will prove that we've no case against any of these men, no foundation for a charge of murder. And, your Honor, I will request that the case be dismissed!"

The judge invited Mr. Abernathy to proceed. Mr. Taylor looked up in protest, and Mr. Abernathy bowed very politely to him. He looked around, opening his arms to the court.

Then Shannon realized that the courtroom was curiously filled with men, officers in blue and gray.

One by one they stood and addressed the judge.

"Sir, I'm Corporal Rad Higgins, U.S. cavalry. I came here to say that I rode with Malachi Slater back in April, against a horde of bushwhackers. I rode with Jamie and Cole Slater, too. I'd like to testify, sir, that I ain't ever rode with better men."

"Sir, I'm Samuel Smith. First Sergeant, Darton's brigade, Union army. I'd been left for dead when these fellows came riding in. The fought and beat Quantrill's offshoots, and they offered me the finest medical care. Their doc even saved my arm, and it had been shot up mighty bad.''

From a man with the stripes of an artillery sergeant on his arms: "I knew Cole Slater in Kansas before the war. I never met a finer officer."

One by one, the men stood. Soldiers in blue, soldiers in gray.

Then a woman stood up, plump, dignified, gray-haired.

"I'm Martha Haywood, and this is my husband, and I come to say that I ain't ever met finer people than Captain Malachi Slater and his bride, and that's a fact. And my husband will testify to that fact, too." Mr. Haywood stood alongside her.

Shannon looked around, incredulous. They were all there. Jamie's Confederate friends from Texas, the people from Haywood, even the professional gamblers from the saloon. And one by one they testified with moving stories to the honesty and honor of the Slater brothers.

When it was over, the judge stood. He slammed his gavel against his desk.

"I dismiss these cases," he told the prosecution. "Lack of evidence," he said flatly.

And he walked away.

Silence reigned for a moment. Then there was a Rebel war whoop as hats were thrown high into the air. The crowd rushed forward to congratulate the Slaters.

Shannon pushed her way through until she reached Malachi. He drew her into his arms, and he kissed her warmly.

"It's over," he said softly. "The war is really over."

"All of our wars are over," she promised him. She slipped her hand into his hands, then turned around, searching for Mr. Abernathy. She hurried over to him and gave him a tremendous kiss on the jowl. "Bless you! And I promise you a dozen lamb chops every year, as long as I live!"

"That would be right nice, Mrs. Slater, mighty nice."

"What's this?" Malachi demanded, shaking hands with his attorney.

"That's a mighty fine little woman you have there, captain." Mr. Abernathy said. "Some temper, though, huh?"

"It's a ghastly temper," Malachi agreed.

"Malachi!" she protested.

"I love it, though," he told Mr. Abernathy. "I wouldn't have her any other way. She's full of fire and sparks."

"Malachi—"

"In fact, I'm going to take her right home and see if we can't get a few sparks a-flying." His eyes fell on her. "Seems like a long, long time since I've been away."

"Scat!" Mr. Abernathy told them.

They still had to fight through the crowd. Malachi had to kiss Kristin, and Shannon had to kiss and hug Jamie and Cole, and the brothers embraced, and then Malachi and his brothers thanked each and every man and woman who had come to their defense. Shannon hugged Martha Haywood fiercely, and Martha told her with shimmering eyes that she should go. "And be happy, love! Be happy."

They came out into the sunshine at last.

Then Malachi kissed her. Slowly, surely, completely. He broke away. "Come on. We can go home. We can really go home."

"And start sparks flying?" she teased him.

"No," he whispered.

"No?"

His eyes danced, as blue and clear as the sky above them. "Sparks are already flying."

She smiled slowly, meeting his eyes, curling her fingers within his while he sun beat down upon them, warm and vibrant.

"Yes, let's go home!" she agreed in a fervent whisper.

Because they could. They could really go home.

Life and love were theirs, and they were only just beginning.

The war was more than over. Peace had truly begun.

Epilogue

June 18th, 1866   *Haywood, Kansas*

Martha Haywood had just locked up the house for the night. There were no guests at the hotel, so she thought she might as well lock up early. She wished that someone would come through. It was summer, and it was beautiful, and it would be nice to be busy and have company.

She felt a surge of nostalgia for the previous year. She smiled, remembering all the hustle and bustle when Captain Slater had come with his Miss McCahy. Maybe she had been wrong. Maybe she and Papa shouldn't have forced the two to enter into marriage.

People had a right to make up their own minds.

She hoped things had worked out. Captain Slater and Miss McCahy had been the perfect couple. A handsome, dashing hero and a damsel in distress. But she hadn't heard from the two of them in a while, not since the letter at Christmas...

Martha started, hearing a fierce pounding at the door. She hurried over as fast as she could, muttering to herself. "People should have more courtesy. Why, I have half a mind not to open the door. Stopping this late along the way..."

But she threw open the door anyway.

For a moment, she just stared, stunned.

"Martha, may we come in?" Shannon Slater asked her. She looked like an angel on the porch, in her light blue traveling dress with a white lace collar. She held a big, blanketed bundle in her arms, and she stood next to her husband. He was as dashing as ever. His Confederate gray was gone, and he wore a well-tailored dark frock coat and a stovepipe hat. He was carrying a valise and held a squirming bundle as well.

Shannon didn't wait for an answer. Smiling, she stepped into the house, pressing her bundle into Martha's arms. "We are awfully late, aren't we? I'm so sorry. It's much harder traveling with the children."

"Children?" Martha sputtered at last.

"This one is Beau. And this—" she smiled, pulling back the blanket on Malachi's bundle "—is Nadine."

"Oh!" Martha said at last. "Oh, twins!"

"Twins," Malachi agreed, and he pressed his bundle, too, into Martha's arms.

"Twins!" Martha repeated, as if she could think of nothing else to say.

Malachi winked at Shannon, enjoying the woman's flustered pleasure. "This is our wedding anniversary, you know, Martha."

"Yes," Shannon said, stripping away her gloves. "So we've come back, eager for our honeymoon suite."

"Your honeymoon suite—of course!"

Beau gurgled. Martha laughed with delight. "Oh, he is precious!"

"Well, you see, Shannon's brother Matthew and Iris were married last week—"

"No!" Martha gasped.

"Oh, yes. We were all just wonderfully pleased. But they're setting up housekeeping now."

"And we've done what we can to pull the McCahy ranch together," Malachi said.

"So," Shannon continued, "Cole has gone to Texas with Kristin and Gabe and Jamie and Samson and Delilah."

"We're going to join them down that way, too," Malachi said.

"Malachi has been offered a job as sheriff in a little town west of Houston," Shannon said.

"Cole is ranching, and Jamie is—believe it or not—scouting for the cavalry."

"Oh, how wonderful!" Martha said. She looked from one of the squirming babies to the other. "Oh! They're just both so beautiful."

Malachi pinched Martha's cheek. "We're so glad that you like them, Martha."

"Like them? Why, captain, I love them!"

Shannon smiled sweetly and kissed Martha's cheek. "Good." She laughed mischievously. "Because we're going to sneak up to our honeymoon retreat."

"Oh, of course!" Martha giggled. "You two go right ahead."

Malachi swept Shannon off her feet, striding to the stairs. "Oh, we'd like to baptize them tomorrow, if we could. If you and Mr. Haywood wouldn't mind. And we want you and Mr. Haywood to be the godparents."

"Oh!" Martha would have clapped like a child except that her arms were full of squirming babies. She looked at them more closely. They both had soft ringlets of gold and immense blue eyes. Nadine was going to be a beauty like her mother, and Beau would be as handsome as his sire. "My godchildren!" Martha cried. She turned around quickly. "We won't mind. We won't mind at all."

She wasn't sure that Malachi and Shannon heard her. Their eyes were locked with one another's as he carried her up the stairs. She was glorious, with her hair streaming over his arms, and he was wonderful in his dark coat, tall and striking. It was so romantic, the way he held her.

"Of course, of course!" Martha repeated.

Shannon had heard her. She looked over her husband's shoulder and winked. Martha waved. A second later the door—now repaired—closed at the top of the stairs.

"Oh, my!" Martha said. "Papa! Papa, wake up, Mr. Haywood. We've responsibilities tonight!"

She sat down with her two little bundles.

And she smiled. She had been right—she had been ever so right. They were the perfect couple, and it was just like a fairy tale...

Ending happily ever after!

* * * * *

COMING NEXT MONTH

#21 LAWLESS—Nora Roberts

In the untamed Arizona Territory, half-Apache gunslinger
Jake Redman held his own better than most. So why
should he let Eastern lady Sarah Conway rattle his nerves?
He tried to convince the refined miss to leave the barren
frontier and head back where she belonged—until he
started thinking that the only place she truly belonged was
by his side.

#22 CAPTURED HEARTS—Deborah Chester

Young noblewoman Anne-Marie de Chalmes had fled the
treacheries of Revolutionary France by the skin of her
teeth. But the peace she sought on British soil eluded her
as she found herself entangled in a perilous game of
intrigue, with roguish spy Max Dayton her only ally.
Through each other they would discover the strength to do
battle with even the blackest forces of the Reign of Terror.

AVAILABLE NOW

#19 RIDES A HERO   #20 SAMARA
Heather Graham Pozzessere   Patricia Potter

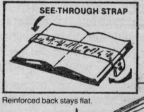
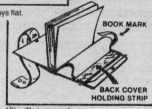

Janet DAILEY

THE MASTER FIDDLER

Jacqui didn't want to go back to college, and she didn't
want to go home. Tombstone, Arizona, wasn't in her
plans, either, until she found herself stuck there en route
to L.A. after ramming her car into rancher Choya Barnett's
Jeep. Things got worse when she lost her wallet and
couldn't pay for the repairs. The mechanic wasn't
interested when she practically propositioned him to get
her car back—but Choya was. He took care of her bills and
then waited for the debt to be paid with the only thing
Jacqui had to offer—her virtue.

Watch for this bestselling Janet Dailey favorite, coming in
June from Harlequin.

Also watch for *Something Extra* in August and *Sweet
Promise* in October.